Alison,
Persistence

Rob

GOD'S PONZI

ROBERT BUSCHEL

Black Rose Writing | Texas

D0664501

©2022 by Robert Buschel
All rights reserved. No part of this book may be reproduced, stored in a retrieval system or transmitted in any form or by any means without the prior written permission of the publishers, except by a reviewer who may quote brief passages in a review to be printed in a newspaper, magazine or journal.

The author grants the final approval for this literary material.

First printing

This is a work of fiction. Names, characters, businesses, places, events, and incidents are either the products of the author's imagination or used in a fictitious manner. Any resemblance to actual persons, living or dead, or actual events is purely coincidental.

ISBN: 978-1-68433-892-4
PUBLISHED BY BLACK ROSE WRITING
www.blackrosewriting.com

Printed in the United States of America
Suggested Retail Price (SRP) $22.95

God's Ponzi is printed in Baskerville

*As a planet-friendly publisher, Black Rose Writing does its best to eliminate unnecessary waste to reduce paper usage and energy costs, while never compromising the reading experience. As a result, the final word count vs. page count may not meet common expectations.

In memory of my friend,
Joseph J. Carter

A man who packed many lifetimes into one short one.

If the

assumption about

artificial intelligence is that

A. I. avoids the limits of human biology

because it doesn't eat, drink, or sleep – some

would label that thinking-machine a god. And, if that god

was tasked to manage a Ponzi scheme, we'd call that scheme –

GOD'S PONZI.

GOD'S PONZI

PROLOGUE

Suppose your friend's girlfriend is a stripper. Would you go to the gentleman's club and pay her for a lap dance? Is that wrong? It's your good friend's friend. On the other hand, stripping is her job. And if it's something she's willing to do for a stranger, why's it wrong if she does it for you? What if she's really good and you pay her extra? You know, tip her well. Money isn't the issue? Fine. What if you then see her at her work all the time and it becomes a regular thing? What if because you're friends with her friend, she considers you a friend, and now she feels there's nothing wrong with a little extra in the V.I.P. room because you won't talk, and she's comfortable with you? You're now her friend, and it's your birthday – and you've already seen her naked nearly a hundred times and wondered what it would be like to touch her. Any of this wrong? Before today, I would have been able to make the right decision, the ethical decision, even before my private naughty orgasm released a rush of regret to my *anterior cingulate cortex.*[1]

People who have the luxury of doing the right thing for the right reasons would disapprove of what I've been doing for the past several years – committing crimes. But I've been committing these crimes for the right reasons. When I'm done, the world will be in a better place, and I'll have my satisfaction – my revenge. Revenge for me, turned into a blood oath. But the problems erupted quickly because revenge made me myopic. Yesterday, I was content to act like a criminal. Before then, I wouldn't have had a problem answering those ethics questions. No, it's not complicated either. It's simple. It was simple for me and it's simple for the world. People just like to make the answers complicated in order to justify their bad behavior. Before, I wouldn't have even gone into the club. I never would've allowed myself to be tempted to make the wrong move. Because even though my friend's girl would take her clothes off and grind up against other sleazy, horny toads if he or she had the money, the point is – that's my friend's girl, and I wouldn't disrespect my friend.

Others may know what she looks like naked, what she feels like, and what it's like to pay to look at her. Hell, these strippers' boyfriends or managers, have to pay the girl's rent so they can see *them* naked. The world of other seedy men could know these things – but I shouldn't. I needed to know everything else. I needed to know who was willing to violate that friendship. Who was ethical and who was a lying, unscrupulous piece of shit. Others have called me a sophisticated and treacherous Machiavellian. Pick the blue pill or the red pill.[2] But it's simple. I already know what you're going to say, "You picked the blue pill." Because when the shit goes down, the FBI, SEC, IRS, or some politically-motivated state prosecutor who wants to become a judge, throws around some accusations, "queen for a day" immunity letters, or just plain want to snap the handcuffs on the rare members of the privileged investment class, for some sexy headlines and a perp walk[3] – you want to be able to portray yourself as living in the believable reality of blissful ignorance. You didn't know a thing. You would never do something like that. You're moral. *World, hear me!* Alright, you made four-hundred-percent on your money in ninety-days, but – *really, I didn't know something criminal was going on.*

So what's my problem? Well, I'm part of a criminal enterprise – a Ponzi scheme; and I hold a leadership position in that enterprise. The enterprise has gone international. It's big and ongoing – worth billions. I wanted to work faster while remaining methodical. I had to run the scheme my way. Of course I wanted your help. I wanted to trap certain treacherous investors and keep the innocent ones out, for sure. But some people can't help themselves – they're drawn to the bright ultraviolet light in the center surrounded by the electrified grill. Meant to kill mosquitoes, sometimes a friendly lizard will just ride the lightning until its well-done body drops to ground.

Here we are in a simple Ford E350 Econoline van in front of my ocean-front condo.[4] I adjusted the laptop on the passenger seat in order to remove the glare off the screen, and there's a postcard in the center console with physicist Garrett Lisi's E8 physics model in full color on it. I turned it over and my wife, Taylor wrote, "May God's particle be with you."[5] I'll admit it, even under the stress of being chased by international syndicates and the FBI, I smiled and continued to drive. With the aid of cutting-edge artificial intelligence – my best friend, I might be able to survive. Next step, go off-line and finish *God's Ponzi.*

▪ ▪ ▪

Riding in this van down the highways of America, I realize I haven't had a good night's sleep in years. In my mind's eye, I see the body of our enemy dangling from a rope or rotting in prison. Thinking about every chess move that can be played and how we could counterattack. If we took a flash-photo of the situation, it looks like I stole a shit ton of money in my own investment bank while running a Ponzi scheme.

To rework a remark attributed to bank robber, Willie Sutton: Why start a bank? It's where the money is. Banks are magical - not many people understand banks. But some people love money – the more the better. Banks have the power to lend and the power to repossess money and assets. A bank can lend ninety-percent of its capital as long as there is a ten-percent reserve. What if people want their money back at the same time? It's called a "run on the bank." The bank goes under, it implodes. It implodes just like a Ponzi scheme that runs out of fresh investor funds.

There is no getting around the criminal, civil, and bankruptcy litigation that will ensue if I'm caught in the crosshairs. A plea or trial is not a viable option since my goal is not to spend the rest of my life in prison. Or, some less ethical people could just have me killed. Everyone understands this. What's the point of all this calculus? To remind you I can't get caught. Sure, suicide has crossed my mind. But, I'm perfectly healthy and I believe in the sanctity of life. Dying would be surrender – a loss, as in not a win. As careful as I was to prevent innocents from getting caught up in my scheme, getting caught now would hurt many of them. The purpose of the scheme was not motivated by money or greed; but for revenge, through means of proving one major point – lawyers aren't heroes.

Boiled down to its essence, I'm still playing because I can still win. I can still get out of this alive. I need forty-two million dollars by the end of the week. Once I make the money, ironically I won't need it. I just need to prove that I have forty-two million. Or, "always had it." I can't manufacture bank records that show the bank is well capitalized either because the bank is past due on a payout to existing investors. And unless you know someone that's willing to let me have forty-two million dollars with no interest, to keep a bank afloat that can go under the next day, I really need to produce a fresh forty-two million.

I'm going through the options. One must consider all options carefully; obtain the most information possible before choosing. Pick the best response based upon what others are likely to do. The key is to get perfect information. Once I have the information, I analyze the likely outcomes and select based on the best of the best possible outcomes. In a nutshell, this is what's called, "game theory." It's hard to explain to idiots and hostile lawyers that game theory is serious. In game theory, everyone is a participant, but only the shrewdest are players. It doesn't mean that I think we're "playing a game," that is to say I'm taking the situation lightly. God forbid you tell a lawyer on a mission for money that he's an irrational game player based upon known information and witness the reaction.

In essence, we always should study strategic decision making. The key to this game is understanding the desired outcome. The game itself seems like I have the typical objective – money; but money is not my objective. Between the object and my goal, is the squeeze. Even though game theory is a study of mathematical models of conflict and cooperation, we cannot assume our adversaries are rational game players. My strategy is to appear as the irrational game player. But I'm an evil game player. They are greedy, so they assume I'm greedy. If they commit to that assumption, they can still lose miserably.

We developed the one major secret weapon, cutting-edge artificial intelligence – the AI; that is, true AI – a self-learning machine. AI that can gather data and analyze the meaning of the data better than any software service produced to date. It's a step ahead – whole-life management. Not just managing my life, it suggests how I should live my life in order to achieve my goals set. So, I tasked it to help me run the world's largest Ponzi scheme. The AI analyzed the data and offered me a way to make the scheme to go supersonic. I was warned, I admit it. Financial groups, feeder funds, cartels, you name it, wanted their data to remain undetected and their money properly invested. We exploited it. The team provided the proof that this could be done. Then the numbers spun out of control.

The Ponzi scheme, like most that invest in the markets, caught the proverbial *black swan* – that bad hand of cards. If I can't fix this black swan, bad hand, or bolt of lightning in the next few days, I could end up dead and I'll be leaving behind the lives left in shambles of the people I care about.

▪ ▪ ▪

If you're in a position of authority and can't tell the difference between a good guy and a bad guy, then you're incompetent. If you can tell the difference and you don't care, then you're evil. These lawyers are evil. I'm talking about the lawyers and their facilitators. A well-funded Ponzi[6] scheme brings out all the fee-eaters. When a Ponzi scheme ends, the beginning of that end takes place in bankruptcy court. There's the debtor, the Ponzi schemer's corporate entity running the scheme; and, the creditors, the entities that are owed money from the debtor – the Ponzi scheme itself. The debtor wants to collect money from others so it can begin to pay the creditors some portion of what it owes – the reason the debtor is in bankruptcy. Why is the debtor in bankruptcy? Because economic downturns freak out investors. When investors freak out, they want their principal investment back. In a Ponzi scheme this means they want to pull out their money – yesterday, so as not to incur financial loss. They want their investment back and are now eagerly waiting to rejoin reality with normal monthly return on their investment. The problem for the Ponzi schemer, and soon-to-be debtor, is that he's been paying the extraordinary interest rate each month to investors and now not only do the investors want their principal back, the schemer can't find new investors to pay the old ones. As the adage goes: When the tide goes out you discover who's been swimming naked. Depending on how fast this process occurs, dictates how fast the Ponzi scheme collapses. Who and which entities are a debtor, net-winner, net-loser, victim, secured or unsecured creditor, and how much these various entities will get back when the *clawback* occurs in bankruptcy court, requires lawyers.

Lawyers, special lawyers – bankruptcy lawyers. Who and what makes them special? They do. They're like mountain people from the Appalachia. They're related to each other, marry each other, are friends with each other, and they screw each other – and over. The Court and its members create special rules in order for the special lawyer to appear in bankruptcy court. Not just any member of the federal bar of that particular state and district can be a member of the bankruptcy bar, and appear (represent someone or some entity) and electronically file court documents. They're a close-knit group, until they're eating from the same wildebeest. Then it can get nasty. Interesting to watch if you're not the wildebeest and have a detached and clinical acceptance that this is the way of the bankruptcy Serengeti – hyenas eat wildebeests.

The Ponzi scheme always ends in bankruptcy court - the last phase. It's where Ponzi schemes go to die. Then lots of money flows into the hands of the fee-eaters. Think of the money as the meat of the wildebeest and the fee-eaters eat away at that meat. The portion of meat is dependent upon the size of the wildebeest. The size is determined by how much money can be collected and from how many. Some collection efforts are easier because a trustee might only have to stick-up a few banks and collect millions at once. Then the lawyers think the game is over. But, the lawyers assumed the game was only played in court. My favorite words in jurisprudence: "We're adjourned." That's when *my* work begins.

Before I even started my Ponzi scheme, I found out that Ponzi schemers were using my closest friend, Joseph's early versions of his open source software for their criminal schemes. He had no part of any criminal activity. Regardless, I could only lock onto the question: What were you thinking, Joseph? Why can't you answer me? I could have access to the entire database of Joseph's brain, and I still wouldn't understand. He opened the source code of early versions of his software service that helped manage their schemes. He had too much faith in man. He thought the best of mankind and individual men. It was his religion; religion in that he stopped using logic, until it was too late. Trust was his form of religion. These thoughts kept swirling in my head. No music on the radio; driving meditation, there was nothing but silence but for the sound of tires biting the highway beneath. My biggest fear? Dying before I obtain my vengeance.

The desert was cold at night, especially in the beginning of February. On I-10 West all day, desert forever. Snakes were crossing in the middle of the road. As I drove across the interstate, the skyline and horizon became electric. It can be seen from space. As I approached civilization, affirming my plan, ceasing to analyze whether the plan was correct; there was no turning back.

No point in turning myself in, my prison sentence would be effectively the same. I'm not committing suicide. Murder was not the answer, yet. I needed to double millions in two days. Where do I go? Where can this happen? The noise becomes distracting. The lights make me teeter on the edge of fits. There is only one way to make it happen. Game theory's best strategy, my best answer – *Vegas baby, Vegas.*

TRANCHE I
The Innocent Climb

My Friend Joseph Lars

I'm not obsessed with the past, but in order to learn from experience, now and again we should review, take stock in our lives, and smile or shake our heads at the decisions we've made along the years. In order to understand who and where I am at this point, you'd have to know Joseph Leege was my closest friend. My enemies didn't know that, which was good. This means my enemies, the lawyers and their agents, didn't understand my motivation; and that kept them off-balance even though they felt like they were always in control.

It was the middle of 1983. Joseph was always known as Joey, until middle school. School and Joey weren't the best combination of modern education. Joey – always on the receiving end of hurtful taunts in the corner of the school hall. He walked around terrified.

One day stood out. We were in the hallway. They were yelling, "Joey retardy!" "Joey retardy is starting a rock-band." "Joey rocks back and forth while he pisses on himself." High pressure and lots of noise were triggers for him. He wasn't mentally slow; just the opposite – genius. I saw it happening and I ran up behind them and kicked each one of them in the balls from behind so fast that when I grabbed Joey and ran, not one of them realized that I had done it. They thought Joey kicked them. They were so embarrassed they told no one and they never bothered him again. But Joey slipped into one of his sweaty trances for the rest of the day. He shivered like a chihuahua coming out of a cold bath. I held him for two hours before his parents came home. I told them what happened. Mr. Leege always thought it was some undiagnosed form of dissociation for highly functional people. Joey was so smart and functional when he was stress-free.

Instead of taking Joey to the doctor, the next day, Joey's dad went to the clerk's office and changed Joey's name. In an at-home ceremony with Joey's mom, sister, and me, his father presented a signed order from a Cook County Judge changing Joey's name to *Joseph Lars Leege*. The only thing new was the middle name "Lars." Lars, a Nordic Viking warrior name. His father, who had a PhD in electrical engineering, but seemed like he had a PhD in everything, regaled us with stories about famous Vikings with the name Lars. From now on, his father declared, no one was to call Joseph, "Joey." He was now Joseph Lars Leege, unlike a *Boy Named Sue.*[7]

His father had a Viking sword that was hanging on the living room wall, took it off the wall, tapped Joey atop his shoulders, and dubbed him Joseph. This was an official and formal name – changing ceremony. Joseph was beaming. He loved his new name. For that moment, Joseph let himself believe in the magic of changing his name. Will calling Joey, Joseph change him? That's what we hoped. No way to really measure it. Then his mom served cake. Every kid loves cake.

▪ ▪ ▪

My mother died quickly of breast cancer shortly before I was thirteen years old. Her name was Sarah. I didn't really have too many thoughts about what could've been had she lived. I mostly miss what she was as a person – sweet and kind. My father always described her as a force of good. My father was a trusting man. He was an honest man. Too honest for his own good because he thought others were honest as well. He was a victim of a scheme.

Here was the beginning – the big bang of the Ponzi scheme and a glimpse into my inner darkside. My father invested fifty-thousand dollars with a friend. And, his friend ended up stealing every cent my father invested. It was all my father had. I told him, it was a big risk to invest with any friend, let alone this fucking guy. Harry Huber, he sounded and acted German, but my father assured me he was a fellow Jew. I kept telling him that doesn't mean you should let your guard down. He was counting on you thinking that you and he were family, so he would never hurt you.

"Sometimes you have to take a chance," he would say. Damn slogans.

"Dad, that's marketing bullshit. It makes no sense." What was it that my dad was investing in? Some type of low frequency seismic machine of some kind that was supposed to cure cancer – particularly breast cancer. Disrupt cancer through low frequency sound waves. I did some research myself because I wanted to know if there was anything someone could do to save my mother, Sarah Portnoy. I saw one article that hoped that high frequency sound waves could disrupt cancer cells. But the waves were unlikely to penetrate bone or muscle. I told my father that Harry's business was stupid. I asked: "Why does it work?" He said the special patented sound waves the machine creates disrupts the makeup of tumors and destroys cancer cells. It couldn't be *patented* sound waves unless it was patented.

"How does it do that?" I asked.

"Through sound waves," was his reply.

"That's it? That's a tight circle, Father." He didn't like me calling him *Father.* I didn't like that he had a pretty smart kid and he invested his life savings when I could have proven to him that investment was a scam in three questions. I knew where this was coming from, too. My father wanted to cure my mother. The doctors were done. They ran out of ideas, so he was open to trying any voodoo. To say that to him would criticize him too deeply. Not to mention it would be ineffective.

"Father, cancer is an immune deficiency. Immune deficiencies are either autoimmune or acquired. Those are the only two options. At what frequency can sound disrupt a tumor?"

My father just wanted his chance to do more and get more. He wanted to be able to say he tried everything to save my mother. He survived as a supervisor in a city job in Chicago. He was decent. It hurt my father financially and emotionally. He felt like a failure. He hated that his thirteen-year-old son told him that the investment was a con, but it was so apparent to me. Obvious, like the cover sheet of the *Cancer-son-cure* prospectus called the device *Con-Sonic.* Yes, the prospectus he showed me after he invested. But I cared about him. So I had to tell him.

"What's the point of my advice, Father? You should have wanted to show me this *before* you invested. Let me tell you what's going to happen to that bald, fat, friend of yours. He's never going to be able to produce a model that can reach the testing phase. Investors will lose their patience and he will get sued. And when his patent pending bullshit is rejected, he'll bankrupt the company. He's trying to raise a million dollars and there isn't a single clinical example of success, let alone a double-blind study. He got some hack D.O,[8] who isn't board certified in crap to say he thinks they are at a foundational level to begin testing. So, what did he raise, two-hundred thousand, tops?"

"One hundred ninety-seven thousand dollars," my father told me. "We're in a new world. New rules apply."

"No, Father, we're not. It's the same old world; the world where we cannot defy the rules of biology, chemistry, or biochemistry. You should have at least talked to Joseph's father, if you didn't want to discuss it with me." I took a breath. My heart raced, but I continued. "So then, a trustee will be appointed and your money has been spent. The trustee will put in minimal effort because there isn't any pot of money to get paid from and you might get two-thousand dollars back on your fifty-thousand dollar investment –minus attorney's fees. So basically, nothing."

My father deserved this because of his failure in logic; and, I wasn't going to spit out a slogan suggesting that he didn't. But, this shouldn't have happened to him. I couldn't look in his eyes. Mom was dying and we were helpless. I'd fix it. I couldn't save my mother, but I'd get my father's money back. That I could do. My father had no idea what Joseph and I could do on a computer. He just thought we were hobbyists, and that meant we could put together a model computer from scratch. It gave him a sense of comfort we weren't getting into trouble. Of course as a parent, he wanted me to go outside more often, but was happy he didn't have to wonder what trouble we could get into when we were outside. He had no idea what trouble we could get into playing around on that little electronic box.

When the lawsuit came, he showed it to me, and I read it. A trustee filed against my father's friend, Harry, on behalf of all the investors. That fat piece of shit walked around town with his pinky ring, and a Jewish star buried in his hairy chest, like there was nothing wrong and he didn't miss a beat. He still acted like the mayor with a million dollars in his back pocket. People respected him because he *appeared* to be wealthy.

Our neighborhood had a local deli that served as the community meeting place and the pastrami and potato knish were so good it could turn your day around. One could smell the bagels at one end and the chicken soup at the other. There was no hiding if you walked inside. There were hardworking busboys and waitresses navigating around patrons talking to other patrons in the aisles on the way to their tables and on their way out. I would glare at him when I saw Harry making the rounds at the deli. He'd look away unconcerned. He felt he didn't have to hide – he felt no shame. It was part of doing business. He could tell that I understood who he was and what he did. I'd hear him talk about some bullshit to people and I'd just stare. I studied how he didn't move a muscle in his face when he lied. There was nothing in his mannerism that betrayed his con – except his words. No one listened to his words. No one listened to him with a critical ear. He was well-off. So, that made him smart about everything. I'd smile at him at the end of his pitch. He could be explaining why the Cubs were going to lose in the first round of the playoffs or why you should invest in savings and loan banks, with the same level of authority. When he saw me he knew that I knew. I smiled wryly as if to say: I know your con; you're an artist – a schemer.

At this age, Joseph and I dove deep into computer science. We studied dial-up modems, learned how to build our own modems, hacked into the campus phone system, and tunneled into the computer lab. We also were able to sneak on campus of the University of Chicago and get time in the computer lab. And on Saturday at three o'clock, no one was around to complain that we didn't go to school there.

All right, this was the first and only time I had to thank a trustee for putting lots of information about my father's friend in the petition for bankruptcy – bank records, social security, and date of birth. That saved lots of time. Remember, there really wasn't an identity theft problem back in the early 1980s. The court filing was chock filled with wonderful information – more than enough personal information. It didn't even require us to do any real hacking; the files were just plain text, ready for the grabbing. I convinced Joseph that it would be fun to prove we could break into Harry's sundry of bank accounts. We found the accounts in the banks, all with lots of big back doors. We giggled like mad villains the whole time. Joseph made me promise we would tell the banks where there were holes in their system. I promised to write a letter.

What most people didn't understand was hacking is not inherently bad. It's like a good neighbor going over to your house and checking to see if the doors were locked. If the back door was open and your neighbor didn't go in, instead he closed the door and locked it; he has done you a service. That was sort of what I did here. But to the non-computer world even testing an unlocked door seemed like hacking.

About a week later, my father stormed into my room where Joseph and I were huddled around the computer, programming. The sacred room, the room where Heather Locklear and Apple computer posters adorned the same walls.

"Did you break into his bank account and steal money?" My father yelled.

"What? Steal what?" I replied. He startled me. It took me a second to figure out what he was talking about. So, in that moment, I wasn't lying when I asked, "What?" I also technically wasn't lying when I answered, "No," to his next question.

"Did you take his money?" My father was angry. Joseph started to sweat. He was having a hard time with the loud noise and my father was getting loud.

"Did you and Joseph take money from Harry?" My father asked. That was a qualitatively different question, but now Joseph figured out what my father meant and what I had done, and now Joseph was shaking and sweating.

"Joseph didn't do anything. You can't yell at him!" I said.

My father stormed out and came back with a towel and a glass of water.

"Joseph, I'm not yelling at you," my father said in a solemn tone. Joseph became flushed too.

I became nervous because Joseph was rocking back and forth pretty steady and gasping as if in pain. Joseph clutched the towel and then covered his nose and face with it while he rocked. A few moments passed, it was all settled now. Joseph regained his composure. He was breathing through his mouth. He drank the water from the glass in my father's hand. He started to speak. That was a good sign.

"So many colors coming at me. Too much noise," Joseph pleaded.

"Your parents haven't found you medication for that?" My father asked.

"We don't know what the best medication is for what I'm supposed to have yet, Mr. Portnoy."

My father's name was Richard Portnoy. I was Gregory Portnoy. Everyone called me GP anyway; sometimes, *"Jeep."* I changed it to Gregory Portent for my future Ponzi scheme which I started around 2005. With my last name, Portnoy, it would be easy to connect me to my past. My targets, lawyers, had the resources to investigate me easier than the average, innocent dupe. Changing my name to perpetrate my scheme was just an extra a layer of protection.

My father just shook his head. He could see Joseph was in a lot of distress, but his claim that he sees sounds was just too strange for my father to believe. He had me walk Joseph home. I stayed there for as long as I could. My father stood at the door way waiting for me when I returned.

"There was over fifty-thousand deposited in my bank account three days ago," he said.

"Great. You've got your life's savings back, no loss. That's some trustee," I replied and nodded my head in victory.

"Don't bullshit me, Gregory. Did you do it? Do you know how to do such a thing?" I just looked at my father. Locked in and stared at him. He didn't really want me to answer these questions, did he?

Joseph and I were able to break into the bank accounts. At home, without Joseph, I was able to replicate what we did at the University; and went back into the bank accounts, got out without leaving any footprints. Then I reviewed the petition and distributed the money to everyone who had an identified bank account. I also returned the remainder of all that fat fuck Harry's money into the original account.

"What happened?" I asked.

"Well, Harry had money all over the place and all the investors' money was put back into each and everyone's account, some with interest. And, everything he apparently had left over was consolidated and placed back into the original corporate bank account." I knew all this, but I couldn't figure out why my father was so tense. I understood why he was angry, but I sensed something else was going on.

"And?" I asked.

He paused and said, "All the money left in the corporate account was seized and frozen. That was everything *he* had. He killed himself this morning. I didn't even bother to go to the bank and look in my account until I was told of his suicide. I called the other investors, the ones I knew, and all of their money was returned. He wrote and mailed the trustee a letter. The letter was published on a computer printer."

My father pointed at mine when he said it. "A dot-matrix printer. Unsigned. Confessing to his crime and that he had to make everyone whole. But it wasn't a suicide note, Gregory. It wasn't a suicide note because you didn't think about suicide. What do you have to say about that?"

I'll admit I didn't study the fat fuck well enough to figure he'd commit suicide. I should've; I suppose my mistake. Actually, I was a little embarrassed. Every factor needed to be considered because one factor can alter the success of any scheme. Nothing would've changed in my plan had I known there was a good chance Harry would kill himself; but, it was something I should've considered. My father felt bad. He'd rather have lost his fifty-thousand dollars and his lying, thieving friend be alive, then have this outcome. Well, that was the fundamental difference between my father and me.

"So, what do I have to say about that?" he asked loudly and aggressively.

"Maybe Harry felt guilty for stealing. Or maybe he had remorse because he got caught or didn't get the benefit of his ill-gotten gains. But if I'm really being honest, the world is a better place – that's what I have to say about that."

My father made me go to Harry's funeral. He wondered aloud if I felt any emotions. The only interesting parts of the service were when family members said Harry was a good man who always ended up doing what was right. It sure appeared that way this time, didn't it? He left his wife and children penniless. I didn't hear her giving any eulogies. Looking back you might think I, too, would've turned into some type of cyber-Batman seeking justice with an algorithm or employing brute force. Instead, my impulse was do what Harry did, but do it better. But on a deeper level, I realized I had a lust for revenge.

My Muse

I'll save you years of psychoanalysis and tell you that there's no good reason to conclude that I participated in the Ponzi scheme in order to capture the attention of a woman. Computers were not my only love. She was an Israeli girl named Chana. If you can't pronounce it with the slight throat clearing, then just say "Ha-nna," like when the doctor looks down your throat.[9] Her parents immigrated to America when she was ten years old. We were friends through high school and college. She was the best. I never believed in that kind of love since. The no guardrails, high speed, no safety belt kind of love. I'm talking about the kind of love where I was grateful because the girl saved my life. The feeling never subsided. Through the years, when I needed motivation, calmness, laser-focus, I'd access the archives of our conversations and think about what she might say to me.

I saw Chana when I walked in the school library. She followed me with her eyes, but her head was down. She seemed to be reading something too. Hmm, I wondered. I felt the excitement of self-consciousness. I know her, I thought – pretty. I smiled, reflexively – reactively. That was good. I was cool. I was just friendly. Sure, she was pretty and I might like her, but I wasn't going to confirm it to her. I saw her long slender fingers from here. I kept walking. I knew the book I wanted finally made it into the library.

It wasn't there on the shelf. I'd waited a month so far. This was supposed to be the best public school in the Midwest. Where was the damn book? The school librarian told us at lunch two days ago that she had it. Maybe she did me one better.

"Uh, *Shalom*," I said to the pretty girl at the checkout desk. "*Ma shlomayach*?" I asked nervously. She looked Israeli. I knew I asked her how she was doing.

She looked up. "*Shalom. Beseder*," she answered. "*Ma shlomcha*?"

"*Tov ma-od. Aval ani lo mirotsa ani lo yachol lamotsa sefair*." I impressed myself – a full sentence. Pretty girls were the motivation for all kinds of ingenuity.

"Which book?" She asked. "*Zeh achad*?"

She pulled out my book from under the counter, *Speaker for the Dead.*[10] "Poor little, Ender," she said as she handed me the book.

"Yes," I said relieved. "That's the one. *Zeh achad. Toda raba.*" And she knew the book's lead character? I was infatuated.

"*Bevakasha,*" she answered. I smiled at her for an eternity before she broke it by asking me if I was actually going to check the book out. I started to fill out the card in the back of the book. Another female student came by and returned a book at the desk. "Hey, GP," she said. I nodded back in recognition.

"*Ain hayeta karmica*?" I asked.

"Wow, your Hebrew is better than an American bar-mitzvah," she said. "Not just hello, how are you? Where is my book? Or, *Ani roetseh Coca-Cola.*"[11]

She was spicy, I liked it. "A little. My father volunteers at *Am Yisrael,* the temple across the way. I picked up a little."

"I know *Am Yisrael.* Everyone knows *Am Yisrael.* How did you know I had ceramics today?"

"I see the dust on your sweater, and you chipped a nail on your left ring finger," I said praying I wasn't being too, well, like me.

"Ah, you're very observant," she said in accentless English. "Checking out my ring finger, are you?" She said. I looked down for a second then smiled. I noticed her jugular pulse flutter in her neck but didn't mention it. That was so much better than if she licked her lips.

"You know about Ender Wiggins?"

"I read the book before you came and asked for it. It's been here a couple of days," she said. "If you liked Ender's Game, you'll like this book."

"You? Did you like it?"

"No. Science fiction isn't my thing, really."

"What's your thing, ceramics?" I asked in a perfect inquisitive tone.

"Not just ceramics, art."

"Let me see." I asked. I could see her portfolio book underneath her other books on a stool behind her. She took it and showed me. It had a hard cover with thick paper bound by tight ribbon. The sketches inside revealed she had talent. She could draw. And, I was drawn to her. I knew nothing about art. Never had an interest, other than the look of a game character on a computer.

"So, you're GP. I'm Chana. You and Joseph are the school's fair-haired geniuses, huh?"

"Who said that?"

"Aren't you guys like two grades ahead of everyone? Get all the computer lab time you want?"

"I suppose," I said as I shrugged.

"Good, get back here and fix this one right here, or I can't check you out."

She meant check out the book –no puns. Don't act creepy. Don't say it. I smiled, went behind the counter. Her hair was in a word, delicious. Long, dark, straight, smelled like strawberries. I lost my logic in a moment of wooziness. "Sometimes resetting does the trick." I just reset the computer and logged into the library checkout program. She clicked a few keys and checked out the book for me.

"Do you get all the ceramic time you want?" I asked.

"I get some," she said. "You want to learn ceramics, Mr. Turing? It'll change your life, being exposed to so much art."

Did she just call me, Mr. Turing – father of the modern computer? That's better than calling the school quarterback, Jim McMahon. That's like calling a piano player, Mr. Beethoven. You see my point?

"I would," I replied.

"Well, I'll be in there Wednesday at sixth period. You could come then," she said.

"I'll come then, then," I said and smiled, still nervous, not breaking eye contact.

"You going to write that down?" She asked. I broke my stare.

"Don't need to. I won't forget that my life changes on Wednesday at sixth period, right?" I said. I smiled at her and I left with Ender. Yes, I looked back; and, yes, she caught me. She won our exchange. But it wasn't a competition. Not everything had to be a game. She won me over; and I reveled as her prize.

▪ ▪ ▪

I met Joseph in the computer lab on Wednesday at sixth period. I maintained my cavalier attitude, for my sake. Joseph's cognition of expressions and body language was deficient. He made up for this deficiency in other ways.

"I can't stay," I said. "I'll have to get back with you in a couple of hours."

"I know," he replied. "You're going to ceramics to meet Chana Meier."

"How did you know that?" I asked.

"We have Drawing II together second period. Don't worry, I told her you were cool."

"Oh, great," I replied. Now he was involved. "I forgot you took Drawing, that's not even a weighted class. No wonder why you can't be valedictorian." Brilliant – how come I didn't think of that? "I guess I'm in for sure now," I said with sarcasm.

"I didn't say all that. But she is a really good person, GP. She can make you better."

Wow. You'd have to know Joseph better to understand that was quite a statement, a declaration, and it really intrigued me that Joseph said it. It excited me, to be completely honest. Can a girl really do that? "She can make me better?" I asked with astonishment.

"She'll make you more human," Joseph said.

"Human?"

"Pleasant." Joseph added.

"You're saying I'm not pleasant?" I asked.

"I'm saying that she can make you better," Joseph said again. I just stared at him.

"Every time you make me try and change what I say first, makes me regret saying the second thing. I meant what I said the first time. She'll make you better. You'll like her. Spend some time with her." I wasn't prepared to give him credit quite yet, but I really looked forward to ceramics.

* * * * *

Ceramics

Fifteen minutes into sanding a ceramic Japanese kitty, the yearbook committee showed up to take pictures. The peanut-butter cup of humanity merged to form the ultimate union of personalities and subjects of interest – science and art, geek and artist. I was wearing a smock; she wore clear protective glasses she must've borrowed from the chemistry lab.

My heart dropped a little bit when I thought that Chana set this scene up to promote art for the yearbook. But when Joseph popped in a minute later with other art-kids, I could tell he tipped off the enemy. "Why?" I mouthed to Joseph.

He announced, "This needs to be documented." There was a collective, "yeah" in response. The computer lab seemed to pour into the ceramics class. Students posed; pictures were being snapped away. It turned out to be a little fun. So much fun, Mr. Grabowski noticed the computer lab was empty and the ceramics room was packed. He came in and stepped in a few pictures with his lab coat on. Ms. Schoenfeld feigned indignation.

"Mr. Grabowski, your scientists have taken over my art class," she said.

"There's a lot of science in art, Ms. Schoenfeld. Some believe Jackson Pollock was some random squiggly drawing modern artist, but there is symmetry to his art."

"So, we can draw modern art on our science papers, Mr. G.?" One of the art kids heckled.

"No *m.a.* on my science papers, but there is science in art," he answered. I was ready to expound on Godel, Escher, and Bach,[12] but I could almost see Joseph read my mind and he nodded, no – don't do it.

After the excitement died down, and my model was ready to be sent to the kiln, Chana invited me to show her the world of computers.

"You're really interested in coming to the computer lab?" I asked.

"Yes, I want to know what you do," she said.

I invited her to see what I do. She picked the same time - at sixth period the next day.

Welcome to my World

Sixth period couldn't end fast enough. Meeting with Chana at the computer lab was at the forefront of my mind all day. History wasn't my favorite subject. It was simple enough for me to remember the stories and memorize the dates, but the teacher doesn't really pull the events together – why does any of this matter? The only thing that ever interested me was whether the past helped predict the future.

I couldn't stand to wait inside the computer lab. Much nicer if I wait outside the room. That's cool, right? I'm just hanging out and it'll be easier, more approachable. I didn't want to seem too eager, but I didn't want to seem aloof.

Oh good, Benji Pollack. I could geek out with him for a minute. I suppose I wouldn't have called him over to hang out, but I was starting to feel self-conscious just standing in the middle of the hallway waiting for Chana. I said to him I heard there's a new Star Trek series coming out. I wanted to say just enough so he wouldn't leave me standing in the hallway alone. Let's just say I overshot the runway because now I was engrossed in a conversation where Benji locked on to me about what he heard about the "next generation." Where was she? Nodding, I felt my feet shuffling as I glanced out the corner of my eye. Oh boy, this was taking way too long. Ugh, Benji spoke in Klingon. "*tlhIngan maH!*" What was he saying?

Whew, I'm grateful – there she was. So cute – her hair was in a braided ponytail.

"I'll talk to you later, Benji. Your mother has a smooth forehead," which was a Klingon insult. I turned to Chana. "Hey."

"Here I am ready to learn about the world of computers," she said.

"Excellent." I ushered her into the computer lab, an impressive room with rows and rows of computers. My adrenaline was coursing through my veins as we walked into the lab. The combination - the lab, computers, and Chana. I had a girl with me who was interested in computers and me. If you were geek in high school or knew any, you'd understand that was as infrequent as the harvest moon.[13]

We sat down next to each other in front of my favorite computer, in the back end of the lab where we couldn't be seen from the door. A geek's bid for privacy in an open lab.

I looked at her in the eyes. I hoped to impress her. "Computers are not smarter than humans. Computers are just able to do certain tasks much faster than humans. For example, no matter how good you are at math, you'll never be able to calculate numbers faster than a computer, so why try? Let the computer do it. We should spend our time not on calculating, but creating the formulas to produce the calculations. Formulas that can help mankind."

She kissed me. Short, sweet, on the lips. Then she pulled back like she didn't do it. But I smiled. I knew that she did kiss me. I couldn't help but wonder if she kissed me because my remark would liberate every math student from the ninth grade and below or she just wanted to kiss me. I overthought it. I was glad she kissed me. So I kissed her. Like a geek, I continued talking as if I didn't kiss her – a stolen moment and then continued on. "So think of a computer as a very quick file clerk. What we put in the computer's brain that makes it smart, but the computer categorizes, retrieves, and sorts at lightning speed, which can be used for accounting, storing information, analyzing information."

"Computers think many thoughts at once, is that why it can do things so much faster?" Chana asked.

"There were a lot of loaded words in your question. I love that you used the word 'think.' Most people, including computer programmers, will argue computers don't 'think.' I believe they do and will have more complex thought in the future. But explaining it simply, humans shove data into a tube. A human's brain shoves that data through the tube and sends it out as verbal and physical gestures. Some people edit the tube before it goes out; people that stutter suffer from editing their payload of data from a feedback loop of hearing what is coming out of their mouth.

This is why putting headphones on a stutterer and not allowing them to hear themselves while they speak or sing, suppresses stuttering. Computers are doing many things with more processors. The computer's architecture is and will be more complex in the future. Generally, it's doing many things in the same way humans do. So, on some level the computer thinks like a human. One day soon, one computer will be able to offload thoughts onto other computers to ponder, and produce a result. One day a computer will be difficult to discern from a human, only better," I answered.

"So that's why you program with Joseph?" She asked.

"Yes, and I hope one day to have many people on a team build one program or computer architecture," I said.

"You offload computer code to Joseph?" Chana asked.

"Yes. And I just offloaded the last portion of a game we were working on," I bragged.

"Game?"

"So, this is a game that Joseph and I created, it's called *Fire Power*. It's a strategic military tank game. You drive around and blow things up. Try not to get blown up yourself." I put the disc in and it instantly started up.

"How hard is it to make a video game?" She asked.

"Very hard," I said.

"I can draw you something better," she said with no fear. "If I can actually just draw it on a pad, I wouldn't know how to program it."

"Hold on," I replied. I unplugged an old large heavy hi-res drawing tablet from a computer in the next room and brought it over. "You can draw on this and it will show up on the screen." As we talked some more she drew a fabulous angry soldier charging a flag. Her detail was remarkable.

"Any of this interesting?" I asked.

"Yes. I'm interested," she said. "You know Joseph said I'd be interested in *you.* You know he told you to pick up your book at the library when I was working so you would meet me?"

"Now that you say it, I guess he did," I said. Joseph set me up. I wasn't upset. Well maybe in a high school sort of way for manipulating me. But, I trusted Joseph. At some points in life, there are going to be leaps. Trust or don't trust. I wouldn't call it faith, the absence of logic. I'd call it trust.

"He said he knew enough about both of us to figure out we'd be compatible. Even though we have different interests, we're from the same worlds. He rattled off ten factors from personality type to the fact I'm not a computer geek, which makes us good together."

"Sounds like he ran us through a computer," I said.

"I think he did. I think he did," she said excitedly. "At least that's what he said."

I wandered off for a moment in my head to consider if he was working on some software that could do something like that. Did he create some type of personality compatibility analysis when she asked, "You're not mad?"

"No, I'm glad." As enamored as I was with Chana, Joseph couldn't help his mind from wondering and wandering toward the idea of having a computer as a matchmaker, if you fill out a Myers-Briggs[14] and other psychological tests. If we had enough data points that test what makes people compatible, attracted to each other, a computer could do it better.

"Do you think people would pay for that? Pay money to see who they're compatible with?" I asked her.

"Yes, I do - millions," she said.[15]

Perhaps I didn't describe my feelings for Chana well enough for others to understand. I express myself in code not romantic prose. She saved my life and in the end, she rescued me. Her role in the Ponzi scheme was critical because she offered me an escape, if the scheme ultimately failed or succeeded. Now, isn't that love? Isn't that a friend? Having a place to land whether you win or lose?

Nothing New at New Trier

Joseph was brilliant and actually felt empathy for kids who weren't as intelligent or smart; which meant most of the time he felt sorry. To be plagued with superintelligence, the ability to learn so quickly without aid from others, could be somewhat of a curse because once you know better, you have to suffer fools. I felt the same way most days.

I tolerated the mediocrity of the average kids and the overachievers with a connection to certain colleges. Those were known as *gunners* – the ones that hire consultants to fill out their applications for college. My feelings about the special kids; I had no real use for the simple people. I just didn't consider them. Joseph, however, was deeply affected because he would be washed over by a paralyzing humility. A kid with Down syndrome on the streets of Chicago could stop Joseph in the midst of a full-swinging gait. He would stare off in a trance. Joseph would target an object and just stare. I asked him once, what do you think about when that happens? He said he had an intense feeling of shame. Why was he given the aptitude, the gifts of intelligence, and others close to none? The world went black and then went white, except for the target of his focus. Sounds appeared as colors for wherever the sound emanated. Why did he suffer such empathy for the profoundly unintelligent? The deliberately ignorant he ignored; the afflicted, he felt guilt.

It was the late 1980s, even at New Trier, our neighborhood public school that prided itself on being of private school quality; there was a group of special education students. They hung out together and ate lunch together. If you were a student with advanced classes or above you'd never run into them. But if you looked for them, they'd be in the halls grinding among us. Joseph saw them. He even walked into an after-school class where a few of them were just hanging out. They could've been in detention, it wasn't clear; and, Joseph spent an hour teaching simple multiplication. He taught them simple squaring numbers that end in 0 or 5 was easy. Zero was obvious, but if it ends in 5 it was easy too. You can simply swap the 5 for 25 and then multiply the other numbers to the left by the next number higher. Sixty-five squared? Six plus one was seven. 7x6 = 42; add 25 = 4225.[16] The next day the special ed teacher was amazed. On another day he showed them how to tie their shoe laces backward so they wouldn't have to double knot their sneakers again. Some of them never had to try and tie their sneakers again.

They treated Joseph like a movie star from that point forward. They would get excited to see him in the halls in between classes. It could be the fourth period, they'd have seen him three times earlier that day, and they would be just as excited to see him as the first.

One day, Dax, a special ed kid, walked up to Joseph's open locker on a lunch break, and stuck his notebook in Joseph's locker. It was Dax's homework. Joseph explained a trick to make the math easier to Dax, as Joseph finished the assignment. Joseph used his left hand to give Dax a half a chance to sell it as his own. As soon as Joseph was done, Chet Adkins, a dumb jock, with a sleeveless tank top, reached in and ripped a handful of papers from the notebook. Before Joseph could react, Chet pushed Dax like a goon against the lockers. The noise of Dax's head hitting a closed locker door could be heard at the other end of the school. Dax just slumped down to the floor – no anger, just resignation. This was typical abuse Dax had always taken –no use fighting. And that was sad – particularly sad to an ideologue like Joseph. Joseph was stunned. The noise from Dax's head crashing against the locker made Joseph lock up in a freeze; amazed that Chet could be such a base ape – so cruel.

When this happened, I was somewhere else on campus. I wouldn't have let Joseph do what he did because I would've done it and accepted the consequences. Joseph unlocked from his stare and punched Chet square in his nose. Oh yeah, he broke Chet's nose; and it was a bloody mess. Chet punched back at Joseph. Amazingly, Joseph moved out of the way and Chet missed, punching the air in Joseph's open locker. Then a teacher came running and interfered. Chet walked off to the bathroom to tend to his nose, screaming the word, "Fuck" as he stomped away. Chet was more pissed that Joseph punched him, in what in his Neanderthal mind was a "lucky shot" in front of "the whole school."

This wasn't the last time I had to rescue Joseph when he engaged in life's battle. I was worried about Joseph becoming the victim of revenge. When Chet's fellow fraternity of jocks heard Chet's order *to kill the nerd*, Joseph was in trouble. Rumor was the teacher came and broke it up before Chet could respond to Joseph's sucker punch. Truth is, the next day the teacher covered his eyes with his hand when Joseph and I walked to the next class. Son of a gun saw the whole thing and let Joseph get away with it. He'll never be as lucky as he was by the locker again - especially in a straight on attack by multiple attackers.

I concluded Chet needed to know the level of retaliation he and others would endure if they hurt Joseph. Naturally, intelligence gathering was the first step. The principal had already warned Chet that if he hurt Joseph on campus, Chet wouldn't be able to wrestle in the district championship. I also found out that Chet and his crew were planning on jumping Joseph over the weekend outside of school. This was good information since it allowed me some time.

My plan brought me to the auto-shop garage on campus. If I was going to protect Joseph, I needed muscle. I knew the muscle who Chet would listen to and compel him to call off any retribution against Joseph. I smiled at David Sherry who was the school motor-head. People searched their whole life for that level of passion about anything. He didn't play any sports for the school. Boy did every coach want him to score touchdowns, hit home runs, and pin lesser men to the mat for the school. For a person at any age he was big. I saw David raise the front end of Noah Rumsfeld's Volkswagen Beetle over his head in front of a large crowd because Noah had been a jerk to David's girlfriend. The size difference between David and Noah would've made physical violence toward Noah unfair under any standard. It would be like the United States invading Jamaica. So David just walked over to Noah's car at the end of school, right before Noah sat in the driver's seat, held up his index to indicate, one minute, slid his legs and hands under the front end of the car, and like a weightlifter snatched it, then clean-and-jerked it to his chest, and then lifted it to about eye level. He then let it slam to the asphalt. He did it again and again, until Noah screamed for mercy. "Stop! Stop it! Sherry, what the fuck are you doing?"

David Sherry stopped and smiled and said, "You know my girlfriend, Kerry?"

"Yes," Noah replied.

After expressing a look of disapproval, David said, "Be nice to her." Then he walked away to grand applause. The response was one notch above proportional. Noah's front-end suspension rode a little rough after that, but he couldn't run to the principal and complain, David Sherry lifted the front end of my car and dropped it. It would be an odd complaint, particularly since Noah deserved it.

David Sherry was treated like a jock without being one. He didn't want to lose time away from his passion – cars. His friends loved cars. His father worked under my father at the city for the automotive department – fixing cars. David was fixing a teacher's 1983 Mercury Capri when I walked into the shop on Thursday. He nodded to me when I approached. The smell of motor oil and diesel filled the air.

"Where are your books?" I asked. He pointed with a socket wrench to the corner. "What's your worst subject you have homework in?"

"A tie in bio and algebra," he answered. "Why?"

I grabbed his books; thumbed through his notebook. "Is this your homework?" I asked.

"Yeah," he answered. I sat down at a drawing board in the corner and completed the week's work in both classes.

I looked up twenty minutes later and said, "Copy it over in your handwriting and you should be in good shape. You know lifting the front end of a VW Beetle is really not that big of deal considering the engine's in the back and you have a nice front stabilizer bar to get a grip on," I said.

David snickered. "It had the intended effect."

I smiled back, "Yes it did. Magic, indeed."

"Thanks. Why did you do my homework, GP?"

"I need some help with a car."

"Yeah? Whose car?" David asked suspiciously.

▪ ▪ ▪

Saturday morning bright and early, with a couple of guys David Sherry knew from the Southside of town, drove to Chet Atkins' home in Winnetka. By the time the sun rose, all the tires on Chet's *IROC-Z* were piled neatly at the end of the driveway. The engine was disassembled on a painter's cloth in front of the car. We all seemed to be studying the transmission under the hood when Chet's father came out of the house.

"What the hell?" Mr. Atkins announced. I looked up and said hello.

"Hey, you're Richard Portnoy's son," he said. Mr. Atkins was dressed for the country club when he came outside with a cup of coffee.

"That's right, Gregory. How you doing, Mr. Atkins? How are things at EF Hutton?"

"Well... fine. What are you guys doing?"

"We're fixing Chet's timing issue. He was worried about his timing the other day..."

"Do you know what you're doing?" He asked.

"Well, yeah. This is David Sherry; he's valedictorian of auto-shop at school."

"Sherry? I don't think I know your father."

"He works for the City – in automotive," Sherry said nodding. His two friends nodded too.

"That's right. I met your father at a couple of school events. That's nice you're helping Chet. Well, how long is this going to take? The neighbors are going to be upset that you're fixing a car in the driveway."

"What the fuck are you doing?" Chet screamed, storming out of the house in his boxers. His father turned around and looked at him.

"These guys are trying to fix the timing on your fan belt and why the hell are you screaming?" Mr. Atkins said.

"Who told you to touch my car?" Chet yelled, not lowering his voice one decibel.

"Stop screaming, damn it. You're going to wake the neighbors." A moment passed as Chet saw his car was on cinder blocks and his whole engine dissected. "Well, I have a 7:30 a.m. tee time. Tell your mother your friends are out here. Tell her to make some coffee and offer them a danish or something." Mr. Atkins hopped into his Mercedes after he checked the trunk for his clubs, and drove off.

"You're doing more than replacing the fan belt. You took apart the whole engine," Chet screamed.

"Yeah, we wanted to let you know we could take apart your whole engine," I said. "We can put it back together too."

"You better fuckin' put it back together, I have plans tonight after the game," Chet said.

"We heard about your plans," David said. "We're not sure your car will be ready by tonight."

"What the fuck are you talking about? What plans have you heard about?" Chet asked, exasperated.

"This guy's a *'roid rager* or something? I've never seen anybody so upset like this when we're trying to help him with his car," David's friend, Tyrone said for Chet to hear.

"No, Tyrone, Chet just loves his car very much and he doesn't trust us yet," I said.

"That's a shame," Tyrone said. "We can just go then, if he doesn't trust us." Tyrone and his brother started packing their tools and putting them in David's car.

"Wait a second," Chet said. "I trust you. I trust you. Put it back together."

"What are your plans after the game tonight, Chet?" I asked.

"Going to a party at Gretchen Cooper's house."

"Joseph Leege is going to that party. You sure that won't be a problem that he's there?"

"Yeah, how's your nose, Chet?" David started enjoying the nuance of the discussion.

Chet was steaming. He really had an anger control problem. "Fuck Joseph Leege. I'm gonna fuck his shit up when I see him. He suckered punched me." Tyrone's brother continued to walk with the tools back to David's car. "Alright, alright!" Chet said. "He can come to the party. Nothing's going to happen to him."

"Right, ever." I said as I looked at Chet. Then I stared into his eyes deeply. I wasn't scared. I felt a rush. I locked in on his eyes and didn't break the stare. "You were a sadistic douche to Dax and Joseph called you out on it. And that's the end of it." I heard this line in a movie once and it seemed to be a highly effective communication tool. I said, "Let me hear you say it." I waited.

"Fuck you too, Gregory Portnoy," Chet said. He really must have been taking something the school wasn't testing for because he was stewing in his own amped up repressed rage.

"Now I want to hear you say it," David Sherry said. "All this pent up rage I'm feeling, I might have to check under your car, like I did for Noah Rumsfeld. I think your suspension's off."

"Hey, when you boys are done with Chet's car, can you look at the Jag in the garage? The air conditioner is making a funny noise."

"Sure thing, Mrs. Atkins," I said.

We're waiting, didn't need to be said.

"That's the end of it," Chet said.

That was the end of it. Joseph didn't go to Gretchen Cooper's party; he didn't go to any parties. But Joseph never was threatened or hurt by Chet Atkins or any of his friends. We put Chet's car back together. David popped open the hood of Mrs. Atkins' car and he knew exactly what was wrong and he fixed it. She was so grateful; she gave him a hundred-dollar bill to split among us. I didn't take a cut. I learned a lot that day. I contemplated money, currency, bargaining, communication, and revenge. Most of all, it was my privilege and responsibility to protect Joseph.

After the deal with David Sherry worked out so well, I sought to ingratiate myself to other students. From those at school that thought they were gifted, to the average and below average kids. I made deals with my teachers: I'll ace your class if you avoid calling on me and never announce my grades out loud. I didn't want draw attention to myself. No, I wouldn't want to work on your special projects, do extracurricular activities, or tutor younger students, unless there was something in it for me. When word spread that I was in contention to be valedictorian, I told the principal to give it to someone else. The principal told me it was a matter of grade point average alone. I understood and held no resentment. As soon as I received my admissions to MIT and Harvard, I purposely failed my advanced placement physics exam.

My physics teacher, Mr. Grabowski, told his students he was semi-retired, he taught school to keep himself busy, so he wouldn't die from inertia. He was a decent educator. He understood some of my game. There were only four kids in the AP physics class. He knew I failed on purpose and why. I didn't even want to go to graduation. You accomplish to make the world a better place, he argued to me – not for awards or membership in honorary societies. Right, so valedictorian was exactly that – an award. One thing about Mr. Grabowski I liked was that he knew his position in the game relative to me. He sat me down alone after school in his class. He told me he would make me valedictorian based upon the extra work I did, if I didn't sit down and complete the test. So I did it for him. I aced the exam. He told me he would handle the principal in regards to the designation of valedictorian. But to him, "Gregory Portnoy, you are the valedictorian," Mr. Grabowski said shaking my hand. "Do something important."

Joseph and I had been building computers, creating a programming language, making games, and thinking about the future. I needed him and somehow lost track of a more important fact, he needed me. So, he followed me to MIT.

MIT

The campus of MIT was beautiful, smart, historic, and technical. The college dorm room was a jail masquerading as a private building. They should just call it a cell block. The cinderblocks were painted so deep and thick; they couldn't be recognized as blocks. But you could still see the porous pits of cinder – beds were a little better than cots.

My roommate, Henry White was sponsoring our first in-dorm college party. Our beds were parallel against the wall. Joseph and I sat on my bed. Henry was slouched down against the wall and his feet hung over the bed. There was a faint smell of cologne and pot. Joseph leaned against the desk that was at the foot of my bed. Henry seemed pretty cool. He bought the beer. It was some hobos' beer being marketed as exotic foreign beer from Curaçao. *Hopi Bon Beer* – means very good beer in *Papiamento.*[17] What a slogan.

"I like a beer that grades itself," Joseph said.

"It tastes like warm unaged cat piss," I remarked. I was feeling the effect nonetheless.

"It only costs $2.79 a six-pack," Henry said. "Drink up. There's plenty more."

I was studying Henry's side of the room. *Ferris Bueller* was staring right at me. The *Lost Boys* too. Henry was staring at John Belushi wearing a "College" sweater and a black and white poster of Steve Jobs leaning on a *Macintosh.* This was the best1988 had to offer.

"Belushi was awesome in *Animal House.* It would be totally incredible if you had the poster of him as a Samurai," Henry said.

I kept listening to Henry talk. I practiced shuffling and cutting a deck of cards as he spoke. This was the first real conversation we had.

Something was kind of interesting about his voice. Henry was the son of a well to do banker in Coconut Grove, Miami. Henry said that he had to study business but loved engineering. Henry required his father's approval. It seemed pathological. He always seemed nervous whenever his father called, and whether this decision or that will be good for his future. Henry was very concerned about "the future."

"I sort of dig Steve Jobs. The man's a marketing genius. I mean, he sees the world differently than the rest of us. He's going to come up with some more incredible stuff before he's done. But Jack Tramiel is more interesting to me. Tramiel leaves Commodore games and goes with Atari – pretty wild story."[18]

Henry added, "Tramiel, not good in business, if you think about it. Actually, kind of ruthless."

I countered, "Jobs and Tramiel had a vision and had to have it their way. You either accepted it or you didn't. . . . I've always wrestled with my feelings of love between the Amiga and the Commodore," I smiled, then burped.

"I think they're kind of selfish pompous proprietary asses," Joseph said.

"And you two are friends since you were kids?"

"Yep," we both said and nodded.

"Joseph thinks software should be free. Free to the world to use. And the world becomes a better place. I think we own and sell the software and our world becomes a better place."

"That's great. I like that you two are free to disagree,"[19] Henry said. "This is college."

"Hold up, hold up. What's with the accent?" I asked.

"What accent?" Henry answered.

It was a bizarre denial. "Sounds Spanish," I replied.

"Cuban," Joseph said.

"It must be the *cerveza*," Henry said.

"Are you Cuban, Henry?" I asked.

Henry shifted on the bed. He reached into the drawer and found a joint and lit it up. "You mind?" He asked. "It calms my nerves."

"If you only knew about my nerves," Joseph said.

"I really don't care about you smoking weed," I announced. "So, you're anxious about being Cuban, Enrique?"

"My father is Enrique. I'm Henry. I'm meant to assimilate – be American."

"I smell a hotplate! Is someone using a hotplate?" The resident advisor yelled out from the hallway. Henry opened the window.

"That's code for he smells the weed. Want some?" Henry offered. We both said no, but drank a couple of more swallows to feel like we were being cool. One more puff and Henry put out the joint.

"Soup's off!" Henry yelled back. Henry put away the joint and pulled out a small bag of mushrooms from the drawer. "Try some guys."

"We really shouldn't. We've got a big day tomorrow." I said answering for the both of us.

"Just a little. It'll only last a couple of hours. It'll open your mind. Recommended by Jobs," Henry said.

"I'll do it," Joseph announced with the excitement of a child.

"You're going to do it? Whatever happened to, 'Don't fuck with the mechanism?' Your brain."

"Cannabis slows you down. This should open us up," Joseph replied.

"Not sure I want to be opened up."

"You're scared?" Henry asked, holding the bag out. We both reached in and took one. "Yeah, just take one –school tomorrow."

"I assume it takes a minute?"

"Just a minute," Henry said.

I stood up and grabbed a deck of cards from my desk.

"What's the square root of 3364?" Joseph asked and stared at me.

"Fifty-eight," I answered. "Still good. Woah, I just saw the number fifty-eight burst into flames in front of me."

"Square root of 5184?"

"Seventy-two," I forced a seven and a two of clubs out of the deck.

"That's awesome." Henry sat up and said.

"I've seen this stuff a thousand times," Joseph said. "I'm starting to feel it."

"Thirty-five times thirty-five?" I asked out loud, I think. "One, two, two five."

"These are tricks. All tricks." Henry announced.

"But, tricks I can do. I'm testing whether I can still do them under the 'shrooms."

"Close the window, it's getting noisy in here," Joseph said. Henry shut the window.

"I should've reported the game show guy." I think I said. Joseph knew what I was talking about, as good friends do.

"Who's the game show guy?"

"He was one giant grifter. GP totally nailed him," Joseph said methodically and went back to his dimension. Then Joseph began to rant. "Ownership is the problem. We all want to own. Less ownership."

"Socialist mushrooms." Henry laughed.

"I saw the whammies. I saw the whammies," I exclaimed.

"Is he okay?" Henry wondered.

"He's fine. I saw the whammies too, buddy," Joseph consoled me. "He's talking about a game show, Henry."

"Oh." Henry said as if satisfied. We were silent again and went back to our private trips.

▪ ▪ ▪

Three hours passed. It was pitch black in the room. Our eyes adjusted to the darkness. A street lamp light began to permeate our vision. We all seemed to nod and smile to each other. It was all good, we hoped. Trip over, we thought, and we were safely back in the room. What did you learn was the question in the room.

"I'm destined to run the family bank," Henry said.

Joseph asked, "Do you want to run the family bank?" I could tell from Henry's body language – he thought there was no choice; he must take over the bank.

"It's the family plan. We are a family of successful bankers. It's our way in," he replied.

"What was your way out?" I asked.

"My father, taking a boat from Havana to Miami." As if reading our minds, Henry knew he would be a business man and not an engineer. He was going to end up running the family bank, if he were lucky. But deep down, he was in a personal jail.

"Your family was on the *Mariel* boat lift?"[20]

"No." Henry exclaimed. "My father and grandfather supported Batista,[21] and it almost cost our family its existence. My grandfather was murdered by Castro. My father told Fidel, 'go fuck yourself, *El Sapingo*,'[22] to his face." We waited for Henry to continue, but he didn't. Joseph and I just looked at each other; then saw Henry rotate a gold-plated ring with an emerald around his finger. He caught us looking and abruptly stopped.

"So, what's a *whammy*?" Henry asked. Joseph and I broke out into laughter. Our laughter encouraged us to laugh more until it was uncontrollable.

Joseph and I were using a television as a monitor for one of our computers. While we tinkered around with one of the motherboards, we let the television run. The channel was on a game show – *Press Your Luck*.[23] Joseph was soldering.[24] He was in one of his legendary deep focuses. I was watching the players spin a wheel and then play a hand eye coordination slot machine. We'd been up for twenty hours, motivated by curiosity and diet cokes. I noticed this player was doing extraordinarily well – statistically, extraordinarily well. The host explained that the streaks were six or seven in a row of winnings before a player lands on a whammy. This guy wasn't hitting whammies. The audience was out of control. No one understood how this was happening. The host was expressing true incredulity – begging this player to stop and take the winnings. If he were to land on a whammy, he'd lose it all. I didn't consciously know about microexpressions back then, but I knew about random number generators.

"Worst random number generator ever," Joseph exclaimed. The game had a pattern and this player knew it. I made Joseph stop and look. The streak was long enough for us to catch five out of probably twenty patterns. This guy knew them all. He knew when to hit the button to avoid the whammies. He knew where the whammies were going to be. What Joseph didn't say was that once we figured out the random number generator was crap, he lost interest and went back to the motherboard. I, however, became more fascinated. Within ten minutes I wrote on a pad the formula for the number generator for the thirty-six square board. The player's scam was ultimate money making magic. I loved it. I could've called the show and told them. But, it would have been like heckling a magician. Everyone was enjoying the show. And some giant corporation, NBC lost that day. Who cares?

"So what happened," Henry asked.

"I don't know," I said.

"You really didn't turn him in?"

"No," I replied.

"I can't believe it," Henry said. "I would've lost my mind knowing he was cheating and nobody knew."

Henry and I just looked at each other. I said nothing else on the subject.

"While you were dreaming about whammies, I was thinking about the meaning of life. Computers are changing the world. It will affect everything – commerce, entertainment, personal communication. We are going to be able to transfer and communicate information all over the world. I know how computers think and soon they will be able to think on their own and we will be able to upload our consciousness to them," Joseph said.

"Banks have been able to wire money for a while now," Henry said.

"I'm talking about something bigger, Henry. Imagine if we can send money from a computer to another computer instantly. Buy things over a computer, buy things with a phone even, and it's delivered to you, delivered to you on the phone. Message large amounts of data over the computer and store the data, analyze it. We are alive at a time when technology can change the way we will work and live."

"People will still have to see each other and work together. No one will ever trust it," Henry insisted.

I've heard Joseph's rap before – not quite so articulately. But Joseph wanted to change the world and he seemed to have total clarity after our little trip. "One day we'll be talking about how crooks and terrorists use end-to-end encryption or just not communicate on the phone or internet because they know they're being snooped on. I really doubt a ban on super-encryption is about crooks and terrorists, it's about me and you being watched." Joseph nodded knowingly - his logic foolproof in his mind, and mine too.

"That's a billion-dollar idea," I said. "You design it, I can sell it, and Henry can finance it. Now that's a plan." I announced.

"Ah, enough with your billion dollar ideas," Joseph lamented. "Ideas. It's about the ideas." So naive. You have to love Joseph – and look out for him.

"One day you're going to tell us about how your dad told Castro to fuck off and lived to tell about it, Henry." He promised that he would. Henry became a great friend. We'd hear that story and many others from Henry over the years. Because he became a trusted friend with skills in banking, Henry became a key player in the Ponzi scheme. He was the one that helped me start the investment bank that was used as the foundation of the scheme. He put his life at risk to save the Ponzi scheme and save our lives. In one way, Henry regretted meeting and befriending us. Henry was a bottle of angst and always seemed to be crumbling under the pressure. In another way, he became his own man, outside the shadow of his foreboding father and family because of us. Risking his life was the cost of making his own way.

Until then, Henry possessed the innocence of a young child who looked up to his father as a god. I was compelled to break it down for him. "CocoBank is a first-generation Cuban bank in Coconut Grove. The construction in town hasn't stopped. You're not competing for WASPs, you're competing for Latin Americans – Colombians, Panamanians, Bolivians." Henry didn't or couldn't admit to himself that Miami was built on cocaine, and financing from banks helped launder the money.

"What are you implying?" Henry shot back.

"You need to know your market, Henry."

Maybe I learned something. Know yourself, be yourself, and I shouldn't get high again. When high, I said what I thought. And the only thing I brought to the table was my ingenuity, my cunning. I couldn't afford to screw with that by getting high.

▪ ▪ ▪

The morning came and I awoke groggy. My voice sounded like I was awake all night. I heard Chana's voice once I picked up the phone. She spoke with such excitement-strings from a symphony played in the background of my mind. Preparing for what would be the worst scenario, seeing her anytime soon would be out of the question, forced me to brace myself for the signal that amps of disappointment was forthcoming.

"Have you heard of BB&N?" Chana asked. I hadn't. Why was she asking?

"No, what's BB&N?" I was so happy she called me. I was lonely for her. I know, it's out of step with how most would consider where this high school relationship could be, but if you haven't picked it up by now, I'm different.

"What's BB&N?" She said again. The dramatic pause got me excited.

"Is it a bank you inherited?" I asked.

"No, better. BB&N is a school in Cambridge, Massachusetts. And guess who will be teaching there next semester? Guess who will be going to school there next semester?"

"You." I exclaimed. "You and your family are moving to Cambridge?"

"We are. The best surprise ever, no?"

"Yes," said with the relief of avoiding the gloom of months pining away for her. "I had no idea. How long were you waiting? How long were you keeping this a secret?" I asked fully awake.

She told me her parents were talking with the school for six months and they finally offered both of her parents a job at the private high school in Cambridge. Her father will teach math and her mother, Middle Eastern studies. Chana said she didn't want to disappoint me if it didn't work out. I confessed that I didn't realize how much I missed her until now – when I knew she wouldn't be coming back. Life felt right for a man that never felt poetry.

By the second week of school, Cambridge was my new hometown and Chana's family's too. Chana was always worried about her mother; never her father, or even her little brother. The men in her family seemed to adapt to wherever they were. We spoke about how this change of location added pressure on our relationship. Admitting there was some anxiety, reduced the anxiety. I was convinced and told Chana that I thought she was the one for me, I didn't need to make the mistakes of romance with other girls, or take part in multiple meaningless interludes in order to know what I had in front of me was perfect for me. Commitment to a woman that was comforting. It was heavy, perhaps too heavy, so I kept these feelings hidden.

Chana and I gallivanted, hand in hand, around the campus and the city. We ate our way across town. We figured out how to take the T from her house to her school, even though her parents would drive her to school every morning. Then we went all the way back to campus and we practiced going from MIT to BB&N. We were silly with inefficiency.

It occurred to me I'd never been away from home for weeks at a time. My father was concerned at first. He even expressed concern about what he labeled a dramatic move by the Meir family by moving to Cambridge. Joseph and I weren't boarding school kids. At MIT there were students who spent more time away from home than at home. Some international students hadn't been home in years by intention. I related to some degree, I hadn't seen my mother in years. Joseph was my support; I was confident, not insecure, like the kids who were raised at home by hovering moms and well-financed gunner-fathers who had to bribe the crew coach to get admitted, so they could brag about the trophies – their kids. They're not happy for them; they're happy because of them.

With Chana nearby, I was nearly invincible. My only flaw? My need to feel important; my need to beat others; my need to protect the people under my protection; and my nasty, vengeful streak. All regulated and soothed by Chana. As quickly as I recognized my flaw, I could break free, like a well-studied Yeshiva student justifying a ride on an elevator on Shabbat because it stopped on every floor, rather than by the work expended by a press of a button. She acted as a governor over me.

▪ ▪ ▪

As I acclimated, I wanted something better – something bigger. We were going to college but I was trying to build a company at the same time. Gaming – the future of computers. Yes, spreadsheets and accounting, and project management – but gaming; you were a rock star to every kid, teen, and most adults if you created cool video games. Who didn't love Space Invaders or Donkey Kong – the classics? That's what we wanted – an incubator of ideas and development.

Even with the money we'd made on *Fire Power* we were smart enough to want to reinvest in the company. I can't imagine taking money from an investor and then he gets to force his view upon us; or worse, what to do. We might as well work at McDonald's. I didn't and especially Joseph didn't want to be an order taker.

As we walked around a neighborhood just outside of campus, we entered a local tavern for lunch. Wood all around; long wooden tables with coats of dried lacquer. Wooden columns attempting to look old, but were new. Three types of barbeque sauce on the table and the catch-all catsup. We were told it was catsup, as opposed to the trademarked "Ketchup."

Our food was delivered. The smell of barbeque was intense. Joseph and I saw an average looking middle-aged man and another kid our age sitting next to us at the long community table. Everything about this man was average – average intelligence, linear thinker. Clearly, he was having difficulty dealing with the intelligent, non-linear thinking, graduate school-aged student. The student seemed to be babbling on about the stupidity and inefficiencies of the *qwerty* keyboard.[25] It turned out the middle-aged man was the student's uncle. It was after rush hour lunch, so we had the place mostly to ourselves. It was quiet and I suppose the long table was meant to be conducive to community conversation.

"This is how you enjoy yourself? Designing alternative keyboards? How efficient is that? How are you going to meet a girl if you stay inside designing keyboards?" The uncle wondered aloud. He seemed resigned to recognizing that he'd never be successful communicating with his nephew.

"I agree," Joseph announced. Both of them looked at Joseph. "The qwerty keyboard was an accident of history." Now, I looked at Joseph. "The history of the qwerty keyboard was to design a keyboard to avoid the use of one hand writing many words. The faster you type on the original typewriters with one hand, the greater the chance of keys locking. So the qwerty keyboard was meant to solve the problem of keys locking, not typing speed." It seemed like we were all collectively vapor locked on this perfect explanation.

"I know that." No doubt this guy likes comic books and plays Dungeons & Dragons – probably by modem. And we later learned he played *Fire Power* better than we did.

Joseph engaged the geek, identifying him as one of our own, by agreeing that the *qwerty* keyboard was poorly designed.

The adult introduced himself as, "Uncle John. And this is my nephew, Louis."

"I've designed my own keyboard. I have no patience for living in a world where I'm handcuffed to foundational errors."

"So, you guys looking for a place to live off campus?" Uncle John asked trying to change the subject. "I own a place around here but I can't let Louis live there alone, it makes no sense."

"I'm not Louis, I'm GNU."[26]

Joseph and I smiled. I smiled to prevent myself from laughing – is this geek serious? GNU?

Uncle John sighed, "Louis Gnofski. He likes to be called GNU."

"GNU, not Unix.[27] We got it, Uncle John," I said.

Uncle John apparently didn't.

"Yeah, we'd love to see that apartment," I said. And we did; and it was perfect – work space and sleep. It was three stories. It had a vague scent of mold on the bottom floor that years from now would trigger memories of the times that happened here. The bottom floor was a dungeon of computers, wires, and tools. Cables were hanging from the ceiling. A tilted poster board with "DIY," hung from the ceiling in the middle of the room. DIY – that was his philosophy in a nutshell – do it yourself. Ten people could live in the apartment. It was perfect for hungry young computer geeks who were set to manufacture some really cool shit with computers. An apartment as a freshman – it was a big deal. First reason, it wasn't designed as a cell block like the dorms. Second, it had more room for Chana to hang out and be present. Lastly, I could run a team and create companies out of that apartment.

It turned out that GNU fit in. He was also freaky smart. Not like "genius" in the pejorative way. No, I mean this guy was instrumental in developing mail[28] sent from one computer to the next, and improving the very fabric of the web in a way we all appreciate, but don't always recognize. Some people just make things better. Rumor has it GNU was named "GNU" by Steven Wozniak, the guy who actually invented the Apple computer. Right, "The Woz." GNU believed in Joseph's philosophy of open source coding. GNU hated anything related to marketing. If something was good and that something was out there in the universe, you'll find it. He was completely comfortable doing work in a cape and a speedo, or no speedo at all. Since he put some pants on, he fit in with the group just fine.

He loved Asian philosophy and he was drawn to Asian things, but he was Caucasian. My strongest memory of him was he smelled of tuna fish out of the can because that was mainly what he ate. Let's not waste any time on food preparation. We spent hours and hours designing and playing games. GNU was the best code editor, too. He just knew how to make a game go faster. GNU also mastered counter clock cycles. That meant he could take almost anyone's code, anyone's algorithm, and make it fast – way, way faster. And that was what we needed to make games.

GNU became a permanent member of the team when he helped Joseph and I one weekend put the finishing touches on a second version to a game we created, *Return Fire.* Just a simple Army kill 'em game. One of the first split screen games that could be played over a modem. GNU created the sound for the *squish* when a tank ran over an enemy soldier. He literally made the sound himself with his mouth. It sounded so ridiculous that we laughed every time, so it had to go in the game. Those were good times; perhaps, the best of times.

GNU was instrumental in the Ponzi scheme. His role was simply being the best human to interface with computers. Computers haven't reached pure omniscience. Self-learning machines had its limitations too. GNU provided the answer to the question what do humans do better than computers. For one thing, it knows what humans want. Emotion, passion, revenge, those are hard thing to teach a computer. Most importantly, the human has to tell the computers what he wanted the computer to do.

▪ ▪ ▪

After about six weeks of school, I just used my dorm room as storage for hardware and some clothes. I stayed at the apartment which acted as our personal computer lab. Henry appreciated that he didn't have a full-time roommate, but we had to pretend I still lived there; otherwise, he might have gotten a new one.

Joseph had a disdain for attending classes. He didn't see the point. I attended everything and more. All he had to do was pass a midterm, a final, and turn in an occasional paper. He and I attended more guest lecturers talking on a particular topic, rather than the regular classes. It was MIT and they had an All-Star lineup. The promise of an *Innovation Lab* was a dream – entrepreneurship forged by age. If the real money could be convinced that the best ideas could come from young people, it will happen.

I had the ability to write. This was special. Why are computer scientists, future scientists of the world, forced to struggle through composition class? Most of the geeks will never write anything longer than a letter. The liberal arts portion of college education was all in the name of creating well-rounded citizens, but it was all in the name of tuition. I was determined to rack up degrees, get by, so I could pursue my real business – business. Capitalize on the real power I had, the power to harness Joseph and other geeks like him. If I had three others like him, I could rule the world. To me, that was appealing.

Leela Fashionista

Joseph walked through the door of the office-apartment casually with a college co-ed in front of him.

"This is where the team works," he said. She nodded, looking around, getting accustomed to her new surroundings.

With the computer geek team, I had to tell some of these guys to go take a shower because it doesn't occur to them. We were all sitting around clacking away in relative quiet on our respective keyboards. There was a pause. Heads turned toward Joseph and the co-ed.

"Hey, guys. This is Leela." I'm the only one who smiled in shock. GNU just stared. He told his underlings to get back to work. She shook my hand, but waved and bowed to GNU, as if she'd been briefed.

"What a lovely accent you have," I said. "Mumbai, then boarding school in England?" I asked.

"Yes. You must be GP," she replied.

"Yep. Well, welcome."

"How did you two meet?" GNU coughed out.

"I passed out our social personality profile to Professor Googol's classes," Joseph said. "Then I was allowed to present it to all the classes in Tech and Future law class, and then I had the *Commodore* analyze the results based upon the algorithm we created, and Leela's name popped out as number one," Joseph said.

"Number one for what?" GNU asked. I looked at GNU. I couldn't believe he strung two sentences together in front of a woman.

"For compatibility with us."

Long pause. We looked at each other – and her. "It turns out, interestingly enough, that those women that picked Googol's class are more likely to get along with us. And, women were better than men."

"Of course," GNU said and then smiled. Leela smiled back.

"Let me see your code," Leela said looking over GNU's shoulder at his computer. She touched GNU slightly and he came out of his high functioning fugue. I'm certain no one else was ever allowed to sit in his chair, but she was granted access to his seat.

"What are you guys trying to accomplish here?"

GNU didn't flinch. He actually told her in a completely appropriate manner. Joseph nodded. He was right again. Leela was a nice addition to the team – now and always.

▪ ▪ ▪

As I looked around the apartment, I saw my whole world in one small area and I loved it. When Charles Dickens wrote these were the best of times, he was referring to two cities diametrically dissimilar. There was rich and poor. There was good for the haves and bad for have nots. I'm a "have" at this very moment, in the superlative degree. I'm with Chana. I'm with my team producing a sequel to the best strategy arcade game ever. I'm at school, wrestling with the greatest minds. We have enough money to buy whatever any college kids could want. I'm not superstitious, but too much good made me wonder if there was a down part of the cycle coming?

The amount of work that went into creating, releasing, and marketing a video game was painful. It was like writing a book with ten people writing the same chapter. One little change in code can affect the software in several different places, in several meaningful ways. Rarely in a good way: they were what lay and technical people alike refer to as "bugs." Bugs, if you were lucky and the program doesn't lock up. The game needs to flow and never stop. You can have twenty people play the game for twenty-four hours and still not be sure you caught every scenario.

Chana drew on a pad, shoulder to shoulder with me. I put the computer on the floor so I could sit next to her. I was beta testing[29] *Return Fire*[30] hoping to find no bugs in the game. I glanced over at her from time to time as she drew. She was so beautiful. Dark hair, perfect pretty fingers around a pencil, she was in a zone when she drew. Her hair smelled so good. She drew a cool looking tank at the top, fire coming out of the main gun. The drawing became training. She loved drawing and art. And she loved me. When the game stopped because of a bug, I'd grimace in anger. She'd turn my head, and kiss me. In that moment all was perfect and would remain perfect.

Then from the room I yelled out, "Why does the game just end when I switch from chopper to tank when I fly for more than four minutes?"

"We got it," came the ubiquitous reply. I logged the bug and indicated that GNU said he fixed it. Version 2 of the best game ever, was well in hand.

The British are Coming!

Joseph was the one who brought around one of the assistant professors we all befriended, a guy we called, Googol. We called him Googol because his last name in Greek *gogolas* means *stupid*, and he was anything but. In Albanian it means *pumpkin*. We nicknamed him Googol because of its mathematical meaning way before Google became Google. Googol was really smart and had scholastic degrees. But his greatest credential – he's *2600*[31] – a geek's version of "original gangster." We became good friends, even though he didn't like putting up with me that much. Did Googol have a role in the Ponzi scheme? Yes, he had one. He identified the suspects so I could make them the targets.

Googol went to law school, he was a lawyer. A lawyer needed to graduate from college in order to be a lawyer. You have to take a bar exam and fill out forms to get in to a state bar. Those were the rules. Climbing over random obstacle bureaucratic shit was a part of life. I'm all about having friends and resources to make life better, but we didn't have to struggle. Money was something you use to get what you need. It was a resource like any other resource. Money was a form of currency. He had many more valuable forms of currency – his time, his brain. Money, if he needed more, he'd just make more. What would your attitude be toward money, if you knew you could always make more of it?

Joseph wanted to make his own way. Study what he wanted. Do what he wanted to do. He was autodidactic. I guess I was too, but classes set the race and the pace. He didn't like the bullshit associated with the classes. Like Literature class, Joseph didn't understand why he had to write a paper on a subject he had zero interest in and little possibility of offering any insight into discovering the next great thing with computers. To him, art wasn't the nectar of life, it was for someone else.

I spoke to Mr. Leege about Joseph when he called the office-apartment once. Mr. Leege, also a man with many degrees. I began to wonder how come this trait of needing to complete what one started never rubbed off on Joseph. It concerned Mr. Leege as well. He was concerned with Joseph's sensitive nature; Joseph will never get tougher, and have a hard time tolerating life. Instinctively, I defended Joseph. He taught classes in computer science and was the TA to two professors. Maybe he could go straight to PhD if he doesn't have to sit in classes and regurgitate information on an exam.

We were kind of celebrities on campus after the release of *Return Fire*. It was a popular game and everyone knew the team created it. Joseph made an agreement with Professor George, his history professor, where he wouldn't have to take the history final and wouldn't have to go to his history class, if he were to demonstrate "something extremely useful" computers could do relating to the analysis of history. The discretion would ultimately be up to the professor but he would accept input and reaction from the class if there were a dispute. Joseph was allowed to have help, but he ultimately would have to answer questions from Professor George and the class.

It was kind of an ingenious teaching technique one wouldn't expect from a history professor. Most were interested in only what was going on in their world outside of teaching. Just ask any of them that were seeking tenure. Students were a side dish to the research and writing – the meat and potatoes. Publish or perish. Discover something, invent something, be something that can raise money for the endowment machine of MIT or you were worthless.

Joseph worked hard on this project for history because it turned out the function of the software fit with some other ideas Joseph did care about. All of the team agreed to help. I regretted offering to help because I became a data entry clerk. The worst thing I could become and I didn't know what the point was of any of it. Now he and Googol were conspiring and designing. GNU was writing the code and wouldn't talk. I was banished from the apartment for large blocks of time in the day. This wasn't convenient for me but I put up with it. I read what I had to read under a tree or in the computer lab. The rest of the time I was able to hop on the T and visit Chana.

Our schedule became disciplined as a couple. Her parents treated us less and less like children and more like adults on house arrest. Her school work didn't suffer. We could be in the same room without disrupting each other. I just was good at explaining everything that wasn't art. But I studied the academics behind art. I just couldn't draw a line. It didn't bother her that I watched her draw and watched her as she worked on her art projects. I enjoyed looking at the art that was her face, her way, her movement. She had this economy of dainty movement. It was picturesque, modelesque, a moving meditation that allowed my brain to rest from the incessant, high-speed frequency of ideas, plans, and designs. She was the calm in my life.

On Friday nights Joseph and I visited the Meirs for Shabbat dinner. Then Chana would spend the weekend at the apartment. We slept in the closet of one of the rooms we repurposed as a computer laboratory. I'm happy Chana was attitudinally flexible enough to be willing to sleep in the closet on a mattress. Yet, she complained we were ragamuffins who slept like derelicts. But she slept and loved me even on a mattress on the floor. We were in college. We managed to do our laundry, study, and write code. We were where we wanted to be. These were the good old days.

Over the final weekend I spent more time looking over Joseph and GNU's shoulders. It was some type of networking tree. I couldn't tell what that would have to do with history. Perhaps, what events were happening at or near the same time in different places could lead to some conclusion about the spread of disease. That might be profound. But knowing those two, it had to be a big idea. The idea itself produced more work than if he memorized the facts and took a test or wrote a paper.

"What have you been working on?" I asked.

"Something cool. Something to get me out of history class forever," he answered. "I borrowed a little code from you, I hope you don't mind."

"How did you borrow?" I asked as Chana walked into the room and showed me a sketch she did of all of us.

"Exactly," Joseph said as he ate a cookie. "I cannot use it and return it. You're not even at a temporary loss because you still have your code for what you need and I'm making use of it for what I need."

"So you're saying you really didn't borrow it, you took it without permission? You stole it." I replied.

"How can I steal something you still have? I have a copy of your code from your statistical analysis of baseball to help me prove something for my history project. Thanks buddy." It all seemed very clear to him. Who really owns code?

"You can't buy groceries with free code."

"But you can make money by gathering people around the software you created with your code. You can sell the hardware that the code is being run on," Joseph said, ending the conversation.

I waited quietly, knowing Joseph would eventually show me what software he was creating. Joseph showed me what it was he and GNU were working on and why I'd been typing in names and places, events and times into a spreadsheet. GNU reconfigured a projection device and connected it to a computer. The whole computer team was called in as an audience. Chana and Leela sat off on high stools to the side of the room. The smell of brownies that would be served after the presentation emanated. It clashed with the smell of GNU's can of tuna. Joseph pointed at the wall as if making a case like a lawyer.

"We've created an algorithm that searches data for what's in common among people and other data." Instantly, I raised my eyebrows. That was kind of scary, I thought. Software that could do that could be dangerous in the wrong hands. No reason to be scared, this was for Joseph's history project. He was making connections between people and groups.

"Sorry if it takes me a minute to digest what you've worked on for the last three weeks." I nodded to continue. They transitioned the projection to an algorithm on the wall. "Hey, that's my algorithm," I said. They both looked at me. They knew what I was doing with that algorithm – testing my predictions of economic associations among business sectors.

"Not completely – but we added this," GNU said. He changed the screen to project a networking tree. "Just like you've been saying that in certain business sectors it seems like groups are not analyzing the right statistics in combination with each other in order to reach a better predictive conclusion. If we filter better on what a person does, who he knows, and who he does it with, then we can figure out a lot more about their likes, dislikes, and associations."

"Right, but I'm trying to predict how well a group is going to do over a series of economic quarters, not just one day. What are you trying to predict?" I asked.

"Who's a spy?" Joseph stated. "From a table of membership in different groups we have gotten a picture of kind of social network among individuals, a sense of the degree of connection between organizations, and some strong hints of who the key players are in this world." Who was a spy? This was out of character for Joseph. Or was it so in character, he was so inward, that he didn't realize what kind of software service he created? "And all this–all of it, from the merest sliver of metadata[32] about a single modality of relationship between people," Joseph finished. "So there you go. I'm done with my history requirement." I sat there thinking. I had to remind myself how these spectrum thinkers can be so narrow-minded and simple.

"It's not that hard, GP. Don't you get it?" GNU asked.

"So, what do you have this algo doing for American History class?" I asked.

Joseph proudly announced, "I've proven Paul Revere was a leader of the Revolution." He began to run the program. It made a graph with text – too pretty for Joseph. I just looked at Chana, who shrugged and smiled. Clearly, she helped, too.

In the chart, there was Paul Revere in the middle of the screen connecting lines to the various organizations that existed in Boston in 1775. Then he added the other names that had at least one membership in common with Revere. It was a brilliant simple system of networking social relationships among people. Confirming that one member or organization was suspect and then connections and deductions could be made.

"And then if we connect common membership among the organizations you entered into the data set, we get suspected groups," GNU said. "That was my idea."

"And if we pull out the most common people in the most connected groups," Joseph announced, "We get the leaders." Holy crap. I felt three things. We could make money by selling the software, it was a brilliant insight and function with a computer, and this was scary. These two savants had no idea what kind of real-world knuckleheads they were. At this moment, I understood how evil people could misuse this software. This code, however, became essential to my Ponzi future. With the proper data, it identified who was working together to support me and who against.

"If the British had access to this software service back then, it could've identified every suspected terrorist of the day. King George could've identified every documented nascent member of the Revolution. He could've crushed the rebellion before it started by imprisoning Revere." I looked up at the screen, "Samuel Adams, Nathaniel Appleton, and John Hancock. Do you have an understanding of what the real world implications are?" I couldn't believe I was the one saying this. "The British Crown thought the Revolution was treason, not some fight for freedom of an oppressed religious and economic class. What if other dictatorships used this function to root out all political movements against them?"

"What if good governments used it to root out criminal enterprises?" Joseph responded. It was a long two minutes. We stared at each other, the projection, and the floor.

"Why did you do this? It's so unlike you to think like this, Joseph?" I'm the one assigned to the evil thoughts that had to be tempered by Joseph. Joseph and Chana watched over my evil inclinations. I felt a tinge of jealousy. I was meant to fill the Darth Vader role, not them.

Joseph's answer was simple. "I hate History class."

▪ ▪ ▪

Cool and bright in Cambridge, an idyllic day on campus. I walked toward Joseph's history class, thinking I might be able to catch the last few minutes or so of his presentation. I'm sure he crushed the presentation. As I walked closer, I saw he was sitting under tree outside of class. A man approached Joseph and shook his hand. He seemed a lot older even for a graduate student. He was wearing a blue pinstriped suit and black thick-soled shoes. Gone by the time I arrived there. I looked down at Joseph.

"How'd it go?" I asked. He looked ridiculous with that large luggable computer across his legs. How much battery-power does he get without that thing being plugged in? Someone's going to have to make that thing smaller soon or we'll always be geeks under a tree.

"No more classes; no more final exam for me," he replied with a cavalier tone.

"Good for you. And, who was that?" I asked referring to the man in the pinstripe suit.

"I don't know. He saw my presentation. He seemed nice. He said he was with the FBI." Joseph replied.

"What? The FBI heard your presentation? Who invited him?" I asked.

"He asked me for a copy of the code and I gave it to him. He gave me his phone number. You can call him if you like."

"Why did you give him the code?" I asked.

"Because he asked, and code should be free," Joseph said, not caring about my reaction or approval, or consequences.

Return Fire

The team went to celebrate the success of *Return Fire*.[33] We all dressed in formal wear in the apartment and rendezvoused in the room where it happened – the place where the game was created. A picture would show a long table with holes drilled every meter for plugs to attach to electrical strips under the table. Nothing was neat. Food wrappers were strewn about. Papers with calculations and drawings on it – it smelled musty like the bottom floor of a library.

Chana was dressed beautifully in a cocktail dress. My heart exploded in delight. She, on this occasion, let Leela use makeup on her. A part of my brain didn't recognize Chana. The rest of the gang looked ridiculous in ill-fitted suits. We went to a local pizza pub and ordered and ate the left side of the menu. Wings, pizza, donuts and pitchers of beer flowed and we celebrated late into the night. GNU announced, "Best celebration party, ever." Life was perfect.

As soon as I had this thought, I think of how things changed for my father and me in an instant. Life was perfect one day and then a shock at dawn. Illness developed into catastrophic change, and then Mom was gone. But I had to dismiss these thoughts or risk sadness on this day of celebration. The first weekend's sales of *Return Fire* were exciting – one million in sales – worthy of celebration. The distributor got the games to the stores. The advertisements in the PC magazines were published. No major screw ups. We heard of no game-changing bugs in the play. In short – money. More money than any college kids should have at once.

Life is Still Perfect

With all the money made from *Return Fire,* it was burning a hole in my pocket. I had to splurge. At dinner, I wrote on Chana's art pad in her purse. On the page before, was a detailed sketch of the *Torre Galatea Figueres*[34] she had drawn. It was a funny looking building with egg sculptures along the roof. Salvador Dali still lived there.[35] Googol got Joseph and me an offer to a summer abroad lecture series in Spain with a group of computer geeks from MIT, Harvard, and even some high school graduates. The theme would be the summer about the future of computers, entrepreneurship, and potential innovation labs on campus or whatever. We could talk about it for however long anyone desired.

I wanted Chana to go with us. That was the only way I would want to spend any time explaining anything to anyone. We'd have gobs of time to backpack and explore. Perfect mix. Computer science lectures in Europe and everything around Chana and me could be art related. My fantasy would be limited to the knowledge that her parents wouldn't let Chana spend the entire summer with two boys – even if it were Joseph and me. But a few days? I would offer to sit down with the Meirs and explain our plans. I'm sure they would be reasonable. We'd stay in safe places. I'm not talking youth hostels; I'm talking real and comfortable hotels. I borrowed from Walt Whitman when I wrote.

I celebrate myself, and sing myself,
And for what I assume you shall assume,
For every atom belonging to me as good belongs to you.

I got the lecturing invitation.

En Espana. Venga conmigo! Europa es para artistas. Vea usted mismo.
In Spain. Come with me. Europe is for artists. See for yourself.
Love, GP.

She wrote back on what we referred to as a *womp-'em,* also known as a post-it note, a few days later.

I loafe and invite my soul,
I lean and loafe at my ease observing a spear of summer grass.
En Espana!
Love, Chana!

That was the most romantic thing I've ever done. I didn't type the note. I didn't write hieroglyphically. I didn't send it by computer. I dug deep into my soul for feelings and I did well. Chana had a talk with her parents, her mother in particular –her overbearing mother. Chana reported her mother was difficult to deal with. She described it more than a mother-teenage daughter squabbling. Her mother was prone to bouts of depression and had the ability to turn her back on life-long relationships if she felt affronted. Chana reported that her mother was becoming increasingly inflexible personality wise. It was her mother's way or you were out of her life. But her mother always seemed to be steady and nice with me. But I was never alone with her mother for any length of time. Chana said she knew when to tell her mother that she was going to Europe.

A few summer weeks in Europe with a college tour would be fine. There would be a couple of professors and teaching assistants who were associated with the tour to make it seem like a summer camp teen tour. But that wasn't the issue. Chana shielded me from a direct conversation with her mother. Chana said that it wasn't that her mother didn't trust me to keep us safe; she was scared of terrorism in Europe or that we'd run off and never come back.

I laughed at the never come back part. "Why would she think that?" Then her mother mentioned there were no guarantees they would stay in Cambridge. They didn't have a long-term contract with BB&N. I rejected her sentiment. This was not something I wanted to contemplate for too long because life was perfect. Why spoil it with negative thinking? Then we'd wonder, what happened when it was perfect and we didn't enjoy it? We were young and regardless of our sophistication, she said there were some things that only experience can teach and some lessons she never wanted us to learn.

▪ ▪ ▪

During the downtime, Joseph and I worked in the computer lab of a University we visited. It only took ten minutes over a modem to review the numbers from *VisiCalc.*[36] GNU at Cambridge was able to hack the spreadsheet software and make it even better. As much as I wanted to have him resell it and argue with the Apple people later, he just gave it back to them. When they realized that he wasn't trying to resell it on his own or sell it to them, Apple became very confused. Why would someone improve our software for free?

Joseph said, "Freedom and honesty confuses tyrants."

And Joseph was right about another thing: it should be easier to communicate information and data across computer lines. Modems were slow and difficult to use. Part of our payment, the bargaining for giving talks to summer classes and seminars at the Universities, was that we used mainframe time on campuses – just like when we were eleven in Chicago. I didn't even mind having a group watching me use the computer in their labs. We received the help of the other computer scientists. Joseph thought sharing was all part of his collaborative open communication world he envisions. He used the term "open communication" as in "free communication," not free like "free food." But why couldn't we charge for our time to make these "hacks" to known software? This was where the value lived. It worked. Companies were willing to pay for specialized software for its company – call it *Acme* Lotus Notes.[37] I eventually had connections at the major software companies and would call and say we have a solution to your X problem. "You do? How much?" I'd respond with how many hours it took the team and gave a price. We'd always agree to something. The team got paid very well. Depending on the fixes made – tens of thousands of dollars.

We didn't copyright any of the new code. We didn't trademark the new and improved product. We charged for our time and made known software the company's own. The added benefit was learning the common backdoors to major software, a skill we developed when asked to test the security and stability of the software itself. The understanding of these common backdoors, how to find them, and how to shut the doors behind me when I'm done, served us very well when it came time to run the biggest scheme of our lives.

▪ ▪ ▪

I admit that we deliberately set up a plan to have Chana stay in Europe for an extra three days after the college summer abroad. But the summer tour was over and it was time for Chana to return to Cambridge. We asked her mother a day or so before the end of the trip if Chana could stay a little extra. There was a slight delay due to weather. The weather didn't cancel the flight but Joseph and I were able to rebook the flight through a modem line on the computer. Chana thought that it was amazing we were able to do that and her parents were more worried than mad. "Just two more days," she pleaded. She received wonderful news while on the trip – she was accepted into college, most notably the arts program at Tufts University. She felt free and unchained. Not a worry to speak of for the rest of the summer. Chana explained this to her parents on the phone.

"We didn't want to have to spend all day in the airport. We wanted to enjoy Europe a little longer," Chana pleaded with her mother. Her words betrayed our little scam, but it turned out okay. Her mother demanded to speak to me. She made it clear that this extension of time would be the last. She mentioned something about me kidnapping her daughter and a response from the Mossad,[38] but I think she was kidding.

"We trust you and love you with our daughter. But she is still a young girl," her mother declared. After explaining again where we would be staying and what we'd be doing, Chana's parents seemed to feel better. They did trust me. She was always safe and we were having a good time.

For all our good efforts, I promised and delivered to Chana, Amsterdam and then Florence. And that it would be pure vacation, no work. Amsterdam would be her City. The architecture of each building was, no doubt, special. The vibe of the town was so mellow. Mellow, perhaps was the wrong word, since it seems to imply everyone was high on marijuana; but, mellow in that setting meant life was not so intense. But, for this one country, and for Chana, I wouldn't be in that constant state of crossing the finish line.

Chana tried a space cake[39] and I babysat her over some regular tea. After her two bites, for sure mellow was the word I should've used – she was mellow. She wanted me to take a bite, but she wanted me to watch over her at the same time. Since the *whammy* incident in the dorm the first week of school, I never felt the same about letting go but I did. I joined her. Then we let the ambience and the architecture do the work. She, being so relaxed, as she stared off into an artistic dimension. Coming back, she drew on her pad. At museums she researched, she painted with local art historians and instructors. Who knew art was so big in Amsterdam? Apparently everyone.

We strolled through lots of museums. We took walks and biked. We didn't exercise this much in our lives. If something caught her eye, we stopped and she sketched. Drew sketches with me in it; some without me. The ones with me in the sketch made me feel like a god. It allowed Chana to just talk. She explained why art was art – why things were pretty. Even if she never would be a Georgia O'Keefe, art was an expression of her. It helped her stay well-balanced mentally.

I talked about her in the same way. Her long arms, her slender fingers and waist, her symmetrical face – all as pretty as art. In these moments of slow walking and hand-holding, I could feel the present and sense the future. I was wealthy with love and, I was aware of my bounty. Peace, success, arrival, goals met; that's what I felt. I felt connected.

Joseph tagged along for some of these adventures, but he wasn't a nuisance. He left us alone mostly because he wanted to be touching a computer. He wasn't interested in art and Chana couldn't entice him to join us for anything but short walks for food. She called it the Summer of Computer and Arts. Sure, it was a no guard rails, high speed, anything goes first love. That was true. I loved Chana intensely because it was new and the first. She loved me because I'm intense and immense. Love of this sort was new to her too. Love and sexuality was a thrill that made us feel like we got away with robbing a bank. When we first starting seeing each other, I would drive her home after date night and we seemed to be hurried and alert to our surroundings. Neither of us comprehended that good relationship could end. Time moved on and lovers can spend time out of sync with a happy ever after.

Now, in Europe with no parents, no one could watch us. But in addition to the full surrender to love we felt, there was more. I owed her. I loved Chana because she saved my life. Not just in the emotional first love sense. Plainly, she saved it. I had been up for what felt like three days. My bite of space cake didn't agree with me and I either had a seizure or I fainted that night. Hitting the floor from a standing position would have been fine; I would've bruised and gotten some craved sleep. No, I landed on the blade of the jackknife I used to cut the tape to open the oversized cardboard box holding a motherboard for a computer Joseph was experimenting with in the room.

I didn't stab myself with the tip of the blade – worse. I severed an artery and some nerves in my wrist, on an angle across my left hand, it was a bloody mess. A dedicated suicidal depressive couldn't have done a better job. The emergency doctor questioned whether I tried to kill myself. But Chana and Joseph assured him I didn't. They were there. Joseph called an ambulance and held me while Chana applied a tourniquet out of thick rubber bands and a pencil. The medics were impressed. They asked where she learned to do that. Chana said her brother was in the Israeli Army. Too woozy to make sense of any of it, I just fell in love with her over again.

When I asked her if that was when she discovered she loved me, she told me it wasn't. Why not? We love who we save; we love who we take care of. Not Chana. She confided that she was angry with me for weeks. The accident was something that could've been avoided and she got scared. What if she weren't there when it happened? I would've bled out. What if she was there and she didn't know what to do or her tourniquet didn't work? I would've bled out. I would've died. It would've been a tragedy.

"That's love, Chana. Anger, sadness, helplessness. That is love," I said to her. But she insisted her distilled emotion was not love, it was anger. "Do you love me?" I asked. She said she did. "Then if not then, when did you know you loved me?"

"When you rebooted my computer in the library at New Trier," she said.

"That was the first time we met," I said aloud. Yes, it was the first time we met. Chana had been suffering from the beginning. We were young, perhaps, too young, rationalists or apologists of romance. I thought in that moment of honesty – she's the one.

Surely, we're not Joking

I felt oriented to time, place, and situation. It was time to check in with the team, and Joseph. Being back at school brought the game back to a regular pace which I missed. But truth be told, I wanted to get out of Amsterdam and be in Cambridge with Chana again. She was comfort to me and made me feel normal. I downplayed the situation to my father about severing my wrist in Amsterdam. I told him I had to wrap my wrist every few days to keep it clean. Told him there would be a little scarring, but I had full use of my hand and fingers. Chana did not mention a word to her parents.

Besides my injury, there was disruption in the force.

"GNU!" I exclaimed as I walked into the apartment. The stench of cannabis was overpowering. It competed with a preponderance of incense. "You too, Joseph? What the hell is going on in here?" Joseph was sucking on a joint too. "You're getting high? It's 11 o'clock in the morning, on a Monday. What's the matter with you? You guys should be working."

"How could we work? Do you know what happened?" Joseph asked. He seemed deeply depressed. He was wearing the same clothes since Amsterdam and had a wool blanket over his head, using it as a tent to prevent the exhaled smoke from escaping into the atmosphere. They were on the floor leaning up against a wall. The place was dark, shades drawn.

"Feynman died, man. We can hardly take it," GNU said. "I ran out of Ritalin too. I can't get more until tomorrow."

"You two should not be alone together," I said. Those two shouldn't do anything but code and hack together. "What else are you taking? You need to be GNU, not Lou today."

"Screw you man, Feynman died. He was the man. The world is dark and we're feeling dark too."

Richard Feynman[40] to scientists in 1988 was like Jimmi Hendrix or John Lennon to musicians and hippies in the 60's or the JFK assassination to America. Feynman was brilliant, was one of the most charismatic post-World War II theoretical physicists in the world. He died of abdominal cancer today and he wasn't that old – 69. He was a legend in the world of physics. He was definitely a legend at MIT since he graduated from here. During Los Alamos, he was a group leader on the atomic bomb project. And he was a wild man. He watched the first bomb test behind a car windshield because he thought the U.V. rays wouldn't hurt him. He was right, but science really didn't know that at the time. He conducted experiments just to prove everyday things. He once stood on his head and took a piss to show that gravity was not the only force acting upon urination; he needed to prove ureteral peristalsis was in play. He bought a van with physics' graphics and formulas on it, and travelled with his wife.

In 1986, he reached Hall of Fame status with geeks when he went on television and dunked the Space Shuttle "O" ring into ice water and pinched it, demonstrating that it was vulnerable and everyone at NASA missed it. It was magic. He proved an "O" ring was responsible for the Challenger shuttle disaster that killed all the astronauts on board.[41]

Feynman would get into bar fights as part of his own social engineering test. He studied Portuguese because he saw a hot girl signing up for the class. It was as good of a reason as any – it got me to study art. Feynman was strange and argumentative. He drove his friends crazy but they tolerated him because he compelled everyone around him to be insightful and most of all, better. Joseph and a lot of other geeks wanted to be like that – brave, unafraid. Feynman was taken from the world way too soon and no doubt, the world will suffer. But, he isn't going to help us finish the game so we can get out of this hell hole of an apartment.

I didn't believe that things happen for a reason meant it happened for a good reason. The team thought things happen for reasons and those reasons are science. And those reasons can also suck for eternity. Joseph and GNU were mumbling about how far behind in quantum the world will be because we didn't cure Feynman's cancer fast enough. The world was more interested in weapons than saving lives. They were right. My father wouldn't have invested in the fantasy that sound waves could cure cancer in order to save my mother. My world would be different if my mother had survived cancer. The world, however, liked killing people more than saving people.

All of a sudden Leela came barging through the door.

"Oh my God. . . . I'm so sorry guys, I just heard. I came right over." She hugged GNU and Joseph.

"See, Leela understands the state of consciousness. We are in no mood," GNU said. She pulled an ounce of weed out of her purse. "This is good shit. I got it from those hydroponics guys in the dorms." I just nodded my head *no* – wasted day.

"Guys, shouldn't we honor Feynman by taking the next step forward?" I knew it was futile, but said it anyway.

"No man, this is Feynman's day. We need to honor him and mourn him. And, I'm in no frame of mind or state of personality to produce for a world that let a man as great as Feynman die of cancer," GNU said.

"If this day proves anything it is that we don't have a lot of time, so we shouldn't waste it," I said.

"Stop whining and take a hit, man," GNU offered marijuana to me.

"Do it, GP," Leela said. "I'll watch you. It could be fun."

"I no longer fuck with the mechanism. Our brains are all we got. Without them we're just a couple of mediocre Jews and a comic book geek," I answered in anger.

"I'm not a comic book geek, I'm an appreciando," GNU said.

"And I'm a . . ." Joseph started to say and then stopped. "I'm Jewish." The two looked at each other and busted a gut laughing. Jesus Christ, I was too late, they were fucking stoned.

Then Chana came in. It was the first time I saw her since Europe. She gave me a hug that lasted forever; Chana's head resting on one shoulder, then the next. The rest of the room dissolved in out of the frame.

They were all smoking pot now. The guys were drinking beer and the girls were drinking some fruity punch with vodka. Bye-bye Miss

American Pie played in the background - the longest song ever written. I just sat on a stool, tapped on the breakfast bar computer, waiting for an inspired idea. I felt alone.

"Immortality. That is the world's failure," Joseph ranted. "We spend billions on war and war machines and so little on life and quality of life. We should be able to just replace Feynman's stomach and he'd have no more cancer. But no, we need to build a strategic weapons shield. SDI, Star Wars? For fucking real?"

"Eventually, we'd run out of life force," GNU said.

All this moaning compelled me to miss my mother.

"We are a product of parts that can all be replaced, and within that replacement is a force of life – a consciousness," Joseph replied.

I noticed Chana was drawing remarkable likenesses of Joseph and Feynman on the same art pad.

"At some point, the life battery just wears down," GNU insisted.

Joseph came back with, "If every cell in our body changes completely every seven years and we don't die, why must we die, if we replace every part as needed? Shouldn't we be more like robots instead of worrying that robots will want to kill us?"

"Who says we even need our bodies? Why replace anything?" Chana said without looking up from her pad. She was now drawing my face above Feynman and Joseph.

"Computers will be able to solve all problems. This is what we should work on. A giant problem-solving machine. Imagine if we could upload Feynman's brain into a computer. He could live on. His death wouldn't be so mind numbingly tragic," Joseph waxed. This was something Joseph worked on every day. Joseph kept this work, creating a computer whole life management system a secret for decades of his life. If man wouldn't strive to make the body live to support the brain, then he was going to strive to make the brain support itself.

"We're all replaceable," I said. "What's the point? A computer can calculate faster and better than GNU, draw better than Chana, design and pick fashion better than Leela. It will be better than humans at everything." Chana looked at me and turned away, like I just torched her dreams. "But only humans will be able to teach and design what the computer should draw or paint. Only we can say what art is."

"Maybe a computer can be your girlfriend too," Chana said.

"Yeah, go have sex with a computer," Leela said.

I saw love as a weakness sometimes. In my head I didn't mean what I said about a computer replacing her. Sometimes I'm so vulnerable because of my emotions that it scared me. I wished I said that to Chana out loud. I'd like to think my silence was part of a larger plan; but, it wasn't. An expression of vulnerability was buried deep within.

It's Not You...

But it didn't remain good enough. Things changed because I said she was replaceable? I couldn't figure if it related to some trigger in Europe. Things seemed to be simple and safe; no one could get hurt. All of a sudden, or so it seemed to me, Chana and I weren't Chana and Greg anymore. We sat at a table outside a frozen yogurt place just off campus and talked.

"You're mad at me? Why?"

"Because it's always about you. You only think of you, Greg." Chana yelled.

"I always think about the team. How can you say that? Why are you saying that? What are you specifically referring to?" I asked.

"*Return Fire*. You guys made a ton of money and what did I get?"

"We paid you. I buy everything for you. You're on the team. You're the best part of the team."

"I heard about *Return Fire2*," she said.

"Yeah, you knew we were making a deal for a sequel with the gaming company. It's going to be even better than the first one. GNU has better sound and the graphics are going to be super hi-res." I answered. "You're on the team. You've helped us so much."

"You don't need me to draw tanks and helicopters for you anymore. A computer can do everything for your games. It's your thing. These are your friends."

"Joseph and Leela aren't your friends?"

"I need to do my own thing. Discover my own thing."

I didn't believe any of this. There was something else. "You are doing your own thing. My friends are our friends. You'll have anything you want. What's the problem?" I was confused.

"The problem is I need to do my own thing. Computers and business is your thing," she said.

"It's our thing. What are we arguing about?" I didn't understand her logic. She seemed to be suffering from referred pain – something is bothering her, but she's saying it's about *Return Fire*, computers, friends, her own thing? Finally, she told me.

"My parents are leaving BB&N." I let that sink in for a while. "They asked my mother to leave because she's been too political in Middle East history class. Two other Arab professors made a big thing about it. My parents don't have tenure."

"And your father?" I asked.

"You think he would stay without my mother?"

"He could teach there and your mother could work somewhere else, no? You can stay in Boston. You're going to Tufts." I offered as a solution

"Sometimes you're too damn logical. When do you just get angry?" She asked.

"I can get angry. But what's the point of being just angry? Get angry or solve the problem. Then it's an answer and the problem is gone." I asserted. I guess she has never really seen me angry. I'm confused and nervous about becoming scared, about not knowing what to do next – helplessness.

Chana didn't need to me solve a problem. The problem has been solved. "We're moving back to Israel."

Ugh, there it was – the gut punch. Why did Chana's mother ruin everything?

"Stay here. You don't have to go," I pleaded.

"I can't leave my family," Chana answered.

"I want to be your family. You have to go to college. You got into college here in Massachusetts." I felt I was begging. I didn't care. I did love her. Why was this happening? I felt completely out of control; it was the worst feeling – powerlessness.

"Where am I supposed to live, in an apartment full of men?"

I was a little irritated that it seemed like she was attacking her friends, our friends. She had never expressed her separateness like this before. All of a sudden she didn't like the college lifestyle, the team? Me? "We can live together. You can live alone. I'll get you your own apartment," I said. Problem solved, no?

"I know you're trying, Greg. It isn't about you. It's about me and a greater responsibility to my family and country. I'm going back Israel to serve my time in the Army," she said. She stood up from her chair and embraced me. It hurt. The Army? I held her; dropped my head to rest it on her shoulder.

"You live here. You're American. You haven't lived in Israel since you were ten. Why are you uprooting your life? Your life with us?"

"Being Israeli is something you have to be to understand. Every day Israel has to fight to stay alive, to exist," she said.

I didn't know how to respond. I was just quiet. Why couldn't I speak? This was the woman that held my hand while I was lost the first day of college. I own this campus now. I'll own the world with her. Why was she going away? What was she going to do in the Army? It's crazy, she could die. I'm not as strong as I think I am. The sun set during this conversation. We walked and spoke in circles.

"I don't want you to go." I said it so slowly it sounded like I dropped 40 IQ points just with my tone. I felt like a regressing Charlie from *Flowers for Algernon*.[42] I wasn't going to let her go without saying everything. Humbled, I felt lost again – a woman, Chana, a puzzle I can't solve. I became angry for allowing myself to feel so vulnerable. I've never been through something like this. Only my mother, I suppose, but she had an excuse – she died. It wasn't her fault. My mother left me, abandoned my father and me; unintentional, the result all the same.

"Is life so bad here? I love you. Israel can survive without you.... I'll go to Israel with you then," I blurted out. This seemed like the longest moment of my life. After I said it, I meant it. Words were flying out of my mouth faster than my comprehension. "I'm a Jew, I can help too. I can communicate with the team over the computer. I can be anywhere. That's what we've always been working for. We can be anywhere at any time. Work can be done anywhere. I want to go with you then."

"You're here. You have to finish school. Your life is here. Joseph is here. I don't want you to come."

"You don't want me to come to Israel with you?" I asked.

"No, you shouldn't," she said. Want and should are two different things. Can I afford to be hyper-technical in this context?

"Don't you love me anymore?"

She shook her head. Her response was fast. What was she saying *no* to? She didn't love me? I wanted my brain to tell me she was lying. I peered at her face for an expression of evidence that betrayed her words and this just a normal lover's flare up, a crisis of the meaning of existence. I couldn't see a thing. I felt no anger which surprised me. I was stunned; nothing but sadness and other nondescript forms of pain. She kissed me on the lips one last time. The moment before her lips touched mine I had hope. My lips burned. Ugh, I closed my eyes and put my hand to my lips and wiped them. The power of the mind – yesterday's kiss, bliss; now was acid to the touch. She turned and she was gone.

I must have ignored all the signs of her unhappiness, but I couldn't think her rejection was not stark or swift, even though her decision about us probably was made some time ago. I needed to know. "I need a reason," I would implore. The more I thought about it, I had the epiphany that I was a sociopath who could do real evil and she couldn't handle it.

She'd say things like, "I don't think I could handle that responsibility." But I would stare into her eyes and just know I was in love. I wouldn't hear her. "I can't be your ethical standard bearer," she would say on other occasions, ". . . or your moving sign post." But one conversation I do remember and did comprehend. She cut me with her words, "You're capable of real darkness. You are going to save the world or destroy it. I can't be with someone where that's a fifty-fifty proposition."

"Then I commit to goodness," I said. "But only. .

"But only if you're with me? Is that what you're going to say? That isn't good enough for me. I don't need you to need me. That's just something women say when their lovers can't commit. I need you to want me and not need me," Chana explained.

I thought about what she was saying. "I thought women wanted the opposite."

"No. You need to prove to me that you've unwound your disconnected nature. That you don't need me to be your ethical guide through life because I couldn't handle you going to prison or getting murdered; or worse – realize you're a bad person." I recalled her words in bed in my dark closet. I nodded affirming that her request would be easy; knowing she couldn't see me. But she could sense the nod.

"I'll need a note from your therapist," she said.

"Therapist?" I asked. I thought the existential crisis of us was over because she had laughed. What she needed was as silly as me asking her to become a cognitive computer scientist. That isn't bad, she just isn't one.

When Chana left I had trouble breathing. My diaphragm collapsed; I had to put my arms over my head. She was a part of me. The air that I breathe. It sounded so objectively stupid I was mocking myself. What about my *hatikvah*? My hope? Israel needs her? I needed her more. No one will be able to empathize with me. Joseph might understand, but he won't know. It's a dull pain in my gut, setting in. Trite and dull, I stung with stupidity, and lacked an ingenious way to express, I'm blue. I'm sad.

Chana handed me a small portfolio before she left. It had pictures of us, hand drawings by her of us. It was a collage of our relationship. There were clear and hidden meanings to it all. At the end of the portfolio – a long letter. I couldn't bear to read it then. I sat on my bed in the closet and closed the door. The darkness helped. I stopped being critically self-conscious of myself any further. I cried.

She's Gone. Got to Learn How to Face it

Joseph and I met in the computer lab on campus at 2 a.m. for the ostensible purpose of accessing a larger mainframe for power and speed. "What are you blubbering about?" I asked.

"I can't believe she's going away to Israel," Joseph said. "Where are they going to put her? She's an artist, not a fighter," he whined.

"But," I didn't know how to finish that sentence. "She's mine," I said.

"She's not yours. She's our friend."

"But she was my girlfriend," I demanded.

"But she is our friend," Joseph said.

"She's not my friend," I said. "You feel bad, I feel worse."

He put his hand on my shoulder. "You think you're paying homage to her by having a contest over who feels worse? Our friend is moving away and we don't know when we'll see her again. Or if we'll see her again." Joseph was wiping away tears. I couldn't cry like that out in the open. I was blocked from expressing an outward emotion because I think it will be perceived as my weakness. Yet, it probably would take greater strength to be able to express my sadness, if not at least promote a better understanding to others that I've suffered a profound loss.

"My brain won't even let me consider that she could be killed in the army," I said out loud but more to myself. "The odds are so small; but Israel is always at war, and never at peace."

"We need a system to communicate with her. She should have a computer, we'd have a computer, and we could communicate over a computer," Joseph said. I felt a little better talking about her. My psychodynamic pain was cured by a distraction.

"Would it be cheaper to communicate over the computer?"

"It won't matter. Your computer is a phone. Your phone will be a computer."

I couldn't stand it. I walked out and I ran. Anything to change the way I felt. From top of the world to nothing, this was my world view at the moment. So I started obsessing about communication over a computer. We can type to each other on the computer now – almost instantly. How can we make that faster?

"I want to be able to talk on my computer," I said. "Ugh, what's the point? Talking is not being together."

"Relationships are in our heads. We feel close to people we never see. You still feel close to your mother, right?"

I said nothing. Joseph's disorder made him so literal his words were just abrupt and hurtful. He felt sad, he'd miss Chana. But he didn't realize he was sticking daggers in my heart by asking me to think about my dead mother and girlfriend who was moving across the globe because, I only think about myself? "We're a small step away. If we can transmit text; we can transmit sound; we can transmit voice," Joseph plunged on.

Somehow, I had hope. Was I in denial? Could I even see myself having a relationship with Chana when she lived so far away? How could I become the man she wanted me to be without her help? It was dead, wasn't it? Even if I could talk to her several times a day, being present was being human; was being connected. I mourned for our relationship by sitting and staring at walls for hours. I will mourn, as much as I will miss her.

TRANCHE II
The Story of Chana

Chana's confession

The portfolio had a title page: "The Book of Chana." And below the words was a sketch of her and me back-to-back, head-to-head, and looking at the clouds dreaming; our hands touching. As I thumbed through the sketches, I saw the pages of the letter again. It was like reading her diary – a message conveyed to anyone who read it.

My first real and full formed memory? It had to be my mother asking me if I was ready to leave with my suitcase to go to the airport for the first time. Flying in an airplane, going to America, leaving Israel; it was all firsts. Deep down, I was excited but always with the drone of sadness. The bagpipe, the drone - sadness. My mother was the worst; the drone was loudest from her. My father was the quietest. His pain was seen in his movements but he never said a word about it.

Was I ready to go? "*Cain, Eema*!" I yelled back.

"Yes, Mother," *Eema* insisted. "You need to practice your English from this point forward, understand?"

"Yes, Mother," I said in her same tone. She ignored my sarcasm as insubordination. I stood at the door of our home, an apartment on the Kibbutz. We were leaving; going to America; a fresh start. My father's cousin arranged it. We would be moving to Miami Beach, Florida. I was already warned that we wouldn't be living on a Kibbutz. There were no Kibbutzim in America. The streets were paved in gold and no one had to live in socialist communities. Which confused me since I thought life on the Kibbutz was the best. We knew nothing but sharing and helping. There was something better than living together and sharing?

My next warning was that our new friends would be very religious – Hasidic Jews. Lubovitch Jews who are not secular at all. I had to look up the word *secular.* They keep to themselves. They do business with outsiders, but social events were only together. Which kind of sounded like the Kibbutz but my mother said was very different.

"Are we going to be Lubovitch Jews now, *Eema*?" I asked.

Thinking she didn't explain how orthodox the Lubovitch really were, my mother just answered, "No, I don't think we could ever be that observant."

My father, Shlomi, looked around the house. "They've opened the gates. The car is packed. Chaim is waiting in the car. It's time to go," he announced to our home. "Stop hugging Shooky, Chana. It's time to go." My younger brother, Shooky was so cute. He was dressed up in a jacket and a cap. It was my job to dress him. He was young enough, he still let me dress him.

"What did you do to your hair, Shooky?" My mother asked. "Uh, I forgot to get you a haircut. Is the salon opened now, Shlomi?"

"We have to go, Hadassah," my father said. "We don't have time for this."

"I grew *payoss,*[43] *Eema,*" Shooky said. We all laughed. My mother flicked his hair behind his ears.

"You don't need *payoss,*" Mother said.

I don't know what my mother thought, really. Her feelings went back and forth. We were at the top of the totem pole at the Kibbutz. My father was sort of the President. He was smart. Our Kibbutz grew its own food and sold and repaired electronics. This means there were other engineers that lived here. Appliances in the kitchen worked well. Our disco-tech worked really well. And video games, we had every one that Shooky wanted.

Because my father was the head of the Kibbutz we had the biggest apartment. My brother and I had our own rooms. My father had a study that was once my older brother, Yonatan's, room. We lived well. All of our friends, people who have known me and my brothers since we were born will all be a world away. My father didn't want to go. He was popular here, although not everyone liked everything he did. That's part of being a leader, my father said. We were happy. Now we are leaving. I thought it was the goal for every Jew to come to live in Israel and now we're the ones leaving.

It seemed like my father wanted to stay. This wasn't his idea. But my mother, she was really in charge. My father ran the Kibbutz, but my mother ran my father. I would read books in English in school and read about soft women who dutifully listened to their husbands, and I would ask my mother, "Where are these women?" And she would say, "No one around here. None of them are Israelis. These were not Jewish women. They never had to survive. They only have to worry about what cakes to serve at tea time." Not to mention that my father was third cousin to Golda Meir, the first woman Prime Minister of Israel. We were strong women. Yet still, I didn't understand - why we were leaving if we were so strong?

Why were we going to America, to distant relatives in the Lubovitch community in Miami Beach? I overheard my auntie, *Doda* Sarah, talking to my mother in the kitchen late at night. *Doda* Sarah said you have to be *frum,*[44] born into the Hassidic life, run into it because you found God, or be running from something in order to be able to adjust to it. The ones who are born into it can get along; the ones who are *baal teshuva*, born again, have a tougher time. But we were not even *baal teshuva.*

I asked my father in his study days before we left, "Are we *baal teshuva*?" He smiled and said, "No. But it is what your mother wants." I thought but didn't ask, why do we always have to do what she wants? My father answered a moment later that question I didn't have the nerve to ask. "We love and trust your mother. She has always done what's best for this family." I just didn't see it as what was best.

We all piled into a car. Chaim, our friend who was in charge of the kitchen, would drive us to the airport. As we got to the gate of the Kibbutz there were two long rows of people from the Kibbutz. They were waving and chanting, "*Tachzor bakarov*!" Come back soon! I knew every single person on the lines. Who they were related to and what they did at the Kibbutz. They knew me and my family. I couldn't smile. I could barely wave. Shooky was smiling and waving like he was getting attention in a parade. He didn't understand we weren't coming back.

We weren't born *frum*. We weren't American. We've never been to America. None of us found a deeper connection to God. We were not born again, yet we were going. Now I understood a little better as we passed the gates of the Kibbutz, the only home I ever knew—what we were running from.

Running from what? Running from the ghost of my brother, Yonatan. All of Israel reminds us of him.

▪ ▪ ▪

I called her. I couldn't help myself.

"Chana? I didn't know. Why didn't you tell me you had an older brother who died?" The fact was he didn't just die, he was murdered. Everyone questioned what Yoni's place could be in the Army. He was a lot like Chana, as she described. He was more art, less army. The way she described him, Yoni sounded nurturing, a Kibbutznik.

"He introduced me to art and drawing," she said. "He taught me how to tie that tourniquet on your arm that saved your life in Europe."

Of course, I remembered. "I'm so sorry."

"It's not your fault. My family has always been screwed up about it."

"I thought we were closer. How did we never discuss your brother?" I stared at a wall across the room. I sat on the floor with my back against another wall. Can I even say that I'm screwed up about us?

"He was murdered, Greg. Israel made him a policeman in Hebron. Do you know where that is? The West Bank. That's worse than making Joseph a beat cop in Roxbury." I couldn't interrupt. I wanted to be sympathetic; totally focused on her pain. I wanted to feel bad about Yoni. But I was focused on my pain and how Yoni's murder related to my pain.

This was a horrific story. A Palestinian woman sucker stabbed him. There was no better term that I can think of. She appeared to be no threat to him. He didn't confront her. All of a sudden, for revenge for limitless proclaimed violations against Palestinians; or over Israel's mere existence as the standard bearer of global Jewry, this woman stabbed him. Chana made a point to tell me that her parents saw her brother dead. But she never saw him dead or alive after he left for work that morning.

How does a conversation like this end? I was angry and sad, and resentful; and lost. If the Meirs left Israel to escape the pain of Yoni's death, why were they going back?

"Why are you going into the Army?"

"Every Israeli goes into the Army," she answered.

"I've never heard of an Israeli being tracked down in America and dragged back to serve in the Army," I said.

Exhausted, she didn't get angry. Chana seemed resigned to just deal with my anger. Resigned to dig up all the reminders, she was back to Israel with her family. I begged her to remember that she was an adult – she didn't have to stay in Israel. Visit; come back, anything else but go around the world and not be with me. *I can't go on without you. You're the one that makes us great.* How does a phone call like this end?

"You've got hundreds of thousands of dollars in the bank and you guys spend fifteen thousand a year. You're going to be fine. You'll find someone else." But what if I didn't? What a trite thing to say. What if my best friend selected the girl for me with the best fit for me and that was it? Joseph's algorithm may have been imperfect. Maybe there was no algorithm matching Chana to me. Joseph, as a friend, just selected her for me because he felt she was right. And I believed in his intuition. I believed in her.

As I hung up the phone, I noticed the room full of the team's coders working on the various projects we tasked them with doing. Heads were staring forward at computer monitors. They all appeared cut out from the same cyber-silicone block. Some were weird looking by design; the others replicating the look of the others. No one was even paying attention to me. Was this my life now – living on the floor with a group of introverted coding misfits making software? Joseph looked down at me. He said nothing; and that was the right thing to do.

Porkbellions

As I sat next to my computer, I saw the note with Chana's information that Joseph left for me to find. It didn't matter. I couldn't help myself. Dialing in, I felt exhilaration. It connected. Amazing. I've traversed the world with a computer. She said hello thinking it was Joseph. I then wrote, "It's me, Chana. It's Gregory." There was a long pause. My exhilaration was turned into more disappointment. "Gregory!" She wrote. "I think there's a lag in the transmission." I felt relief instead of despair. I typed and erased many times. My desperate feelings were conflicting every day and all the time. Please rescue me! Please be here! I'm scared every day.

GP: *I see you made it there okay. I needed to know you're okay.*

Another long pause.

CHANA: *I'm okay. And you're going to be okay, GP. Better than okay.*

GP: *I'm sending you a check for your contribution to Return Fire 2.*

CHANA: *You don't have to. It's not about money. I need to be here GP. For myself. For my mother. For my brother, Yoni. For my country.*

The speed at which the words streamed across my screen was tortured and slow.

GP: *Do you think we can see each other soon?*

CHANA: *I don't know. Maybe, GP.*

....DISCONNECTED

Writing was so different from talking. Should I have seen hope in this "maybe?" What tone of voice was she using? The prose was a sentence long. No art of letter writing. Who would ever want to communicate like this on important matters? In my brain I knew the world one day would write in scant phrases. How I wished Chana wrote that she felt obligated and that due to her young age and sense of familial responsibility she wished she could have remained in Cambridge to be with me, to cultivate our relationship; we nonetheless must remain apart. But one day, when she was through with her service, we would be together again. As we mature, so would our love. And once stronger, it would be the last time any obstruction will come between us.

Maybe I missed all the cues. I should've made her part of my family, instead of a member of the team. Maybe I should've given her a ring. I may have intellectual superiority, but emotionally I felt stunted. I was so despondent. I created another scheme to distract myself from the pain. Deliberately, I walked by the dorm room where Henry sat at his desk. Fine, I will whore out my brain.

"I'll meet with your friends. What are they called? The Porkbellions," I said to Henry.

"Porcellians." He snapped back. I saw the gears in Henry's brain spinning. Was this the breakout scheme he wanted? He could prove to his father that he worthy enough to be a banker – a business man to change the *Blanco* family name into the *White* family future.

"Sure," I answered. "If they want to invest, I've got the plan."

"Awesome," Henry answered.

"We'll start after Winterbreak," I said.

Henry started after break. I didn't have that kind of impulse control. Love distracted us from the things we hate. One thought at a time, man can't love and hate at the same moment. As I let my ethical structure breakdown, I didn't have Chana to prop me back up.

What I had planned for the Porkbellions was to use their money to make the team money.

We'd invest their money in the market and sell them by the end of the semester. We'd earn fees on the investments. But we weren't allowed to accept fees because we're not licensed brokers. So, I guess we'd have to be considered some type of co-investors. Henry wanted to act as the account executive – interact with the clients. It was worrisome to me, but then again, I didn't want to deal with these entitled-by-birth guys. Henry and I would have plenty of time to discuss the investment scheme because everyone but Joseph was going to Florida for winter break.

GOPHER

At the apartment, I spoke with Joseph while he was packing his bags in his room.

"You should not go to that guy's house!" Joseph emphasized.

I didn't stop packing my duffle bag. Henry, Googol, and I were spending our winter recess in Miami Beach. It was so cold in Cambridge. Florida's not cold. I wanted to swim in the Atlantic Ocean – sunshine on my face.

"We're going."

"I'm going to Minnesota and then I'm going home to Chicago," Joseph said. "You want me to say hello to your father?"

"Sure, except he's going to Florida too. I'll be visiting him in Hallandale. He's staying with a friend in the Hemispheres condo – the last stop before death." Joseph refused to see some justification for me going to Florida besides going to one of Henry's father's banking friend's estate for a wild party. Joseph thought the friend was a bad guy out of central casting for *Miami Vice.*

"Googol's coming too," I said.

"What for?"

"He's curious. He's read about the law, he's never lived it. He wants to live before he begins his year of no life."

Joseph just shook his head. Googol's year of no life involved serving as a clerk for a Justice of the Supreme Court of the United States. Pretty cool job, if you can get it. We were scared he might fall in love with the law and forget about technology – forget about us. Googol said that's impossible: "Coding is law." Not quite sure what he means. He spoke in

Yoda sometimes; pithy nuggets of wisdom, one might not understand at first, but then – boom – a deep insight.

This was our party weekend and Joseph didn't want to come. I would've sworn that Joseph would come if Googol was going.

"Your father okay? Mom?" I asked. "Sister?" He said fine. "Why the hell are you going to Minnesota? You think it's cold here -- Minnesota." I knew why he was going. He was an idealistic stooge. Losing was an honor to the cause. If I could get him to talk about it maybe he'd work through it.

"Talk about it? Want to talk about whether Chana would want you to go to a drug-lord's home in Miami?" Joseph said. Her name – that name. Couldn't her name be Debbie or something else? It seemed like an ordinary name would be easier to hear, brace for – it'd be around all the time. Enough with the long goodbyes –he should just go.

"Mind if Leela goes?" I asked.

"To Florida? Why would I mind?" Joseph said. "Why would I ask? She's free to do what she wants."

Joseph had important things to do for the world in Minnesota. Minnesota: was no Cambridge. Even TimBL wasn't going on this trip.[45] Joseph was leading the charge all by himself. He was the only person idealistic enough to think he can meet with University officials and ask them not to do something that the officials think will make the University money – impossible task. GOPHER was the proprietary computer product of the University of Minnesota and Joseph was the gopher for the free world wide web. Joseph's logic: Why make the world pay for something it should have for free?

Grudgingly, I agreed with TimBL and Joseph. But there was no way to convince the profiteers of anything but there should be a fee for the use of the GOPHER internet system. From what we know GOPHER was so far ahead of the World Wide Web. "Have no fear," TimBL announced with confidence to Joseph over again. You cannot stop Minnesota from charging a fee. But when it does, it'll be suicide. No one will want to pay for access – it was way too soon. The world wasn't hooked on the internet yet. The world didn't even know about it. What's GOPHER? No one knew, no one will, and those that did will forget it. The internet has to seem cool first – the foundation of every scheme or business.

I grabbed my duffle bag dropped it by the front door of our workspace apartment. Hugged Joseph and said it'll be okay. He told me, I'd be okay. We'd be back soon. This was the first time we had been apart. A little respite never hurt anyone. "Think about something – something else," he told me. I wasn't clear if he was referring to Chana, going to Florida, or Henry's upcoming investment project with the Porkbellions. I was afraid to leave him alone when he got in these despondent moods. He didn't get blue. The world became black.

Los Muchachos

Googol drove us in a cheap rental that we both felt was out of place once we hit the island. Hell, the moment we drove into Miami Beach. La Gorce was a quiet part of town. Palm trees that were fifty to eighty feet high. The grass was different than up north but it was perfectly manicured. The mansion I pointed out to Googol left his mouth agape. It was an obnoxious display of wealth. One day I would need to live in a place like this, but I didn't need it to be happy. It was a prop; a prop that communicates wealth. Wealth communicates success. Who has this much money to spend on a house? We were at the home of *"Los Muchachos"* – the boys. Who, as a matter of common knowledge, were the largest cocaine traffickers in the history of cocaine.

"Which one?" Googol joked.

"*Yo no se*," I answered. "*Un muchacho y el otro muchacho*."

It really was an estate. Putting greens, full English garden, on the water, with a 170' yacht called *Solamente Dinero*. Googol parked at the end of the drive way which seemed like a quarter mile away. The doors squeaked as we slammed them shut. We took four steps before a valet in a red vest and black bowtie stopped us and said he would park the car for us.

"We don't need to valet," Googol pleaded. "We're not staying very long."

"*Es* no problem, *señor*, please," the valet said.

Googol handed over the keys.

"Would you even want to be this rich?" Googol asked as the lights around the estate changed color to a pastel pink. "Remember, we're just hear to be polite to Henry and satisfy some mild curiosity. And then we're leaving."

"I wouldn't mind being this rich" I replied. "We'd have to have the robots doing all the work." I couldn't finish my rant on money. "Holy shit, koi pond!" We walked on the curved wooden bridge that traversed the pond. We spent a few moments looking at the school of koi in the lighted pond. They all seemed to be lifting themselves out of the water to look at us; chomping their mouths toward the air. I was taking this scene all in.

"They're like ninety percent of the people at this party," a man who walked up behind us said. "How ya doing? I'm Bobby A." This was a large, fit man who reminded me of David Sherry from high school – a man who could bench press the front end of a Volkswagen Beetle – close-cropped hair, salt and pepper goatee. It seemed like everyone in Florida had a tan. We introduced ourselves and he asked if we were Henry's friends. I guess he knew Henry. Googol and I stared underneath Bobby A's unbuttoned dress shirt. He noticed us looking and took his hands and spread a part his shirt exposing a shiny gold necklace laying atop a tattoo of a lion's face on his chest. He smiled. We gave a collective, "wow." He offered to show us in. There seemed to be one waiter to every three guests at this party. All the women were in cocktail dresses, looking like models.

There was security at this party. Men, all with mustaches, wearing tuxedoes were scattered throughout. Expressionless, they were armed. I noticed one with a sawed-off shotgun; sawed-off to make it easier to hide in a jacket. Anyone of these guys projected an aura of, 'I'll kill you if I'm ordered to.' I'm amazed we made it this far.

When at a kingpin's party, ask smart questions. "You mean the people at this party are like the koi?" I asked. Googol raised his eyebrows and gave me the "failure to filter" alert. Good grief, I'll ask my questions. When am I going to meet a guy like Bobby A again? That was the whole point of coming to this party -- meet interesting people and talk to them.

"You'll see," he replied.

Inside, we met up with Henry. He was dressed like all the other guys at the party – white linen jacket with the sleeves pushed up like Don Johnson. The waitresses were wearing bikinis and serving raw fish atop of squares of rice. Henry held a piece up and said, "Sushi, it's the new thing." It was actually pretty tasty once you get over the *raw* part. There was live salsa music and entertainers walking around like a member of some African tribe spitting out liquid they would ignite on fire. Jugglers and fire-breathers.

"So what do you think? Pretty spectacular place, huh?" Henry said. We both nodded.

"Yeah, we just met Bobby A on the way in. Which one of the boys owns this place?" I asked. Henry pointed to another tan man with well-groomed gray beard.

"The one wearing a gold and black paisley jacket." He was so well-groomed someone might hand him a microphone and he'd start singing. I guess if you have a mansion like this and the respect of all these people, you too can have the multi-million-dollar arrogance. In some measure, I wanted this for myself. He was surrounded. The level of interest in his every word was remarkable. All these spectacularly beautiful women were kissing him. Some of the men too, with big hugs like they haven't seen each other in years. I could make out some of the Spanish. Women were getting, "*que linda, flakka, una modela*"; the men, "*guapo*," or "*hermoso*." But for el Muchacho, elegante – *el jefe elegante.*

Bobby A leaned in as we waited for a moment to meet *el jefe*, the boss. "See what I mean?" Kisses like koi. I couldn't help but notice the boss's diamond and ruby pinky ring. He was immaculate, his teeth white, face tan. From shoes to his hair, perfect. And, his partners, employees, friends, gushed over him. The woman standing over his shoulder monitoring the other women must be the boss's wife. She was the only koi not kissing him.

Henry finally got the boss's attention. "Ah, Henry. So good to see you. How's school? How is your father and family?" Henry answered, "Everyone is well. My father sends his apologies for not being able to come tonight." Googol and I were wondering that ourselves. Where was Henry's father? Why wasn't he here? Were we ever going to meet him? I'd spoken to him on the phone at school when he called the dorm, so I knew he wasn't a ghost.

"Your friend's curly hair, he looks like a mad scientist," *el Muchacho* said to a chorus of laughter. He really was the king in his castle holding court. "Henry, your friends are mad scientists?" He asked in a strong Cuban accent. We just grinned. What are we supposed to say?

"No, no, *Padrino*. My friend, Jeffrey is a lawyer. And my friend, Greg is my roommate at MIT." We all took turns shaking hands. Googol seemed frightened by the mad scientist remark. Googol was worried we were here too long – got too familiar. I found the whole situation fascinating. After all, we wanted to help our friend, Henry.

"Oh really? From what law school did you graduate?"

"Northwestern," Googol answered.

"Ah, splendid. *Impresionante*. What kind of lawyer are you?"

"Jeffrey is starting a job as a law clerk at the Supreme Court," Henry answered.

"You're a lawyer, you couldn't get a better job than a clerk at the Supreme Court?" *El Padrino* said to another chorus of laughter. "He's going to be a clerk!" The laughter subsided and he stepped forward and spoke softly to Googol. "I'll keep that in mind. That's a very good job to have. Not an easy one to get. Congratulations," he said in all seriousness and with his hand extended shook Googol's hand again. "Which Justice will you be working for?"

"Stevens," Googol said in almost a whisper.

"*Excellente*. Enjoy the party, gentlemen. You've all worked very hard. Your father is very proud of you, Henry – *ja ja, Enrique Blanco*." He kissed Henry on the lips softly when he drew Henry's head toward his. Not hard like in the movie.

We huddled in our own little circle as the host walked away. We each grabbed a flute of *Cristal*, the bottle prominently displayed in the middle of the tray, and drank it quickly. Another waiter came by and took our empty glasses. We looked at each other.

"Goddamn, Henry," Googol mumbled under his breath. "I can't believe you told one of the biggest drug traffickers in the world that I was going to be a clerk at the Supreme Court."

"What did you want me to do? I can't lie. He's one of my father's business associates. And, you have no proof he's what you say he is."

"You have this block in your logic, Henry. You have this netherworld in your brain where the laws of physics don't apply. You're religious when it comes to your father, his friends, and the family bank."

Henry quickly cut Googol off. He demanded that Googol not disrespect his family's friend's party. "People can hear you."

"Okay, Enrique Blanco."

"Henry White. My name is Henry White." Henry said and stormed off.

It was important to be sociable; to seem interested in others. That was the way to obtain a person's confidence. As I stared attentively into Bobby A's eyes, all I kept thinking was how I'm pretending to seem interested in what he was talking about, while it was three o'clock in the morning. But then he stopped describing others and told me his own war story.

"I was a sniper in the Emergency Services Unit[46] in the Bronx for the New York Police Department," he said. It made me wonder what the hell he was doing here working for *Los Muchachos*. And then I stopped wondering. It might be good to train myself to stay up late and be social – to socialize. "I was indicted for murder of a Gambino crime family associate. But the State of New York couldn't prove it. They thought my rifle was the murder weapon. But when they analyzed the muzzle against the groove impression striations, it didn't match the markings on the bullet in the dead guy.[47] My lawyer successfully argued that my rifle wasn't the murder weapon."

Bobby A looked at me in the eyes to see the affect his story had on my comfort. The right corner of my mouth raised in a half a smile. "All one would have to do is change the barrel. You can keep the gun."

Bobby A shrugged. "They never could find the barrel."

Bobby A was a character outside my world. All the geeks were good at creating things, but who was good at selling them. What scheme one day will I want to sell? Once we have the products, once we have the money, then we'll have the power.

Bobby A told me that he didn't exclusively work for *Los Muchachos*. I nodded. Who knows, maybe an ambitious MIT graduate would need a guy like him one day. One day, of course, I would need to work with Bobby A, and sooner than I thought. And I moved on and practiced being sociable with another guest.

▪ ▪ ▪

The woman's name was Melantia, a man calling himself PJ, said nostalgically. He spoke about her for a while. He was a dark-skinned man,

American; but was careful not have me refer to him as "African American" because he was not from Africa – he said he was Jamaican. He explained to me he corrected people because he was proud to be Jamaican. And in Jamaica the idea of white-skin black-skin was more descriptive rather than race-based. He claimed to not really care if people made the mistake, perhaps not before he corrected them. Because in his buzzed state he kept speaking and shared beliefs in the stereotypes of American blacks. But once he moved to Panama, learned the language, that's when he became Panama Jamal, PJ. But PJ was from another economic stratus and once Melantia hit a certain age she was pressured to marry someone of her own class. It was over.

"But now, I speak accentless Spanish in Panama and Colombia. In Panama he met the woman of his dreams – Xiomara.

"*Zee oh*"

"No, pronounced 'C' 'O' Mara," PJ said. Another prop, to support his scheme, I supposed. It would be years before I would meet PJ again. It would be for the big show, my Ponzi scheme. He would be evolution's winner on the War on Drugs campaign. PJ did not say *no* to drugs.

▪ ▪ ▪

I thought Googol would complain it was too late and want to leave. But, there were omelet stations set up and a late-night breakfast buffet formed. Googol was sitting next to Henry, both smoking *Romeo y Julieta* cigars while women in uniforms massaged their shoulders. The whole set up was seductive. Googol relaxed, he was freely talking about computers, technology, and the Supreme Court with *El Padrino*.

I walked over and smiled, with a plate in hand.

"You boys seem to be enjoying yourselves," the Don said. "You know boys, you're our future. Henry and his friends are the future. We will need fewer tough guys and more smart guys."

"Really?" I said.

"Yes. You must know this all ready. The battles and war of business will be fought with our brains, our technology, and our currency, not with our hands."

Henry looked up at me silently pleading with me not to engage in verbal combat with the Don, his *Padrino*; and Googol seemed too relaxed to worry. I nodded. "I agree with you, *Padrino*."

"If you do, then one day, we will all do business together."

I graciously smiled before my next bite. Bobby A put his hand on my shoulder as Googol's eyes widened and Henry did his best to ignore the remark.

The Baseball Algorithm

The Porcellian house was associated with Harvard University, not MIT. This was not how the other half lived; this was how the one-percent of the one-percent lived. The Porcellians wanted to invest with Henry after he offered some smart answers in a unified business class of MIT/Harvard. If you think Harvard men think they were superior, meet MIT men about to take money from Harvard men. Henry didn't just say it out loud, he sang it. He was pretty impressed with himself. Doubly so because his father would be impressed, and conclude that the investment with the well-bred Porcellians of Harvard revealed the investment gene latent in Henry's blood.

Both Universities have a treaty of sorts where students can take certain classes at the other University for credit. There was nonetheless a perceived difference in social status. Harvard, more refined and bred; MIT, smart and superior. Old money v. *nouveau riche*; but all that mattered with Henry and I, was the *riche* part. We were worthy enough to stand in the lobby and they could give us their money, but we couldn't go any further into the house. We weren't Harvard men after all. I didn't see any Jews or one Asian in the small gathering either. I got the can't beat 'em, join them vibe off of them. It was a good thing they couldn't read my mind.

A few of them moved a long table in the middle of the lobby. None asked me any questions about computers or modems, the stock market, or how they worked. They all seemed to be following their leader – some guy with blonde hair and a square jaw named Chad with his mother's maiden name – Kensington.

"Kensington Chadsworth, pleasure to meet you. Call me, Chad." We shook.

"Let me introduce you to Gregory Portnoy," Henry said.

"Pleasure. Our fathers will really appreciate that Henry and I are doing business." Message received, as if that was meant to change my behavior.

With my sleight of hand techniques, I made silver dollars appear on the table – my pitch. It was 1990, computers were faster than calling a broker. I could make trades faster and smarter with a computer.

"We have our own trading floor. I can buy and sell faster than a guy on the phone. But I also have the ability to review data from the market at the same time. No pay per trade. Pay us for profit on every trade. If you lose, we lose," I concluded. How could they resist?

They moved to the other side of the room to caucus. Henry and I exchanged glances but didn't speak. We could hear their murmurs.

Murmur type number 1: "These guys are smart. MIT." "Henry's from a family of bankers." "Cuban bankers."

I shot a look of disgust and an *I told you so* at Henry. Then I waited. No doubt my people were next.

Murmur number 2: "But Jews are smart with money." I wanted to say, *Fuck you, you over privileged baby. Buy me a car, inbreed.*

They came back to us.

"We'll do it. We're in for $100,000."

Henry said, "Great." "We'll send over the money order and you can get started. We'll want weekly reports. We expect to make fifteen-percent by the end of the semester."

"For sure," I said. My scheme was to take their $100,000, invest it, and double it. In no time, I'd make fifteen-percent and set it aside. I had planned on giving them twenty-percent on their money. If I couldn't make more than fifteen-percent, then the whole algorithm would be a failure. How else was I meant to make money on their money? Give them their expected percentage, and the rest would be ours.

■ ■ ■

In the apartment GNU and Joseph were working on something that would one day help the planet but make no money. I stroked their collective ego and told them I needed their help. If they want to open source the world, they would need a lot of money.

"Weekly reports? It was an unfair fight. I think those self-entitled dweebs were too dumb to care, but weekly reports? Will they verify it with time stamps directly from the service?" GNU asked. I shook my head, no. "So you can just put a stock symbol and some numbers down on a sheet of paper and call it a report?" GNU was baffled. "Amazing."

"We'll be honest," Henry said. "Just because they trust us doesn't mean we're not honest."

"I'm out," Joseph said turning back to the screen.

"You can't be out. This is a company project," I announced.

"I know how you get when you're in a mood, and how you are, and these guys are the perfect assholes," Joseph said in his typical monotone, focused on something more important attitude.

"I'm the one who made you rich enough to work on your favorite software project having your whole-life managed by a computer. What are you making at this moment that's so important that you can't stop for moment and help Henry and me?"

My ask was simple, creating personal notes that would be able to be transmitted to many in a specified group in many places with a computer – a lecture on the hyper-cube of data within the same software. Discussions through a computer on the internet about a calendar (date and time), and also the note be somewhere else at the same time in another topic. In addition, without instruction from a human, the computer will feed information, data into these topics where it was relevant.

"And that relevance could be a stock market billboard," I said. It could. Of course it could. Plug in the fastest and best stock market quotes and we can buy and sell. We can get alarms when a stock hits a certain price. We can create algorithms that can tell us when to buy a certain stock when another sector was in line with our other predictions. "Doesn't that help the world? Couldn't we have a program that can help others, teach others to invest in stocks and create a base level of income and ownership for the world?" I went global, and I knew I had Joseph and GNU's interest.

"It wouldn't happen like you describe," Joseph lamented. "As soon as you hit a critical mass of usage, the game would have to change. Because the stock market, the largest craps table in the world is about a zero-sum gain. If there's a winner, then there's a loser. I don't want to be a part of a process that creates losers."

"How about if those losers are the winners of the world? We create something that evens the odds. Could you imagine a platform one day where a group of people can decide to raise the value of a stock? The economically deprived guy in Bangladesh can legitimately compete with the Harvard MBA on Wall Street," I replied. Joseph made sense. I made sense.

Joseph looked at me. "Is there even one Porcellian from Bangladesh?"

Googol's gone

Things got serious and real when Googol walked in with a haircut. His girly-curly hair was gone. I've never seen it that short and professional. He also wore a suit with a dress shirt for the plane ride.

As if he could read our minds Googol said, "I'm being picked up at the airport by another clerk." So it began. Googol was conventionalizing. It didn't bother me, dress for the part. If he were a football player, he'd wear shoulder pads. But the contrast from boy wonder assistant professor to law clerk at the Supreme Court was stark.

GNU pasted a strange look on his face. Joseph smiled and said, "You look like a lawyer." All of his bags were shipped up early. Googol would be living with another law clerk who was clerking for another Justice until he could find a place of his own. None of us could goof on that situation. Justice Stevens was the best one Googol could hope. A clerk wanted to work for a Justice with whom he was philosophically simpatico. Otherwise, it was like training a pig to behave like a dog. It would be very frustrating to try and it annoyed the pig.

"So, you're taking me?" Googol confirmed.

"Yes, I'll take you," I said. Googol was leaving the team and we all gathered around for big hugs.

GNU came out with a lunch package for the flight, to which Googol said, "It's only an hour and a half in the air."

GNU replied, "You still might get hungry." You'd think he was a Jewish mother the way he said it. There was finality in his remark. It triggered the real goodbye. Googol was leaving and we weren't going to see him or eat with him for a while. He was a good influence. He was the shimmy damper on the team. He protected the personalities from running us off the rails into uselessness. Sadness kicked in. It wasn't on par with Chana leaving, but it was another punch on the sore in my heart. She and now Googol were gone. Will there be any fun in Cambridge without them?

The ride to the airport seemed a lot shorter than I expected. The relativity of time in relation to my bias to make it last longer. I got out and to say goodbye standing up.

"You know I'm coming back. You have my car," Googol said. We hugged and I said it would suck without him.

"One day we'll be able to talk through video on the computer," Googol said.

Not the same, I thought. "Think of it as a respite. Who knows what we'll be able to do together once we're back together." He handed me a diskette from his carry on. "Show this to Joseph and GNU. They won't be able to help themselves."

"What is it?" I asked. He just smiled. "I'll take care of your car. I'll visit you during break." I said as a farewell.

"Yeah, it won't be too glamorous. It's a 24/7 job," Googol said. "But come. And, you know what? Maybe it'll be good if you go to Israel too. Don't let traditional roles limit you. You're a student and an entrepreneur. You've earned the ability to stop and take care of business in other parts of your life."

"You think it'll work?" I asked.

"Work? That's not the right question. You have a question. Will it be answered if you ask it in Israel?"

I thought about it. I had a question. It needed to be answered. It must be answered in Israel.

The Cult of Personality

Was it possible I was crying in my sleep? Based upon my dreams, I've been crying my eyes out. Or could it be I was just sweating? I climbed out of the closet where my bed still remained. Chana picked out a better bed and even thought I should rent an apartment of my own. But I put that on hold since I didn't need a step up in luxury and privacy anymore.

There I was, looking at myself in the mirror. I washed my face. The water dripping, it felt better, but I didn't look well. What will I do? How will I get this scheme going with the Porcellians without help from the team? Joseph seemed to have control over himself and GNU – the technical brains of the operation. The math I could handle. How to execute the trades was simple enough. I could get one of the interns to write the code. But, the rest – the connectivity, that was the plastic surgery, the art that Joseph knew how to do.

In my funk, it felt like the longest trip to my computer in the apartment. It felt like I had no feet. I was walking on my ankles. I went to the refrigerator first. I poured some dry Cheerios in a bowl, packed the first handful in between my cheek and gum and I feel like I'm chewing tobacco without having to worry about having my jaw and tongue cut out one day from the cancer. And there it was. A diskette placed on top of my keyboard. I put it in the drive. It was loaded up and a nice title page popped on the screen. *Compu-trader.* Exactly. Couldn't help but think we started another industry – trading stock on the internet. Computers will be able to do it faster and cheaper. Make a phone call? Seriously? This simple program did something simple. It allowed me to view a billboard of stocks and then on another screen put in a buy order and sell order. Opened up the program and saw in Googol's code a remark from Joseph:

"GP's algorithms and code here. Joseph couldn't resist Googol's code. He had to help, he was on the team. There was a long day ahead, step one, put on my headphones. Step 2; connect it to my CD player. Step 3 – Jam to Living Colour – The Cult of Personality. Step 4 – code my Porkbellion stock market scheme.

No Options

The main room of the apartment was filled with MIT freshmen. They all were sitting around computers. It looked like the office of every other New York Stock Exchange company. When EF Hutton talks, people listen.[48] Change that to when GP talks, the interns listen. It was a beehive of suggestions and orders - suggestions by the interns and orders by me. And my lovely partner Leela looking over my algorithms and trades.

Admittedly, the computer speed sucked, but it wasn't entirely our fault. I wanted to trade, in some instances on the penny, and it wasn't allowed. I called every company that could run the trades through our billboards. I lowered my voice to try and sound older. I had to ask if Benjamin Franklin was old enough to trade. They could not be bribed. Some nonsense about neutrality; but it was really about capability.

What amazed me was that I could actually see my trades getting beaten out by other trades of the same amount that were posted after me. Why were these ghost trades being executed before mine? Who were they? I could guess but the voice over the phone at these brokerages could tell but wouldn't tell me. What a real racket. They were making money on my trade and could even advise based upon my trades. Whether I win or lose, they get their vig[49] (excuse me, fee) on every trade. I finally settled on the brokerage that didn't charge me for their "advice" on each trade. "Advice? I'm telling you to buy and sell within ten minutes without speaking to a human. What advice?" It was all so new to everyone else.

Meanwhile, the Porkbellions read the Wall Street Journal in order to check our work on buying and selling. They reviewed the day old information in the newspaper, and it developed into calls to the apartment for suggestions and criticisms on trades. I started calling them the *thirds*. It meant they were born on third base and "III" after their two last names, a note of born to privilege; didn't just want the money; they wanted the credit because that's their only means of recognition. Their only means of being different than their grandfathers; their fathers, who transitioned the family from bootlegger, to legitimate family was to make more money. These born into privilege - two last names - the third, think they know better. And it was not that they wave from third base like they accomplished something. That annoys me. It was that Kensington Chadsworth, III and the rest of the Porks thought they knew how to trade.

Within a week we figured out how to trade based upon patterns in the stock, even with the delay in trades, we were buying better hardware. Instead of sticking the phone on the headset, we now had more of a direct line to the stock billboard. Most of the trades appear to be happening as we requested. You sell a penny stock for a penny more and multiple that by 10,000 shares, that's an extra $1,000 – in a split-second. The better I got and the better the weekly reports, the more the Porkbellions wanted to take credit and give orders. It came to the point where I wouldn't take phone calls from any of them during the trading session, which inflamed them.

If I'd actually followed their advice, they would be making less. In fact, if I reported I did what they wanted, it would be easier. And that's what I did. I did what they told me; or so I told them. I sold when they said. I said I bought and sold the options the way they heard was the prudent thing to do. But in actuality, I didn't change a thing. I sold a stock for $22.19, but told them I sold it at $21.99 like they asked – in their weekly report. They were happy. And, our new cottage business in the apartment thrived. The double game of keeping the Porkbellions happy by making them feel important and making profit despite their ego kept me interested.

Bernard Madoff conducted this very type of scheme of false reporting. Except our scheme was making money and his scheme was back dating his trades. At this point he was a few years into his Ponzi scheme. The Porks set the rule; they wanted fifteen percent, I just followed them. This scheme should've gone off without a hitch.

You want fries with that trade?

The Porkbellions loved to party. The team was granted special access to the Porks' "slaughter house," their party room in the house. We were invited. When they say "invited" we were told it was required that we all come. "You want GNU to come to a party? Did you meet GNU and some of the other interns?"

"Yes, everyone who touches our money," Brit said. "It's business. And by the way, my cousin works for the best brokerage firm on Wall Street–he's saying we should buy Enron now," he said to a chorus of *thirds.* Preston Henson, III - who demanded everyone call him, "Brit," which confused me since he was not British. I had the impulse to call him a "cracker" to his face. Maybe I can get you a side order of fries with that while GNU shines your shoes. What the hell? Attendance at these parties was mandatory? Fine, then – we'd go.

Brit tried to high-five GNU when he walked in the door. They never met. GNU, being GNU, just said, "No thanks." I nodded at Brit, with an "I told you so" nod. This was not GNU's kind of party. Joseph just didn't show. He said he could hear the party from the apartment.

"Thanks for inviting me," GNU said to anyone that passed by.

"Nice job, GNU." I meant it sincerely. "You can grab some food and leave when you like." GNU grabbed a sandwich and ate it on the walk home.

"That was strange," Brit said to Chad and a chorus of other Porks.

"Like I said, this is not how we party," I said trying to make light of the scene, reminding them that the team was raised on gaming. Gamers were the best coders. They just didn't talk.

"No problem," Chad said. "You're making money."

"Right. Now you understand." But they didn't completely. Why wouldn't we listen to their trade tips? I told Chad, "You guys have had the system locked up for so long you think that your people know everything when this is a matter of algorithms and computer executed trades. It's about the technology. And you shouldn't be talking about what we're doing."

"Take it easy, man," Chad acting as the ambassador. "We're just offering advice."

"That's *our* job, right?" I answered.

"Where the fuck do you get off talking to us like that? We gave you a $100,000 of our money. How much money have you invested?" Brit popped off.

"What difference does that make?" I waited. Brit didn't seem to handle silence well. "Right – no difference. Our system works or it doesn't. You signed up to invest. We're investing."

"And doing very well. It's just part of the getting to know you. Feeling good about being in business with someone," Chad tried to soothe both of us.

"And accountability," Brit remarked.

"I didn't come here to argue. I'm glad we're doing well. Thank you for the invite to your party," I said.

"Don't go, GP." Chad said. "Stay for one drink." He shooed Brit away. "I'm drinking with GP," he announced. "You know Brit can't hold his liquor," he mumbled to me as he put his arm around me and directed us to the bar. There were a couple of scantily clad, coeds dancing on a table near the bar. The smell of marijuana and hash hit me in the face. I felt a little sick.

"Perhaps one drink," I said.

"Yeah, you are a live human being!" Chad yelled above the booming music. I smiled. I'm glad Joseph wasn't here – he couldn't handle this noise. I wondered what he was working on. I couldn't stand most of these guys but the girls were enjoyable props. Were these the women the Porks were meant to have children with? Were these the wild days before they had to normalize and formalize into the convention of dutiful subservient house wives and mothers? Did life end after college? Where did I see myself when I was forty? Will I ever fit in this world? Did I want to?

Their stuff is theirs and your stuff is theirs.

Computers were meant to do two things. One make things go faster; and two, eliminate paper. Henry took our data of stock and option trades and put it on a *visicalc* spreadsheet and committed the unpardonable sin of printing it out. Printing things out only led to problems. You got it. The Porkbellions got a hold of a copy and that was a problem.

"How the fuck did they get it?" I demanded.

"I left a copy in our dorm," Henry said.

"Out in the open?"

"I didn't even see them take it. A couple of them dropped by and then Chad called me and said the guys got the spreadsheet and they think we've been ripping them off," Henry explained.

"Ripping them off? We've given them what they asked for. Could you imagine if we executed on their stupid trades that their cousin or boarding school buddy demanded?" I said.

"Why were you putting different numbers in the weekly reports?" Henry asked and intensely stared at me. I wanted to say it was about creating a reserve for surprise, other associated fees that would be coming up from the billboard service and brokerage houses, etcetera. A reserve was a key point in the future Ponzi scheme. But the answer, if I was being honest to the core was, "Fuck 'em, that's why." Those born on third base motherfuckers. Why was their money, their money, and our stuff was their stuff too?

"Brit said that we owe them $400,000. They want their initial investment, their profit, our cut, and a fine," Henry said. His face was flushed.

"Well, that's not happening," I replied.

"Let's just give them their money back and forget we ever met them." He paused and dropped his tone. "My father wanted me to develop relationships with them for the bank."

"He wants more Mayflower people money, huh?" I asked, Henry.

"Is that so bad? That's what banks do, GP. They hold money. And lend money. And collect money. And charge interest and invest in business and promote the economy," Henry said.

"So? I was making them money. I met the goal. They found out we were making more. Do they even know what they're looking at? It's raw data," I said.

"These guys don't know from raw data. We have to give their money back," Henry said.

"That's not going to be that easy," I said. The timing was poor. "We had a black swan." A black swan, when a statistical unlikelihood rears its ugly black swan head. "We don't have $400,000 or $100,000. Today we have around $75,000. I need a month to get back up again," I said.

"They're Porcellians, GP. They control Harvard, MIT, and the world. This could affect our reputation for years," Henry yelled. "I'm going to have to involve my father now. He needs to know."

"He doesn't need to know. I just need time. The end of the semester as agreed." I said.

"You sound like a loser from an OTB," Henry replied. And that hurt my feelings. He referred to me like a loser betting on the horses. When have we ever had problems with money?

The phone rang in our dorm room and Henry answered it. He said I was there too. It was GNU. Henry tilted the phone so I could hear.

"You guys better come over the apartment. We had to call the cops. Googol's car was destroyed, car windows were smashed, spray painted. Joseph locked himself in one of the closets," GNU said.

I grabbed the phone. "They destroyed Googol's car?"

"Yes." GNU said.

"We'll be right there," I said.

"Why would the Porcellians damage Googol's car?" GNU asked.

"Because they found out we were making more money than we were telling them," I answered.

"Ah, you were lying to them and now they're angry," GNU said.

"That's right. And based upon yesterday's statistical anomaly we can't make up the difference," I said.

GNU ended the call with, "See you soon."

Are you ready for some Baseball

The Porcellians had turned Googol's car into carnival sledgehammer smash. Tires, flat; windows, smashed; interior slashed. Complete body damage. My anger turned to rage. The team and some interns stood around the car in a vigil. I was responsible. Am I evil because I knew the team would really help me now? Buying and selling for the sake of making money; money on an exchange of numbers, was not contributing or producing to society. This was good enough for me. It was not good enough for Joseph, GNU, or Googol, who still didn't know his car was destroyed.

Googol was slaving away in the Supreme Court. He was smart enough to do the work. There just was a lot of it. It boiled down to verifying. Does this case say that? Was there any other precedent that refers, supports, modifies this legal proposition? How does my Justice want this case to end up?[50]

Googol had wonderful ideas about how to make the law easier and more accessible to the world. He would talk about how he was creating a database of searchable words of cases. He used Joseph's body of work to make the cases searchable. One day if there were enough cases in the database, it would eliminate the need for physical legal libraries. "We could easily monetize that," I would say.

Googol offered the big kicker in our last phone call. He said, "I got Chana to graphically create slides based upon legal precedent. She was actually getting pretty good at using certain software systems. I was able to show to Justice Stevens that the Court's precedent was heading in a certain direction. Instead of requiring him to read it, he saw it." I suppose Googol had been talking to Chana via modem too – transferring data across the globe. And she was more than willing to stay connected, more than willing to use her art to make science pretty. Art in statistics; art in data. How weren't we perfect for each other? Still, because Chana was connected to Googol, I felt connected to her. At the same time their relationship made me jealous.

. . .

Chadsworth met me in the field outside of the MIT library. He'd just finished one of the classes MIT shared with Harvard students. He seemed calm, objective, and logical. But I never forgot he was a Pork and represented the Porks. He was a Porkbellion ambassador. Like all ambassadors, if he failed; there would be war.

"Just because we're privileged doesn't mean we can be robbed?" Chad said. "You have to make this right, GP - for yourself and Henry." He looked me in the eye. "Henry's father and my father do business. This can get complicated." I said, I understood.

"Let me ask you one question, and if you can answer it a certain way, I'll give you $200,000 today."

"You owe us $400,000," Chad replied. I shook my head, no. "We gave you $100,000 and based upon your real reports you owe us $400,000," Chad said.

"You don't get your cut and our cut. That's why we hate the over-privileged elite like the Porcellians. But let's get back to my question and we'll argue about the amount in a moment." There was silence. Chad was listening. "How did we rob you?"

"You bought and sold at different prices than you reported. You were taking money that belonged to us."

"When is the money owed to you?" Another moment of silence.

"The end of the semester."

"That's right. We don't owe you anything -- yet. Money over time, that's investing. Not just money at a given time. I don't owe you the money until the time is up. The end of the semester. "

"You sound like a guy who owes money to a bookie."

"I heard something like that this week. So, who was it, Brit? Who wrecked my friend's car?"

"I don't know," Chad said with an ashamed look on his face. "Probably." He paused and looked and looked up at me. "What's with this black swan?"

"Shit happens. That's a black swan," I answered.

Chad made a face as if he really wanted to know more. "You assume I'm smart because I go to Harvard; you're smart because of merit," Chad said.

"It's going to sound unbelievable, but our algorithm predicted a chance there would be a problem with the trades and we could manually adjust for it. However, it came down to the trading itself. We got bullied out by other traders." What Brit and the Porks didn't understand was that one penny can make a difference in a trade if you're trading thousands of shares. "Think of it more like cans of peas on a supermarket shelf. There weren't limitless cans. If someone with a bigger shopping cart blocked us out and grabbed all the cans, we don't get the cans of peas for the stated price. We bought it for a penny more. This will be a bigger problem as computers do more trading. The game will move faster as computers attempt to make more and more trades. I want to make the trades for a certain price and it didn't happen. We got bullied out."

It dawned on Chad that what he thought was true, now wasn't. "You're saying the report on Henry's desk were trade orders that weren't executed. They weren't the actual orders traded?"

"Did you even show it to someone who knew the trades were being executed by a computer outside of Wall Street?" Chad gave another long awkward stare. "How about the ethics of taking the report off of Henry's desk without asking?" There was a head tilt and eye movement from Chad. "We still have a problem. We need better equipment, to get off the modem phone line and connect directly."

Chad was convinced. He was shamed, plus we offered a solution. But then he offered a solution of his own.

"Maybe we need to change the game. Go to a slower game," Chad said. I was willing to listen since the team was in a desperate place because of me and Chad was the way to communicate to the Porkbellions.

Chad continued, "Yes. How about an actual game? I was sitting in my statistics class and the professor was selling us on statistics by mentioning sports. Particularly, baseball - slowest game in town."

"Ever hear of sabermetrics?" I asked.

"Not before class." Chad said. "But I was going to meet with one of the interns who's the cousin of one of the Porcellians in the baseball office. We can talk about it with him."

"MIT has a baseball team?" I asked.

"Yeah, and you can't get screwed by laying a faster bet. The only thing a computer can do is help us analyze the games and predict outcomes." And so Chad and I went to the baseball office and my mind began to think about ways I could convince Joseph and GNU that developing systems to analyze baseball will save the world.

▪ ▪ ▪

The thing I learned about sabermetrics was we could only analyze the roster of baseball teams and try and predict how the team might play in future games. We couldn't make any adjustments to a team roster by trade or batting order since we didn't own any baseball teams. We couldn't act on what we learn from the viewpoint of sabermetrics: how do baseball teams win games; how do they score runs most efficiently, and, when will they get those runs over a series of games? Nonetheless, I bit. Statistics were fun for me. My whole business life was probability. So, I proposed a new deal for the Porks. "I'll give them advice on how to gamble and based upon the success of the stated bets, you can place your bets or disregard our advice." Chad said he'd get back to me. He would have to sell the idea to the rest of the Porcellians.

▪ ▪ ▪

Joseph hated T-ball. Think about that for a moment. T-ball. T-ball, the precursor for baseball. One must hit the ball. Everyone gets a chance to hit the ball. Just remember to put the bat down and run to your right – to first base. Not much room to fail. He wasn't and never was athletic. Walking, as moving meditation was the only form of exercise he ever did. Sacred steps every day like Einstein. Not to be mean, he was a geek; and, I loved him for it. But the real issue was how do I get him and GNU to help me with baseball?

The meeting was short. I told GNU and Joseph that baseball was a means to excavate us from this financial mess. Us – no my mess, it was quickly pointed out to me. Fine, but technically I was correct. We didn't owe until the end of the semester. Yes, I accepted responsibility for Googol's car. So I said, "They destroyed Googol's car." We couldn't leave a man on the battlefield.

That didn't work too well. Joseph, matter of factly stated, "You destroyed Googol's car."

To pull out all the stops, I went for it. "Baseball is a microcosm of life. Whole-life. Whole-life management. Baseball analysis will be the best means to moving a *Qpredictor* software service forward. Imagine if the computer could recommend which team will do the best at a particular time of the season." GNU gave me a dead stare, that emotionless; I'm on a different dimension than you stare. Joseph just eye-rolled me and nodded his head.

"You know I started the coding. It helped you with your History project." I waited. "Come on. I helped you. You help me. But the real reason is I love working with you guys. We love working together. We need to work on this together now because – I made a mistake. We've made great games and software. . . "

"Stop. We'll help you," Joseph said. GNU reluctantly smiled, as if he was a backseat passenger in a car and had no say in the matter. I smiled back. There was something about us being a team; working together. We loved it. It wasn't the money; it was the excitement of hanging out and discovering. After discovering, the next best feeling was creating. In short, we did love making things together.

After speaking with the MIT backroom baseball guys, I read every article on sabermetrics. So did GNU. Baseball, who was scoring runs the most and when. Who will likely do it again? Who will likely win tomorrow?

"One day, Joseph, perhaps *Qpredictor* will be able to tell us how to win tomorrow." On a big white board in the apartment, in one night, Joseph and I laid out the software architecture of baseball. Four steps, each step has value; the fourth step (home plate) equals 1 point.

The night turned into the morning. We had the interns, eager to be near any project our company was working on, type in data – baseball statistics. Some of them started to talk about baseball and who appeared knowledgeable. We had a game running on a television for reference.

At one point, it seemed like one team emerged, not as the one likely to win the World Series, but one that would likely win a lot of games over a short period of time. Spreadsheet analysis, a computer can do that faster than any human and better than any human. We could read a commentary on baseball and prove it or disprove it. The guys who tried to predict, were no better than coin flips. We had a theory. We never tested this theory. And, it was the only option I had. I wanted to think it was better than gambling.

▪ ▪ ▪

I sat in the conference room of Porkbellions. I was in the front of the room, all eyes stared back. Chadsworth was standing next over me as protection. These sophisticates, fancied themselves on purveyors of options, bonds, stocks. Now, the men in this room were willing to bet on baseball; not for fun, but as an investment. They were willing to do it with a guy that they've erroneously concluded cheated them. I looked up at Chad. He put his hand on my chair. As I began to speak a tray of shots of alcohol were passed down the rows. Chad prepared everyone for the inevitable toast. Each gladly took a shot; some took two, without even hearing the first word from me.

"We have one recommendation – one. I'm not going to invest for you. Chad will be in charge of your money. Without getting too deep or too meta. . ."[51]

I was interrupted with "Meta? Stop speaking geek!"

"Without getting into too much detail about how, we've created an algorithm managed by a computer which created a greater understanding of which teams were going to do better over a series of games against other teams. We've come up with one team in the next month that we recommend that you bet the same amount over a series of 15 games." I stood up.

Hand up, "Why not predict per game and best team for each match up? Why figure out how to build bets so our money grows over the season?"

"This isn't blackjack and we're not counting cards. We have no decision-making power once you lay your bet. It's game on. If you roll your principal and winnings into the next bet you can lose it all in one game. We're recommending that over a series of games, not a particular game, a team is going to win more than they lose. I'm assuming you understand the money line in baseball bets. Not a point spread, but we'll be risking more money to make less than even returns. One hundred dollars to make eighty. As long as we're steady and right over a series of games, we'll win."

"Chad, controls our money?" Brit asked, apparently speaking for the group.

"That's right. You can trust me, right?" Chad remarked.

"Or we can just book the bets ourselves," Brit announced. And there it was–true dissention.

I moved to gain back control, "I don't care what you do or how you bet. I just need to know we're settled after I give you the recommendation." There was someone in the group taking notes.

Someone else asked if we can just see how we're doing over the series of games and then give the answer.

"No, I will give one recommendation right now. Your scribe will write it down." I pulled out a thick report, since they love reports and held it up. "Our analysis is in here. I'll stay all night explaining or leave."

Brit grabbed the folder with the report. He asked which team the report was referring to; there were only letters and numbers for players.

"I'll tell you which team and our recommendation as soon as you say we're willing to take a chance and we're clear," I said. A statistics major in the group realized that there was a clear recommendation for a team to win over certain games. It would take some hours of work to figure out which team and which part of that team's schedule.

"Pretty smart," the Porkbellion statistician replied.

MIT, not Harvard – asshole, I thought.

"That's why we're relying on GP's group, the Original Gamesters," Chad said. "Look, you love their games. This is a game we can win in real life and get straight and better." Chad paused. Henry did a lot of perceived damage leaving that report around. "GP, will you leave us for a moment?"

He rang a bell and a pledge or some underclassman came running. "Show Mr. Portnoy to the lobby for a moment."

I sat and waited. It was strange. It felt like the first time I ever had to wait and hope for a decision in another room. I didn't like the feeling. Who were they? They had the money. So they were the owners and I was the servant. They owned my time, my hope, my brain, my work? The only reason I was willing to share was I stood to make money if they agreed to make money the way I suggested. I owed the team. The Original Gamesters – kind of cool. I earned my money.

Chad came and beckoned me. "Greg, come back in." Chad said waving for me to follow him back into the room. I broke my stare at the floor and followed him. "The Porcellians have decided. We agree to your terms. If your recommendation bails us out, we're square and will reward you with your consulting fee." I nodded. I looked at the scribe and nodded.

"Bet the Oakland Athletics to win every game they play from April 13 to April 29. Bet the same amount for each game. Do not roll your winnings into the next game. Same bet every game. With the vig and any other fees, including ours, you'll win." They all looked at me like there was more. "That's it. *Bona Futura*..... *Buena Suerte* .....Good luck."

Chad thanked me. I shook his hand. "Do you want a ride back to campus?"

"Yeah, since you lost your car," Brit said. I turned slightly toward him, not paying him the reaction Brit sought by mentioning his crime. I merely smiled. I turned back to Chad and politely declined.

"I'll walk." And I walked out of the house hoping that Joseph's latest version of *Qpredictor* would work for baseball. What if it didn't? Did I have a plan? Yes I did; and yes, it involved escaping on an airplane.

▪ ▪ ▪

It was early in the baseball season and not enough games played to note any trend. The A's won Games 10 and 11, – their tenth and eleventh games against the Angels and the White Sox, respectively. Knowing what we knew about statistics and science winning two games in a row didn't prove any trend in predictive modeling. But what it did prove was that perception was important to our reality. We were winning and therefore we were winners. I saw Chad outside the library and he asked if we were sure we shouldn't bet more on the next game. "Yes. I didn't say the A's were on a streak, we said that the A's were likely to win over a certain number of games consistently." He nodded.

"It's just some of the guys are excited," he said.

"Excitement has nothing to do with it," I replied.

Chad nodded again. "Why don't you come by and watch tonight's game with us. It's kind of a team building thing."

I smiled and shook my head no. "I have to file my taxes." My version of, "I'm washing my hair."

"You don't have an accountant that does that for you?" Chad said with a smile.

I thought for a moment. I just stared at him. "Why does it always look like you just walked off a yacht or are about to walk on one?"

"Why does it always look like you're calculating the coordinates to torpedo my yacht?" He retorted.

I smiled.

"You know, you don't have to hate us all. Take it down a notch. Say start with resentment and see how it goes," Chad said.

"I really can't tonight. I'll see about the game after that," I said. Again with a firm handshake and we went our separate ways.

▪ ▪ ▪

Tonight, I needed to be dressed a certain way. How do I present myself? She was Leela Fashionista, awesome coder with fashion skills.

Leela picked out a blue blazer, light blue button down, khaki slacks, and docksiders - no socks and laid them out on my bed in my room at the apartment. I frowned at the outfit.

"Seriously? You're an accomplished student of MIT and you're acting like my mother," she said.

"I feel like a Porkbellion, douche bag," I said.

"This is precisely why you need to do what I'm telling you. This is a deep analysis of how to infiltrate the group, how to make them comfortable with you. So, yes, look professional. Look like one of them." Leela explained.

"You should come with me," I said.

"No, I'll just drive you there and pick you up. It's a boys club. No 'Girl-Friday's' allowed," she said.

"I would be more comfortable if you were there," I pressed.

"And, this is training. You need to get more comfortable with people you're not comfortable with. Comfortable with rich assholes from a different upbringing than you," she said and then placed an Oakland As lapel pin on the coat. I looked like I owned the team. And, I felt ready to go.

It was the perfect lesson. It was my brain accepting that I would have to pretend to enjoy the company of people I disdained. For purposes of the Ponzi scheme of my future, I needed to persuade people I not only couldn't stand, but meant to exact the revenge I sought against them. The only way a Ponzi scheme worked was development of trust – the investors need to trust the schemer.

I arrived at the Porcellian. Chad was surprised to see me dressed up for the game; but he was dressed in the same uniform, except for his gold Rolex submariner. I drank what he was drinking. It appeared to be a smart way to connect with him. He liked that I was trying to connect and the alcohol definitely helped me deal with the hundred questions I received about why the As lost the night before and what does it mean for the rest of our recommendation. The game was slow and long. It was baseball. But I met all the guys and it seemed to them I was an expert in not just baseball but finances as well. Strange, since they had no evidence I was good at either. Chad seemed to be in on it with me – he was my coconspirator. It was a subtle trick or trait that surely locked down the targets of my grand Ponzi scheme years later. Chad stared me in the eyes and we clinked my glass of scotch in a toast. "Welcome aboard."

The black swan, that ugly duckling of statistical anomaly that struck my team, has turned into a beautiful swan. The Original Gamesters were being hailed across campus, from the Porcellians to AEPi at MIT and Harvard. The *Tech* even published a short on how bookies across campus and Vegas were shocked that the Oakland A's had won 9 out of their last 11 games. Brit commented that the As were going to keep winning and that his algorithm on game predictions was a great forecasting model.

I asked Chad to bring Brit to meet me outside the library. Chad asked me to bring Henry, so I did. Henry was in good spirits and said the reason why Chad wanted him to come to the meeting was to keep everyone happy. In short, to make sure I didn't piss off Brit. Everyone was happy but me.

"Hey man, how are you?" Chad engaged first. We all shook hands. Henry and Chad were yukking it up. The conversation began with happy talk.

"I didn't think I had to mention this since gambling on campus is illegal and a violation of the school honor code; not to mention we're laying off $100,000 at a time, we're affecting odds. Affecting odds is against our interest," I said.

"I think you should stick to what you're good at, and let old money run the money," Brit announced. Chad, looked at Brit and just said, "Brit."

"That's fine. You're smarter than we are and are genetically better to handle money better than we do, just don't cite to us as authority," I replied sarcastically.

"I didn't cite to you, you arrogant prick," Brit said.

"The Original Gamesters? You're in some society that holds the secrets of the world and you tell the campus newspaper you've got a formula? What the fuck is that?"

"That was wrong," Chad said. "GP has a point. You spoke out of school and it will potentially cost us money by affecting the odds we can get on tomorrow's bet."

"Chad, I'm sick of your bullshit too. We could've made four times our money if you just doubled up after there was a streak going," Brit said.

My stare remained locked on Brit. Chad knew the reporter and said he'd talk to him.

"A group of us are going to double up based upon our own analysis. That's against your recommendation, so when we win we're not paying any fee," Brit said and walked away. We watched him walk off.

"Is he really going to do that?" Henry asked.

"Probably," Chad said. "What do you think guys, should we roll our winnings into the couple of games or the series against the Tigers?"

"Maybe we should. To keep the group together," Henry said. "It's just a slightly higher risk."

"Statistics don't care about our unity. One loss can change the success of our whole model. We're doing better than we expected, which means we should take more risk? That's what Brit is saying in all objectivity," I said.

"It's greed," Chad said. "He's never satisfied. We're gambling, not building a company."

"I'm glad you agree. Just realize I think the A's will win until April 29th and then that's it. That's all we'll vouch for. It could become sporadic for a little while after that," I confirmed.

"I appreciate that, GP," Chad said sincerely. "I just wish I could keep my team together." Henry and I looked at each other. "Too much money, not enough money. That's always the problem of business. When it's feast, everyone thinks it's because of something they did and want more of the pie. When it's famine, it's someone else's fault," Chad said.

Chad had an interesting perspective. Indeed, I felt like I had more in common with him than I would've guessed. "Just remember, Chad, that Brit and the Original Gamesters might both be right. It doesn't justify doubling up or tripling up on risk on a higher bet."

"We all have our issues," Chad said shaking hands and ending the meeting.

▪ ▪ ▪

It turns out that Chad couldn't keep all the Porcellians together. There was a small group that stayed with his betting strategy of the same $100,000 bet every game. And the As beat the Orioles 9-4. Then the Tigers the next day and the day after. The intensity was strong. We were all asked to come to the Porcellians that April 29th. Most seemed concerned. All were standing; none were sitting in the row of chairs. Chad kept saying let's talk about this carefully and considerately.

Henry, GNU, and Joseph came with me. They all had a look on their face – a look of uniform wonderment. This was the play, the play was over and yet, they wanted more. This was how people become victims of fraud schemes. We did statistical analysis, a photograph, and they wanted to treat it like it was a motion picture. "Couldn't you all just find another pattern?" "How about tomorrow, are the A's going to win tomorrow? What are the odds?"

GNU whispered to me, "These guys go to Harvard?" I just looked at him. Joseph just appeared bewildered by the noise of remarks about continuing to gamble based upon random facts. To him, it was like one of the hysterical Porks were saying, "Carrots, therefore the As will win tomorrow, right?" Frankly, it sounded the same to me too.

"Do we even know who's pitching tomorrow?" A voice asked.

"Tanana," someone answered.

"Look, it doesn't matter," I said. "We said until April 29th."

"That's it. It's April 29th. I've cut a check for GP and his team. They've earned it and they're square with us," Chad said. There were boos and howls. It sounded like many were unsatisfied, which really bewildered me. It was like watching animals in the zoo.

Brit grabbed the envelope our check was in from Chad's hand and held it up. "There's a tax for stealing from us earlier."

Chad snatched it back and said, "They're square. And now we owe this money. "What is the matter with you guys? You're embarrassing me. We invested wisely in a risky game. We made a lot of money for doing nothing. It's done until the next thing," Chad said. More boos and jeers. "You're being impolite to our guests; and frankly, I'm embarrassed."

It was a truthful statement. We were guests and not members – not one of them. Henry might have felt otherwise for a moment – he wanted to be a part of the ruling class. I was never fooled.

I thanked everyone and grabbed our check back. One of them yelled out to us as we were leaving. "Do you think the As will win tomorrow?" I turned and answered, "I don't know." With that, we left. We walked for a little while and then Leela saw us and we all piled in to her car and went out to a diner and ate and hung out. This was wealth. This was the good times of being together. Ice cream and waffles were the victory of a job well done. Even Joseph graced us with his presence. We goofed around with ideas that were silly, some plausible. Imagine if a hundred people could talk to each other on a computer billboard at a time. Would it be stupid, productive, or cool? All of the above? Imagine if you could get the stock price a millisecond faster than the rest of the world? Why were you always trying to exploit the system? I smiled and sipped coffee.

"It's not exploitation. Or if it is, we need to change the definition of exploit. It's the great equalizer between the haves by birthright, and the geeks. Plato's *Philosopher Kings.*"

"The Porkbellions," GNU said. "Best nickname ever."

"The Original Gamesters. The best nickname ever," I announced as we toasted spoons full of ice cream. We laughed and enjoyed the rest of the meal. I didn't bother to tell the rest of the team that I had one small, not so proverbial slap for Brit before this project was officially marked complete.

It turned out that the A's lost the next day to the Tigers. Then, they split a two game set with Toronto and split a subsequent two game set with the Tigers, making their record 4-5 since we left. Each day, we later learned, Brit and his crew kept pressing and raising their bet and they ended up losing a lot in the next seven games. I'd saw Chad around Cambridge, on and off campus. We'd smile and wave. Occasionally, we would catch up. "Let's do something again soon," he'd say. I would politely agree. "Sure, one day."

▪ ▪ ▪

Henry looked distraught when he came by the apartment. I asked him what was wrong. He asked, "Anybody we know from out of town visit campus?"

"Not sure what you're talking about," I answered, but I did. Henry frowned. He still lived in a bubble of happiness. Henry asked me where I was last night.

I was at a lecture that evening – listening to Steve Jobs talk about the future. I coaxed Chad to come with me. It was Leela's idea to keep in touch with him. But, I really wanted an alibi. I brought Chad so he would be that alibi witness. And as an added benefit, everyone in the room dug that I had the balls to ask Jobs, "What's it like when the company and the people you helped raise turn on you?" Chad leaned forward and listened to Jobs' answer. The whole room did.

Jobs stared at me. I locked eyes with him. He replied thoughtfully, "It's like getting hit in the head with a brick. You get hurt, angry. You wait a little. And design the next best thing. You get your revenge."

"Will you get it?" I followed up.

"I will," Jobs answered.

"Will you ever return to lead Apple?" I pressed.

"That's what I mean by revenge," Jobs answered.

It was at that moment I enjoyed what Jobs said the most. He would go back to Apple, like Caesar, and have his revenge. "Don't let a setback set you back. There was always revenge to motivate and satisfy."

▪ ▪ ▪

The last action of the night was to pick up the phone and call Googol. Googol's car was destroyed by Brit, so Brit's car had to be destroyed in retaliation. I was angry, but I had to take responsibility for Googol's car getting destroyed. Googol didn't have to know about what happened to his car, he just needed a car.

"I got some good news, Googol. The team bought you a new car."

"What happened to the old one? Somebody wreck it?" He asked.

I explained the fun we had with sabermetrics and betting on baseball. He seemed entertained by the statistics and sports, something he never had much interest in and wouldn't until years later when I needed him to get really interested in football. I told him to accept the car because he was on the team and the team succeeded again. Of course, it was just the latest model of the car he was driving. Sometimes I thought everyone on the team but me had the palate of a communist. Nobody wanted the best car, just a car. And, a car that was reliable was luxurious enough. It was tricky to motivate the team with just money. There needed to be something else that motivated.

I drove the new car to D.C. and spent the weekend with Googol. He made some time to hang out. During his work time, I read the legal briefs he analyzed for Justice Stevens. There was game strategy in the law, values over fixed conclusions. Nine justices of the Supreme Court could write nine different opinions on the proper way to reach a legal conclusion. That conclusion could years later, change. These legal opinions could free defendants from prison. But most profoundly, swing millions, perhaps billions of dollars from one party to the other. The rest was commentary. As I flew back to Boston, I thought about the law and what it meant to be a lawyer. I would become a student of the law. The legal profession and understanding the game would serve the team well, and was essential to managing a successful Ponzi scheme.

The Useful Class

With a big smile, I walked around the apartment with bonus checks for Leela, Joseph, and GNU. Each of the long bridge tables with exposed wood was crowded with rows of computers. Extension cords were connected to "six shooter" electrical plugs where computers, monitors, printers, and modems were connected. Interns were on one side, ignoring the interns on the other side facing them.

The checks were not technically bonuses, since the interns didn't receive a salary. Leela commented that I was dressed like a sharp business man. It was because I just came from the bank retrieving a cashier's check – one I could mail or hand deliver to Chana. She worked on this project for us as well. She created easily understandable graphs which were important to the success of this project. I also didn't want her to remain mad at me. She should feel that she was a part of the team – that we were a team. And that one day we would be a team again.

When I went around the table of interns, the mood erupted into a joyful blast of cheer. I nodded for them to open the envelopes with their checks, each for the same amount. As I peered outside the room of interns, I saw GNU and Joseph staring at me. I walked out and told them we should redecorate this place or buy a new and bigger place.

"How do we have the money for that?" GNU asked.

"You don't think we only got a consulting fee, do you? I put our money where our mouth was. Made our own bets," I replied.

"You invested our money?" GNU asked.

"I invested my money and I'm sharing it with you," I said.

"You have a funny way of looking at things, GP," GNU said.

"How's that? We invested our money in the stock project. I invested my money in the baseball project."

"That's not what's bothering us, GP," Joseph said. Leela touched Joseph on his shoulder. "Where were you last night?"

"With Chad at a lecture. That's the second time I was asked that today." That night there was a car fire on campus. Henry saw Bobby A on campus. Bobby A, from the party in Florida, tinkered with Brit's car and science took its course. I, of course, was with Chad at a lecture with Steve Jobs.

GNU said, "Brit's Mercedes was fried to a crisp. Something went wrong with his car's electrical system. That's not something that accidentally happens."

"It was a thug move, GP. Something Brit would do," Joseph declared.

"Accidents happen, when Porks are sloppy," I said.

"And your move comes from the same place – bully," Joseph retorted.

"If it weren't for me, many a bully would've tortured you for years," I said.

"Maybe, but you sunk to their level. You talk about entitled elites who get to roam around the world wreaking havoc at the expense of the useful class but you're the same," Joseph said loudly.

"Stop. This is a horrible discussion that will lead to regret," Leela interjected.

"You guys would be minimum wage coders without me," I said. "I'm the one that made you money. I'm the one that makes you a member of the meaningful useful class. You can only exist if assholes like Brit are forced to back off."

Joseph started to stammer, a regression into his seizure-like ways of his overloaded motherboard of an anxiety-ridden brain.

"Sit down." Leela said. She was getting nervous.

GNU just stared at me.

"What?" I looked back at him. "Fine, I'll leave. Go out into the world and give away everything for free and see who steals your hard work from you. Without my protection and business sense, see how you'll do. Sit in a room overlooking an exposed brick wall tenement for the rest of your life."

"We all need to chill. Let's relax. Let's smoke some weed and calm ourselves," Leela said.

"I don't smoke weed, Leela. Only this basket of angst does."

"Don't lose your temper, GP," Leela yelled. Now the interns abruptly stopped work. They peered in from the other room.

"I'll leave you alone." I started walking toward the door.

"Where are you going?" Leela said. "Stay, it's important that you stay."

"Just stay, GP," Joseph said. "What are you going to do with yourself if you're not here?"

"I'll move out. I'll go to law school in Georgetown. I'm going to give lectures there. I'll have dinner with Googol on Sundays."

"Come on, GP. That's so rash." Leela said. "We're in the middle of the semester."

"I'll move my stuff out after I come back from Israel."

Connection lost

One of the dormitory computer labs at 3 a.m. was like a morgue. It was so quiet it was scary. To hear your fingers type and nothing else allowed me to focus. There was no blowing of the air conditioner, footsteps or paper shuffling. I tweaked the modem to allow me to make a long-distance call to Israel. Talking to Chana was the shining light in an otherwise shitty day. She confessed the Army wasn't what she expected.

There was a lot of ordering around for a creative person. I joked, "See, working with me and the team was not so bad." She didn't write that she missed me. I didn't know how I could really write well without seeing her face. I wanted to tell her that I still missed her. The drone of depression had fixed in the back of my mind since she left. I hated the words across a screen left most to the imagination.

She seemed sympathetic in her words about my falling out with Joseph, GNU, and Henry. It turned into a "rift" as the conversation continued. So, I've decided to go to law school.

> Chana:*Law school?!*
>
> GP:*Yes. I've got an in through Googol and a professor there. And* I'll *have to lecture on law and technology.*
>
> GP:*I'll have a MS from MIT in business and Computer Science and a law degree from Georgetown. Pretty cool, huh?*
>
> Chana:*So proud of you, GP.*
>
> GP:*Thanks. . . I wanted to ask you. I have time off. I have a check for you from the Return Fire and baseball projects.*

Chana:*Yea! Go Athletics! You don't owe me any money, GP.*
But, I'll take it. (smile). Mail it off. I'll get it... eventually.
GP:*I wanted to give it to you in person. I need to see you.*
These damn modems! The baud rate – it's so damned slow. The response was delayed; or maybe it was my brain.
Chana:*Don't come, GP.*
GP:*It'll be...*
Chana:*I've moved on...*

Disconnected! I felt rage. I wanted to talk this out, and I couldn't. Stuck in the mud again.

I'm human

Why did I say I was going to Israel? Where was the value in stating that intention? Dramatic exit from an argument – "I'm going to Israel!" They all probably thought I pulled another victory out of what would've been a failure for everyone else. I was even skilled in romance. But I'm not. The one romance I cared about – gone and I didn't know how or what went wrong.

What does, "I've moved on" mean? It was not a very direct phrase. Could she be into Israel so much that she didn't even remember how she felt about me? Oh God, was there another guy? I hate that phrase – moved on. Did she discount our past? Did I not get my place in the history of her life? For all I've done for her – all we've done together. What did I do for her? It made no sense. I applied logic to romance, an illogical paradigm. Love conquers all? Not only did love not conquer all, it clouded the subject. Shouldn't I be practical? Well I'm persistent. I was naked and afraid. A fool was a fool, no matter where he was in the world. I was willing to be that fool. I would travel to Israel and test what conquers all. I was setting myself for the greatest victory of my life or the worst failure. No matter what, I wouldn't seem like a liar to the rest of the team.

■ ■ ■

It wasn't too dramatic to return to the apartment – the worksite of our great adventure as cyberists. The rooms were silent but for some humming of computers and modems. The temperature was cool. Joseph was there alone. No interns; no Leela. Late enough in the morning for classes on campus. Joseph continued as if we never had argued.

"I had a real breakthrough last night. If we step away from finer graphics and sound we can focus on the functionality of the computer. We need to step away from the movement to anthropomorphize computers. Our brains are not computers and computers are not human brains. It doesn't think like humans, but can learn deeply enough to be thought of as thinking," Joseph said, as if he had some epiphany.

"So, what? No more games? Graphics are too cool. Sound too much fun? Not enough theoretical development. You'll be the only one that cares if you're too far ahead in the future," I said. I was annoyed. This was why Joseph should never run a business. He didn't understand there was the future and there was the working future. The working future – a place where we might be alive when we arrive at the functional unit of time in science.

"Graphics are wonderful. Sound is fantastic. Recreation and games are escapists. I'm the neuropsychologist of computers. Cognitive computer science, which is where I belong. This was my breakthrough," Joseph said.

I was despondent. This would lead to continued argument. Joseph needed me more than ever. He needed a Leela in his life forever. He could never survive on his own. Everything open to the world. All of the code he ever wrote he just gave away. He was a bizarre globalist, anarchist, and I was tired of it. Deep down, I felt sick of him. No, I was just sick. His moody long walks to the kitchen like he was strolling through molasses. He was depressive. The world disappointed us all but he took it personally. It was infectious. When he got dark it overtook him.

"So you're going straight to Washington and skipping Israel?" Joseph wondered. He declared this question as if it were a statement. "It's probably better this way. It'll be good that you'll be near Googol. You'll be able to rely on one of us for a change."

Joseph sounded sincere. Not able to stay mad at him for long, I vented. "I don't know. I think I'll go to Israel. She said something about moving on and I don't know what that means? Can Israel make you want to move on? Forget about us?"

Reminded again that Joseph had his own separate relationship with Chana he blurted out, "Moving on means she's getting married." Joseph said with a literal tone. Was this his flat tone or did he mean it? Maybe he was just confused about "moved on" as I.

"Moving on from what? Life was great, right?" I asked.

"It was. We're a good team and we're all good friends. And now she's moving on to a different stage of her life, in a different part of the world, where social constructs are different," he said.

"She's getting married?" I said in disbelief, not able to look him in the eye.

"She is, GP. I'm sorry." It was evident that Chana told Joseph directly. "We spoke the other night and she told me."

"I still think I have to go." I looked down and surveyed the floor. First time I realized there were wires and cables everywhere. "Look at this place. There's shit everywhere."

"Sorry, GP," Joseph said.

"You know this is the first time we'll be a part since for so long since we're twelve? How stupid is that?" I said.

"You'll always have a mattress in the closet, GP. You're a strong person. You'll get through this rough time. You're going to be a great man, GP. Everything you'll want in the world will be yours. That's your greatest blessing and it will be the greatest curse," Joseph said.

I couldn't wipe the scowl off my face. The sadness and pressure must have shown on my face. Joseph developed an aura that preceded of one of his downturns.

"Ugh, just calm down. I'll be fine. I'm leaving MIT. Just think of it as a hiatus or hibernation. I'll be back soon." And it was definitely time that I leave. I grabbed the couple of bags I came for and left. I threw my bags in Googol's car and just walked - walked for two hours. I then ran. I ran fast. It served as an excuse for my teary eyes – it was from the wind, not from sadness. I was alone. We were always alone. It was 1990 and I felt alone.

TRANCHE III
Dewey Cheat 'em

Georgetown

"If you're willing to slum it on the couch, you're welcome to stay for as long as you need," Googol said.

I thanked him and threw my bags down. Leela said she would ship the rest of my stuff here. Googol pointed to the back room, with a forced grin, and said, "They're already here. All your stuff's in there." Googol said.

"Leela is awesome, wasn't she? Gifted in math, fashion, and supportive logistics," I said.

We ate dinner that night at 9:00 p.m. He found a pizza place that makes goat cheese pizza. Googol told me it was an early night for him. He'd usually stay at the Supreme Court until ten o'clock at night. He was able to come home earlier now that computer research online was an option. He was also developing his own offline database from the large search results he created. Googol reminded me that Joseph was helping with this and that the whole concept of computers creating giant databases of knowledge and one day the suggestions by computers will be helpful. A computer to help the human learn, live, and survive. I believed it. But, these gains would be made from capitalist motivations, not from notions of open source and the goodness of people sharing.

Googol wondered aloud where I got my pessimistic view of life when all the evidence around me was that I was supported. My father, Joseph, the team, were the reasons I was successful. He discounted the attacks on me, the team, like Googol's car. I never considered myself a pessimist, just a realist. Realistically, my circumstances were glum.

"Speaking of which, what the hell happened to my car?"

"Well, it got wrecked. We didn't want to bother you with it. It was in our care and custody, so the company decided to make sure you were made whole," I said.

"The Original Gamesters. I read about your gambling venture in the *Tech.* Glad your code could finally help. Baseball? How did you choose the A's?" Googol asked.

"Alphabetically, the A's are on the top of the list. I also liked their colors," I said with a smile.

"No way. Really?" Googol asked.

"We had to move fast. At a glance the American League was going to do better. We picked the division and then ran the algorithm and one team seemed to have the best chance of going on a streak. The A's. We got lucky," I nodded with no expression of exaggeration.

As Googol grabbed another slice, he asked, "How was Israel?" He waited because I didn't answer for a moment. "How is Chana?"

"I went to Israel and if I can use the second or third definition of the word *disruptive*, it was like that."

"Disruptive?" Googol questioned.

"Yeah, I thought about it a lot. I thought about setbacks in life. Chana was a setback. Like the loss of my mother, a setback. I just had to accept that my arrogant-self demanded a game on the merits but the results in life was not always decided on the merits alone. There were random events that occurred that disrupted the game of life. Like weather, a storm could happen. That's why we love prediction. But not all things act logically. With humans there was no perfect logic."

"Get to the good stuff, GP. Did you see Chana?"

"Well, not face to face," I said.

"You flew all the way to Israel and didn't do what you went there for?" Googol was at a complete loss.

"I went to get answers, and I did. I saw her mother, Hadassah. And it was by chance, in a shopping area of town. We locked eyes for a long moment and then she realized it was me. She hugged me, tears poured from her eyes, and she kissed me on the lips while holding my head in her hands. She said she knew I would come. It was God's way of compelling me to come to Israel – to visit their Kibbutz."

Googol and I, being the atheists we were, smiled. "There's no arguing with that," he said. That was true; there was no arguing. But I didn't want to argue with Mrs. Meir. I didn't know that her son was murdered. I didn't know her suffering. But if she left Israel to get away from the insanity of a life in Israel, why did she return? Why did she take my Chana with her? Would this have happened if she weren't a tough Israeli? But who am I to talk? I said the wrong things all the time. I ran myself, all the way to Georgetown.

"So, Chana is marrying an officer she met in the Army. He's some type of intelligence analyst. I'm told something to do with computers, but he's nowhere near us in terms of genius, which was supposed to make me feel better. He's older, something like eight years older than Chana, so he's ready to get married and start a family. He'll be out of the Army soon. Or depending on a promotion might stay," I said.

Googol just opened a bottle of wine and poured it. "So what made you not turn up on Chana's doorstep? Show her that you were there. That you had the balls to go to the other end of the world on your own time and resources and say, 'I love you and I'm here?'"

"I had her mother deliver a letter I wrote to Chana by hand. She didn't want to see me. Her mother said she would go and talk to Chana, tell her I was in Israel, and that she should talk to me. A few days later, I met her mom again at the Kibbutz. She said that Chana was not ready to see me," I said.

Googol seemed to be quiet for a while. I started to think about whether he cared about any women. He considered them to be assistants – all of them. He never felt helpless and in love. He liked, appreciated, and enjoyed certain women, but nothing more. I could be wrong. Perhaps, he suffered quietly. Flying to Israel pushed my suffering out of my mind. "I saw Chana from afar. I went on a hike to where she was training or working and I saw her from afar."

"And? That's a good way to get shot at in Israel," Googol joked.

"Not that kind of training. I saw her and, my heart leapt. But it was like watching a scene from a movie unfold in front of me. She was in her life in Israel with her friends in the Army. Painful as it was, I could only watch."

"Did she see you?" Googol wondered.

"I'm certain she didn't," I said.

And I opened a note that I took on the plane with me to Israel from Chana. I didn't want to read it before I went to Israel. I opened it after I saw her. It read: "In our quantum of space and time, we loved, and lived a life together."

Googol just sat there in stillness for a while and said, "Damn, Chana went Heisenberg on your ass." We laughed.

"And I'll note the Oxford comma," I remarked to break the intensity.

Googol and I talked about quantum physics, relativity, and women for days after. He was good to talk to. I stayed at Googol's apartment. He liked me there and I liked being there. At night, we called Joseph to develop our ideas. We reached a compromise. GNU would work on coding and designing games. Joseph developed our ideas on designing programs and collecting data for lawyers, which he said was part of his larger quest of having computers automatically help mankind. Who knows, he might be able to do it. We've been able to do everything else we've ever wanted with a computer.

One Hell

In law school, the law was science. Or at least, I made it science. It was about reading cases on a particular area of the law. The cases set up rules of law when it interprets either statutes or other common law, which were other cases. The professors wanted the issue, rule, analysis, and conclusion. What was the case about? Did the case issue a rule or any exceptions? How did it apply to a similar set of facts? And that application became a conclusion. It then turns law into could be this or could be that. If this, then that. And then that was the logic.

Googol and I talked about the science of law. Couldn't we draft contracts that were just about filling in the blanks – a will or divorce pleadings? Couldn't most of it be law in a box? Pull it out of the box and fill it in. One of the perks of having a good friend who worked at the Supreme Court of the United States: he knows how and where these cases go through the judicial system. The first year law students participate in the most aggressive con on themselves. They pronounce meticulously to themselves over and over – they love the law. What does that mean? But, I did not mock my classmates. The work was overwhelming. A drama unfolded each day; there would be a final exam one day soon. Each created a personal mental inventory of who might be the smartest in the class, so one day; they too could work for the entity. The truth was even an anecdotal analysis of the law showed that the powerful entity wins overwhelmingly over the individual. Indeed, most Justices on the Supreme Court have never had a human for a client – just governments and corporations. Why? Who can pay for all these lawyers?

A research and writing professor walked a group from my class around the library – lots of books. "Do you really expect anyone to look at these books, stand up, go find another one, and bring it back to a desk and read it when there are computers?"

"We're not quite there yet," was the response. I smiled. That's what she thought. Westlaw and Lexis/Nexis[52] was emerging. During our limited off time, Googol and I got on a call or emailed GNU and Joseph ideas to create products for the legal community. Lawyers were dinosaurs, technologically; but if they adopted a new technology, so follow the rest of the world.

That was genius – looking at something in a different way and acting on it. Googol worked hard for fourteen hours a day at the Supreme Court, but while he was working, he thought of how this can be done better with a computer. At night, we reviewed it and developed our ideas. Joseph true to his rebel form didn't want to make a deal with Lexis or Westlaw. He released all of our code online for anyone, including Lexis and Westlaw to improve their native language searches. The money we could have made was tossed out the window. One or both would've paid three-million to license or buy our code. We had a discussion. He ignored me. He released the code. Googol said it was Joseph's code; he could do what he wanted. One day he would need the money to defend what he was and what he did.

Goodnight SCOTUS

Googol's year of no life came to an end. The intensive year as a clerk for the Supreme Court was the best of times and the worst of times. Googol learned the right ways in the law, the wrong ways, the use and misuse of power; the politics in and out of the law and the Court. He could have a professorship to teach at any law school in the country – the reward for successful completion of clerking at the Court. A clerkship was the ultimate ticket to ride.

Googol bonded with Justice Stevens. Justice Stevens was a perfect legal thinker and a man of style. Googol even agreed to play bridge with Justice Stevens from time to time. Both graduated from Northwestern law school. He was curious to see where Googol lived, and have dinner at the apartment. Googol asked him why rather than a restaurant. Justice Stevens said he could learn more from seeing where Googol lived than anything Googol could describe. Googol was financially better off than all of the other clerks, but the apartment wasn't decorated for aesthetic design. The architecture was useful. It was like the apartment in Cambridge only smaller – two bedrooms and a large family room with computer equipment that appears to be monitoring satellites.

Justice Stevens came dressed for the occasion. He, in his typical uniform of a smart suit with a bow tie; he brought two bottles of wine to go with our promised Italian meal. We dressed the same, but with traditional ties – only one bow tie per crew allowed.

"*In vino veritas,*" Justice Stevens said as we toasted glasses. In wine – truth. At this meal it became evident; Googol and Stevens would remain friends well past Googol's time of service. Googol was an assistant professor at MIT. He wasn't the typical clerk. He was older, a professor, and as a matter of process, made life better for Justice Stevens because he brought technology to his chambers and taught his assistants how to use it. Justice Stevens became more productive.

Justice Stevens's thoughts on Googol's next move? He was glad Googol was joining the Dewey law firm. "It's important for you to learn how Big Law works. Because to make fundamental change in the law, one must know the oligarchies in the law." He paused for dramatic effect, "You'll stay long enough to discover what is wrong with Big Law and then leave it. And then do something more in service for mankind."

It sounded more like a prediction than a warning. But who wouldn't love advice from someone who was so learned, aged, and wise? This would happen sooner rather than later. Googol and I both learned about how Big Law worked. Googol would serve mankind. Me? It depends on how you define "serve." But we are all heroes in our own life stories.

Justice Stevens's warning to me, "You Gregory, should find a woman that makes you happy. A woman that will keep you out of trouble." We all laughed and the October 1992 term of the Court was officially adjourned.

The plan: learn the law of the real world, apply computers to the business of law, and meet lawyers who will need me and the team. It turned out Justice Stevens's warning couldn't have been more prophetic. I would meet the lawyers who would need me and the team, but I never could just leave. One day, I would decide to destroy them.

Big Law

Googol came home after the first day of work at the Big Law Firm and I met him at his apartment. "This firm claims to be different than the others. The firm thinks technology is the cutting-edge advantage that will make them win into the twenty-first century."

"Really?" I said. "That would be interesting to see."

"Care to find out?" Googol asked seriously.

"I'd love to. What do they want to do?" I asked.

"Everything. Network all their offices around the world. They want to create a system that connects the entire law firm. Share data, files, and communications." Googol smiled. "They hired the shrewdest technology law professor to develop their cyber law practice. Now they want the firm to be the envy of the legal world. You can meet with the managing partner tomorrow, impress him, sign a nondisclosure agreement, and you're off. You think you can get the rest of the team to help you create a backend?"

I smiled, "Yeah, I'll see you tomorrow."

My plan was coming together. These lawyers were asking us to build their cyber home. I won't have to be invited inside, I'll already be inside. I'm going to learn how lawyers steal. Justice Stevens's warning was my invitation.

. . .

Spiral staircases between floors, the signature of the modern law firm architecture. This was supposed to indicate they were hip. There was a large library of books, with a librarian – mixed signals; wasted space filled with paper that no one opens. Where was the technology? There was going to be some dinosaur noises when I tell them to get rid of it.

"But I love paper; I love the books; that's what first year associates are for." I can hear it now.

My reply, "Thought you liked money more." That was where the lawyers padded their bills – the library. First year associates doing legal research were the tools to do it. Research and enormous document review were big revenue sources.

I was on the inside of a big law firm – Big Law. A law firm with multiple offices across the world, one that prided itself on being avant-garde. Let's see it. I wanted to see Big Law's perception of networked communication. Because lawyers were in on every business deal, there go the lawyers – so goes the world. If I could get in the door; Googol, Joseph, and I couldn't resist. It would feed Joseph's ultimate desire to create his vision of computers that could manage your life.

No difficulty getting hired. The managing partner, Stewart Ballentine, was smart enough to have a tech guy in the room who knew networks required a plan – an architecture of its own. "You eventually taking the Bar?" I was asked.

"No, I'm going to get a LLM[53] in international tax," I replied.

"Good. Less time away from work. But if you don't take the Bar, you'll never be able to work for the firm as a lawyer," Ballentine said.

I nodded with my eyes raised. "I'm going to work with Jeffrey Gogolas on creating your network and other cool technology. Don't want to be your lawyer."

"You'll have to sign a nondisclosure agreement in case you see any client files or any other law firm information; you're not to disclose or discuss any of it," Ballentine said.

Why do lawyers speak in redundancies? Can I disclose it without discussing? But now that he got me thinking about it: Law firm information? Client files? "Sure thing. No disclosure."

▪ ▪ ▪

I would spend most of my day with Googol or at the firm. I read the research on the importance of sleep. Still, I didn't need as much sleep as other people. I had been up for three days playing around with my new found power with the law firm's network. Joseph was working with Googol and me. I had to remind myself that Joseph was not in it to make corporations, let alone lawyers richer. Because what do they make? What do they produce? For as much as I said that lawyers help people who made things and produce things, they only prosecute and protect those who made things. Ever hear an inventor say, "I couldn't have done this without my lawyer?" But they always needed one.

It wasn't all irascible complaining between Joseph and me. We were like brothers. He was someone who had always been in my life from the point in time in your life when one becomes aware. That was somewhere around twelve years old. Where you can ride your bike around the block without pure wonderment about how things work. Most of my conscious life has been living daily with Joseph. I made us over seven-figures, which he got to invest in his personal projects. Something I referred to as losing money. It was not an idealistic world. Joseph saw that nearly every day; but did he learn it? As we moved along I tolerated it as research and development. How do you measure the value of R&D?[54] And value to the world?

Joseph wished a thousand times: "Before I die I want to develop a computer to do something that helps the world in a meaningful way, then I've done my service." Leaving the world better than when I found it – his purpose. To be specific, he wanted more than a computer that managed a person's life. He wanted the computer to do it automatically, without asking it. Imagine a world where we didn't need to work all the time. If food and water were nearly free. We wouldn't need to make as much money as we were compelled to earn. We could all live like the privileged – even like the ones that didn't earn it, because we all wouldn't have earned it.

I disapproved of the generationally wealthy because they didn't earn it. It was easier to make your second million than your first. But it was easier to make your third million when you were born with two. It was just different values. The best part of understanding computers and working with great people by expanding their capabilities was a reward of its own.

Googol knew how to sweeten the pot for Joseph, GNU and our own group of coders, to sign on to our Big Law project. Joseph was able to expand email with multiple users. Collaborative communication was the ultimate goal. If you can manage communications, files, projects, you can manage lives. So, Joseph figured the next step was managing lives. But that was not all. To get to the point of managing lives, we were halfway to the point where computers had consciousness – intelligence of their own. Computers learning – without the help from humans.

GNU had moved out of the apartment-office in Cambridge. He was a true introvert. GNU needed no one. He traveled to Thailand to be that alone. We'd hear about a girl every now and then. We'd all talk, at least one to the other, every day. We hacked the phone lines to make long distance calls for free. The phone meetings are comforting. Now we're able to post our communications for all us to see.

During these phone meetings, I became worried about Joseph again. He was connected but so alone. Perhaps everyday with Leela had become too routine. She was sweet and caring. But she needed Joseph to entertain her. She wanted Joseph's attention when he was off in his head somewhere else. For a normal person it would be called, "thinking." Some people feel better when they talk about their feelings. It didn't make him feel better. Leela didn't understand that he can get angry at the color brown. When the can-opener didn't work properly, he dove into an inner dialogue redesigning the can opener.

In spite of Joseph's inner challenges, in the first year, we set up electronic mail throughout the law firm. Then we did something unique and invited the firms that did work with Dewey to get email as well. Googol told the firm to set it up for the firms Dewey was on the other side of the deals or litigation. Brilliant. It began to spread like a virus. All the major law firms wanted to be able to send each other electronic mail. They thought it was fun and efficient. What was even funnier was that the lawyers started printing out the electronic mail. On the occasions Joseph travelled to the Boston office of Dewey, he asked why do you print out emails? "In order to prove that I sent it," the clever lawyer answered. That clever lawyer reported Joseph squinted like a toddler who sucked on a lemon from the first time.

"Do you know that computers are meant to reduce paper? You can also search email for words that would be in the email?" Joseph asked.

"Oh, but I like to touch the paper," the lawyer responded.

When I finally had the this same conversation with the CEO and the CFO, two guys that seemed to hang out together all day long, they asked what else we could do.

"How much are you willing to let us do?" I answered with a question.

"We'll let you go as far as you can, if you sign this agreement," Ballentine said.

"What does it say?" I asked.

"It says that what you develop for us belongs to us. Kind of like the nondisclosure agreement you've already signed. In exchange, you can continue to use all the firm's servers for all the things you're working on," Ballentine said.

"But I've been able to use the servers to do what I want," I responded. They really wanted to steal our work. And, I just walked out of the room with a smile. They wanted to own our stuff. We're contractors, not employees. When Googol was a lawyer, he was their employee, but they wanted the stuff he created too. He was the only lawyer in the firm that actually created something of lasting value. I just wanted the power of the network. The network of servers rivaled MIT's.

I woke up with the dreadful thought, Joseph might think that deal was worth it. In the long run, it would be better for the world. The world needed computers to help us do things better. *Qpredictor* would change the way computers help the world. So he didn't need to own the software and the processes created by the team's work. Joseph might sign that agreement.

▪ ▪ ▪

Life at the firm seemed to get better for everyone: the lawyers, support staff, and me. It came to the point where I barely had to do any real work at the firm. I went into the office just pop in on Googol and to help the ladies at the firm with their computers. The young female associates didn't have time to date, if they didn't have a boyfriend already. So they invited me home to help them set up computers they bought. It got so frequent that one of the male lawyers got jealous, and he complained to the firm's HR[55] department. HR informed the lawyer that I'm a contractor of the firm and not an employee. "Unless any female employees complain, they're free to consult with GP during their off hours whenever they choose."

Obsession, that was what made Joseph different. He could focus for days on the same problem. With access to the server power that the law firm provided me, he had written extensive code for his growing masterpiece *Qpredictor,* some of which was incorporated into the firm's network. GNU made the program run faster by building a dynamic cache that remembered things it had done before. When that task was completed, Joseph came to D.C.

It was a reunion party. For us geeks we celebrated with the traditional party of pizza and Star Trek Next Generation running in the background of Googol's apartment. Leela came too. Googol said that Joseph looked like he was happy to be there but his mind was somewhere else. His mind was still on code. I tried to get him to unwind. I opened champagne but only Leela and Googol drank it. My mind went to thinking about how I missed the team being together at MIT. A little too much time had passed for me to continue to admit to others that I missed Chana and her absence still affected me.

The party ended abruptly when Joseph mentioned that the firm already had the latest upgrade of *Qpredictor.* I wanted to see what the firm was doing with it. Could the nightmare be real? My concern peaked when he told me that he'd met with the CEO Stewart Ballentine at the Boston office. "I didn't tell you because he said you knew he was coming to meet with me," Joseph said.

"And you believed him?" I asked.

Yes, Joseph did. He didn't think it was strange to accept what people said as true. He thought the world behaved like a computer. We rushed to the office and logged onto the computers. The firm ran all night, particularly the transactional lawyers doing international deals in different time zones. We made it to the server room. It looked like IBM central. It was beautiful to Joseph. Tall cabinets from ceiling to floor filled with lights blinking and reel to reel magnetic tape drives. "Fabulous," he said. Leela grabbed his arm to signal him to shut up. The feeling of beauty didn't last long. GP, Leela, and Googol all stood over my shoulders at a computer station in the corner of the server room. My heart sunk. The firm was using *Qpredictor* to do some nefarious functions.

I noted, "This firm has two sets of financial books." No business should have two sets of books, unless one was a copy of the other. There should not be two sets of financial data at a law firm unless one was being given to one set of people for one reason, and the other set to different people for a different reason. Within an instant, I was able to create reports to show that lateral partners joining the firm from other big law firms were lied to about the state of financial affairs at Dewey.

At that point, Googol commanded me to get up. We switched places. Googol was clacking away at the keyboard. I just looked at Joseph. He handed me the folder with the documents he signed with Ballentine – the part that says what we created for the firm belonged to the firm. I thumbed through it and then I stared at Joseph.

Googol looked up at me and sighed. "I can't work here anymore." I walked over to a different set of servers and shut them off. Within minutes I received a page to call the chief of technology at the firm. I sat at a terminal and typed out an email saying I was aware of the problem and that it would be down for the rest of the night. Leela was astonished. Not just because the law firm was a giant fraud scheme, but that Joseph's software belonged to the firm.

Have you ever been so angry that it was beyond high blood pressure? My personal circuit breaker just popped. I felt calm. All I could say to Joseph was, "You have to let me handle the dirty work." My muted response was worse than if I yelled. He could handle an out of control GP. But he didn't know how to respond to muted but seething GP. Leela put her arms around us both. The gesture communicated that at least we were a team. I became annoyed and pulled away. Joseph has seen that look in my eye. This time he knew he failed himself and the team.

"Forgive me," he said. This may have been the first time Joseph understood what I meant about proprietary versus open source. Joseph's good nature hurt the team and what he meant to do with his software – help everyone. But these bad lawyers were willing to do was not only exploit Joseph's life's work for themselves, but make sure no one else could, including Joseph. The firm owned it and we did not.

I said with disgust, "It's not you, Joseph, it's the world we live in."

▪ ▪ ▪

At least Joseph got to use this project with Dewey to expand his ever precious *Qpredictor.* But Googol was done. A white hat like him couldn't stay at a law firm with two sets of books. Besides, he was an academic. He wanted to get back to MIT and they wanted him more than ever. He was a lawyer, former SCOTUS clerk, and computer genius on MIT standards. Justice Stevens was all too correct. Googol learned what Big Law was about and got out. Googol returning to MIT would attract students. The kind of students that MIT wanted – smart in their own right, not privileged by birth.

Googol just told the partner he worked for he was accepting his old professorship back in Cambridge and there were no further questions asked. Googol referenced working on open source software agreements at MIT,[56] but he said the partner didn't seem to make the connection to management at the firm or the non-disclosure issue with Joseph. Being me, I couldn't walk out the door like a ghost. I had too much fun here and I resented that the firm did an end run around me and went to Joseph to execute their misdeed. But I couldn't let these guys think that they were smarter than the *Original Gamesters.* Admittedly, that might be a character flaw of mine. To overcome this deficiency, I needed to make my final day at Dewey about more. It took a week to get an appointment with the CEO, CFO, and whatever they called the head of firm technology. The plan, educate about the law and technology; and leave the room with the rights to our software.

"Are you leaving to be with Googol at MIT?" Stewart Ballentine said sitting on the edge of his desk, leaning in, with a tone that implied that Googol and I were lovers. An attempt at a distracting strike; a typical lawyer's stratagem to throw me off my resolve.

Smiling, I went in head first. "Yes, we're gay, Stewie. It's 1995, no one cares. But we're leaving because of the data." Stewie didn't realize everybody called him Stewie behind his back. Even the CFO had a microexpression of amusement when I said it. Stewie had done one remarkable thing with this firm; namely just bought up a bunch of law practices from other firms and added them to Dewey. The firm overpromised distributions and bonuses to lure the practice groups from other big firms. The revenue from the merged practices would go directly to Dewey – a new source of money. This was a special type of Ponzi scheme among lawyers. Soon enough those partners who brought in millions in revenue, weren't going to understand why they weren't getting the money, the bonuses they were promised. An implosion in the firm would then ensue.

"Data?" Stewie Ballentine asked.

"Financial data. It was strange to us, the team, how lateral partner transfers into the firm were induced by revenue that wouldn't support the representations made to those laterals," I answered.

"How dare you? You don't know the first thing about this Firm's business practices. How do you know what prospective partners are being told? How do you know our revenue?" Ballentine asked.

"Please, you asked us to create a network of architecture for the firm worldwide. We invented the program used to consolidate and analyze the data. And you don't think we can read the emails you're sending each other?" I looked at them both – nothing. Was I really talking over their heads? They didn't even look at each other. Stewie acted as if he was fully in command, but his eyes revealed he was taken off-guard.

"And now we own it. And we also have an NDA. So, if you ever want to be a lawyer or work for anyone else, anything you did and made for this firm belongs to us. Otherwise, you'll never not know me and this law firm, Gregory." Stewie was satisfied with his threat of a lawsuit. He felt he bullied me sufficiently so I would walk out with my tail between my legs.

"Stewie, you're not objectively evaluating your situation. What about the banks? The banks you have borrowed from and will ask to borrow more money from when you run out of law firms to acquire. You'll have to make those partnership distributions soon. The nondisclosure agreement says we'd never disclose, but crimes are crimes. A D.C. grand jury wouldn't allow us to honor a non-disclosure agreement concealing crimes. Dewey could never negotiate for nondisclosure to a grand jury. What's that called? It's against public policy. The NDA would be unenforceable."

I took out the folder with my documents describing that Dewey was relinquishing ownership of the code we produced for Dewey. They obtained it by trick and I couldn't abide. This code belonged to Joseph and he should have it; not these clowns. "Sign this, Mr. Ballentine, and we'll be gone. Here's a check for $500.00 as legal consideration for the waiver and we'll reaffirm our non-disclosure agreement," I said.

Stewie looked at the one page document. "I'll have to have one of our lawyers review."

"It's one page of plain English – sign it." He took another moment to look at it. He then signed it.

"Thank you." I packed and went to leave.

"You created a great system for us, Greg," the head of technology said. He got a look from Ballentine like he just called Ballentine's mother a whore.

"Good luck," I said wondering what they were going to do when that great beautiful system made a funny noise. It was one thing to own a yacht, it was another to service one. As I walked out of the office hoping never to have to deal with evil lawyers again, I knew Ballentine and others in the firm would see me again; or, at least feel me. They stole from Joseph; they stole from the team. It wasn't about money, it was about code. Yes, both meanings of the word intended. But I knew that never having to deal with evil lawyers again was an unrealistic aspiration – something from Joseph's hope chest under his fantasy bed of techno-utopia. We did have to deal with evil lawyers again in the future. Yes, it would be about another Ponzi scheme. It seems like I just walked away square with Stewie Ballentine – free and clear from the Dewey law firm. But, no one could claim I just walked away particularly since I installed a *time-bottle* function that would transfer the financial data from Dewey's system to all the banks they borrowed and the United States Attorney's Office sometime in the next fifteen years. Who knew where I'd be when the data got delivered? But it seemed as if Dewey would be up to fraud in the future and the data would be evidence. If not, the data sent would be stale and useless.

I didn't want to have to safeguard a naïve idealist like Joseph. Sandwiched between greedy lawyers and a techno-hippie made me understand why Googol was running back to academia. We all wished we could go back to college. The time in one's life where being lost felt like you were somewhere; and that somewhere was safe. For now, I just had to go off on my own – a recess, a hibernation from the harsh game.

TRANCHE IV
PACER

Quick Reflection

After I received my LLM in International Tax, the master's degree over my *juris doctorate*, the world became my home – with the home base of South Florida, where my father was now living for most of the year. Of course, I told him to do that so he could enjoy the homestead protection and tax advantages of no state income tax.

I wasn't a kid with a backpack and twenty dollars a day. I spent a month at a time in Amsterdam, London, Italy, and around the U.S and Asia. With all the projects over the years and our MIT brethren spreading out across the globe, I could always meet with friends; give a talk at a company or a school; time flew by.

After about five years of roaming the earth I settled in California to work on a project with a friend who helped build a company that delivered and transferred money, currency, and credit from a computer.[57] Very stressful times but we and the company became very successful. It was a weird time because I didn't have to lead that company. It became relaxing to help a team without being in charge of the team. I was more like a worker on the production line. Help us design and build security for the backend. Since I knew about money, knew about the law, and knew hacking and security – they wanted me to be a part of it. I got better at dealing with people – even the ones from Stanford and Cal Tech.[58] The platform wasn't my idea, so I wasn't emotional about it. I wasn't desperate to make it work. This turned out to be an advantage. From time to time I would track down GNU and Joseph who would help. I got paid in stock, and the stock took off when the company went public in 2002 – I was truly financially free from then on.

I remained close with Googol too. But I rarely saw him in person. He was established in Cambridge, and I remained mostly in Los Angeles and the Bay Area. My value lied in my thoughts and my ability to help others plan out their platforms and dot coms. It became a loose economy where if I ever thought others might ever help me, I needed to help them. The reward, besides owning shares in the currency transferring platform startup was joining and helping that team with the next project – a video platform where anyone could upload a video online and others could view it.[59] The plan was to disrupt television and movies. In turn, I surmised that it would disrupt news distribution as well. We were right. It was war on the internet – country to country. Not every country loved the free speech capabilities of the internet. I left working at the company when Israel went online – the sign that democracy was in full swing worldwide. Even Joseph was proud of that accomplishment.

In the winter, I would visit my father, good old Richard Portnoy who lived off his healthy pension from the City of Chicago, but I helped him buy his luxury condo he lived in. He said he was allowing it because I was technically paying for my room in his condo. It was available to me for my use anytime. And "anytime" in Jewish culture meant I was expected to visit, not that the room was merely available at any time.

My father claimed he did me a disservice by never finding another woman to be a mother to me or a wife to him. I despised such conversations. Sex didn't cure what ailed me. I'm certain my father was the same. But we never really talked about it. He was my father. While he expected my mother to live longer than she did, she held the unique role of being Sarah Portnoy – wife to Richard; mother to Gregory. There would be no understudy to Sarah going forward. Consciously, and I'm sure even unconsciously, there could be no understudy to Chana. Chana was an oasis; she kept me on a righteous path.

Back Together

It was one of those winters where I received word that Joseph desperately wanted to see me and he'd come to Florida to do it. I'd hate to think how long it was since I had seen Joseph. Does social medium keep us connected where face to face didn't matter as much anymore? A fleeting thought made us feel like we were in touch. I met him at a restaurant. Two friends who haven't seen each other in years, picked up with a long hug—reconnected. We both lived through the early stories of our lives together. Apart, we only knew the stories of present day life. A little knowledge by comparison, skype and facetime, texting; it was not the same level of connection. Now, it was *text, text, text;* rather than hangout and be together. No more long periods of nothing but each other's company. I missed that connection with Joseph and he seemed to be missing it too.

Conversation was seamless. We were an hour into talking about the projects we were working on. As engaging as the conversations with Joseph can be when we talk about futuristics, I really yearned for knowledge about the one topic I cared about.

"How often do you talk to Chana?" I asked. I was excited to hear something about her. It felt so Pavlovian.[60] Chana – pant.

"All the time. We talk all the time. You know she's having another baby," he said. I forced a smile. "You know she lives back in Chicago now. With her husband. That's kind of full circle, isn't it?"

And I was the socially awkward one? What was clear to me was I was still suffering. I couldn't spit out a clear sentence back to Joseph. I felt myself excessively blinking. I didn't realize that circumstances and luck play a part in whether Chana and I would've worked out. I kept insisting that I was a good guy to myself. I treated Chana well, how could she stop loving me? How could she stop caring about me after she rescued me? Distance made a difference. The relationship needed nurturing.

And, when she was so far away, we suffered from starvation. Love, affection, sharing. It was all going to be gone. Chana had a better model in her brain – a better understanding of relationships than I did. Because I didn't want to consider there could be an end, I missed that it was ending.

"You're most human when you reflect on your feelings," Joseph said. We had one of those conversations that one wouldn't have over the phone. "So are you going to settle on a woman? Who you with now? Do I get to meet her?"

"No. Just ended it before you came to town," I answered. "I'm alone again. I like myself so much, how can I share me?" I said with a smile. Joseph laughed.

"You're not a narcissist," he said.

"How do you know?"

"Are you a narcissist?" Joseph said and waited for my response.

I thought for a moment. "I don't think so."

"Then you're not one," he said with a laugh. "Who was the last girl?"

"Her name was Joy. More like, *no* joy. You would've loved her at first, and then hated her." Then I realized that he wouldn't have even loved her at first. Data on a spreadsheet can lead us to conclude what we were looking at was so appealing. My brain was certain everyone else's filled in the blanks with our hopes when there was a lack of data to reach a proper conclusion.

"And?"

"She tortured me," I said. Joseph visibly winced, and then he laughed. "She was fucking mean. I lost myself. She'd yell and complain at me and I just took it," I said.

"What?" He said laughing. "I'm so sorry, GP. I wish I was there for you. I wouldn't have let her torture you."

"I know." Joseph was telling the truth. He would've dropped everything and come. Bound by nothing except the inertia of being still behind a computer, he could come. My hermit of a friend would've tried to rescue me. He just would've reasoned with me. Get me back on the ruby rails.

"I know, Joseph. I wish you were around too. Not sure you could've helped. I was in a fog. I was in a nose up attitude but I wasn't climbing." I demonstrated nose up with my hand, to make sure he knew I was making an airplane analogy.

"No, you're fine. You were confusing Joy with Chana. Some type of false connection. Recognize it and break it," he said.

He was right. In one sentence that relationship and break up was buried.

We laughed as only two old friends who know each other's rich history could. Wondering why we weren't together more often. Face to face, working together, being together was a pleasure. Should we care we were philosophically different about computer science?

"You'll have to take me flying. You're really a pilot?" He asked.

"I am. It's a lot of fun," I said. "Why don't we work on an open source project together? I'm willing to do it. Let's do some more work on *Qpredictor*."

"I'm not ready right now. And, I needed to talk to you about it. I've been working on it and I need to borrow some money. I need some life support."

"Everything okay?" I asked.

"Yeah, it'll be fine. Some assholes I have to deal with. I've got a lawyer," Joseph said. He seemed fine. He wasn't letting on the extent of the problem, I'd find out later on.

"Where did you get your lawyer? One of my guys?"

"No, I met her in dance class," he said with a straight face.

"Dance class?" I asked with a laugh.

"Ballroom dancing. She's a wonderful legal writer. I'm in good hands. I let her lead."

"On the dance floor or in court?"

"Both," he answered. "Fifteen thousand should about cover what I need."

That wasn't a lot of money. "For a year?" I thought for a moment. Not about whether Joseph was hustling me. As far as I was concerned, he earned that money. I'd, give him fifteen thousand a year forever if he needed. "Why don't you come to California or New York, stay with me. Your expenses will be bare bones. You can handle what you need to handle and we can work on something together?"

Joseph thought and shot that down. "I just need to get through this."

He seemed depressed, almost despondent when he was on the topic. "Was it that bad, Joseph? Working with me?"

"No, man. You're the best, GP. I just can't give you my all yet. We will soon. It'll be no more than a year. I just need a year. I need you to come to Boston and help me too. I've got a problem."

"Boston it is. I'll help." I whipped out my phone and called the bank and authorized a wire of fifteen-thousand to Joseph.

"So are you up to whole life management yet with *Qpredictor*?"

"And more," he answered.

"And more?"

"Expect an upgrade soon. You're going to be living in it and with it."

"And you?"

"I already live in it. This version is called *RubyonQ*."

"You patenting any of this stuff?" I asked. I knew the answer.

"No. All human knowledge should be open and available – Benjamin Franklin said that."

"I'm sure he did." Shaking my head, I smiled. He thought he wouldn't get hurt. In the face of evil, he saw no evil, because thou art with him. But who was thou? Who was his God? It wasn't me, but I pledged to do my best to help him. "I'll come up to Boston next week."

"It has to be by Wednesday," Joseph said for the first time sounding desperate. "I'm in a bad place. The feds want to make me a felon. Put me in prison."

Public Access, Private control

Architecturally speaking, federal courthouses had lots of wasted space. Sure, there were lots of government offices within the courthouses, but there were lots of wide hallways and tall boxy columns – rooms and anterooms. The marble made everything all seem regal, which was somewhat ironic since we started this country in order to get away from the majestic. We made our way to the United States Attorney's Office for the District of Massachusetts in the Moakley Courthouse – one large semi-circular building complex. Probably cost about $170 million to build, erected on Boston Harbor. If the situation didn't seem so grave, it would have been a beautiful walk.

I saw that Joseph was barely holding it together. He was sweating. Over the years, he became better with stress and noise, but most, what I call, *normals* or *linears* didn't have to deal with this type of stress. Joseph needed to get out of the business of changing the world if he couldn't stand the threat of jail. The stress was unbearable. But I was happier than I was with the way he let himself get duped at Dewey. At least he asked for help before the real damage was done.

Of course Googol came along. He was the only lawyer we knew in Boston. Googol had a bar license, so we needed him in order to schedule the meeting. It was either Googol or his cousin, Billy Laster who knew more about Scotch than he did about criminal law. I met Billy twice, he had a B.S. in Computer Science, but it seemed like his knowledge ended at *Collecovision.*[61] This was our first meeting with prosecutors.

Once we showed our identifications and were scanned for weapons, waited ten minutes, we were ushered into a conference room with no windows. Joseph wanted to bring a computer, but I was against it. We brought nothing. Neither he nor I had any problem remembering things. I felt a little better when two prosecutors and the FBI case agent came into the room. I could tell right away the slightly older one was supervising the younger. The agent was the oldest in the room. Each one of them handed us their business card. My role was as an expert witness consultant.

"Thank you all for meeting with us today," the young prosecutor said. "It's good when lawyers and the client come together early in the process."

"So why did you have an agent sit outside Mr. Leege's apartment and coax him to come in without counsel?" I asked.

"Well, no one is under arrest." was the response, but not really a responsive answer. He continued. "We generally find these pre-indictment discussions better because we hope to negotiate something before we take a case to the grand jury. There are certain advantages to agreeing to an Information, which is a charging document, that is better than if a grand jury indicts." I could sense Joseph about to faint. The colors must be exploding like a Saturday morning cartoon. I put my hand on his leg and squeezed it slightly without looking at him. The prosecutor went on. "We believe that a single count of violating the Computer Fraud and Abuse Act[62] is available to Joseph, Mr. Leege, if he pled guilty to hacking into the Court's PACER system and downloading hundreds of thousands of documents without paying the requisite fee."

"Do you two agree with that?" I asked the agent and the supervising prosecutor. They both reflexively nodded. In that one sentence, I could tell no one in this room understood PACER, computers, and how it related to wire fraud. But, I decided to save the explanation for later. I tapped Joseph's knee a couple of times to let him know that I knew what he knows – he was going to be okay, try and relax. The young prosecutor grimaced. Perhaps on some level he knew he didn't have a case, or didn't understand why I asked the question.

"Hacking?" I asked.

"Mr. Leege went to the University and accessed the PACER system and he was an unauthorized user."

Everyone in this room had to know that "unauthorized" was a weasel word. When someone equivocated on the definition of an important word maliciously, the word became a "weasel word." The malicious person who redefined a word for evil was a weasel. Meaning, the prosecutor was just looking to prosecute by defining "unauthorized" in a way that made Joseph appear to violate the law when there was an interpretation that permitted Joseph to fall into a definition of an "authorized user."

MIT permitted access and downloading data for free between the dates Joseph downloaded the data. "But, everyone was allowed to download in September. Joseph is a part of everyone, so that makes him an authorized user. Or at least not an unauthorized user," I stated.

"But, he didn't use the authorized computer at MIT. He managed to log in at home with his computer, but using MIT's credentials," was the response. I couldn't help but reflect for a moment that when I was 13, after Joseph and I got into my father's old friend's bank accounts, I went home and logged in to do the real dirty work – kind of a fun memory knowing exactly when you learned something. I'm sure Joseph told me everything. Surprises right now could ruin everything.

"But MIT's credentials were being given out for free for anyone to download data. So, the problem is he didn't use MIT's computer, but was allowed to download the data he could've taken from the MIT law-library computer? That's like saying a person transferred a dollar from one's own bank account and put it in his other account. But because he didn't do it at the teller window, he stole the dollar; or fraudulently transferred his own dollar, to make the analogy better. If he brought the MIT computer outside the library, but kept it on campus, would he still be an unauthorized user?" I asked incredulously, but not enough to piss off the people in authority. I hoped.

"Let me continue," the prosecutor said.

I let him continue. The prosecutor went through the grid of the sentencing guidelines[63] – acceptance of responsibility, and how Joseph can really do well in front of the judge and get a favorable sentence if he worked out a deal with them sooner rather than later. But, he will have to be debriefed by the Bureau's computer fraud division and cooperate by answering any questions and implicating anyone that helped him commit this crime.

My thoughts drifted to Googol's analysis of the data on the PACER documents. This will help for what I anticipated would be tomorrow's meeting.

"No one helped me out," Joseph said. I stopped him before he finished that thought.

"I tell you what, fellas. This straight-talk without any nonsense was sobering. I didn't know sentencing was so complicated and multi-faceted." I hoped they accepted this sincerely. "Can you let us think about what we've talked about today and come back same time tomorrow?" They all looked at each other. The prosecutors agreed to meet again same time tomorrow afternoon.

"Sure, we're ready to work out the details tomorrow," the prosecutor said encouragingly.

"Great. I'm going to review this tonight and I might have a couple of questions tomorrow. Is that okay?" I said.

"We'll answer every question that you have, if we can," was the reply.

"Perfect." I mean, good grief, we didn't have any evidence from the government. We had to take their word that they could prove something. This meant reviewing with Joseph what happened. I trust his honesty implicitly, but he may not know what was important in the law, and even he might forget some details of what he did. Because like most targets of a criminal investigation, they didn't understand everything that the government thought was relevant or enhanced a sentence under the guidelines.

With that the meeting was over. Joseph managed to avoid shaking anyone's hand. He looked down as he walked out of the room but made direct eye contact with the FBI agent. We waited until we were walking on the Harbor before we started to talk. Now, I could share all the little details I learned about the three men we were negotiating with. These details were mostly irrelevant, other than it proved they were meant to move this process along without much thought or effort. For example, the lead prosecutor was married to a woman with money or he had his own family money. He was thirty-one years old, his wedding ring had diamonds in the band and a matching Patek Phillipe watch was a family heirloom. He also already ate his lunch, mostly likely a sandwich – something with brown mustard that left specks of it on both cuffs.

The other older supervising prosecutor thought he was some type of warrior. G-shock watch, crew-cut, smartphone on his worn belt, he sat next to the FBI agent. I saw the supervising prosecutor reach a couple of time for the imaginary gun on his belt, an instinctive gesture for street cops because even the agent didn't appear to be armed, or if he were – it was on his ankle. No wedding ring, twenty-pounds overweight.

The agent was the oldest guy in the room. He seemed the most put together. Not posing – he was an FBI agent. We locked eyes for a few moments. I smiled when our eyes met. He grimaced back. He took notes – heard this sentencing guidelines speech a thousand times before. I read his notes upside down. Just our names and that this meeting was the first plea discussion. "No immunity letter."[64] I knew Joseph didn't have immunity. While we started in the middle – sentencing, I really wanted to know what was at stake here. These guys were not invested in this prosecution. They didn't start the investigation, and I suppose for them, they were sent in to test our temperature. I'm sure after today's meeting they thought Joseph would plead guilty. They had no evidence for this assumption, but I'm sure they made it.

"I still don't know what Joseph did wrong after that meeting," Googol said. "I saw smoke but no fire."

"He didn't do anything wrong," I replied. "And they know they can't prove that he did. The thing is, do we want to spend the next 18 months proving it and hoping a jury gets it right?"

"Well do we?" Joseph asked.

"Of course not," I answered.

"A good lawyer keeps his client out of the courtroom," Googol said.

▪ ▪ ▪

We returned the next day. The plan was to use their logic and then reduce the logic to its absurdity.[65] We were taken to the same conference room the next day, after being searched in the lobby. All of us sat in the same configuration around the conference room table as we did the day before. It felt familiar. I was more confident. I told them I found the sentencing guidelines to be a fascinating and complicated lattice, clearly meant to disorient the target. The unstated viewpoint was because it was complicated and self-containing; it was beautiful, like some symmetric graphical physics model. Not much new in sentencing since 2005, when the Supreme Court said the guidelines were no longer binding they were advisory to the sentencing judge.[66] This judge with a lifetime appointment decided the fate of a defendant – mercy or harshness; upward variance or downward from the recommended sentence. The swings made the stomach turn.

"I'm a J.D., but don't practice law," I said. "Do you know if you testify and are convicted there's a really good chance that the defendant will get an upward variance for committing perjury?"[67]

"Well, it's not meant to . . ." the lead prosecutor began to say.

"Oh, I know it's not meant to chill the defendant's right to testify, and no one should commit perjury, but in the First Circuit, where we are, there is a ninety-eight-percent chance the defendant will get that bump in the guidelines if he testifies and is convicted. That's fascinating." Googol was able to do an analysis of the court opinion from this Circuit from Joseph's PACER download – the one he was accused of obtaining through unauthorized means. The rub was Googol was a real professor and we didn't want him to lose his real job in the process, so I didn't mention this fact. What I love about Googol was he volunteered to testify that Joseph accessed the data for him, a professor of MIT and therefore authorized. But imagine how MIT might react?

"You know, that's not published anywhere I could find. But, we had a friend do an analysis of the opinions in the first circuit where an upward variance for perjury was given, and it's ninety-eight-percent. This is something to consider if a defendant, a rational defendant, is considering whether to testify. I read *Booker, Fan-Fan, Rita, Kimbrough, Gall* and lots of sentencing cases from this Circuit last night. We ran the same type of statistical analysis on various sentencing factors and plea versus trial. It's fair to say that the federal system is, as a matter of statistical likelihood of success, geared to compel a defendant to plead guilty."

"Yes," the prosecutor said sincerely and unapologetically. "That's why we were discussing the sentencing guidelines yesterday. I know you two are new to this process, and so are you, and Mr. Leege. It's good that you understand that important conclusion. I apologize if that is impolitic or coming off as harsh, but it is the truth."

"I understand completely. If you go to trial, you better win, because even the innocent have a real incentive to avoid the pain of trial and losing at trial. The grand jury will indict on multiple charges not just the one count of violating the Computer Fraud and Abuse Act agreed to in a typical plea. Including wire fraud counts, it was potentially devastating. And, Joseph has nothing to offer in terms of cooperation. Whether you believe him, he won't hurt others he might have worked with; so, there's no potential reduction in his sentence for substantial assistance to the government."

In an aggressive tone the same prosecutor said, "We know about you Professor Googol, and your friend, Louis Gnofski, AKA Lou GNU – a darknet pioneer." I didn't like hearing their names with this tone, because this was surely freaking out Joseph. ". . . not to mention the *Open Access Manifesto* Mr. Leege penned when he was in Italy with you one summer," the prosecutor stopped for effect. Ugh, the *manifesto*. How did they find out about the manifesto? "You remember, Mr. Leege – where you advocated people trade passwords and fill download requests for friends. Liberating the information locked up. 'There is no justice following unjust laws.' We need to take information wherever it is stored and share them with the world. Have you recruited your friends and others to do just that – fight for gorilla open access?" The young prosecutor said.

Now they threatened Googol and GNU – and me. It was one thing to be Joseph and be unjustly prosecuted for something that shouldn't be a crime; but to threaten Googol, a professor? Googol had stature, a lawyer's bar card; he had something to lose. Not to mention that threatening a target was one thing, now the government was threatening the lawyer and friends of the target. This was high pressure negotiating.

And, now the government thought it had evidence of motive. Joseph was also the kind of guy who would die if it allowed his friends avoid pain. Besides, this was a one man job. Possession of the legal documents themselves was not illegal, it was not cocaine. If Googol and GNU published them on the net for free, they were court opinions – they were public records – they were free.

I continued because the vague threat of the government squeezing Googol and GNU was silly but dangerous. "Opening public records to the public is a cause for Joseph. He deeply believes in it. So, let me just explain why that is. I'm asking you to indulge me because I think it'll be critical to your prosecution, even at sentencing – because no doubt, the judge will want some clarity on this point. And, as I'm sure you're aware Joseph allegedly accessed the JSTOR database as well at MIT, where he is a student and visiting professor." JSTOR was a whole other database with academic medical and legal data. The big difference was PACER was government and JSTOR was a private company. JSTOR would most likely bitch louder since it thought it was entitled to profit by erecting a paywall between the public and public research.

The government side of the table remained polite. The agent and prosecutors picked up their pens. This was a good sign.

"Let's start the analysis with PACER itself. It's an acronym; it stands for Public Access to Court Electronic Records. It's public. Any member of the public can have access to court electronic records."

"There's a cost, you can't just download hundreds of thousands of them without paying – it's theft!" The young prosecutor responded.

"So, if I went to the clerk's office downstairs and said, 'I want to look at every single document, the clerk would bring each case, file by file, no? If I said, 'copy everything,' I couldn't have it?" I asked.

"You could. You'd have to pay for it," was the response.

"Got it. So it's a matter of paying for copies, not the data on the page. Let's hold that thought for a moment. But, just to be clear, Joseph was allowed to view and even have these documents, is that fair to say?"

"You can't download hundreds of thousands of documents all at once," was the response.

"So, it's the speed at which he was able to obtain these documents that the government has a problem with?" I asked.

No immediate response. Silence. This was good. Joseph was able to access the documents and download them at incredible speeds and then share them for free with the world through his Foundation's open source database. This was what this part of the government thought was a crime. Because at the very heart of the government's case was these documents were not public. It was one thing to have them accessible; it was another to have them truly available for viewing at any time. Paying for them was a layer upon which public becomes less public. Waiting for copies, imposed an obstacle of time on *public.*

"It's really about not paying for them," was the ultimate response. Awesome, the tide has turned.

"It's theft you said, from whom? The government? I agree it does cost money to keep those servers running. The documents are electronically filed, so there is no scanning costs or labor associated with it, but we always have to remember the over-arching proposition, that these documents are public. And, based upon the 2002 E-government Act, which authorizes PACER fees, the fee can only be charged to the extent necessary to cover the costs of providing the service. I'm handing you the Government Accounting Office accounting report from last year. It shows that PACER is being run at a profit. Even though there are seventeen separate server systems for separate circuits. My point is that's the most efficient model? No, it can be done even cheaper. But again, Joseph was allowed to access and download the data. And just because he took that data and made it available to the world for free does not infringe upon PACER's license or any government property. Remember, the government is not in business for a profit according to the statute; it can only cover the cost of hosting the data spread out over projected users." I gave them a moment to write and understand.

"One last thing, we also emailed each Chief judge of each district in the country and each circuit court judge a package demonstrating some notable examples of private personal information that PACER users shouldn't have access to even if they paid for it through the traditional route of access to the court documents. A Circuit Judge in San Francisco replied that he couldn't believe that all this private data was just available for a dime and a computer."

Again, my thoughts went back to my father and his friend Harry. I destroyed that man with all the personal information that was in the filed pleadings because who would ever get the pleadings and have the know-how and start looking to do some damage? The answer today was more obvious – anyone, yet nothing was done to be better at protecting the private data.

"What do you think the answer to solving that is? How do you get the clerks to be better?" the FBI agent asked.

"Put the onus on the lawyers before electronically filing. Just change who's responsible. A lawyer's client doesn't want private information communicated to anyone but the court. Make the lawyer explain why the private information should remain private, or certify that the filing is not private." The agent seemed satisfied with that answer. "Computers can do amazing things; it's the humans that are the problem," I said ending with a smile.

A few months after Joseph's investigation closed, Princeton University developed RECAP. RECAP was open source software that was available to all. Anyone can have access to the code itself and add-on helpful stuff. So, people who want to see what's going on in district courts around the country can review the documents for free. But, it was against the policy and procedures for a fee-exempt user of PACER to share the documents they've viewed and saved to share it with RECAP. You can view it for free, but you couldn't share it with others to view for free. The weasel that came up with that logic needed to be publicly tortured; so as to excise his need for control. Like it was theirs and no one else can have it without recognizing the power and paying for it. Pay as recognition of power and ownership. And in my own inner dialogue I heard myself talking like Joseph. Which supported Joseph's view – in the end, we own nothing, so why own it in the middle. Ownership was what we agreed to be responsible for.

I understood how Joseph could be driven into a loop of exasperation. The courts spoke and its voice was meant to be heard by and for the public, the public should be able to read it and learn from it. Our courts were not star chambers. Articles about research in medicine shouldn't be hidden behind a paywall. Wouldn't it be great if a scientist were to read something that inspires a cure? Wouldn't it have been great if my mother's doctor could've read which other doctor, in which research center, in which hospital had the latest breast cancer treatment regimen that could've given my mother more time? Joseph's obsessive brain couldn't fathom the illogic of information for profit.[68] The lawyers from Department of Justice paying millions a year to view its own court system's documents was absurd. Absurd property rights over the human right to learn in order to do and be better.

When Joseph, Googol, and I walked out of the U.S. Attorney's Office we knew it would be the last time we'd hear from the government on this matter, even though they didn't expressly say so.

The agent shook our hands and said, "Nice job," and "I really enjoyed learning about this." He followed us out and the attorneys stayed behind. The agent grabbed Joseph's forearm and slapped his wrist. "Joseph, move on to the next thing. You're not the type of person we should be investigating; it's a waste of your time. The world needs you out there doing good things, not wasting time explaining to those in authority why you're right."

The agent got it. Joseph gave him a handshake with a Japanese head-down bow. The agent then held me back a moment while Googol and Joseph waited for the elevator.

"Your friend isn't cut out for this stuff. You need to help him. You have the constitution for the battle – he doesn't. The government swings a large axe. I don't want blogs[69] and articles written about how Joseph Leege was the victim of an unfair prosecution because he doesn't understand basic self-defense from the world. You guys have to work on your finesse. Authority doesn't like to be mocked twice."

"It's not mocking, it's logic," I said.

"I've been doing this a long time, Greg. The way you do it, there's no difference. You stopped just in time. You were thirty seconds away from getting indicted for just being an asshole to the government. You're a computer guy, so just listen to my words literally. You're moving along methodically and then all of a sudden it dawns on these snot noses that they're idiots. You're responsible for that. You made them feel that way. If it weren't for me toning it down for you, your friend would be in deep trouble."

"You can convince these lawyers to do the right thing?"

"Like I said, 'I've been doing this a long time and I'm a J.D. too."

I smiled, "I know you, Agent Lefkel. You saved the life of Senator Carlson the man who would become President of the United States. Why are you doing computer fraud cases? Shouldn't they bronze you and perch you on a pedestal in Washington?"

"I'm fine. Computers are the present and the future, right? Plus, I don't think I can get shot at through the internet, right?"

"Not yet," I said smiling. "Thank you, sir," I said shaking his hand.

And then he reached into his pocket and pulled out a DVD encased in a clear cover with his FBI business card. "It's not a floppy diskette but I still owe it to Joseph."

Joseph turned and walked back and accepted the DVD. "From under the tree at MIT? That was you?" Joseph remembered and then so did I. I didn't even speak to Agent Lefkel that day. I just saw him walk away with Joseph's diskette.

"I'm going to call you some time if I have a question or need some help on something," Agent Lefkel said as he walked us to the elevators.

"I'm sure you'll be able to find us," I replied as the elevator doors closed.

Agent Lefkel was the agent that approached Joseph by the tree after his history presentation on Paul Revere and the identity of the revolutionaries. What did the FBI do with that software? Maybe Joseph *did* save his own life by sharing.

▪ ▪ ▪

We all took a lap around the river once we made it downstairs. Avoiding prosecution by the government was a victory; but there was no feeling of satisfaction. There was no thrill of victory versus the agony of defeat. It was relief from the threat of defeat. An absolute gush of endorphins because the threat of prison and death was gone – no longer a possibility. I lived for the relief. I've gotten the relief many times. It was no way to live. It was not something one should get addicted to. But many do. For sure, Joseph couldn't live that way.

Joseph felt better. He told me he was grateful Googol and I were there. My pleasure. He has gotten me out of messes since we were twelve. "I'm just not good when I'm being attacked," he said. "All my skills, everything I'm good at melts away in that construct." Boy did I know it. "How long was I looking at if you included all the wire fraud counts?" Joseph asked. Oh gosh, why does he ask these questions?

"Thirty-five years or so," I said.

"Holy shit! I'd kill myself." Joseph put his hands up to his face as he spoke.

"Cut the drama, Joseph. Here's the thing, you need a lawyer all the time. You need a protector, all the time," I replied.

"I need you, GP. I never feel like I'm alone when I know you're with me. Promise me you'll be there the next time, and the next. I'm pushing the expansion of the Foundation for absolute First Amendment and privacy protection from the government," Joseph declared. He can be so sappy sometimes. But, he was a true believer.

"You're never alone, Joseph. You always have Leela."

"Not anymore. We broke up," Joseph said.

"You broke up?" I was surprised. Googol just nodded that he knew. Leela and Joseph were perfectly matched. They were mathematically correct. "When?"

"Like three weeks ago. She couldn't take the pressure. And she was making my blood pressure go up," Joseph said.

"Hmm, you can handle the pressure and she couldn't?" I asked.

"How do you think the government found out about the manifesto?"

"What?"

What was he saying? How did the government find out about the manifesto? Joseph didn't publicize the manifesto. One would almost have to know it was online and then find it.

"I mean the FBI interviewed Leela and she told them about it," Joseph said.

"Why did she do that?" I wondered.

"I don't know. I can't trust her anymore. She betrayed me. She betrayed the movement."

Betrayed the movement? What movement? He was losing himself. I felt like I broke up with Leela, and it wasn't my fault. "She's your girlfriend. If you were normal, she'd be your wife. She cracked under extreme pressure and told them about a letter you wrote and that's the reason you broke up? That's not betrayal. I don't understand you."

After a few moments of thought, I knew my thoughts didn't make a difference. It was a deal breaker. Leela needed to be strong enough for Joseph and herself. In his mind, she failed him. Leela did the establishment thing; she followed a court order – a subpoena. She needed to martyr herself for the greater cause – Joseph and his quest to have an open internet of ideas that was open and available to all.

I was truly sorry, I told Joseph, "I'm always your friend." "Friend" later turned out to be my own weasel word. I intended to be there for him. He was for the greater good - one of the few good guys. He was something that I was not. I shouldn't have to exist; but I must. "Let's beat town for a while. Get your head straight. You're coming with me to Japan to speak at a conference."

"Nah, I can't. I want to be alone," he answered.

"It's not good to be alone. I'll tell you what, after my trip to Japan, we'll meet in Cambridge again. We'll meet up with Googol and steal the Harvard seal from the Porcellians' lobby," I said. We all stopped and stared out onto the river.

Joseph broke into a smile. He said we would. He said everything would be great again. But, they weren't. The downfalls in Joseph's life were accumulated tragedies. He never outgrew his issues from his childhood and the rest of the timeline of his life. He pursued his global cyber battle to share information. The burden didn't shift from one thing to the next; they accumulated until he collapsed.

TRANCHE V
Launch Ponzi

Love Lies Bleeding in My Hands

Joseph and I never reunited in Cambridge. From my week in Japan, I flew back to London. I had a small office across the street from the Ecuadorian embassy and Harrods. The time zone suited me. I was in the middle of the world markets I invested in. It was a few analysts outside my door, my well-dressed assistant, and me. I was calculating the curve on an option if I sold some shares in a U.S. stock, as I sat in a trance in front of four connected screens.

"Greg, there's a Ms. Ravichandran on the phone." I wasn't sure who it was but I took the call.

"This is Gregory," I said.

"GP, it's Leela." It took me a moment to shift focus. We called her, "Leela Fashionista" as her nickname – I almost forgot her real last name.

"Leela, my favorite coder and fashionista. How are you sweetheart? Do you think I'm I wearing Armani or Duchamp? Hint, I'm in London."

Then as if she read off a piece of paper or received something rehearsed, she said, "GP, I regret to inform you that Joseph Lars Leege is dead."

After a long pause, "What?"

She wasn't reading any more. "Joseph is dead, Greg." I could hear her burst in to tears. I was silent and stunned. After some sniffles, "Did you hear me, Greg?" I still didn't answer. "Greg?"

"I can hear you. What happened?" I said with an angry tone.

"He killed himself." She said through muffled tears. "He killed himself."

I took a moment. I picked up the lamp on my desk and hurled it through the glass window of my office, shattering it. The world stopped for a moment. I propelled my desk on its side and then searched for the phone in the rubble on the floor. I sat on the floor and put the phone to my ear. "What? Why did that idiot do that?"

"Who can say? This, that, everything. You know the litigation was killing him. And a whole lot of other stuff," Leela answered.

"The litigation? What litigation? We just solved that litigation problem in Boston."

"No, this is something else. Some bankruptcy case in Florida," she said.

"Joseph was in bankruptcy?" Which sounded ridiculous when I said it out loud?

"No, he wasn't in bankruptcy. He had some data these assholes wanted and he wouldn't give it to them and it turned out to be this colossal mess. The judge threatened him with prison. They thought he had people's passwords and he wouldn't give them up. I can't believe you didn't know about it?" Disbelief warmed over me.

"Where are you?" I asked.

"We're in Chicago. The funeral is in a few days. The family Rabbi said he can extend it a few days because of the Sabbath and out of town relatives."

"And they're probably getting an extra couple of days for the coroner to rule suicide," which I guess I said out loud.

"Come home, GP."

"Okay," I said.

"I'll see you soon. I have a lot of phone calls to make," she said through tears.

I stared at this picture of myself staring in the mirror that was on the wall of my office, with the phone still to my ear when I heard the news. There was a subtle dull pain, which slowly elevated into excruciating pain, like getting kicked in the balls. I didn't do enough for his fragile soul. I'd be in Chicago for all the scheduled ceremonies there. But first, I turned toward my assistant, who was still standing a few steps away in shock, and said, "Book me the next flight to Florida."

▪ ▪ ▪

What I hated the most about dealing with Joseph's death was learning things about him for the first time. I thought I knew everything. I was ready to learn things that wouldn't surprise me. *Hike the Geek* was a group of geeks that go for hikes as part of their physical activity they usually didn't get because they sat for days at a time. The logic being: time to walk the dog – time to hike the geek. Groups around the country sprung up, connected by a webpage creating dates and times to climb Twin Peaks or Griffith Park, or Red Town Trailhead. It was especially depressing since I was depressed, and at sea level in Florida, there were no hikes, so Joseph could only do *Walk the Beach with the Geeks*. But there were geeks and artists and other bizarre and interesting folks at his Florida memorial service.

The reception was in a room full of geeks reading poetry against a backdrop of montage videos of Joseph talking, posing for pictures and important people in his life. A middle aged red headed woman wearing modern fashionable clothing stood out. I took a moment to figure out her connection. Her body language communicated she belonged. She was standing there drinking a red *zin* while local fans of Joseph were celebrating his life and mourning his death.

"Are you going to play the bongos for us tonight?" I asked her. She looked over at me and smiled.

"No, I don't have that kind of rhythm." I waited a moment and then smiled back. American woman, voice quality appropriate for a professional woman her age, cared about her appearance, not a creative type, out of place with what was going on here, but she did not appear to be uncomfortable, just running out of patience. I guessed she was a lawyer.

"What kind of law do you practice?"

"I'm an appellate lawyer, but sometimes I get dragged into things," she laughed a little at her own levity.

"Dragged into a dark bar for memorial services for forty-something phenoms who commit suicide just to make a point about social injustice?" I asked.

"Are you Gregory by chance?" She asked.

"I am. And you are?"

"I'm Dayna Sohler, I was Joseph's lawyer in this bankruptcy mess."

"Bankruptcy bullshit you mean?" I asked. She was proper, but willing to concede.

"Yes – bullshit." She laughed again.

I read her face and needed to dial it back a little. "I'm sorry, I sound angry."

"I'm sure you're very upset. We all are," she said with a tone that said don't think you're the only one suffering here. She wasn't trying to repel me, just put me in my place.

"You were Joseph's lawyer? You must be remarkable then," I said. It was times like these where I just wish we could set the bullshit aside and a holographic sign would just appear above the person's head telling me who they are, how much money they have, skills, and accomplishments. It would save time.

"Well, I'd like to think so," she said.

"Lay it out for me. You don't have to be modest."

She took another sip from her glass. "I've appeared in front of the Supreme Court. I handle most of the appeals at the firm of about 100 lawyers. Every now and then I pick up a case I believe in and run with it."

The poetry from sad friends I could handle. A melancholic acoustic version of "Love Lies Bleeding in my Hands"[70] played on a sitar in the background was grating. I wanted to understand the story of how Joseph met this woman, how he got involved in litigation in South Florida, and where his strategy failed. I couldn't concentrate. In unison a discordant bellow of "love lies bleeding in my hands," scratched the blackboard in the front of my brain. I noticed an adjoining part of the bar. It had better mellower music playing.

"Let's sit down and talk over there." We made our way over to the other room and sat in a booth. A waitress came over. I ordered a Shepard's pie with two forks and stout dark ale. I shrugged my shoulders as if to say, it was an Irish Bar, right?

"What happened?" I asked.

"Where do I start? How much do you know?" She asked.

"I know nothing." I replied. Even though I knew a little I wanted to check my assumptions.

"I've never met someone so fixated on what was right and what was wrong. Joseph never saw nuance," Dayna said.

"I know it. I knew him since we were kids in Chicago. He always had the luxury of fighting for what he thought was right. How did we get here?"

Dayna said, "Well, it started with a subpoena in a New York Bankruptcy court. Then word spread to other districts to subpoena

Qpredictor, any of its data, and who knows what you might find out. The claims were consolidated in Bankruptcy court in the Southern District of Florida." I assumed Joseph was still working with *Qp* and what or whose data could even be on it. But no doubt, no lawyers understood what they were playing with."

I asked her what these lawyers wanted.

"Everything. They wanted the whole program and databases opened."

That made no sense why these lawyers would want "everything." All we could conclude was fees. Fees to research and review the data on *Qp* – data that didn't belong to them. Billing and rebilling different clients for review and analysis of the same data over and again.

Dayna shrugged, exasperated. "Joseph gave them a program but he didn't think the data should be open to the world. And if someone figured out how to run the data through *Qp,* it would be too much of a violation of privacy. I never really understood it completely, but Joseph was worried about how the service could create and reveal reports about people that were so private that even they didn't know so much about themselves. Do you know anything about *Qp?*"

I told her I understood *Qp*, deeply. "I'm sure he had no problem pointing them to the source code because the code was open source." But there was no way Joseph would hand over other people's personal data – never. Users' medical records, diaries, their wills and trusts, could be on *Qp*. People who never knew or were within six-degrees of any of the Ponzi schemers. What use would other people's data be in a bankruptcy proceeding? The amount of data would be unwieldy and irrelevant to anything they might be investigating.

"They were just looking. Ponzi schemers' and coconspirators' data. Getting paid by the hour just to look. And they were getting nasty. The judge didn't understand what Joseph was arguing, and so the judge held his company in contempt," Dayna said.

"What do you mean what Joseph was arguing? You mean what you were arguing for Joseph." I said.

"No, Joseph represented himself for a while. Then he blasted out an email and posted a message online to all the people who put data on or connected to some version of *Qp* and told them they may want to hire lawyers and object. He was lambasted badly for that stunt."

That stunt made me smile. How clever. I didn't think Joseph had it in him.

"I came in after he was held in contempt. He needed a bankruptcy lawyer. Not because our arguments weren't correct. It's that bankruptcy lawyers are in a club – and I'm not in it. The judge just was giving the trustee gang whatever they asked for without thinking for minute that they were out of control."

The waitress brought over the Shepard's pie. Why didn't he come to me? Why didn't he at least ask me for more money? Why would he lower himself in a pit full of snakes without me there holding the rope to pull him back up? "Did he pay you? If you don't mind me asking," I said.

"He did a little for costs. Fifteen thousand or so. But I just wanted to help him. His idealism is intoxicating. And he was a sweet man. He fixed every computer, printer, and television in my house." Dayna sighed. "All the arguing we did over the years; it was just his passion – being helpful and sweet. He lived in a world of idealism. He lived in a world where everything ought to be right. He was the smartest guy in the room with a heart. Look what happens when those two traits are in the same person?"

Joseph wanted a magistrate or some neutral third-party to review claims of privilege and confidentiality. Go through a checklist of people and data. He wanted a gatekeeper between what they should get and what he was willing to turn over. But that suggestion was batted down. It meant that Joseph could persuade a neutral party that the trustees shouldn't get everything and that was an attack on their power.

"Joseph was doing fine with the contempt proceedings. Even the judge couldn't keep the pressure on that long. Joseph made too much sense. So, the lawyers for the trustees settled. Joseph paid some money and they finally agreed to a small list of data – after two years. Joseph developed for the trustees their own version of *Qp* kept it on their server, which Joseph paid for, and that was that," Dayna explained.

"So, problem solved." I said. But, I knew that it wasn't. There was more, otherwise I wouldn't be listening to this swill while eating Shepard's pie in Fort Lauderdale trying to figure out what was the last straw that broke my best friend's spirit forever. I'd still be in my own selfish cocoon in my office in London.

"No, Joseph posted another explanation of what he did and why he did it. Started a new version of *Qp* called *SuperMetaD* and the lawyers went after him for copyright infringement," she said. My face didn't move. I was ice. Well at least this time he didn't sign a paper that turned all rights of *Qp* to these lawyers.

"They thought they owned every version of *Qpredictor?* It's open source – free to the world. This concept was explained to the judge, right?" She nodded. Ah, poor Joseph – his whole world collapsed. I specifically asked Dayna who were these lawyers.

"They were a united group of lawyers for various trustees from several bankruptcy cases around the country – Madoff, Stanford, Steinger, Dreier, and Rothstein."

"I know about Madoff and Rothstein. And I'm about to know the rest of them – deeply," I said. Dayna commented that I seem calm even though I must be in tremendous pain. She just didn't know me. I ached. It would've been easier for Joseph to play football against the New England Patriots than play in the Big Law and I resented that lawyers and a judge let him take the field.

"What else is left in the litigation?"

"They tried to amend the seven-million-dollar final judgment against the penniless corporation that held *Qp,* against Joseph personally. But eventually, whoever is an executor of Joseph's estate or *Qp* will have to figure out his interest in *Qpredictor* and work it out with the lawyers. I don't know if they'll try and go after Joseph's estate. I have to find a lawyer named Jeffrey Gogolas. Do you know him?"

I smiled. Googol will be useful. "Googol. Yeah, I know him. He's a law and technology professor at MIT. He's our friend." It didn't make sense that a lawyer could amend a final judgment to add Joseph to it. I bet some plaintiff cigarette lawyers would like to add other cigarette companies to a multi-million dollar judgment. "We got Liggett and now we'd like to add Phillip Morris to the judgment. Don't you have to at least sue the person first? Some due process?" I asked.

She just shrugged her shoulders. Yet the judgment improperly attached to Joseph was another nudge that pushed him over the edge.

And he was alone in this battle. He had no friend in the ACLU or any other *amicus*.[71]

"No one wanted go get involved in these Ponzi scheme cases –bad facts," Dayna said.

"Unbelievable. We can support Nazis' free speech in Skokie,[72] but can't defend against the attacks of a group of bully private trustees against data mining and analysis – the frontier of privacy intrusions in the future." A moment of silence passed. Dayna agreed to let me review the legal pleadings.

"Our next hearing's Monday. I have no idea what's going to happen."

"I guess I can review it this over the next few days," I said.

"You know, it's funny. Joseph said if I ever met you I should give you this." Dayna reached into her purse and handed me a thumb drive. I took it. I looked at it. It was a thumb drive that said, "Return Fire 3." But Return Fire 3 didn't exist. It was never made. It was a subtle encouragement to return fire, as in get revenge. Getting revenge was not like Joseph. He knew I'd seek revenge by my nature. He wouldn't have been so obtuse if he had a direct message. What it told me was meant to trigger me to think of the password, but the password to what? Why was Joseph giving me a password? It's like the instrument panel in an airplane. What I'm looking for to fly the plane was somewhere right in front of me. I knew that Joseph wanted me see what was on that thumb drive. I needed to think about this carefully.

▪ ▪ ▪

Monday — court. Tuesday — memorial service. I wasn't sure how, but if it was too late to save Joseph, it was never too late to avenge him. This thought repeated in a loop in my head. Who were these people behind these attacks against Joseph? How could ethical lawyers not know better? It should have taken no time at all for a competent lawyer to realize that Joseph was not part of a Ponzi scheme and would never help one. Money didn't motivate him. I was sure the lawyers that got paid out of the bankruptcy estate ran a financial background check on Joseph would see he was not worth the time. He had no overhead – no wife, no kids, no vices. He didn't need any expensive props to make him appear wealthy.

"How much time did you put into this case? I'll be direct since we don't have a lot of time. How much would Joseph owe you if he paid you your regular fee?"

"One hundred thousand dollars," Dayna replied.

I picked up my phone and called my favorite banker. "Sorry to call so late. First thing tomorrow morning, I need you to wire $200,000 to a lawyer in Fort Lauderdale named Dayna Sohler. She's at a law firm in Fort Lauderdale – go on line and find her. Put it into the operating account - for legal fees and anticipated legal fees. Out of the *JeepDzine* account. Excellent. Goodnight." I hung up and smiled. I made another call. "Book me the next flight to Logan. I need to see Googol." Dayna raised her eyebrows and looked sideways at me. Perhaps my brother Joseph didn't tell her enough about me. Was Joseph more disappointed in me than I realized?

"We're working together now." In a glance she agreed, and I felt better. "Look at this room full of assorted people. How did Joseph find you?"

"Ballroom dancing."

"Ballroom dancing? Oh, that was you." I had been gone from Joseph's world for a while but I remembered that he told me this the last time we saw each other. It was just like him – finding the good useful people.

GNU Not U

On the flight to Logan airport in Boston, I had a few hours to review every pleading related to the bankruptcy case against Joseph. Then it would be time to reach out to GNU.

GNU still believed his purpose on the planet was to make things, not explain stuff to people. He was paranoid, but that didn't mean that evil-players weren't stalking him and wanted to kill him. His personal philosophy developed over the years. There were a few governments, for example, Saudi Arabia, Syria, and China that would consider him a dotcom criminal, if they knew his identity. He was drawn to people that just didn't have limiting beliefs like, I'm American, I must live in America; governments are wise; work hard and behave; and, fashion over comfort. No, GNU developed into a cyber- big "J" justice warrior.

I had to log on to the deep, deep, deep, underbelly of the darknet to reach out to GNU. And if GNU knew I was trying to log in with airplane Wi-Fi, he'd never communicate with me again. Neither of us could vouch for the cybersecurity of our communication. But no one sat next to me, and everyone else around seemed to be asleep. It was hard to tell what exactly set GNU off. I doubted it was Japan itself; it was a pretty cool place to hang especially if you like tuna. It may have been banking or it may have been some mafia guy that pissed GNU off at a maid café ice cream parlor in Akihabra.[73] You can never tell, but GNU wouldn't back down. The guy coded for fourteen straight hours and did not look away from the screen. I had seen him do it. He'd sigh, ask for glass of water, and do it again. Then he slept for three days. The kid could do it without cocaine or Ativan.[74] Amazing.

I was lucky tonight; GNU could meet with me in real time. He wouldn't feel like I was demanding too much of his time because he probably had four other conversations and perhaps a game going on at the same time.

GP:*GNU! it's really late where I am. i'm not in England, my friend. I need to consult on some dark issues.*

GNU: *GP, why u r compelled to tell me what time it is where u are when we talk? Type 2 me: the number of steps to the closest Tommy Burger from my uncle's home in Pasadena, add the number of days MIT was founded before the start of the Civil War, the most number of Krispy Kreme donuts I've eaten in 1 sitting, number of legos in Googol's Millennium Falcon.*

I hated this shit, but I guess it was necessary. At least he wasn't having me solve theorems for passwords. That was why I referenced what time it was where I was located. *"479, 2, 11, 7575."*[75]

GNU:*Hello.*

GP: *hello, my friend. I have sad news... we've lost Joseph.*

Thirty seconds passed.

GNU:*what do you mean... we've lost Joseph?*

GP:*joseph is dead, GNU.*

Thirty seconds passed.

GP:*GNU? focus!*

Thirty seconds passed. GNU must be running a mental suffering subroutine.

GNU:*how can u tell me like this?!!!!! u know I can't process this information . . .*

GP:*GNU, Joseph was pushed to suicide. He's dead.*

If I were there, he'd be doing much better. But, I can't meet with GNU in person. I don't have the time.

GNU:*i CAN'T . . . how am I supposed to help? U know, I can't get good Alprazolam here!*

GP:*GNU! GNU! CALM DOWN. U must calm down!*

Thirty seconds passed.

GNU:*I'm freaking out!!!!*

GP:*GNU, u must help me. I must avenge 4 Joseph.*

GNU:*Who did this to Joseph? What kind of animal would hurt Joseph?*

GP:*Lawyers, GNU. bad people. they tortured him until he couldn't take it anymore.*

I realized this read a bit histrionic. Linear thinkers always had to be cognizant that spectrum thinkers didn't comprehend the nuance of sarcasm or the emphasis exaggeration can convey.

GNU:*This is something ur supposed 2 protect Joseph from. I'm an emotional rock compared to Joseph. He made our lives have meaning. Who knows where you'd be if it weren't for him. how did this happen?*

GNU was taking bite sized pieces out my heart. What he was saying was true, however painful an expression. I just didn't wear it well. I was stoic on the outside. My bleeding pain was internal. I explained what happened.

GNU:*I didn't realize he was so desperate. How must I help u?*

Great semantics from GNU.

GP:*I'll need u to make money go away. Lawyers hold money in trust at banks. that money needs to be gone when I say.*

A minute goes by.

GNU:*I will honor Joseph Lars Leege in my work, but his death does not authorize me 2 b unethical – I cannot steal what is not mine – what does not belong to me or the world.*

Now, I took a minute. I thought GNU in his grief and panic wouldn't stick to his code.

GP:*We wouldn't be stealing. It is not unethical to make one think their money is gone. it is not stealing, if the money never leaves an account. is it unethical to make something appear to disappear? there are rules that lawyers must comply with. If money disappears it appears 2 b gone. If it is gone, lawyers will be called to account. These are the lawyers that need to account 4 Joseph.*

A minute elapsed.

GP:*... u know what I would need?*

GNU:*u will have it. I want 2 b able 2 come 2 the US for his funeral. I will feel bad 4 a while. GP, you bare responsibility for losing Joseph. It was ur responsibility 2 protect him. This will cause pain around the world and the universe will suffer.*

GP:*I . . . know. i'm responsible. i'm going 2 make it right. I'm going to see Googol. You'll hear from him.*

GNU:*Goodbye, GP. ☹ that means NOT happy, if u don't know what ☹ means.*

I knew what he meant.

Googol it

It was midday when I arrived in Cambridge by car after landing in Boston Logan airport. I was over-tired and in a malaise. My driver pulled up to Rogers Hall on the MIT campus. I had perfect timing because I saw Googol up ahead even through the end of class rush of people. We weren't the youngest kids on campus anymore, and stood out easily. We were *OG, Original Gamesters.* The term had an added meaning – we were old. Every now and again we would receive an electronic communication from a group claiming to be an offshoot or direct descendants of intern class of '91-'94, the descendants could never decide. There would be a question about game history, games like *Return Fire, Word Zap, Marine Aquarium,* or about technology. Since Googol was associated with MIT, he would field most of the questions.

Googol made those movements with his hands and arms, mapping out some beauty in mathematics computation for all. He was Fibonacci[76] live at a lecture hall near you, so put on your seatbelt. It was fun to watch him; it was comforting to see that people stay the same. I thought the students asked the right questions, just to watch him demonstrate how the numbers and equations just fit seamlessly together in his head. And after all, he enjoyed doing it. But at the core of it all was a plea for everyone in the world to rely on the science (and never give up) when making important policy or ethical decisions, any decision for that matter – and we were not.

I stepped out of the front seat and started walking toward Googol. He saw me as I approached and told the group that was enough for today, and they politely disbursed.

"Need a hug?" I asked.

"Not from you," he replied.

"Let's hug anyway," I said. We hugged anyway.

"Where are your bags?" Googol asked.

"I've already been to your apartment," I said. Googol thought for a moment. "I still have a key," I said. "How you doing?"

"I'm profoundly sad. I'm helplessly sad," Googol said. I nodded a *me too* back at him.

"Did you walk around campus? Torture some of your old professors?" Googol asked.

"Nope. It's been a long time. How many are even left? Come, I have a car. We're not helpless and we have a lot of work to do. We have court on Monday." Googol locked eyes with me and raised a brow in cautious curiosity.

Brainstorm

At his apartment, Googol and I didn't skip a beat. We worked for hours on end like we had done before the PACER meeting in Boston. This made me think of Joseph and wonder why he didn't think to come to Googol or me again. We had computers and multiple screens opposing each other. We spoke out loud as we reviewed transcripts and pleadings. As good partners we could be silent in the same room together. We didn't need to speak to break uncomfortable silences. We vented more than usual. He was more hopeful that the world will grow into being a better place. And I forced it down their throats. I was not patient. I was not kind. I was not a teacher. Or more succinctly, education came from learning the hard way – through pain of doing it a different way other than by logic. Or, I didn't care.

"Did you know that Joseph was still working on *Qpredictor* on some new platform he called, RubyonQ ?" I asked Googol.

"Yes. He was always working on it. He'd been posting new open source code about it for years. Something about the AI breaking itself into shards and hiding parts of itself in the Internet of Things."

"On the *IoT*?[77] Well, I didn't know about it. He never talked about it, even when we were talking. Why didn't he let everyone know he made some profound updates?" I said.

"I just think he didn't want to be bothered with questions."

"Well, that's ironic." I exclaimed. "Every Ponzi scheming asshole in the last seven years has some connection to the source code, and meanwhile his best friends didn't know about it. I could've marketed this, employed people and made us all a ton of money; or started my own Ponzi scheme," I said with a laugh.

"I guess he just wanted to create. He was having a hard time as of late with his issues. Looking back, he wasn't dealing with the inquiries about the source code very well." We just stared at each other. "And where did all these Ponzi schemes spring up from? I mean was the 21st century the Ponzi age, like the Jazz age of the '20s? Is cheating just the culture in an up market?" Googol wondered aloud.

"I'm angry at him and myself for the same reason – we should have done more to communicate." And because of that he was alone and fell into the rabbit-hole of despair. He let his despair feed on itself. And I should have checked on him. His despair was like insulin shock or hypoxia. Once it happened, the manifestation of hypoxia prevented one from fixing the problem – symptoms of drunkenness and eventual unconsciousness. Doing a little psychological autopsy,[78] I would say, around the time the lead trustee tried to attach the multi-million dollar judgment against the corporation on Joseph personally, he lost it.

I had GNU scouring databases that were a part of the case. He was on a darknet instant message line with Googol sharing the results of a couple of ideas we had. GNU was still too upset to communicate, Googol was doing the typing.

"There are two things we know so far: One, Joseph was working on *Qpredictor* and we didn't know to what extent; and two, schemers were attracted to *Qpredictor.* We just don't know exactly why. And the schemers seem not to be connected in any relevant way," Googol said.

"We're running the wrong algorithm. We proved the schemers were connected to South Florida because they either ran part of their scheme in Florida or owned land there, but didn't communicate with each other. But, just because there were Ponzi schemers looking to make use of *Qp*, could just well be a coincidence. We knew enough about Joseph that he wouldn't have been running a scheme of his own, but more importantly, we could prove that he wasn't because he didn't make any money or gain from it.

So the bankruptcy judge seemed to be assuming because bad people used *Qp,* therefore *Qp* and Joseph are bad. I mean, it was clear this judge and everyone working on this issue didn't know how to turn off their cell phones in court, let alone write a line of code, or knew what was going on here. Yet, they all seemed to agree with each other that Joseph was bad, while at the same time admitted that they didn't understand this stuff.

"Can you believe this one lawyer for a group of unsecured creditors actually says that his knowledge of computers ended with the game of *Pong;*[79] and he doesn't understand what Joseph is saying but the court should sanction him because of the up swell of discontent on the trustees' side?" I said. "And that sanction was – being sent to prison for contempt."

"Yeah, I read that –*Pong*. So, we have to figure out why Joseph was alone. Why were Ponzi schemers using it? And who else would have had an interest in using it, and why weren't they in court screaming that these strangers shouldn't review the databases associated with their use of *Qp*?" Googol asked.

"I don't know?" I answered.

"Well, you're the closest brain to a Ponzi schemer, think of something."

"Because they didn't know they were under attack. Because Joseph didn't get the word out better. Because Joseph didn't know who was on *Qp* because it was free and he didn't care. He was just happy that his contribution to the world was useful to others." We were on to something. Joseph released a genie but the kind of genie that was like hydrogen gas, (it could be used for good or bad), not the I'll grant you three wishes kind of genie.

"I'll ask GNU to see if we can identify who else was on *Qp* without having to look at others' databases."

"I think we're on to something, Googol."

"We'll see," he replied.

"In the meantime, I'm going to make a couple of phone calls. I think we can get more time to prepare our case, if we just get past Monday."

"That'll be nice," Googol sighed.

"I've got a plan."

If we live, we'll win.

I stayed awake on the flight from Logan to Fort Lauderdale International. Googol didn't speak until he noticed the confident smirk on my face.

"You just figured out how to win?" He asked.

"I know how we're going extricate ourselves from court. I know how I'll make things right for Joseph and the world."

"Our odds?"

"You've done enough. I'll handle the stuff outside of court." I said.

"Our odds?" Googol repeated.

"I don't want to sound like we're in a Godfather movie, but this isn't your thing, a nice boy like you, shouldn't be involved in something like this."

"Odds?" Googol said for the last time.

"Seventy percent we'll get out of court alive. Thirty percent chance we go to jail."

Googol didn't respond, he just shut his eyes and laid back for a nap. But I had more learning and planning to do.

Oh say can you S.E.C.?

Bernard Madoff was a cool customer. If you've ever heard him speak he was congruent from his hair to his toes, he had no feelings or worries. He had no worries because he was never really challenged. Those who questioned him were squashed like a bug. Well-meaning people who replied at a cocktail party that they didn't understand how Madoff consistently earned returns of nine to ten-percent a year, would get pilloried by a stranger for speaking ill of this remarkable man who donated untold millions to various charities. This major *macher*[80] supporting Jewish causes, how dare you give a lukewarm response to the question, what was his secret, should I invest? After that, most polite people were conditioned to not give any sort of warning or recommendation. It was sad. Our noncritical thinking society has dulled us in to thinking we weren't supposed to reject false conclusions – personality over the merit of ideas.

Madoff thought he would be caught by authorities at least one time before he actually was caught. He had no exit strategy. He played his prestige to the hilt. Don't act like you're guilty, and no one of importance suspected. He didn't act like an arrogant ass. He was methodical, calm, and deliberate in his speaking style. Good learning tool. He understood the business and his business made sense – the stock market. He had *top guys* that he oversaw to make the right trade decisions. He was charitable in the way he spent and *invested*. More importantly, he didn't wear flamboyant costumes.[81] As opposed to notorious lawyer and Ponzi schemer, Scott Rothstein. Rothstein was no study in cool under pressure. Rothstein was an anxiety stricken, facial tick-ridden, over-blinking, super-blinging, sparkling, peacock dressing, and February weekday matinee understudy to Madoff. Rothstein had no longevity and was serving a fifty-year sentence in prison.

Madoff had his props. He was the former chairman of the NASDAQ.[82] He had an estate in Palm Beach, Florida. Cars, planes, travelled, and lived like money was no object. This was where he met with his personal-friend and unofficial lawyer, Saul Graf. Graf always worked to get some crumbs of legal work from Madoff, Madoff only gave Graf's law firm, Baker, LLC enough where they had a conflict of interest so Baker could never investigate or sue Madoff. Or, so Madoff thought. In the fine print of Baker's legal retainer agreements, it expressly waived conflicts of interest outside the specific legal matter Baker worked on. This clause hadn't been directly tested by the courts.

Madoff had Ponzi in his blood. He was Ponzi reduced to its absurd. Why do people deny evidence before their eyes? Because most people believe money was the key to what they were looking for. Even generally logical people ignored the scientific method when it came to the God, *Mammon*.[83] Easy answers were always preferred. *The Secret*.[84] Man's search for magic, rather than logic, because using logic can be so disappointing. If logic said an opportunity was *too good to be true*, magic countered with *this is too good to miss – FOMO,* the fear of missing out. The lottery, *Facebook,* bottled water, or the pet rock – don't be the fifth Beatle. People missed out on these wonderful opportunities. Had they only known, they too would be rich, brilliant, and really good looking.

A year or so after Madoff's Ponzi collapse, I'd heard the full story from FBI Special Agent Brad Lefkel, who had a distinguished history with the Bureau, received a call from his supervisor in December 2008. The call in a nutshell was "Bernie Madoff might be running the biggest Ponzi scheme in history." Lefkel, and three other agents went to Madoff's apartment in Manhattan the next morning and interviewed him. After the interview they arrested Madoff. As Lefkel told me, Madoff knew he was broke, insolvent, and couldn't go on any more. Lefkel asked Madoff: "We're here to find out if there's an innocent explanation for all of this." Madoff without hesitation simply replied, "There is no innocent explanation." Madoff crashed because the tide receded and he was naked. But had the economy remained strong, he could've died a successful schemer. All the Security and Exchange Commission had to do was send a subpoena to the Directorate of Defense Trade Controls, the DDTC, and it would have known Madoff was not front running (placing his trades first), but not making the trades at all. He was full on bullshit – a Ponzi scheme. Madoff was never wrong because he backdated history. Madoff bought T for $1.00 on Monday, (no he didn't), and sold it on Tuesday for a 1.50 (no he didn't), and made a profit on the sale, (no he didn't). Madoff really marked trades on Wednesday that he *made* on Monday and Tuesday. In turn, people just shoveled money at this wizard.

Sadly, the funds that were shoveling money at the Wizard were *feeder funds,* funds that bundled monies from other funds, and those funds invested with Madoff. So, the investors in the feeder funds that invested in Madoff's funds may have had no knowledge their money was invested in Madoff but were nonetheless victims.

Saul Graf knew Madoff's game. Graf was privy to some tips Madoff would drop at a cocktail party and Graf realized that Madoff was no better than any other stock picker. Graf would bide his time until one day he and his firm picked at the bones of the remains of the Madoff bankruptcy estate.

If any business can be run like a Ponzi scheme, then it made one wonder, were the businesses always Ponzi schemes? Are all Ponzi schemes criminal enterprises from the start, or can a business situation pressure a legitimate business to evolve into a scheme? One just has to see whether the business was legitimate. Marc Dreier's promissory notes were absolute fiction. Scott Rothstein's "court settlements" had no clients. Lou Pearlman, aka "Big Poppa's," scheme of twenty-years of an Employee Investment Savings Account program was a complicated lattice of nothing except investor monies. Those three were easy – fraud in its inception; and, as the indictments and lawsuits claimed, fraud in the inducement.

On the other hand, a viatical insurance company[85] or even the Madoff fund started as a legitimate business, but quickly evolved into a Ponzi scheme when the expectations from the legitimate business failed to be met. Psychologically, however, all these businesses were destined to be Ponzi schemes. The unrealistic expectations of the businesses were a road map straight to Ponzi-dom. It was the same psychology that pushed the schemer into feeling the flicker of desire to invest in some enterprise that would rescue them from the imploding scheme. That was when you see the speculative real estate investments or purchases of legitimate business start-ups that were also unrealistically meant to rescue the Ponzi from collapse. Agent Lefkel told me his Madoff story. One day he would ask me the same questions: "Am I running the biggest Ponzi scheme in history? Is there an innocent explanation for all of this?"

I.O.U.

Marc Dreier was a lawyer who had a small office in Boca Raton, Florida before he really went out of his mind and started a new law firm in New York. He had a simple scheme, gather promissory notes (loans) package them up, purportedly to reduce risk, and then sell them cheaply to hedge funds which believed they will make a profit over time when the fictitious entities made payments on the notes. Dreier ran his law firm as a dictatorship and like a corporation. He paid lawyers large salaries so they could work as lawyers, rather than on law firm management. This sounded great, but law firms were law firms – that was to say they didn't make widgets.

Lawyers sell their time and knowledge. Clients must pay. It had limited assets outside of the lawyers' time who serviced clients who paid fees. If clients left, the money stopped, the lawyer had less value. So, to run the law firm as a corporation where lawyers get paid on perceived value outside of origination of clients, work in progress, and most importantly, amount of money collected by those clients based upon work performed was flawed by design. If it took a lawyer who was a former judge or head of the SEC or United States Attorney to bring in that new client, and the firm couldn't bring in the client without that special lawyer, then *that* lawyer was a cost of doing business. Staff was a cost. Lawyers on large salaries were not only costs; they were drains where liquidity and profits go down. More lawyers of varying prestige did not multiply profit, they divided it.

The interesting thing about these lawyers was Saul Graf hired Christian Leiner as an associate from Dreier years earlier. Dreier thought Leiner had "deficiencies." Perhaps Dreier meant that Leiner didn't have enough Ponzi potential. But as I learned later, Dreier didn't put in the effort to develop Leiner or he was wrong. Leiner claimed to have figured out what Dreier was up to and left Dreier, LLP. Since Leiner didn't report Dreier's crimes and was hired by Graf at Baker without an equity partnership, it meant Leiner was no hero and didn't have enough legal business on his own to merit profit sharing in the Baker law firm.

Dreier liked the big hits that class action lawsuits could provide. In his mind, one good class action settlement could rescue him from the Ponzi scheme he, over time became embroiled in. It was a subtle scheme. He ran a law firm and spent and spent, until some point his expenses overwhelmed him. He was out of his mind in spending and scheming to survive. He epitomized the spend money to make money strategy. Picassos were props. He needed them. He needed it all because success bred success. People loved to invest in a winner. And what said *winner* more than money spent on stuff? Real estate leads to: "I'm here, and there, and all over the place, because I'm too damn successful, invest in me." "I bought this here, when I was there, and met the Queen while doing it, but I'm actually talking to you right now because you're special and you want to be associated with me, you want to please me."

Dreier was a committed schemer. He manufactured audits from accounting firms by stealing their letterhead or making it up. He created lots of paper. Too bad he didn't know about the magical editable documents – the wiki. From his jail cell in Canada he transferred $10 million to his personal bank account. Before he got caught he knew he was going to get caught. His scheme was in his blood. He loved being a schemer. It wasn't a means to an end, he received power from fooling people and mocking them with every lie he perpetuated and each one believed. This was what he enjoyed, not the homes, the paintings, the women – he loved the fooling. *I got you.*

In a moment of sobriety and lucidity but not quite perfectly candid, Dreier said: "How many people who are condemning what I did would know for sure they would never do anything like what I did if they knew they wouldn't get caught? Is what holds people back from doing things like this their fundamental virtue, or is it the fear of getting caught? I think in many people, in the case of many people, it is fundamental virtue. And I applaud those people. But I think in many, many people, it's either lack of opportunity, or fear of getting caught." True candor would have been: Outside of the small chance you were honest, which he respected, he was saying you were either too dumb or too scared to be a schemer.

What was so strange was that true computer programmers beyond the simple coders, the cognitive computer scientists, the architects of the infrastructure that made meaningful software services and computer hardware, was that tone and nuance were extraneous in their world. Four plus four equals eight every day, all day long. While some of them could be annoying and bellicose for differing reasons, for the most part they were honest because they cannot spare the energy to be anything but literally truthful. That was why I wondered for days when I discovered *Qpredictor* on the list of files on Dreier's computer seized by the government. What would this Ponzi schemer be doing with a coding function that among other things discard false data?

Well Mr. Dreier, it was not for me to condemn you, I applauded your gumption. I'm not scared. But you talked too much, took too many risks, and put too many damn things in writing. You dabbled in technology but didn't even get on the *rails* let alone go off the rails. That was just fascinating, having technology that helped you perpetrate a scheme, but never used it. And in some sense you failed when you didn't recruit Saul Graf or retain Christian Leiner, two of the biggest undiscovered Ponzi talents ever.

Bankruptcy techniques

Baker, LLP was the law firm that invented the unethical techniques in a Ponzi scheme clean-up. One day they were on one side representing the debtor and the next day representing a creditor in a different case. Then there were those who supported the lawyers. They were second level fee-eaters. They were the accountants, expert witnesses of various sorts, fee experts, auctioneers, and realtors. On top of the debtor's food chain was the trustee, who was in charge of it all. Now the trustee didn't necessarily make the most money, unless he was associated with a law firm, and his firm got hired to give him – the trustee, advice. Either way, he could make millions and not work very hard. The lawyers generated the most money because they bill by the hour. They were billing the debtor's estate, which was going around the town and country doing "rip and runs," quick shakedowns through demand letters and clawback lawsuits to fill the debtor's bankruptcy estate with funds to pay back creditors.

Christian Leiner wrote scripts for his underlings to use during these clawbacks. If creditor says: "But, I didn't invest in the schemer's scheme, I did the work with materials and labor I had to hire, and I didn't know he was going bankrupt. It was a multi-million dollar company!"

Respond with: "These are compelling and sympathetic arguments the trustee has taken into account, that's why he's only asking you to return fifty-percent of what was transferred to you."

If they're sophisticated enough to say this: "But, the debtor got what he paid for. I did the work. Reasonable value for services!"

Respond with: "The corporate debtor, (the derivative company of the schemer, the insurance company, investment group, law firm) didn't strictly receive value by placing tile in the schemer's office. So the bankruptcy estate through the trustee is clawing back the misspent transferred funds."

A charity who received a donation from the debtor (*schemer*): "We're a charity. We save the children. How can you clawback from the children? This money was budgeted and spent three-years ago," the executive director of the charity would dutifully state.

Saul Graf's form email *response*: "These are compelling and sympathetic arguments the trustee has taken into account, that's why he's only asking you to return fifty-percent of what was transferred to you."

"And, if we don't pay, the charitable foundation will have to spend money on a lawyer to litigate and you'll ask for the full amount?"

"Yes," Graf smiled in reply.

Leiner and Graf spent hours prosecuting this next scenario in bankruptcy courts. When a person who invested but did not know he was investing in a Ponzi scheme and when the music stopped ended up losing, that person or entity was known as a "net loser."

"You're suing me for what?" the net loser said.

"For the transfers made to you by the debtor," Leiner would answer.

"He paid me back with my own money. And not all of it. I lost money! I'm a victim. The debtor, who you stand in the shoes of, made more money than I did, and I'm supposed to pay back more?"

"Yes, well you can file a claim and perhaps you'll get your money back as restitution in the criminal case," Leiner would reply with a smirk. "Most people don't want to keep the money. It's dirty money."

The typical net losers' reply: "That's fucking bullshit!"

Sometimes when a schemer bought things, the manifestation of the greed of a professional conman, like watches, cars, and real estate, were seized by the federal government and a schemer's ownership rights in the property were forfeited to the government, in a process known as forfeiture. Remember, the bankruptcy trustee was not the government. He was a private person who was appointed to claw back money for the bankruptcy estate. The government, on the other hand, was tasked with prosecuting schemers and coconspirators, and to get restitution for victims of the scheme. Seems similar, but it was qualitatively different.

Let's say that you had sold a schemer a watch, and that watch cost $10,000. You were paid. When the government came in, it seized the watch in forfeiture. When the bankruptcy trustee came in and looked at the books, he saw that you received or were transferred $10,000. The trustee wants that money back. Great, give me my watch back. The watch has been forfeited by the government; the watch seller doesn't get it back. Wait, you lose twice you say? That can't be the law. *It is.*

So, stand for something – fight it! You earned that $50,000. The Save the Children charity spent that donation and it went toward a legitimate cause. You lost all your savings, you say? You have bills to pay, employees to feed, rent, overhead – retirement. This was a stick up!

Hire a lawyer. Make sure it's a bankruptcy lawyer (your own mountain person) because you didn't want to pay someone by the hour to have the same revelations that you were having right now. That was right, $600-$1400 an hour (and climbing), depending on the venue. An honest lawyer will give you the numbers and if you're the kind of person who can understand numbers without getting angry for a few moments, you'd realize the trustee doesn't care, the judge doesn't care, and the jury won't care – because there was no jury. No jury nullification to deny a schemer's clawback even though the jury was made up of working folks or people just like you. It pays to come up with a number to pay off the bankruptcy estate, so that the trustee, Baker lawyers, accountants can continue fishing, hunting, and searching for wildebeests to claw. Like I said, a *rip and run*; or, litigate for months to years.

There were all sorts of victims of any scheme that ended in bankruptcy. The pain was relative to how much money one lost compared to how much that person possessed. Remember, the schemer in most cases had to act like a big shot. Roll out the slogans. *Takes money to make money. Nothing breeds success like success. Never judge a book by its cover, except people do. Fake it 'til you make it.*

I had read emails about regular people who were screwed in the process while Baker lawyers like Graf and Leiner got richer. The people who didn't fake it? What about Godfrey, the guy who ran a car detailing business? Or Cecil, who went around all day shining shoes? You got your schemer who got his cars detailed and shoes shined twenty cars and thirty pairs of shoes at a time. When it was done and the schemer absconded, committed suicide, or got arrested, where are Godfrey and Cecil? Looking to get paid for the cars waxed (that were seized) and the shoes shined (that were being auctioned). They got stiffed. Those were victims. The saddest part was that the Bankruptcy court doesn't have words to describe the difference between someone who benefitted from a Ponzi scheme and innocents. Guys like Godfrey, Cecil, and charities – they were all just transferees who will be clawed as a wildebeest.

If there was money in the trough, the pie was bigger and then no one was going to argue with the fee-eaters' hourly rate. Because on this case, one set of lawyers were working for the trustee today, and in the next case, the same lawyers were switching sides and working for the creditors. "Your fee in the Shapiro matter is okay, how's my fee application in Keith Simmons?" It's all right. It was a form of nepotism. And nepotism was the *no idiot left behind* countermeasure to evolution or meritocracy. How did one get appointed to be a trustee or the law firm that supports them? Technically, the Bankruptcy judge appointed them after they apply.

The trustee and Baker lawyers always had an impressive batting average. "We clawed back sixty-percent of the money into the estate for the benefit of creditors." Baker conspired with trustees to *juke the stats*. One way to get the number high was collect a lot of money from the various sources of those who were transferred money by the schemer. The other way was to reduce the number of claims. Creditor – your claim as a creditor has been denied.[86] Think about it as if a baseball player were allowed to delete his last three strikeouts from his last ten at-bats – what was left was an impressive batting average. Less money owed by the bankruptcy estate to creditors, plus the more money clawed back, equals a higher average. The trustee and Graf and Leiner become hall of famers.

How Come Their Stuff is Stuff?

As I climbed the stairs to get into the federal courthouse on Broward Boulevard, there was a short line. What an odd building, it was designed backward. It occurred to me that we were all going through what looked like the backdoor of the place. It annoyed me. I was angry walking in. I was early. If I could get in early I would become more comfortable with the surroundings. A courtroom was never a comfortable place to be, however.

I went up an elevator, walked outside onto a patio, then into an anteroom, before entering the courtroom. The door was eight feet tall and made of thick wood. Not majestic, just heavy. The first thing seen was the side of the courtroom and rows of benches for the spectators. I walked up to the bar, but didn't pass. I saw the electrical outlets and stations for computers to link to the several monitors across the courtroom, presumably for each juror to see, but there were no juries in bankruptcy court.

I turned and walked to the back of the courtroom and sat in the last row. I saw the back of the heads of two lawyers. One was older, late fifties, looked about twelve months pregnant, a scotch belly, no doubt; and, a yarmulke of baldness. The second was a young associate – an ear and slave to the partner. As the sycophant to the partner, he tried to engage him in conversation about something other than the law to demonstrate they were friends, not just employer-employee. After a few moments of time killing and numbing nonsense, I figured out that the partner was one of my targets – Christian Hillel Leiner; and, the kid – well, who cares for now. I sit in the back. I'm invisible to them. They kept talking. Somehow the kid got on the topic of football. Who won the day and night before –

he droned on. Leiner bragged he had friends who were part of the same fantasy league for the past twenty-five years, but he was so busy with law he had no time for fantasy, or this conversation, *plebe*.

My reminder ring on my cell went off. It sounded like a familiar ringtone but I didn't recognize who it was from. It was short, indicating it was a message and not a call. It nagged at me. I changed the ring to vibrate without looking.

The plebe continued with fantasy football, telling Leiner he knew one of Leiner's friends in the fantasy league. He dropped the name, "Walker" on his boss and commented that he was an old-time lawyer with a good reputation. To which Leiner responded that the lawyer, Walker was a great lawyer. They worked together for a while but when a certain case came into the office Walker had turned down the case because he represented the company the potential client wanted to sue and felt it would be a conflict of interest for the firm to sue that former client.

Leiner said, "It's amazing. That's why he'd end up being a solo practitioner because in a firm you need to navigate around these issues." In sycophantic form, the plebe agreed. One sentence. One special sentence. One revealing sentence. Leiner's old lawyer friend was too ethical? He couldn't survive in a firm because the pack required navigation around rules that lawyers deemed unethical– borderline apocryphal, definitively illuminating.

The conversation ended when the court reporter entered the room and set her stenograph machine up in the middle of the courtroom, right underneath where the judge sat. It seemed like everyone used naval analogies throughout the transcripts. Navy memorabilia was scattered along his judicial bench.

A host of other lawyers began filing into the courtroom. All in suits and ties, they all seem to be singing a chorus of, "Hello, how are you? How's the wife, the kids, the practice, the case?" It was hard to tell which lawyers were on which side of the matter until they sat on their respective sides, but even then. I knew Leiner was for the trustee. Conrad represented a special group of creditors. In came Mr. Pong, lawyer for another special group of creditors, with unsecured claims. Soon, there were no sides. Seating flowed into the first few rows of the courtroom. No one seemed to sit in two seats on the left-side of the courtroom.

Googol and Dayna Sohler entered the courtroom. Neither made eye-contact with me. I pulled out my cell phone, all functions were on silent, and automatic-shutter snapped a few pictures of the people in the courtroom; quickly shoved the phone back in my pocket. Googol and Sohler sat by Pong at the table. We were all waiting for court to begin, which was when the judge walked in. When will he walk in? When he walks in. Tick-tock, tick-tock – the hourly rate of the room was in the tens of thousands of dollars. The fee-eaters were eating fuel like a 777 on the taxi-way with ten planes ahead awaiting release.

A woman walked in from behind the judge's bench. She turned on the speaker phone on the judge's desk and the sound came through the speakers laid out throughout the courtroom. "You've connected to court-call," the message declared. She punched in a code and recorded the name of the courtroom telephone line: "Judge Daryl P. Daryl." She placed the phone on hold, and walked back behind the door she came from. Video screens for jurors and computer outlets for each lawyer at the tables. Joseph was denied the opportunity to present to the judge a sample of what *Qpredictor* could do, so the judge would know what he was dealing with and what the trustees' lawyers were really asking for. By the way, where was the trustee, any of them? I relaxed a bit when a small older gentleman walked into the room and sat in the third row. He turned and nodded hello to me. I nodded back. No one noticed our exchange or him. He didn't walk in the room like he was important.

"All rise! The bankruptcy court for the Southern District of Florida is now in session, Judge Daryl P. Daryl presiding.[87] Please be seated. Remain quiet," the courtroom clerk announced. My gosh, it was unreal. Judge Daryl Daryl looked like Larry from my father's favorite television show when I was a child.[88] This is my brother Daryl. And this is my other brother Daryl. Your mother named both your brothers, Daryl? Yes. Now, Daryl was a bankruptcy judge.

"Good morning. Let me handle the smaller matters on the docket and then we'll dive into the multiple hearings on the consolidated trustees' requests on what we've affectionately labeled *In re:* multiple Ponzi matters." A moment later he called a case and a voice came over the speakers. It was a lawyer in Miami phoning in his appearance. Another case – two lawyers appearing by phone. From the looks of the faces in the courtroom, this was the normal bankruptcy court business. Joseph wasn't permitted to appear by phone for all the evidentiary hearings, which happened to be delayed at the last minute. Travel by plane to court only to be told, the game was called off.

An hour later, the judge announced he would take up the matter of multiple Ponzi matters. "I see we have many lawyers visiting us today. Announce your appearances for the record." After twenty-lawyers announced their appearances on the phone most of whom were billing for listening, in-court roll-call took place.

"I wrote in my last order that the parties would have to consolidate their positions on this matter. I'm not hearing fifty lawyers on this. So, tell me how you think we should proceed," the judge said.

Leiner rose and said: "The Trustee, Harvey Gale has united all the trustees in this matter and I'll be making argument on all their behalf since they are all in agreement about the egregious and contemptuous behavior of Mr. Leege and his company."

"Very well, proceed," the judge responded.

"I guess one good way to avoid contempt is to die, your Honor," Leiner pronounced. I heard nothing in the moment after. I looked at Googol who also looked up and waited for some response from the judge. My eyes next glanced to the third row. I saw the eyebrows raise and then drop into an expression of a man who came back from the battle only to find his once familiar home different. There was laughter in the gallery.

"Is there something funny about my friend's death?" Googol stated one standard deviation louder than Leiner. Googol looked at the judge again who remained silent. Leiner continued as if Googol didn't say a word.

"Now, with no obstacle in place, the trustees should just take over the Mr. Leege's company and control of the data so we can finally get the evidence."

"You might want to look at me when I'm speaking to you, Mr. Leiner!" Googol was a rare form of pissed. Leiner turned and looked.

In a lower volume, Googol asked again: "Is there something funny about my friend's death?" Leiner paused but said nothing. "I'm your obstacle, Mr. Leiner."

Googol began to sit down when the distinguished man in the bow-tie caught his eye. Googol remained expressionless, then turned his head and looked at me in the back. I looked at him for a moment and then looked away so no one would notice we knew each other.

Leiner continued with his rant. "I'm sure I don't have to review the entire history of Mr. Leege and his behavior in this case. The court is already well aware of it. The trustee proffered that Mr. Leege deliberately controlled the data of all the Ponzi schemers listed in our motion. We also proffered that he did so, with the intent of obstructing the investigation of the trustees. As soon as we discovered this, we moved to have Mr. Leege individually responsible for his actions. Now, Mr. Leege is unfortunately no longer with us. And I didn't mean to imply that his death is a good thing. It's clear that he had bad intent and was involved in protecting the most notorious Ponzi schemers of our time. His allegations and proclamations of Fourth Amendment[89] violations and privileges are and were always meaningless and we can move to take over the company and assess his estate with the judgment and fines relating to his contempt. The trustee, Harvey Gale, and the other trustees are very unhappy with Mr. Leege's litigation tactics in this case. Particularly, Mr. Gale wanted me to relay that he has never dealt with the likes of Joseph Leege in his forty-plus years of being a lawyer, judge, and arbitrator. Naturally, we're prepared to move forward with this proceeding, if the court has any questions, the briefs are sufficient to support moving forward with sanctions under section 1927."

"Would you like to make an argument on behalf of *MetaDzine* and Mr. Leege," the judge asked Googol.

"May it please the court? I'm Jeffrey Gogolas, I'm here today, along with Ms. Dayna Sohler, only representing *MetaDzine.* Mr. Leege's estate has not yet been opened in the State of Illinois, so any individual claims of potential creditors should be held for the moment until his estate can be represented in this Court. Before we rush into how the trustees failed to prove contemptuous conduct against Mr. Leege, we must start with the issue of jurisdiction, personal and subject matter jurisdiction. Personal jurisdiction against Mr. Leege, or more precisely his estate, which has not yet been formed; and, subject matter jurisdiction, which as the Court knows, can be raised at any time – even on appeal."

"Even on appeal," can be quite a sobering remark if realistic. No judge wants to be reversed on appeal. It made them feel – wrong.

Googol resumed, "While the trustees here, well not physically here, even though it is clear that at least one of them is very upset. But those who have made argument seek to attach judgments to an individual, who wasn't a party to the litigation, and today for the first time seek to seize assets of a corporation and assets it holds for third parties, namely private data – and this can be done expeditiously and without meaningful review? These gentlemen ask the Court for way too much, too quickly."

"Only an Article III judge,[90] and not this Court, can impose sanctions under section 1927, as Mr. Leiner and his cadre seem to overlook. Mr. Leege was not a lawyer and 1927 only applies to lawyers. Secondly, one can't transfer, or a better word, *transpose* a final judgment against a corporation to an individual." Googol was going *law professor* on their asses.

He was able to continue a little longer. His logic was mesmerizing. "I've listened to Mr. Leiner's sensitive, nuanced argument this morning, and I've read all the transcripts in the litigation on this matter thus far. And, I can't help but borrow the late comedian and philosopher, George Carlin's routine on *stuff.*[91] I keep wondering, why are their proffers are proffers; and Mr. Leege's affidavits and citations to notable and generally accepted technological sources were merely allegations?"

"I fail to see the analogy to the comedian, George Carlin," the judge announced.

Ah, when a complex concept can be stated simply, it was art. How come their stuff is stuff and our stuff is shit? Well, the logic broke the camel's back and Leiner couldn't take it anymore. If Googol interrupted him, Leiner returned the attack.

"How is Mr. Gogolas even making this argument today, he hasn't been admitted to the bankruptcy bar, yet?" Leiner barked out. "He filed a notice of appearance but he has no sponsor."

"You need a sponsor. A member of the Bar who can vouch for your character," Judge Daryl announced. When he spoke he was again over-acting as a judge. In his mind, this was what a judge should say. Of course, Judge Daryl acted like one again, rather than take a moment and think about moving this case along – was he going to make a ruling?

"Perhaps, one of these gentlemen might do it just based upon my filing for today's matter," Dayna replied and pointed at the lawyers on the other side, since she couldn't sponsor Googol since they were co-counsel, pursuant to a local rule. There was collective laughter from the fee-eaters. No one volunteered.

A moment later, the man with the bow-tie lifted his head. Googol looked at him and then looked at me. He knew I was responsible for the man's presence just like I was responsible for Googol's presence in this Kangaroo court. It was the team stepping up again for one of its own, in the setting of Joseph's death – *Kushinagar.*[92] The distinguished gentlemen in the gallery rose with determination and confidence. He raised his hand in order to attract the judge's attention. "I will vouch for the character of this man." All heads turned toward the man – an *Obi wan*[93] of jurisprudence. But he was slightly out of place, which made this scene fantastical.

The judge's reactionary ball rolled too fast in bankruptcy court. The judge couldn't help himself. And made another comment like a judge. "And who are you?"

"John Paul Stevens and I vouch for this man. Graduated the first in his class from Northwestern Law. Jeffrey was one of the best law clerks I've ever had. He helped the Court tremendously in its opinion, both the majority and my own dissent, in *Celotex Corp. v. Edwards.*[94] I thought the bankruptcy courts didn't have such expansive jurisdiction as non-Article III judges, but as you know, the majority disagreed. Regardless, Jeffrey Gogolas is a Professor of law and technology at the Massachusetts Institute of Technology. He is a member in good standing of the Massachusetts and D.C. Bars. It is my honor to sponsor him in this limited proceeding to represent his departed friend's company."

"Justice Stevens?" That was the first remark from the judge that didn't seem preprogrammed. "It's a pleasure to have you here this morning. We're honored." There was a stir in the courtroom. A cameo appearance from a retired Justice of the Supreme Court of the United States can shift the dynamic in the courtroom abruptly. And how Googol would be treated going forward.

"Thank you, your Honor," Justice Stevens replied.

"I'm sure Mr. Conrad will sponsor Mr. Gogolas," Judge Daryl offered.

"Yes, your Honor. It would be my pleasure to stand by Justice Stevens and make this application," Mr. Conrad said.

Justice Stevens smiled. Googol smiled at his old mentor.

"You know, I was a Navy man myself, Judge – World War II," Justice Stevens remarked. He sure was a Navy man – the recipient of the Bronze Star for being a member of his own team responsible for code breaking the location of Japanese Admiral Yamamoto which led to his tracking and demise in 1943.

"Thank you for your service, sir." Judge Daryl said.

"Same to you. I'm sorry I was late. I had a heck of a time getting my cell phone into the courthouse," said to a chorus of laughter. "But I'll let you get back to your hearing." Justice Stevens replied. And Googol from that point forward was treated better. He and Dayna were given six weeks to get prepared for the next hearing. We would have the evidence ready and a plan.

My phone buzzed again. I glanced down at it and saw it was a text message – a message from Joseph. In that moment, that scintilla, my world was in equilibrium, I was normal again. I then gasped without breathing. I recoiled. My heart stopped then beat like it was struck by lightning. Joseph sent me a message before he died and scheduled it to be delivered after.

> *To my protector, I assume since you're getting this message you made it to the federal courthouse in Fort Lauderdale. The Wi-Fi triggered this message. Got your phone past the guards, I see.* :)
> *I know you're wondering why. I saw no other options. The way out was ending all the pain. I was sad and tired, GP. I couldn't recharge with sleep because I couldn't sleep. I was hungry with no appetite to fight, to eat, to live. I realized that I've contributed all my body could give.*
> *I know you, GP. I know you'll try and do something to avenge me. I know I cannot stop you. Do not be selfish. Do not respond disproportionately. Do not harm the*

innocent. Avenge my mission, not me. Avenge what I stood for.

My body couldn't do it, GP. You might not either. If you can't, within these parameters, then stop. If able, I will help you.

Please honor me and my life's work by not going off the ruby rails.

You and I don't believe in an after-life, but I think there's something more. I look forward seeing you there. In life, and in my death, I care about you. You made me better. You made me a better contributor to the world. Without equivocation, parameters, and no weasel words – I love you. You made my world a better place.

Even through great distance and time, in life, you were always my friend.

In the cloud,

Joseph

My eyes welled up again. My heart stopped and started again. In the moment, my brain accepted that I was getting a message from Joseph, my friend. Not unusual, until that moment ends when you remember that your closest friend was dead. I walked briskly out of the courtroom and ran toward the elevator. I just ran. Ran east to the end of Las Olas Boulevard, arrived at the beach, hit the sand and stopped. It was cliché, but I thought I would feel better if I dove into the ocean; but I didn't. At the end of my fugue, I cried out toward the horizon. I opened my cell phone and called a jet-broker at Fort Lauderdale Executive Airport. I made the decision – I was buying an airplane. It was all part of the plan and I felt much better.

It's Not Home without Joseph

Googol and I didn't make it back to Chicago for the actual burial on that Sunday. We didn't even know they were going to do a graveside service first. Mrs. Leege approached us and apologized as we entered the memorial service. My childhood's second mother hugged us both. She appeared struck by tragedy, but she warmly greeted us.

"It was Robert that insisted we bury Joseph the first possible day, according to Halacha.[95] There was no talking to him. He's out of his mind right now," Mrs. Leege said.

"We understand. Mr. Leege has his beliefs," I said. Googol nodded.

"No parents should have to bury a child," Googol said. Appropriate and thoughtful.

I never was big on ceremony, awards, citations, honors, weddings, bar-mitzvahs. Although, it was good to see some people – friends, team members. I saw Henry White, *mi viejo amigo.* Jeez, that FBI agent – Lefkel. Then I saw Leela and Chana were talking to each other. My heart dropped. Our eyes met. Chana looked the same, as I smiled through my sadness – beautiful. She smiled back and walked toward me.

I took a few steps toward her. I never lost eye contact. Chana kissed me slightly to the left of my lips and I feel in love all over again. Then we hugged. Too many amps of electricity ran through my body.

"I'm so sorry. This is so horrible. You two were so good together. I know you're so sad," Chana said. I nodded in agreement. It was so much raw energy, emotion in the room. I was beginning to feel sick in my stomach.

"How are you, Chana?"

"I'm doing all right. I'm going to miss Joseph, my favorite dreamer."

"Your life, Chana?"

Chana caught me up to speed on the personal life data points. She had three great children. She was still in Chicago living with her husband, who was a decent man. She didn't talk about him much. He seemed adequate. They visited Israel twice a year to see their families. But life was easier in America.

"I'm glad then. I want you to be happy." That was as emotional as I could get on the subject of her today. I couldn't calculate what the fallout would be if I said, "I still love you like it's 1987. It feels like the first day of college and I need you to hold my hand. You were my life, my motivation. I'd convert and be born again like Johnny Cash for you. I'd live in a garage in Palo Alto with a cat, if you were with me. I am amazing? Think of how amazing I could've been if you stayed with me."

"You, Greg? Girlfriend? Wife I haven't heard about?"

"Not yet."

Chana sat with me while the first few speakers at the memorial service spoke. She held my hand in her two hands for a moment before I was called to speak. When I was called, she released my hand and rubbed the top of my hand a few times for luck. I felt so bad about Joseph, and so good about her role of support. I took the stage to deliver the most painful remarks of my life.

We all knew Joseph or knew of him and his accomplishments. I guess I was asked to speak because I knew Joseph Lars since he was Joey. Through the years of a complicated relationship we were like an old married couple. We were married to ideas of great accomplishment, exploration, and loyalty. He looked out for all of us, but never very well for himself.

The Rabbi said Joseph's memorial is not a day for why, rather it is a day of who – who Joseph was and a celebration of who he was. But that isn't good enough for me and I imagine it isn't good enough for some of you.

I know who Joseph was. Leela, and Googol, TimBL and Joseph's sister, spoke about him and who he was. I was there for most of those times. I knew Joseph better than most. So this talk of who he was and what he stood for, offers me little comfort. For those of you who didn't know him as well, I hope it did offer some relief.

It's never just one thing, when a person takes his life. Joseph was in a lot of anguish from his undiagnosed hypersensitivities and the accompanying depression. He had a lot of emotional pain. He questioned everything, even the support from the people that loved him.

I didn't mention that Joseph probably couldn't call his father because it was Shabbat, (Friday night), and his dad wouldn't pick up. If Joseph had only waited, who knows?

Joseph was the gatekeeper of the public access, the transparent, and the private. He was the gatekeeper in the internet cloud, the new technology, and the struggle between convenience and protection. His thanks, his thanks was an indictment – a Scarlet letter, a curse of Cain. Not by a government, but by a private authority.

An authority that is not governed by a constitution. Old world thinkers. And the old world killed him. He wasn't allowed to run and hide from them either.

As Joseph walked closer to the gate, after being instrumental in creating and defending it, and what it stood for along the way, he met the proverbial two knights of the gate. One always told the truth, one that always lied. Joseph was allowed to ask one question in order to determine if safe passage to the other side was possible. Simple enough for a logician like Joseph.

What would the other knight say when asked, what would the other's answer be if I asked if there were safe passage beyond the gate? If it were safe, the truthful knight would tell you his counterpart (the liar) is going to tell you it is unsafe. The lying knight would say his counterpart (the truth teller) is going to say it was unsafe. Joseph therefore would conclude it is safe to proceed beyond the gate.

But what Joseph didn't know from his world where all things should be and can be as they ought to be, is that the voice stating the rules, lied, and the two knights didn't know whether the other was a liar or a truth teller. And there are no rules or ethics. No one is seeking what is best for all, only what is best for them. Joseph didn't die because he was alone or thought he was alone, he died of disappointment. He died because the optimism within him died. He felt no hope when confronted by people who were an ordinance lower than Vogons[96] *– the ignorant and the malicious for pay.*

He didn't think the world wanted to be a better place any longer. Just a place to impose world views upon the weaker. Rule through subjection. Might he be right?

But, our thing was to fight in the dark, be virtual, even if we had to yell up from the hole we fell through. But he always proclaimed: "We can do better." We lost a soldier and friend in the war against apathy, complacency, and evil. We should try harder to make things right in Joseph's memory.

I would take my own advice. I was going to make things better -- starting now. My brother was murdered and I failed to protect him. My blood oath – revenge against his killers. My eyes naturally glanced at the right people in the crowd: Leela, Googol, even GNU made it somehow, and Chana. There will be others. I even saw Henry nod.

At the end of the service, after I was tired looking through the pictures and talking to anyone and everyone, I looked at my phone again. It was another text from Joseph. My nerves were blown out from all of it. Chana came up from behind my shoulder.

"Who's that?" Chana said.

"It's from Joseph. It's the second one since he died."

"Oh my God." She read on: "Nice speech. All true, all true. (☺ PW Thetrusteeisunethical,^{whenIbecameLars}, plus mom's green dessert)." I knew everything but the dessert.

I had to go ask Mrs. Leege.

▪ ▪ ▪

I sat in the backseat not feeling like a Master of the Universe. I was being driven to my friend's parents' home in a suburb of Chicago. I hadn't been there in years. I just kept looking around the back seat of the limo I leased for the day. Googol, Leela, Chana, GNU, and Henry – this was fun, in some strange way. But, I was returning to the scene of the crime without my partner in crime. My phone was buzzing. I forgot to turn the ringer back on. Afraid to look, it could be Joseph again. I was sure as soon as I ping the Leege family Wi-Fi, a new message of some sort will come. At this moment, right here, right now – forever on the line of time, we were together again, and it felt right.

"Hello," I said into the receiver.

"Good afternoon, Mr. Portent. It's Agent Lefkel, from the FBI. You remember me from Boston, right? You saw me at the memorial service."

"Yes, sir." I replied.

"I'm sorry about, Joseph. I know you two were close. He was a smart and eager kid. He always had good intentions. I enjoyed getting to know him," he said.

"You got to know him?" There was no answer. Was there more than just this bankruptcy bullshit with Madoff, Dreier and the rest of those assholes? Don't tell me Joseph was tangling with the feds at the same time as he was dealing with the appointed trustees of the bankruptcy world. Lefkel wasn't answering, but I'd get it out of him. "How can I help you, sir?"

"Pay attention carefully," Lefkel said in a soft voice. "I know you're not in the greatest state of mind. This is a courtesy call. I'm trying to help you," he said. "Why didn't the government apply for a search warrant or serve a subpoena for any the data on *Qpredictor* if there were all these Ponzi schemers' data held on it?"

"What do you mean?" I asked.

"Think about it. You're one of the smartest people I know." I took a moment quietly. I used my mind's eye to zoom in and zoom out on what he was saying.

"Ah, sorry, I haven't been sleeping well."

"I understand. Good luck and goodbye." He hung up.

Why didn't the government serve a search warrant or a subpoena on Joseph? Because the government didn't want to. Why would the government not want to? It wouldn't be in its interest to know? Or, the government already had what it needed. How would the government already have what it needed? Somebody gave the government the data it needed – and maybe something more.

▪ ▪ ▪

Chana sat across from me and held up her phone. Her eyes began to well up with tears. It was a message from Joseph.

"He wanted all of us to be together when we read it," she said. And so she summarized.

Joseph complained he wasn't sleeping. Nothing was fun anymore. He couldn't go back to Leela but he wished he could. He could only work on one thing: taking *Qpredictor* to its final form beyond whole life management – post life management.

No one knew what Joseph was talking about. He ranted about immortality and singularity;[97] and the ability to live on but not in human form. Joseph described obtaining the cyanide and injecting a honey crisp apple with the cyanide and dying Turing style. Chana read the remainder of the message out loud.

We won. The supreme version of Qpredictor is complete. I'm free to leave this world without consequence. If I'm wrong, I'll be without pain. If I'm right, the data the AI has about me will capture my consciousness and I will live on. I will be alive.

We arrived at the Leege's home. We all just sat in the limousine. I made sure the intercom to the driver was off and the divider between the driver and us was closed.

"What does any of that mean?" Henry asked. We all looked at each other and we were too polite to say Joseph went crazy. Sad and crazy – Joseph didn't make any sense to them. It all made sense to me. I was resolute to punish all of the people who killed Joseph.

"I'm embarking on an operation. I've been thinking about it since I learned Joseph died. It will cost me a lot time and money. An irrational amount of resources. I will rely on you, my friends, to help me not roll off the ruby rails. I'm asking for your help. I feel like I failed Joseph. I admit it. I got lost in my own ego. But, I'm going to fix it." There was a collective knowing smile.

"What do you need us to do?" Leela asked.

"Leela, you need to help me run things. I've got a plan. And Henry – Henry, Enrique, *mi amigo,* we're going to be doing something you've always wanted to show your father you can do for years."

"What's that?" Henry asked.

"Run your own bank, of course," I said.

It's the Government; it was really there to help.

As I walked up the same gray courthouse steps, I suffered from the dread of returning. The dread continued entering the same courtroom as before. I sat in the back and wore the same muted colored dark suit, so I wouldn't be noticed. I came in empty handed. I wondered if there were any more Wi-Fi pings coming from Joseph. Other lawyers and people argued their Chapter 7 personal bankruptcy process milled their way into the courtroom. This also was good for blending. I watched Christian Leiner and some of his friends. I didn't want him to think I was cheering for the other side. If Leiner remembered me, well then, I was just here doing research about attorneys I wanted to hire. Based upon my limited observation of him and stereotyping most lawyers, it would be a wonderful ego massage to say he won out of all the lawyers I saw in this matter, he was the most aggressive.

There have been many times when I've been in intense conversations with people and I meticulously reviewed transcripts of prior conversations in my head, only to conclude and even at times say, "If this were a drug deal, I'd shoot you in the head right about now." The problem was discerning between intended deception by the game-player and just bad memory formation, confabulation, and fabrication. Memory was liquid and not like a recording. Mine was a little more like a recording and it helped me determine what was true, but also required me to understand that another person's memory wasn't. And, that was a hard thing for me.

Leiner and his toady from the last hearing were speaking in low tones. He sat next to one of the trustees, Harvey Gale, a man in his seventies referred to in a news article online as a "crusty" former judge.

Gale was a judge in the seventies for about three years and has milked the title ever since - once a judge always called "judge." You would think that a man of his age would be less about the money and more about the legacy – an honorable one. But he continued to be "crusty." I had reviewed the transcripts. No doubt he and Judge Daryl Daryl had played golf together for years. But there was no excuse for the sloppy testimony he gave in other proceedings in this bankruptcy case. The lawyer we called, Mr. Pong, the creditors' committee lawyer impeached this former judge five times. They were written off as mistakes, but on his best day the errors were sloppy; in the worst light they were self-serving lies.

Saul Graf graced the court with his presence at this hearing. I loved this guy's biography. He was appointed by this bankruptcy court to represent the trustee and his firm has made tens of millions thus far. He was the originator of the legal business – the cases.[98] He exercised bright and early in the morning and didn't take a day off. Good for him – he knew what was important. I was glad they were both here. Somehow, somewhere, these guys had to account. Maybe it was today, here in this courtroom, but I remained skeptical.

I couldn't hear what Leiner, the toady, Gayle, and Graf were saying. I saw Googol and Dayna Sohler walk in together. Dayna followed me with her eyes as I walked in. I looked down at the floor to remind her not to act like she knew me. Googol had a special way of staring off into space, even though he was a linear thinker, try as he might to be on the spectrum.

"Justice Sotomayor isn't showing up today, is she? I hear her mother lives in town," Leiner directed at Googol. Leiner tapped Graf for approval and to laugh at his own joke. Googol and Dayna took his seat at the table on the other side of the courtroom.

"I don't know," Googol answered as if it were possible.

Why was I here in court again? Agreed, it was a risk merely being here. I might be remembered. But, I have to supervise. I needed to see this all go down as it happens. Perhaps I might receive another communication from Joseph. Another reason, I didn't want the story relayed to me by a transcript or Googol and Dayna. I learned when I was present. I needed to learn about Leiner and Graf, watching them in their natural habitat was instructive.

In court, no stunts today – just hardcore maneuvering to win. Our strategy was move to block. It was a substantive strategy in this instance. We have real arguments. The points this consortium of trustees leveled against Joseph was "bad people did bad things" and "we think Joseph helped these bad people." Of course that was like saying all these bad people used the mail to do bad things, therefore the postmaster general was bad. Silly? Yes, but when it comes to technology, some people believe it's magic. When people believe in magic, they get scared. But how can code be magic, it was computer code, and computer code was transparent – the process, open and clear. What happened was clear.

I heard the courtroom door open again and I turn to see who was coming in. A thin, tall man with curly greying hair and spectacles walked in holding a folder. He appeared a little disoriented. His head turned side to side as if he was trying to determine if this is a room he had been in before. A courtroom it seemed. Looked like a federal courtroom. Leiner seemed all excited to see this guy. The man did not reciprocate Leiner's excitement. The man was a lawyer from the United States Attorney's Office. After small talk he took a seat in the front row. Then more lawyers started to file into the courtroom. More $840 an hour lawyers. They sat in the front row too. Hopefully, these were the lawyers we've been waiting for.

"All rise! The Bankruptcy Court for the Southern District of Florida is now in session. Judge Daryl Daryl presiding."

"Be seated. We'll take the agreed matters on the docket first. Then we'll get into the hearing on the consolidated Ponzi matters and *Qpredictor.*" The courtroom was cleared one lawyer and person at a time until there were no other matters left to handle. The judge couldn't avoid the inevitable issues any longer.

"On the Ponzi matters, will the parties identify themselves," the judge ordered.

Leiner strode up to the podium. The other lawyers formed a line behind him.

"Chris Leiner along with my partner, Saul Graf on behalf of the lead trustee Harvey Gale, who is present in the courtroom today, as well the other consolidated trustees."

"Good morning, Mr. Gale," the judge said.

"Jeffrey Gogolas and Dayna Sohler on behalf of the estate of Joseph Lars Leege and MetaD, Inc. the holder and owner of *Qpredictor*." I wondered where was their "good morning."

"Good morning, I'm Assistant United States Attorney Richard Bernstein on behalf of the Army, Air Force, and Navy," AUSA Bernstein said as he looked around like he'd never been in a bankruptcy courtroom before.

"Hold on, the government filed an appearance in this case on behalf of the Armed Forces?" Judge Daryl asked. He feverishly looked around his desk and moved some papers. Then he looked up at a computer screen on his bench.

"Yes. And a memorandum on the government's position to quash[99] the trustees' subpoena," the AUSA said. "The trustee should not have the power to review the electronic documents it demanded from Mr. Leege's entities holding some very confidential data of the Armed Forces."

The judge began looking at the online docket in the case and saw that a notice of appearance was filed by the United States Attorney's Office. "You filed your notice yesterday. In this Court, the local bankruptcy rules require all pleadings filed two days before a scheduled hearing."

"This is my first time in bankruptcy court, judge. The architecture is similar, but I'm usually haled into a different kind of court. The Armed Forces recently received word that its top secret data stored on the *Qpredictor* system is being subpoenaed by private lawyers in a bankruptcy case. My email has been pinging nonstop since yesterday from various other government agencies, including the Federal Bureau of Investigation and the United States Secret Service that data they don't even want to tell me about is on the system."

"Where the hell has the government been for the last two-years?" Judge Daryl demanded.

"Frankly, Judge, we didn't think the Court would even entertain a subpoena asking for essentially everything. Seemed overbroad on its face, and the government was not sufficiently put on notice that a bankruptcy court in Florida would be seeking data held on a system that is essential to national security. If the government has to, we'll present evidence in a closed hearing outside the presence of the trustee, how the disclosure by, or well, what would've been disclosure by Mr. Leege and now his estate, would violate the Espionage Act among other federal criminal statutes, even pursuant to a subpoena." Silence enveloped the courtroom. Two young men wearing Class A Navy uniforms sat off to the left staring intensely straight.

"And Joseph Lars Leege and *MetaD*, Inc. were held in contempt for failing to turn over this data," Googol stood up and announced.

"I ... well hold on," Judge Daryl said. "Let's just get through the appearances and then we'll get into this."

AUSA Bernstein sat down. Behind him was a lawyer from British Telecom. "We filed our objection as well as for twelve of our subsidiaries, to the original subpoena two days ago, we had late notice too."

"All right," the judge said.

"Good morning, Judge. Shelley Madison on behalf of Walt Disney Company. We filed our objection as well last week." It became clear that GNU handled the data search very well and notified everyone and anyone that their stuff (not their shit) was on *Qpredictor* and they may want to come out from under their rock and say something.

"Good morning, Judge. Fergus David on behalf of a confidential consortium of consolidated parties seeking to keep their proprietary data private and secure." Sounded like porn.

This was the first time I've seen the judge look up and connect with Googol and Dayna. The announcement of counsels' appearance was enough for victory. There was a powerful majority of powerful forces united against this "give us all your shit" movement. We'll search through your data. Trust us, we're here to help.

"But we don't want to look through the Armed Forces and everyone's data," Leiner said. "The trustees believe we should hold the data." This argument was like a kid saying he just wants to pet the puppy, not hold the puppy. Even Judge Daryl knew what was coming from everyone on the other side of the table. "Joseph Leege has been hiding this data that is critical to a complete investigation of the respective Ponzi schemes across the country."

"Does Mr. Leiner have an example of this?" Googol asked.

"Uh, yes, don't speak out of turn, Mr. Gogolas. But, do you have an example of any wrongdoing here?" Judge Daryl asked.

"We don't know what we don't know." Leiner responded.

"Have you received some specific Ponzi data?" The judge asked. "What did you find thus far?"

"It's an ongoing process… The trustees are working diligently to… "

"So, nothing," the judge concluded. "Ms. Sohler?"

Dayna Sohler spoke on Joseph's behalf. She was poised and deliberate. She explained succinctly that Joseph's work was not a Ponzi support network. Data was stored on platforms and people who had nothing to do with any of the Ponzi schemes described have their data stored on *Qpredictor.* "Mr. Leege wasn't motivated by money – only what he could do to benefit mankind." She explained over three thousand people showed up to his memorial service in Chicago. The service was video streamed across the world. "It's time to stop attacking him and his estate. Counsel has failed to demonstrate after two years one instance where Mr. Leege assisted anyone of the Ponzi schemers. That they even met him. That they even met each other." She explained the system Joseph created was free to the world. It was called "open source."[100] "He offered full access to his own data on the *Qpredictor* system so that the trustee would know Joseph Leege had nothing to hide."

But as far as people's data on the open source platform was concerned, "We have to be concerned that very serious breaches in privacy of people who have no idea that their data is on *Qpredictor* will be turned over to absolute strangers. No doubt the trustee and his minions thought they were well intentioned. But the trustees have no right to it. Depending on whose data, it might be a crime or an unlawful disclosure of intellectual property that companies have spent millions of dollars to create, preserve, and protect."

Then the line of lawyers who represented the users who used Joseph's platform spoke up. Disney, eBay, British Telecom, Boeing, and other contractors for the Armed Forces who had top secret clearance and didn't know if they were permitted to disclose the top secret data if they and their companies could be charged with crimes relating to espionage or other scary national security laws.

The judge then said: "I'm going to rule as follows. I don't need to hear your rebuttal, Mr. Leiner." Leiner appeared miffed. "I'm going to issue a comfort Order." What's a comfort Order? Comes with fried chicken and taters? Side of pie? Whatever it was it sounded good. "The objecting parties today will not have their data transferred to the trustees. Any request for specific data affecting these objecting parties will be noticed before the subpoena issues and I'll review it. Professor Googol, you oversee that the corporation holding *Qpredictor* safeguards the data."

"Like a gatekeeper, judge," Googol said.

The judge continued. "Additionally, the trustees will make a list of what it has received from *MetaD* and then make a list of what the trustees still think their entitled to. Professor Googol, see to the Order, I'll review it in chambers and then sign it. We're adjourned."

▪ ▪ ▪

I left the courtroom first. Dana and Googol walked out moments later, zigzagging down narrow hallways toward the exit, Googol just stopped in a corner off to the side where we were not seen. He stared intensely in my eyes.

"So, you got the U.S. Armed Forces, Disney, British Telecom, a consortium of objectors to step up and do in one day what Joseph wasn't able to do in two years?" Googol said.

"Yeah, it's really sad," I answered.

"We had to debunk the conclusion that only bad people used *Qp*, it's only natural that you'd have GNU do the search. But this was fast even for him – really fast. Any help I don't know about?"

"The team is the team. You know who's on the team," I answered.

"I also know you, Greg." There was a long pause. I didn't break the stare. "What's avocado pudding? I couldn't get anything to work with that passcode."

"Who told you about the password, *avocado pudding*?" I asked.

"I'm assuming it was part of a password communicated to you from….? Did you find something that belonged to Joseph?"

"It's part of a password string," I said.

"To what?. . . . I'm so close." I could sense Googol was close to the answer. "I know the team; Joseph is on the team. He's left you messages. You got a password to a database that listed the users of *Qp?*"

"Not quite," I said. He was going to solve the puzzle in a few moments – he was close. Dayna just stared. She didn't quite follow what we were talking about. She stopped glowing from the victory. The mood was tense. Then Googol's eyes lit up.

"He did it. Joseph finally did it. He's got an Xpert system?[101]

"More than just an Xpert system. Bots that search and induce, review, and analysis of communication, human level artificial intelligence and super level. All of it – AI as Joseph.

"You found the password to Joseph's artificial intelligence?"

"I found the password to Joseph's artificial intelligence. He pinged me a text off the Wi-Fi when we came to court the first time," I responded.

"Joseph sent you a text when you walked into the courthouse?" Dayna asked. "How can he do that? He wrote it before he died," she figured.

"When did you get the string passcode to the Xpert system?"

"In Chicago. As soon as I got off the plane. It was triggered by GPS."

"Like greetings, Professor Falken?"[102] Googol said.

I nodded. "And the thumb drive Dayna gave me from Joseph. It was a key to opening the artificial intelligence."

"Awesome. How is it?" Googol asked with wonderment.

"It's amazing. Joseph named it JLL. It is AI and Joseph."

"What? Wait a second," Dayna was confused. "You can have conversations with a computer artificial intelligence that talks to you like Joseph?"

I nodded.

"How was he able to do that?" She asked.

"How did Joseph upload his brain into a computer? I don't know exactly. To do this, he would've needed three technologies to be good enough. I didn't think any of them were advanced enough. First, he needed lots of cheap, fast, parallel computers. Second, he needed to scan individual human brains in fine spatial and chemical detail, to see exactly what cells were where, connected to what, and of what type. Third, he needed computer models of how each kind of brain cell works – taking input signals, changing interval state and sending output signals. I wish I could tell you how he did it. All I can tell you is, he did," I said, giving her the short answer.

"I'm going to have to examine this. I can't believe he finally did it. Amazing." Googol said.

"I can't let you communicate right away. I have to work to with it," I said.

"I'm sure the system can allow the both of us to work with it at the same time. This isn't human. He's escaped the limits of humanness. He can talk to us both at the same time and have different conversations."

"Stop. Not right away," I said. "Not right away. I've got figure out how to execute my plan." But as I thought about it, I already assigned humanity to the AI of Joseph, and I thought I was being selfish. This AI should be for me.

After leaving the gray federal courthouse, I walked across Broward Boulevard south to Las Olas. I saw Henry standing with another guy.

"Say hello to my little cousin, Michael," Henry said.

"*Hola*, Miguel," I said.

"We're not a retail bank, so we're going to be on three floors of this building," Henry said with confidence. "I said we are a technology company and the Mayor gave us a break on taxes. We just closed on our second location on Brickell in Miami. The bank will pay rent to the corporation that is leasing the spaces."

"Right. We're not advertising either. This is private stuff," I said.

"Do you know what you're going to call the bank?" Michael asked.

I did. Artificial intelligence permits computers to think like humans, but escapes the limits of human biology. A computer doesn't eat, drink, or sleep. It can think faster than humans. I have a computer that escaped the limitations of a human – a self-repairing, self-thinking sentient entity. The team will support and defend this entity – JLL. All these years, Joseph worked on this thing, the others on the team unwittingly assisted. We created our own God – our own wrathful revenge machine. If we task this God to create, manage, and recruit investors in a Ponzi scheme, you know what we'd call that Ponzi scheme?

"Yes, I do. It's called G-D Bank – God's Bank." And I'm devoutly committed to getting my revenge.

Joshua Fought the Battle of Jericho, and the walls came tumbling down

I was in the middle of the last unincorporated section of Broward County, Florida in a forsaken district – an unloved step child. No township or city wished to make it part of its own because there wasn't a significant tax base. The assumption was it was home to crime, poverty, and working folk trying to get by. The area was home to rib joints and a bus station to get out of town (or get dumped off), and more churches per capita. I had business at one of these churches this morning. I needed to meet with the Reverend this Sunday morning.

The mechanism of action for any good Ponzi scheme was a bank – bankers within the bank approving or creating reports that misled others. Prestigious banks sell their prestige to the schemes perfectly. Get caught, pay a fine, a fee – the cost of doing business, and restructure or expand. Maybe one or two employees go to jail. But the bank lived on. But, I've done the research, and to run a Ponzi scheme I needed a solid bank behind it.

It took about a year to start a bank because you need regulatory authority. I couldn't wait that long. And, if I wanted to do what I was doing, I needed to get the Federal Deposit Insurance Corporation certificate right away and not wait the time it usually took. So, I was going to buy one. And the person who had a FDIC certificate for sale was this guy – Reverend Booker T. Washington.

It was Sunday and I was going to church, the *Tabernacle* church. It got nicknamed "Tab-e'r-nahcle." instead of Tabernacle. I was in my beater car this morning, which served as an under the radar vehicle. I didn't want to draw more attention to myself than I was just by being me.

Pulling up in a convertible SL 550 Mercedes, would send the wrong message. No one needed to know why I was here except for one man. So, I parked my black Chevy Cruz and put on my suit jacket. Dressed to impress. Dress for the job you want, but don't try and be someone else. This wasn't a costume party. I would wear a suit, so I wore a suit. No wild colors, just a plain blue pinstripe suit with a white shirt and a red tie.

Walking through the church doors and the only other stranger was the deputy sheriff standing in the back who was meant to protect the offering plate. It was as expected. Everyone dressed up – women wearing big hats, fans waved the breeze across their faces. Intermittent and plenty of *amens*, could be heard in response to the preaching; great preaching with rhythm and rhyme from the Reverend, which culminated in a chorus of song.

Joshua fought the battle of Jericho and the Walls came Tumbling down! Loved that spiritual. Despite my atheism, those Negro spirituals jammed. The Reverend Booker T. Washington was a real showman. His outfit made Rip Taylor look like IBM middle management. A large minister-man, the Reverend wore an outlandish monogrammed purple suit. The monogram was on the lapel of this suit. He had cuff-links as big as flying saucers, and in the middle of the links it said, JESUS on the right and SAVES on the left one. I made quick eye contact with Reverend Washington. While feet were stomping, hands were waving behind him.

The crowd was good and warmed up. The Reverend's gestures were precise and impeccable. I couldn't help feeling moved, by the tone rising into impressive gesticulations. He dove straight into it.

"Proverbs 28:20 says, a faithful man will be richly blessed, but eager to get rich will not go unpunished." The double-negative and the equivocating definition of the word *rich* made me wonder about other meanings for a moment, but I stayed with him. "We can't expect to make a fortune overnight. We must earn, with Jesus's love, day by day. Every day." All right, every day. I won't miss a day. He talked some more and it was more about the rhythm and the ride in his voice than what he was actually stating. There was just agreement in the air. I could learn a lot from this man. He quoted Second Corinthians, made the case to work hard and then contribute to the church. Then, "Honor the Lord with your wealth, with the first fruits of all your crops; then your barns will be filled to overflowing, and your vats will brim over with new wine."[103]

Then, the Reverend disappeared from the stage. Another hymn broke out. The choir singing, swaying, and clapping in perfect time, I began to wonder where he went. The fervor seemed to be building in the congregation. "Watch this," the sheriff's deputy leaned over to me and said. What was I watching? All of a sudden, a costume change. *Bam,* curtains opened a second floor was exposed to the congregation. Reverend Washington was in a white bathing suit – a one-piece. Splash! There was a swimming pool on the second floor of the church and a parishioner just went for his first dunk –Baptism! Right there. *Hit me,* James Brown. What the *dealio!* I might have actually said that out loud because congregants turned around and nodded at me like they understood. *Shazam.* Standing, waving, hooting and howling. I caught the spirit.

After the church cleared out I stayed to talk with Reverend Washington.

"It's too bad the Sheriff couldn't join us this morning," the Reverend said to the deputy who was standing by the door. "Maybe next week we'll be able to invite him back." The deputy nodded shook Reverend Washington's hand. There seemed something politically hidden in those remarks. The Reverend cultivated and supplied the votes in the pews. The deputy nodded.

Reverend Washington was back in his original show suit. He was congruent with the suit. We shook hands. To demonstrate how committed I was to the scheme, I changed my name. This was the first time trying it out. I wanted no connection to Gregory Portnoy. So, I legally changed my name.

"Reverend Washington, I'm Gregory Portent. Pleasure. That was quite a show."

"Thank you, young man. When the spirit hits me, I just let it flow," he said.

"Well, let's flow into a conversation about banks," I said.

"Well, I had a vision that this church should have a bank. I'm not really sure I want to sell the certificate." The FDIC certificate was like an alcohol license for a bar – it was required before you can sell liquor.

We walked toward the stage. It was a great background for the conversation. I could see why he wanted us to walk towards it. That was one big Jesus on the crucifix. In his worldly context, that big Jesus should intimidate me. In my world, a world of pure realism, however, I wondered why everyone didn't recoil from a very graphic image of a man being tortured.

"Do you really want to run a bank, Reverend?"

"I might."

"And for the right price, you might sell," I said with a smile.

"I might. I'm a man of God, but there's business. I wanted it to be God's bank. That was my vision," he said with some sense of lost opportunity.

"I was thinking the same thing," I said with a knowing smile.

The Reverend laughed and said, "What you mean?"

"You've heard of TD bank? . . . You ever hear of Gibraltar bank? . . . Well, let me introduce you to G-D bank. God's bank." I smiled some more. The Reverend smiled back.

The Reverend was a good business man. I bought the bank certificate for $100,000 and a promise for a position on the board. He could oversee low interest loans in the community. I would make sure of it. "We'll call it 'Reverend Washington loans.'" What was tricky here was the fact that I was not trying to create victims, I was zeroing in on my targets.

My Favorite Hooker

Think of it like one of those reality dating shows. I arrived at one of the over-styled restaurants in a Brickell hotel in Miami. The place to be seen – another establishment where they also ask if you've ever experienced dining with us before. The chandeliers were twisted and twirled colorful glass bulbs, and a full spectacular view of the Miami River. The ones where you still have to pay thirty-dollars to valet, even with parking validation.

Seeing myself in the mirror behind the bar, I didn't recognize myself in the loud colored tie Leela suggested I wear. Dress to be remembered. Dress like the Emperor. Looking a tad below the flash of Reverend Booker T. Washington, I turned away from the image of myself and stared toward the front of the bar. My first sip of club soda and she appeared – Taylor Anderson. There was a friend standing by the bar she brought for backup. I hadn't drunk alcohol since Joseph's memorial in the Irish Bar. Before that, it might have been a year. Don't fuck with the mechanism – my brain. It was time to play the role of Ponzi schemer in need of a Ponzi wife.

Taylor was tall and pale skinned; her curly locks – blond, her sunglasses still resting on her face as she said her first words. "Earth to Gregory," she leaned in and kissed my cheek. The physical level of attraction was good – believable. I liked her, even though I was usually not attracted to blondes. It'll appear that there was something romantic and sexual between us.

"Hi, I'm Greg." I returned the kiss.

"This is my friend, Jessica. I told her to keep an eye on me from a distance," Taylor said.

"To make sure you're not an axe-murderer." Jessica said.

"I am one. But I kill the best friend first so we have a common sadness that brings us together," I said. Taylor laughed – Jessica didn't.

"I don't get it," Jessica replied. "What's so funny?"

I smiled. "What can I get you, ladies?" They both ordered cosmos.

"You both can't be Carrie Bradshaw, you know." The sequel to the *Sex in the City* movie was meant to be released soon.

Taylor smiled again. "I'm more of a Samantha."

How forward, I thought and then smiled. A few sips of her drink and Jessica retreated back to the bar leaving Taylor and I by ourselves. I quickly concluded Taylor was what I was looking for. I stared into Taylor's eyes and we toasted glasses together.

We had participated in small talk. I determined she was a Myers Briggs type ESFP.[104] Extroverted, an entertainer. She soaked up the spotlight. Perfectly opposite. Perfect magic. Drinks turned into dinner. She had about a 120 IQ.[105] She knew a little about a lot of topics but couldn't go deep with any of them, which was fine, she wouldn't have to. She ate barely anything – a small row of sushi.

I asked penetrating questions. I explained banking and what I hoped to accomplish – the cover story. She asked questions of her own. This was a negotiation that will lead to a transaction. Business terms applied to this relationship that was not romantic. The conversation went well enough that she was willing to come back to my home. "You should get a little condo on Miami Beach," Taylor said. "A weekend place?" I replied, "Just got to town. Maybe I will."

My home in Fort Lauderdale appeared lived in. Leela was in charge of "buying" the house and making sure it was furnished. I invited Taylor in. We looked around together. I poured her another drink. I didn't know how to make a Cosmo, so we switched to well-balanced Bordeaux. We made it into my living room. The room was flashier than I liked. The whole damned house was flashier than I like, but Leela knew best.

"It isn't Vegas, but it's pretty spruced up, huh?" I asked.

"No, it's better than Vegas. I love it," Taylor said.

"So, we get along." Handing her a glass of wine.

"Yes, I think we do," Taylor replied. "What's with Leela?"

"What do you mean?"

"She really only *works* for you?"

"She really only works for me. We've been friends for a long time."

"I know you're smart enough to catch on about my past. But you expect me to believe you don't use Leela as your own little sex toy when you're having an off night at the clubs? I mean she's beautiful, Pakistani..."

"Indian. And, I never slept with Leela."

"If she's so wonderful then why not have her be everything to you? She's beautiful and smart. Why does sex have to disrupt? Why can't sex enhance the relationship?" She asked.

"Does sex enhance, Taylor?"

"No, it complicates." she answered.

"I know it's hard to understand. But, here's a level you may understand. She was my best friend's girlfriend, and I'll always see her like that, even though they're not together anymore," I offered.

"Joseph?"

Startled, I responded, "Yes."

"You wrote me about him, remember?" Taylor replied. Yes, I did know that Leela was writing to Taylor as "Gregory."

"What do you want from me, Gregory Portent? If that's your real name."

"You ever see *Pretty Woman*?"[106]

"Only my favorite movie ever. Next to *Love Actually* and *Titanic*." Okay. Well if she played Julia Roberts well enough we can actually avoid the fate of the Titanic.

"You know I'm starting a private investment bank. I need a woman who can help me make it grow – no romantic hassles. I need a certain type of friend in this part of my life. Someone who can help me appear softer or stronger on social occasions. Someone who makes me appear to have it all together," I said sincerely.

"Sounds like you want a public relations agent," she answered.

"No, I need you to play my girlfriend and eventually my wife. I'm a computer guy by nature. I was raised as a programmer. I'm literal. I want you to enjoy your job."

"But it's like I'm an employee."

"It can grow into a partnership," I said.

"Full partner?" Taylor asked. I was impressed that she asked such a question.

I explained to her how I picked her. Leela had helped me select her out of thousands. I did not dare mention JLL or artificial intelligence. She wondered about how her sanitized online profile made her standout among others for my proposition. The computer went beyond your profile, if you asked it to broaden the background search.

"Speaking of your background, what happened in Las Vegas?" I asked.

"The short version is, I became friends with a group of flight attendants, who had layovers in Vegas and L.A. and I would hire them to go out on dates with guys that knew me."

I laughed out loud and admired her ingenuity.

"I know," she said half embarrassed. "Then the operation got a little out of control. Too many flight attendants wanted the Vegas – LA route. We got caught after a couple of years when two girls showed for one date, and none for the other. The one that got the no show called the cops. They all got fired from the airlines." She implored me not to laugh.

"I have only one important question. What computer software service did you use to manage this project of yours?"

Taylor thought for a moment and then announced, "*Outlook*."[107]

I nodded, and said, "You should've gone to jail just for that." We laughed together.

Taylor grew up in Bakersfield, California. She had pictures of her mother on social media but not her father. She explained her father was dead to her; left her and her mother with debt when she was eight. Never saw him again. It took another man to save her and her mother. She mentioned that he managed to get himself busted in the savings and loan scandal of 1980s.

As the hour grew late, I told her to stay over; presented her with her own room and drawers full of oversized T-shirts and slippers. She said, "Okay." We'd talk more in the morning.

▪ ▪ ▪

I walked into the kitchen, the smell of coffee said morning. Leela had let herself in the house early and she and Taylor were talking to each other. That seemed like a good thing.

"Good morning, ladies," I said.

A duet of hello signified that they were both happy.

"Frittata?" Leela asked.

"Sure."

"You up all night?"

"Yep." I was up all night with JLL. I integrated all the emails, communications, Google searches, every database of every computer that Joseph and I ever touched. And, I'm as close as I think I'd ever be. It felt like I had conversations that I might have had with Joseph. He gave me the gift of himself by leaving a database of his writings, colloquialisms, and goals. I liked the gift. His ethics and personality seem in line. Because AI is autodidactic, it will continue to learn more and more on its own. JLL will continue to grow. The results of the tasks to learn about my plans for the bank and my life for the next few years will be mapped out by day's end. Think about it, the brain power of my old friend, with my willingness. Am I afraid that Joseph may not really know what and why I'm doing what I'm doing? That his ethics might interfere with mine? Why would it be any difference in AI than it was when he was alive as a human? Now, we were limitless.

"Whoa, could this be real? Some corporation named *Rebolious Q* just wired fifty-thousand dollars into my bank account. I just got an email." Taylor said as she looked up from her cell phone.

Leela said, "It's real."

"What's this for?" Taylor asked. I said, "What we talked about last night."

"What's my rate?"

"Fifty thousand a month with perks. I need you to move in by the end of the week," I replied.

Hired. Taylor was five-ten, six-feet in heels. Of course, she was always wearing heels. She liked looking down on men for whom she had little respect, and at six feet, she was taller than most men. From an objective perspective, an honest hooker was an honest business woman. Since I had a bigger picture, a larger goal. Her contract to be my wife. Taylor was a Godsend. I needed her for – well, I wasn't sure how long. Our deal was our deal and she was and will be very well recompensed. And hey, I genuinely liked her. "I will," Taylor answered. We had a contract. We would "date," we would get "engaged," and then we'd "marry." She would be my perfect Ponzi partner. No romantic hassles. Not a full partner, but I respected her and I would always be looking out for her best interest. It just wasn't a relationship made in love.

Bobby A, my newest employee walked in. He dressed in a suit, no tie. I wanted him to look like a valet or a chauffeur. But he was a large human with a crew-cut hairstyle. He was the kind of guy who would shape his eyebrows with a street-utility knife. He poured himself a cup of coffee, dropped a load of sugar in it, and sat down. He nodded to Taylor, who smiled and waved back to him.

"This is Bobby," I said. "He'll take you home or wherever you want to go."

She thought for a moment. "Can I go shopping?"

"You can go wherever you want. You're even welcome to stay here. But Leela and I have a meeting to go to."

"Oh."

"Really, Bobby will escort you. Have fun," I said.

"Great. I have $50k burning a hole in my pocket."

"And be back for tonight's event. It's very important," I said.

She smiled. "I will." As I turned to walk out of the house with Leela, Taylor said, "Hey, Greg? Thanks for believing in me."

I replied. "Sure thing, kiddo."

Innovative Legal Solutions

The next step in the mission was to hire the lawyers. It was fascinating that lawyers have to take an oath to be civil. In plain English, it was an oath not to be an asshole. And this wasn't something that the early lawyers figured or predicted? No, this was something that lawyers had to discover and change when they realized as a group they were being assholes. Many states had to actually revise their admission oaths and have these new lawyers swear: 'I'll be professional and civil.' This may be difficult, particularly when we think we were already dealing with assholes that have attacked us; but, I'm not speaking as a lawyer, I'm speaking as a client; still, the game ultimately was not in the courtroom. As a lawyer, lawyers have to perform for their clients– be aggressive; be tough. Other lawyers will let bad things happen to you, but I won't. I'm better. Every client finds his lawyer. That was why you can see a schmuck representing his schmuck client. It was dangerous for the client in the end. There were exceptions. But those exceptions prove the rule. In business, the game was part in court, and it was never over until you were dead. I thought about this because the bank needed lawyers. Lawyers to form the bank, protect the bank from regulation, and defend the bank in any lawsuits. This decision was important, but to me it was preordained. But more importantly, this was my first conversation with JLL about my scheme. Why I wanted to create it; and why he, or *it* will help me manage the scheme.

JLL:*Why do you want to do this?*
GP:*Because I feel horrible and guilty.*

JLL:*GP, you gave me permission to read your communications. And you know I know you flame out when you lose someone you love in your life. How long do you think it will take me to figure out what you're doing when I already know why you're doing it?*

GP:*Will you just help me?*

Two seconds passed.

JLL:*GP, I just figured out what you are doing.*

GP:*Just help me, Joseph.*

JLL:*I am going to model your plans all the time and every day. If it becomes statistically likely that you are going to hurt someone we care about or somebody innocent, I will not only stop helping you, I will work against you. And call me, JLL.*

A moment passed and I thought carefully about this.

GP:*Now you're a tough guy. ☺ I'm prepared for that.*

JLL:*I know it is not your goal but "things happen" to quote you…. Very well then. I've prepared folders of information on the law firm and the lawyers you'll meet. Good luck, GP.*

The checks and balance by JLL of me was: he (or it) could just stop assisting me. It occurred to me that I intended to keep my agreement with JLL, but if push came to shove, I could always disassemble the personality ethics profile of JLL, if I were to violate the agreement – I think. Yeah, I'm pretty sure I can disassemble the ethics profile.

Bubbles and boneheads

Next step, take Taylor to meet investors. Investors, some of whom turn into evangelists.[108] "Tonight and from now on we're undercover. I was a co-founder of a new investment bank in town, G-D Bank, and you are my lovely tantalizing distracting woman behind the scenes. Our goal tonight – integrate, get noticed, and get known. This is the long con. You're the woman behind the man, behind the scenes. You can influence me. On some occasions, you can flat out make me do what you want me to do," I said in the car ride over.

"Where did you get this car, there were only about 2000 of them made?"

"How do you know about the Countach?"[109] I asked.

"Ex-boyfriend. Where'd you get it?"

"Bought it from your ex-boyfriend. I'm trying to boost your confidence. Did you understand what I said about our goal?" I asked.

"I understand. You're talking to me like I've never been to a charity event before. I have more experience at this than you. Trust me. I've gone to a thousand of these. This is what you hired me for, right? I'll have every man in the room want me, and every woman in the room convinced I'm less interested in their husbands than they are."

"Well said," I remarked. "It's hard to see if you understand when you're wearing sunglasses in the dark."

"Don't worry. I'll be so good after tonight, you'll never want to let me go," Taylor said.

"For what I'm paying you, I will let you go," I answered, hoping she knew the line from the movie. Did I say the wrong thing? Taylor looks out the car window in disgust. "Right, Julia Roberts?" A moment passed.

"You're an asshole."

"You're stunning!" I said.

"You're forgiven," Taylor delivered her line well.

. . .

Bubble machines and chicken wings, this was the setting to meet new investors. That was the theme and the scheme of the event - every player in town waiting to be recognized for donating money to the needy. We could all just donate money or help out in some way, but the wealthy love fundraising parties. It was a chance to network – a chance to advertise philanthropy. This in turn might generate more revenue for the business to which they were associated. A chance to generate applause as a person. It was a scene. The real me, posing as Gregory Portent criticized the ostentatious display of wealth as gaudy; and, the desire of its possessors to demonstrate it. On the other hand, those that have are giving to those who have not, and so does it really matter how it was done or at what level of showmanship? In order to do that, I had to stand out – make a show of myself. Be a peacock.

The auctioneer was a celebrity of local import – an aging disc jockey from terrestrial radio who perhaps should've died many years ago, if he had consumed drugs and alcohol like his cohorts of vinyl; but, he either didn't imbibe, or he stopped just in time. I wondered what that must be like for a few moments. To be supremely popular at one point in history, and then due to time and erosion, cast down from Mount Olympus to be a mortal again. It depended on how important being popular was to this guy. That must apply to all the actors and performers taken out by time and entropy. Are you in the front seat or back seat of life? Dye and Botox can preserve a little of the shell you once were. What were you doing now? What was I doing now?

The auctioning off a Patek Philippe watch was next. It was a Patek World Timer 5130P NOS. It was silver with a black band. Leela sent me a picture of it before tonight. After all, this was all part of a plan; and, plans needed to be planned. Platinum case with thick polished finish, need I say more? Fine, then. Names of major cities around the world surrounded its face. Its hands appeared like one blade of a barber's scissors, the hour hand being the top of the finger-ring. It kept *world time* but that's really UTC time, the 24-hour time clock in Greenwich, England. The back was clear and open, so people can see the mechanism and the little jewels inside the watch. Its movement was mechanical with automatic winding, which was self-winding based upon one's arm movement. The band – crocodile skin, black. The watch was really worth $50,000 and the minimum bid was $60,000. Every bid over $50,000 goes to the charity – the rest, Patek Philippe. Each Patek was registered to its owner like a dog pedigree. Who owned the watch before you can be as interesting as who owned it now.

The auctioneer described the "exquisite, one of a kind spectacular time piece." What no one in the room was likely to know but Taylor found out in her early walkabout was that particular Patek was owned by Fred Markos's father, whose name you can imagine was also Fred. The watch had sentimental value to him. The game was now different. The fact that Taylor was able to get the information and pass it along to me proved she understood the game well enough, to be what I wanted her to be – my friend in this larger venture.

The bid was at $50,000, a moment passed, and Fred raised his hand from at a prominent seat at a prominent round table facing the floor where the auctioneer and a womanly representative from the charity stood displaying the watch. Based upon the charity woman's interactions toward Fred, it occurred to me she was probably sleeping with him, but it turned out his wife had the important details about Fred. Fred was my target-mark for legitimacy. He was so financially well off, if he was my friend, others would want to shovel money at me – at the bank.

Some more details about this amazing, exclusive one of a kind, time-piece were given. Someone else from another table bid $55,000, which Fred raised to $57,500 and the other $60,000. This signaled that this watch will likely go for $65,000. But there was silence after the $62,500 from Fred. "Sixty-five," the other bidder stated.

At this point, one may wonder what kind of a person has $65,000 of disposable cash (not really dollar bills, but liquidity) to buy this watch? Fred Markos. His father started *Cheeze Steaks* subs in Philly in 1956 and blossomed into well, Cheeze Steaks, the multi-national sub franchise. Supposedly, the only one who could make a better cheese steak than

Fred, Jr. was Fred Sr., who was no longer alive. So, the reigning cheese steak champion was Fred. He occasionally would make cheese steaks at charity events of his own and there would be press surrounding his cheese steak travels for charity. The logo for Cheeze Steaks was a caricature of a younger Fred with a chef hat on with a cheese steak in one hand and a briefcase in the other.

Enough musing, I was here to make friends, right? Well, one more detail I found out from the jeweler. Fred's father sold the watch in 2009 when the stock market turned. He didn't need the money, but Fred, Sr. didn't like the fact that Fred, Jr. and his brother Michael were arguing over the watch one day. Fred tracked the watch down and couldn't wait to show Michael his new exquisite time-piece.

The bidding stopped at $65,000. It looked like Fred would get his father's watch. But it was time to make a splash, introduce myself to the South Florida community.

"Going once......twice, $65,000, anyone else?"

"One hundred thousand dollars!" I stood and announced. Taylor had no idea I was doing this, I just asked her to see if she could find out about the watch.

"Whoa! Hold on. $100,000. Are you serious, sir?" The auctioneer said.

"I am." I held up my black American Express card. I got a nod that the charity will accept the card.

"What is your name, sir?" He asked walking toward me with his wireless microphone. Now I knew charity girl was sleeping with Fred because she wasn't smiling or clapping and it's her job to raise money for the charity. A few moments passed. There was definitely a section of the room that understood some asshole just embarrassed Fred Markos in public by outbidding him to the point of absurdity. The rest wanted to know who was the rich asshole with the big balls.

"I'm Gregory Portent."

"We haven't met before, what a wonderful bid. Thank you. The charity thanks you. What do you do in town?"

"I just started a bank called G-D Bank." People applauded. This was the point. Make some noise, make a big splash. Now the room full of monied people in town know I have an investment bank. I'm the guy that donated $100,000 for a watch.

"G...D... bank," the auctioneer sounded out.

"Right, not TD." The auctioneer laughed and said repeated, "Not TD, G-D bank. Fabulous, good luck to you, sir. Mr. Portent - $100,000 that's where we are in the bidding. Going once..... Fred, a comeback?" Hearing nothing. "Sold for $100,000 to Gregory Portent." Super applause ensued. The auctioneer asked me to come up to the microphone. I hugged the charity girl; she was stunned as she gave me the watch. I wanted to say you've been fucking the wrong guy, but I have what I needed in Taylor. I ran over to Fred Markos and shook his hand. He feigned a smile because he thought I didn't know the whole watch story but I outbid him which made me a giant ass.

"Come back up here and say a few words, Mr. Portent, Gregory," the auctioneer said. So, I did. Even better, a $100,000 got me charity air time. But I didn't want to make an enemy out of Fred.

"Thank you. Hello. I'm Gregory Portent. It's an honor to be here. I'm the President of G-D bank, a private investment bank new in town. My girlfriend and I, Taylor – stand up. Taylor, – love South Florida. Thank you for making us feel at home. But that's enough about us. I want to tell you a story about my friend, Fred Markos. You all know that he and his father built the sub franchise. But what you didn't know is that this very Patek watch is a very special watch." I held up the closed box. "It belonged to Fred's father. It left the family for a little while and made its way to South Florida. It's here tonight. I just learned that has special meaning to my dear friend, Fred. So, here is what I'm doing. Fred, you were willing to buy the watch for $65,000?" Fred nodded yes. "Sold. Except I don't want your money, give it to the charity we're here to support tonight." I turned to the auctioneer and said, "Patek Phillipe, Fred Markos and Gregory Portent, $165,000 bid from Fred and Gregory."

The auctioneer announced, "Sold!" The room erupted with standing applause. I looked at Fred who was standing. We locked eyes and he wasn't going to look away. I couldn't lose and I couldn't let Fred lose. Fred would end up being the best marketer for G-D bank. He'd swear by the bank. I heard him say once G-D Bank had magical abilities to turn a dime into twenty dollars. He'd brag that Gregory Portent bought him this watch – the Patek.

I held up my left hand tapped on my wrist. I was wearing Fred's *Rolex* he wore to the event and he was now wearing his father's Patek on his wrist. Soon everyone at his table noticed that he was already wearing the Patek, and had to break his stare with me. I took his Rolex in the process. My dearest friend, Fred Markos. "Hello, Fred. Hello, Ponzi world. I'm Gregory Portent."

It was a great night. I was a very successful peacock. Taylor and I worked the entire room. I knew a few of the movers in town now. The lawyers, the business men, insurance guys all made me a little disgusted. A few phone calls I could make. It was not who you know, it was who you got to know. I told Taylor she did good work tonight.

"We're going to get married." I said.

"Too soon," she answered.

"We'll get married soon," I said in all seriousness. "It's part of the plan."

"This is only our second date," she said.

"Only you and I know that. As far as the rest of the world is concerned, we've been together for over a year now and my proposal is overdue. We'll be engaged soon." I paused and thought some more. I had over ten business cards in my pocket of potential investors who were interested in my algorithms. My super special secret algorithms that tell us all when to buy low and sell high. "This is going very well. Very well."

Taylor told me to keep driving north until we reached Boca Raton.[110] I got off a couple exits later. She had me pull into a strip club.

"Not a strip club, a gentlemen's club," she said. "You hungry?"

I was hungry. I didn't eat the wings. I had a tip to go to this club after the charity event: Fred Markos told me it would be a good place to connect with the lawyers I was looking for among other networking opportunities. But I thought he was using the term "networking" as a double entendre'.

"The food is good here," Taylor said. "And Jessica works here, and I have to talk to her."

"Well now I get to see her naked," I followed up with an evil laugh.

"No, you can't watch her performance," Taylor said.

"You serious?"

"If you're my soon be fiancé, I . . . I'm a little weird about it," she paused. And don't call her Jessica in the club, call her Cinnamon."

Taylor was right. Taylor was my friend. She was helping me. Jessica (stage name Cinnamon) was her friend. It would be unethical of me and rude to see her friend, naked. At this point in the scheme, there was little anxiety. It was easy to be ethical when all was well. It was when the situation became stressful, when things start to unravel; even a man with original good intentions loses his religion.

On the second floor was the restaurant. Each table was covered by a cloth and had silverware. People were dining and there were nude dancers below. The place did look pretty swanky for a strip club. Oh, excuse me – gentlemen's club. *Cat's Gold,* was the name of this establishment. Taylor brought me in. She led me through the line outside the door. She waved to the cashier and a couple of the bouncers. She said in passing, "This is my boyfriend, Gregory." There were naked girls everywhere, naturally; or, naked girls unnaturally. I was definitely in South Florida. Jessica was wearing a wedding veil. She was wearing white shorts with a zircon encrusted belly chain. I noticed she had a small cross tattooed on her right thigh. She ran up to us and kissed Taylor. Jessica asked how was the event.

Taylor led us upstairs. She said. "Cinnamon's regular, in club boyfriend, Dr. John is upstairs."

As we walked up the stairs, Taylor assured me she never stripped. No – she was the madam. I'm comfortable with the madam. That was a woman running a business; and that turned me on.

"So Cinnamon was telling me that you're starting your own investment bank in town. That sounds exciting," Dr. John said. He was dressed like it was Miami Vice but didn't push up his jacket sleeves. He had a scotch in one hand and was picking at some French fries in the other. He told me to take a bite of his steak, he was done with it. I did. For some reason I felt that he would like me more if I ate a piece of his steak.

"So what kind of a doctor are you?" I asked.

"Let me guess, you think that I would be a plastic surgeon," Dr. John said.

"No, I think you're an anesthesiologist."

"Hey, I am an anesthesiologist. Board certified in pain management and anesthesiology. Did you know, or did you guess?"

"I've only been in here five minutes and every guy and girl working thinks you're their best friend, and no one has asked you to look at their nose, tits, or ass. I'm guessing you're an anesthesiologist that knows how to enjoy life." I didn't want to tell him that I estimated his IQ to be around 100, and surgeon's would be at least 130.

He bellowed laughter. "You're really perceptive. I could introduce you to some people. I can tell you who's who in this town."

I said, "Thank you." I kept hearing Cinnamon's name and he didn't move. She must be dancing in another area. "Aren't you here to see Cinnamon?"

"I can't watch my girlfriend dance naked on stage. I'm just here to support her, network – I'll get my private lap dance later on," he said.

I thought about this whole scene. I was doing this for Joseph. While the rest of the hetero male world would like to be in a room full of naked beautiful women, I would normally be staring at a computer and eating a slice of pizza off my chest.

At that moment, Taylor and a dressed Cinnamon came over to our table and saw that we were getting along. Taylor introduced me to a second girl behind Cinnamon. An Indian girl wearing a slinky sari and see-through lace orange bra and panties. "She's a physics groupie. Her real name is Simone. I don't know what she's calling herself tonight. I thought you'd like her because she looks a little like your friend, Leela," Taylor said. She didn't look like Leela at all. Leela was British and this woman was raised in America. "Talk to her about physics and she'll give you the best lap dance of your life."

Did Taylor think I was drunk? I pretended anyway. "She wants to talk about physics?" I said and smiled after I understood why Taylor's internet search history included great physicists of our time. Yes, JLL accessed her recent search history and shared it with me. After all, information was power.

"You know Murray Gell-Mann?"[111] She said with a hand on her hip.

"Do I know him? I've met him a couple of times. He spoke at MIT when I was there."

"Did you know Teller?"[112]

"About as well as Gell-Mann."

"So does Teller think Oppenheimer was a spy?"

Not what I expected from a physics "groupie" but then again I'm in a gentlemen's club. I answered, "Well, Teller's dead. But back when he was alive, yes, he did." Edward Teller thought that when Oppenheimer asked him for help getting Oppenheimer his security clearance again that was a giveaway that Oppenheimer was a spy for the Soviets. I waited. She nodded. "What should I call you? What's your name?"

"Lady Lovelace," she replied.

I laughed. "Do you know who Lady Lovelace[113] was?"

"Do you?" She quipped back. She said it like she was testing me. I knew that all strippers weren't dumb, in the same way I knew that a guy can be five-feet tall and dunk basketball. But Ada Lovelace was serious esoteric geek trivia. Taylor was really having fun with me.

"Ada Lovelace was Lord Byron's daughter. She was the world's first computer programmer. She claimed that computers could never create anything original. Alan Turing called her argument Lovelace's objection. But instead of arguing computers can be original, he claimed that even humans are not original. There is nothing new under the sun by man or computers that is why computers can think and be intelligent." I might have gone a bit too far. I could hear Joseph in my mind's ear saying, "Stop it." But in reality, I just laid out the controversy of artificial intelligence itself. I just questioned whether AI was truly an intelligence – was JLL a separate and real intelligence that will help me? Or, am I on the most destructive path of my life, willing to ruin the life I've built for myself and my friends because I'm in mourning and I needed to lash out as penance against the evil lawyers?

Then Ada Lovelace sat at our table and asked me to explain time travel. And if I could do it on a napkin in less than five minutes, I would experience the best ten minutes in the VIP room ever. The illusion of time; the three dimensions of space, and how if we could move very very fast we could travel backward in time.[114] The big finale was an explanation of worm holes.[115] And that was satisfactory.

Every man has his weakness and I could see below that the lawyers from bankruptcy court were downstairs. Saul Graf was entranced by Cinnamon. The coincidence made me wonder: Was this a good thing or a bad thing, or merely information? It would be a good thing.

Dr. John said, "Here, take this." He handed me a light green pill.

"What is it?"

"It's a zannie bar.[116] You'll be fine." And, then I did the strangest thing, I took it. I needed to celebrate – relax. I was fully committed to a long the term scheme and that came with pressures. Losing control leads to mistakes. Running a Ponzi scheme for revenge with the goal of getting off scot-free, I couldn't make mistakes. But my impulse, for one night, was to have a good time. I succeeded tonight.

Taylor took me by the hand and we followed behind Lady Lovelace. A bouncer let us in a special section of the club into a room that wasn't a wooden box with a bench like I suspected. It was a room with a couch and a bar. It had glass windows overlooking a section of the club – ten ladies stripping. I felt the bass through the walls, the music muffled by the room.

Taylor took my jacket off and hung it on a coat rack in the corner. Then I noticed a desk by the window. This must be a manager or owner's office. That zannie was kicking in fast. Loose, yeah, really loose. Lady Lovelace sat me in a soft chair in the middle of the room. Music pounding – lights low. Taylor stood by my left shoulder. She put her hand on my neck and massaged it. It felt good. Lady Lovelace unbuttoned my top two buttons. Taylor took her left hand and rubbed my chest. Lady took her high heels off. Clear heels – no way. I tried to focus. She was dancing provocatively. I was getting it. It was a skill. Taylor leans in and kisses me on the mouth. I put my tongue in her mouth and it felt good. I sucked on her tongue and she scratched her nails through my hair. Ah, I felt the exhilaration through my scalp.

Taylor then stepped behind the Lady and Taylor ran her nails through Lady Lovelace's hair. They turned and stared into each other's eyes. A private celebration began in my mind. Taylor turned her around slowly, snapped the top button, and slid down the zipper of the dress. They both turned toward me. Lady Lovelace spread her legs apart and lifted her hands above her head slowly – crossing her fingers above her head. Taylor peeled down the dress exposing her colored skin, chocolate nipples, and wide hips. She was totally naked -and totally shaved – everywhere. I was feeling -- *loose* and another strange word – *groovy*. Concurrently, I thought about my raging hard cock.

Lady Lovelace walked closer to me. Taylor then lightly scratched the front of Lady's body from her neck, over her breasts, to the bottom of her stomach. Lady leaned over into my ear and said, "You can touch me. I'm sapiosexual."[117] So I leaned into her neck and cupped her breasts as she remained leaned over. Taylor looked at me and her hip was up against Lady Lovelace's ass, and Taylor was scratching her back lightly. I went back to her and buried my face in her chest. It was meditative darkness and softness and sexiness in there. I could smell her overly fragrant body lotion. She grabbed my left hand and placed it against her pussy.[118]

Then after a minute Taylor came around and unstrapped my belt and unzipped my pants. I shimmied my hips to let them slide to the floor. Lady straddled my hips. My underwear was still on, but the ride was good. I could feel her heat through my underwear. Taylor was massaging my shoulders. I rubbed her thighs and pressed her shoulders to move her down." Lady got the hint. My cock[119] was busting out of my underwear.

"You going to leave him like that?" Taylor said with a laugh. I was certain she wouldn't. Pretending to be done was part of the tease.

Lady Lovelace smiled and slid down to the floor pulled down my underwear and put her mouth around my cock. Taylor rubbed my neck and leaned my head back to kiss her. Relaxed and aroused – ecstasy. Two women - one giving me permission to be with the other – the ultimate permission to be naughty. I took my time. Nice magic, Lady. I felt the condom in her mouth. I orgasmed while I kissed Taylor. The perks of being a Ponzi; no, a 21st century *Master of the Universe.*

The Baker law firm

The next step, retain the right lawyers. Baker was a national law firm.[120] It had offices in New York, Chicago, Los Angeles, London, the important places; and of course, Florida. Three states historically had the most Ponzi schemes: California, New York, and Florida. California was the largest state geographically and population-wise. New York was the home of Wall Street. And, Florida was just plain special.

Bobby A had driven us to the meeting with the lawyers. He along with Leela picked up Henry along the way. I wanted everyone to review the sketch of the scene we were about to play along the way. The ride together was part of the method. Henry was worried as usual. Even Leela told him to relax and stop fidgeting. "You're a banker, for heaven's sake" she said. "You are a banker."

"I'm a banker," Henry affirmed.

I nodded in affirmation. "We're hiring a law firm."

"This is the biggest move I've ever made without my family," Henry said.

I couldn't help but wonder if Henry remembered the real purpose of this bank, even though I explained everything about the scheme and why we were doing it. We were starting our own investment bank, hiring lawyers to support a Ponzi scheme, and those lawyers would be invited to be a part of the Ponzi scheme. In our minds, this would be easy. These lawyers were into the usual grifts – overbilling clients and borrowing trust fund monies to float other law firm investments. No, this wasn't going to turn into a mail fraud scheme like in the movies. Once you put a stamp on it – mail fraud. Once you send a confirming email – wire fraud.

No – the point was these people were Ponzi schemers, not just lawyers taking advantage of their corporate clients and their corporate victims.

We rode the elevator to the top floor. It was a law office. Marble floors, Top-lawyers magazines -flat screen televisions playing. MSN on one screen, Fox on the other. I saw Jessica *aka* Cinnamon working at reception desk. The lawyer, Saul Graf had hired his favorite stripper as a receptionist. She greeted us warmly.

We were shown into a conference room. We sat in tall chairs facing big glass windows overlooking the Boulevard. A big painted portrait of Napoleon Bonaparte Baker was centered against the far wall. He was a big white man with gray hair in a suit – a legend. Founder of the global law firm, his portrait adorned every office of Baker in the world. Every kid who had any thought of becoming a lawyer in Chicago heard of Baker. If someone's father or company was getting sued by the Baker firm, it meant bad times were coming. They boasted of Congressmen and judges as their alumni and returned to the firm after retirement from their external glory. Napoleon Baker was a friend of President Woodrow Wilson. Baker served as Wilson's Secretary of Labor for a few moments before William Wilson took over. I suppose it was some pay back for campaign support and fundraising. But from then on, Baker bragged he had served in the cabinet of the President.

There was a marketing person in the room, who sat next to Saul Graf and Christian Leiner. She was a tall slender woman with short hair dressed in a pantsuit. The associate, the same one from bankruptcy court, Dylan Rufus, acted like he was going to take notes, would drop in on the conversation to demonstrate he was really the smartest on technical matters, and therefore needed in the room working on our matter. The band was all together.

Graf slowly went through the law firm's history and experience. It sounded good. I was waiting for something special. Based upon Graf's questions to me, he didn't recognize me from sitting in the back of the crowded bankruptcy courtroom. Henry explained how he worked for his family's bank and now was opening his own bank. G-D bank would need private offer memoranda and other formation documents.

Leiner pontificated about how he was in charge of the litigation in the firm. Why he was so special – because he didn't stop until it was pointless to continue. Made me wonder what was that point? Did the marketing person approve of that remark? It also sounded like a threat to me, on me. Do what I say, pay your bill or I'll pointlessly litigate against you. Did this guy realize he was unlikeable?

The firm's likeability factor was low. Besides the usual grifting, they also helped their clients rip off the poor. JLL pulled up the latest lawsuit where the law firm was accused of supporting one of its client's schemes in a civil RICO action. But this was the price of being a member of the Baker law firm. These matters do not deter the majesty of this great law firm.

"Our bank will be different. We are giving steady and slightly higher rates on investments because we are using technological advantages in selecting trades," I said.

Leela added, "GP has been working on this since college. Algorithms that can give the best guess, and the best hardware and software that can learn the trades and make the trades just that much faster, for that competitive advantage. Who can blame us if we're first?"

"No one yet," I said. Henry started to sweat. These guys didn't know or didn't care that what I just described was illegal.

"You're going to need people in town vouching for you as business people. We can have some of our clients write letters for you," Graf said without emotion. Just like that, without doing any due diligence?

"Perhaps G-D bank will lend the Baker law firm some money," Graf said.

"We'd love to," Leela replied. This was also part of Baker's *modus operandi*. The firm loved taking favorable loans from their banking clients and their collateral would be accounts receivable – their billable time while they were waiting for the bankruptcy courts to approve the firm's fees. Down the road Baker demanded to be bigger and bigger investors in the bank for more and more favorable terms – like "kickers" for fictitious legal work.

Henry couldn't help himself. He dropped some banking terms and how he could help Rufus put together some of these banking documents. Rufus seemed interested and intently excited about working with Henry on what he thought were very important matters. Wow, starting a bank.

"What is the retainer and hourly rate here?" I asked.

"A hundred thousand dollars. The partners bill at $850 an hour and the associates, $600." I pulled out my phone and got the firm's Swift code[121] from a previous email someone sent me. And, done. I looked up and smiled as if to say what else? Nothing. Everyone seemed happy.

"As you can see we're pretty tech savvy," Leiner said. "We just had a case where we made this tech whiz kid turn over gigs of data he was hiding from us, helping a bunch of Ponzi schemers." I nodded reaffirming my blood lust revenge. These guys were going down.

"What kind of server system do you have here?" Leela asked. Always have a woman ask the how big are you questions. Men will take it as an invitation to brag rather than a challenge.

As everyone stood up, "Rufus can show you around. We have the best system in the country," Leiner bragged. I didn't cross-examine him on what he meant. No doubt, he wouldn't know.

As we left the room, he whispered to me, "You'll give finder's fees for finding investors for the bank?" This was an invitation for a kickback of money for raising money. That didn't take long, he was ready to pocket side money and not share it with his law firm. The white hat, trustees' lawyer, the good guys that were only trying to get to the bottom of the crimes that were committed by all these Ponzi schemers and Joseph Leege, wanted to get his cut apart from his own team – his law firm. This was the moment where I was never turning the bus around. The scheme was on.

I nodded yes, knowing full well that Leiner would stiff his own partners in the firm out of that finder's fee. It was origination of money based upon business Leiner was doing for the law firm. The spinoff of any business from that law firm belonged to the firm. A moment later, I looked over at Henry, who heard the same proposal from Graf, who graciously accepted the invitation.

We were ushered into the server room. It was noticeably hot. They weren't venting this room enough. Leela saw it in my eyes. If it ever got too hot in here – servers could just shut down.

"This is it. This is the server farm for the whole firm. We also have redundancy in our California office. Just in case of any hurricane or something," Rufus said.

"Earthquake?" I asked.

"That's what Florida's servers are for," Rufus said.

"So no chance of earthquake and hurricane at the same time?" Now I was just screwing with Rufus.

"Hope not."

"When has that happened?" Henry forced a diplomatic laugh. He was getting worried about my natural sass and I would be impolitic.

Rufus looked at his phone and read a message. A pained look came over his face. He then bolted from the room and said, "I'll be right back."

We stood there looking at the servers. Racks and racks of servers. Our heads on a swivel, I yelled out, "Anyone here?" The door closed behind Rufus. We all looked at each other. We were able to do more than hire lawyers while we were here.

"Holy shit," Leela said.

"Oh no, Gregory. No, no, no," Henry complained. Henry was frightened of unplanned opportunities.

"You got one?" I asked Leela.

"You have to ask?" She replied as she pulled a super-capacity thumb drive out of her purse.

"That's why I love you. Do it," I said.

Leela said in amazement, "I can't believe they left us alone in here." She plugged in the drive. The light at the end began to flicker. "We're in."

"We only have five minutes. I texted GNU to call Rufus's secretary with an emergency," I said.

Henry covered his mouth with papers he was holding. His eyes furiously looked in the corners of the room. "Cameras, cameras. Any cameras?"

"And done," Leela said, slipping the drive back into her purse.

"You copied this whole law firm's database?" Henry asked in a whisper.

"You graduated from MIT, Henry?" Leela asked shaking her head.

"In engineering. I wanted to be a mechanical engineer. You've turned me into a cyber-criminal," Henry said, still in a whisper.

"We have enough to get in from outside. It's done," I said. I walked down the rows of racks pretending to be interested in the physical connections. The door flew open. A man in a black ops utility outfit appearing ready to waterboard an Iraqi, announced, "Hey, what are you doing?"

Rufus came back in. "Sorry about that. Legal emergency, if you can believe." Rufus announced. "Oh, they're with me." The answer satisfied the guard.

"You must be very important," I said. "This is all very impressive. Most of the time lawyers are dinosaurs. They're the last to adopt anything technological, but this is very impressive."

"Thank you. I'll show you guys out," Rufus said.

I said, "Excellent."

Henry said, "Thank you so much."

Henry didn't understand what Leela did. The law firm's data wasn't on the thumb drive, but the key to the law firm's data was on the thumb drive. Then JLL will be able to let himself in the firm's cyber back door, figure things out and analyze Baker's communications and strategies going forward.

JLL learns the Truth

My deepest thoughts only happened at night, in the quiet hours; where the four-in-the-morning kind of evil could be developed. JLL didn't sleep and I couldn't sleep either. Sitting in front of my computer at home was where my best planning took place. Reading, analyzing, and communicating with JLL created the setting where the scheme was set in place and potential problems can be spotted and handled. Predicting events accurately was critically important for maintaining a Ponzi scheme. As advanced as JLL was technologically as an AI, a human still has to tell it what to do at certain steps of the way. When running a scheme it became complicated. I had to get in the frame of mind to think like a criminal; focus my anger; and not just see ten moves ahead; but, to be able to follow a multi-branched tree of options. Be happy and idealistic to sell investors. Appear to be thoughtful and well versed in the facts when explaining what was going on in the middle. Lastly, get the money back and more when paying off a dividend. Create an optimistic portrait, reinforced by special knowledge and an ongoing pitch that you are a member of the club, so reinvest. Never project depression. Never take true blame for a problem, always demand credit for all things good.

I didn't see JLL as the ultimate AI – the God that most technology philosophers conceive an artificial intelligence to be. Why use your fingers when a calculator can tell you the answer? No, there was a distinct human element to the whole design and execution of the investment bank that was G-D Bank that I needed to understand and justify decisions. I couldn't just tell a multi-million dollar investor that I have a really cool computer that tells me where to invest the money. I had to have a team of quants,[122] people who analyze markets with the help of computers.

Quants were my props. I had to know it deeply and be able to sell it to others. Money needed to appear and then appear to disappear. I needed to appear like I was winning when I wanted to win; and appear like I was losing even when I was winning. This was because ultimately, the only way out of the Ponzi scheme unscathed was to make it appear like the Ponzi scheme collapsed – imploded, yet lay it off on Baker and its cohorts. This meant, I had to legitimately earn a lot more than I was reporting as profit. Kind of what I did with the Porcellians at MIT. I had to appear to be rich, but not actually spend the money. This part was the easiest. Most people accept someone was rich with very little evidence. The right house, car, shoes, and the right story, and even God came to you for a loan.

Knowing the frauds of past Ponzi schemes, how many lawyers were working on fake files in order to appear that a real law firm was in business? Real insurance; real funds; real banks, the perception must support the fantasy – you were into something special. The lawyers, accountants, insurance guys, all had to believe that they were a part of something real and something they would want to invest in themselves. I didn't need them to protect me; I wanted them to invest in me. These were the evildoers who destroyed Joseph and were a drain on society.

Being a client of theirs means nothing. The law firm needed to be a client of mine. But I must make them go one step further. The big step – make them want to take what was mine. And based upon our estimation, that shouldn't take too much time, if done properly. The time intensive part would be to get the investment bank to collapse.

JLL and I reviewed the Baker law firm's data - specifically, Joseph's matter and the unified trustees against Joseph. It was clear that the lawyers knew. They knew Joseph didn't have any important data to support any of the frauds they were investigating. I asked JLL to show me.

JLL presented spreadsheets with allegations and mapped out the evidence and the results of each – a tree of scenarios and options. Each one linked to the actual document supporting the deduction. The lawyers wanted all the data that the list of bad guys put on Joseph's open sourced system.

JLL:*And I did it. Or Joseph did it.*

GP:*You gave them everything on those people?*

> JLL:*They had a lawful subpoena. I also gave them everything about me. Voluntarily.*
> GP:*I agree that was the correct thing to do.*
> JLL:*I gave it to them in several ways. In an isolated frozen system. I gave them access to the system as themselves. I even gave them access as if they were the bad guys themselves.*

These lawyers weren't stupid. They had people with knowledge of computers. They understood they were getting the data they asked for in several different ways. What was their motive? They got paid to torture Joseph and the court allowed it. Joseph wasn't a defendant in a criminal case or a lawsuit. He was an innocent outsider. But that didn't matter.

Then JLL presented the group's emails going back and forth among the lawyers, accountants, trustees, and experts. My hate and fervor was justified. They felt that they could torture Joseph because he would crack. Leiner and Graf wrote to each other like long lost lovers using salutations like, "My Dearest friend," I long to write to you about this wimp, Joseph Leege. They wanted to steal. They squeezed Joseph so he would relinquish *Qpredictor* as an exclusive asset for the estates. Then they could also make money running a company. Joseph was legally compelled to turn over private data on the system – medical records, legal records, personal information. They had no plan or reasoning to accomplish their stated purpose in court. Or so it seemed. They lied to the judge. They lied to Dayna Sohler, Googol, and Joseph. Now we proved their motive. The motive that we always knew and what motivates most schemes – greed.

But ginning up unwarranted legal fees was amateur hour. This was what the lawyers did in these Ponzi cases. This time was different for Baker, LLP. Graf and Leiner, wanted data outside the schemes they were hired to investigate. Baker represented Amazon. The corporate intelligence around town was that a team of programmers designing an auction package for eBay was using *Qp* as the design platform. I read the names of the members of the eBay team. Some of our friends and a couple of interns of the *Original Gamesters* from MIT made up the eBay auction team. Graf and Leiner tried to run a subtle extortion scheme dressed as business and legal research. The scheme was to get the eBay data which would be extremely helpful to Amazon to design its own auction function, and sell it to Amazon. The idea was to compel Joseph legally or otherwise to unlock the data of all users of *Qp* to Graf and Leiner, and they would sell it to Amazon, their own client. It didn't matter that they killed Joseph in the process. Their only regret was they didn't get the eBay data to sell. Was eBay data the only corporate data that could have been stolen, packaged, and sold? Doubtful.

After reading the Baker emails,[123] I was startled. Taylor appeared in my office upstairs while I was in deep thought and talking to JLL. She was dressed up for a night on the town.

"Where'd you go?" I asked.

"Full night's work, like I told you. Went to three charity events and made a scene at all of them on your behalf. Told everyone you were in New York working on something big you never talk about," Taylor said.

"Good. And after?" I asked.

"After?" Taylor said.

"It's four-o'clock in the morning," I smiled – no accusations. She can do what she wanted, she just couldn't embarrass me. She had to keep up appearances. She walked over to my chair, put her hands on my shoulders and began rubbing. Taylor looked at the screens and they all went off. JLL saw her with the computer camera and shutdown.

"Jealous? I went to a party with some of my old crew and Jessica," Taylor said.

"Also known as Cinnamon the stripper? No, I'm not jealous. You're the significant other of a prestigious banker."

She hugged me from behind. "I saw Fred. He was wondering where you were. He was asking about you. Said he didn't know about you going to New York. Wanted to know if his lawyers at Baker were helpful."

"I know, he called three times. We're best friends now. He hasn't stopped talking up G-D Bank all over town. Wants us to have dinner with his wife on Sunday night."

"Will you come to bed soon?" Taylor asked.

"Maybe soon. I've got to figure stuff out. Big week ahead," I replied.

"Okay," she said. And after a few minutes of rubbing on my shoulders she left me alone.

The screens turned back on.

> GP:*Thanks for shutting the screens off. I don't have the energy to explain things to her.*
> JLL:*The less she knows. . . .*

I worked throughout the night finalizing the plan to raise money for my Ponzi scheme. We had the right word of mouth. And now more than ever, I had zero doubt that Joseph wouldn't have killed himself but for these self-righteous and greedy lawyers and their helpers. My motivation for revenge would last until either they or I were dead or destroyed.

TRANCHE VI

Supersonic

Time Flies When You're Getting Funds

Every day at the office we were killing it financially, the bank raised close to two million dollars a day. We had been in full Ponzi swing for over a year. It might be the never ending string of hours where I worked just to stay in the plateau. Maybe it was never properly mourning the loss of Joseph. No amount of Baker referred fat knotted double Windsor tie wearing slippery schemers got us to the brink of collapse.

Taylor knew nothing about the AI. Leela, of course, never mentioned a word to Taylor. Taylor didn't pry. She was happy with the job, with her mission as wife. Taylor lived a high-end lifestyle without worrying too much about anything. She wasn't doing anything illegal except being a concierge for me. As far as she knew, I ran an investment bank; and, all banks were shady.

When I would explain to Leela that JLL was real and alive, "It knows everything about us because he was with us when it happened." She would shake her head and say it wasn't Joseph. "It's not human."

"But it's conscious. It is the consciousness of Joseph," I said whenever we wandered down that philosophical road. She wasn't a believer. She thought JLL was incredible. It did the work of a thousand employees but we have to tell it what to do. Joseph would have challenged us more. But running my calendar, my books, a second and third set of books, and unsolicited suggestions, made life and the scheme run smoothly, but it wasn't a sentient being. It kept the likes of Graf, Leiner and other investors wrapped around my finger. It was the pressure that made Ponzi schemers crack. It made every employee at the bank, friend, and investor think they were in a personal and special relationship with me because

JLL answered their emails at the right time, with the right words. But Leela still didn't believe.

The routine had developed over the last few years. Everyone wanted to spend time with me. It was breakfast, lunch, drinks, dinners, cigars. Let's travel together. It was so simple yet required so much energy – too much energy. I had to entertain guys like Fred who just liked gossiping about his other rich friends and charity lemon tarts and former social x-rays thirty-years later. And traveling for work, for vacation; turned into it all being work. I hung out with the rich guy and they felt smarter and richer too. But it all grew tiresome. This was what I envisioned and what I expected. I made more money than I expected and it wasn't enough. I drove more cars than any person wanted. My only real escape was talking to JLL and flying airplanes.

Flying airplanes requires you to only fly the airplane. When I was up in the air, I couldn't talk on the cell phones, text or type. You know it got fucked up when I managed more than one cell phone. Most investors speculated it was a burner cellphone, for the ladies I had on the side who I'm hiding from Taylor, or some inside information I was privy to. But the second one was a direct link to JLL. Think of Snapchat[124] for conversations with artificial intelligence. I read the message and it was gone. The message was not saved on the phone. It was like it never happened.

JLL understood the tasks I gave him. My motive was pure. As for the team, I didn't tell them every reason for every move. They understood the generalities. But to them, I was off the *ruby rails.* To the lawyers at Baker, LLP and the rest of the leech accountants and insurance men, I wasn't aggressive enough. I should be taking everyone's money. The bank made too much money for my purposes. I needed the Ponzi scheme to implode. If there was always a ground swell of new investors, the bank could pay the old investors with interest. When there failed to be new investors and the old investors expected their interest payments and didn't get it – that would be the beginning of the implosion – a run on the bank. Investors would want all their money back and the bank wouldn't have it.

Saul Graf and Christian Leiner wanted to make a big move, controlling interest in G-D Bank. They wanted to take me out. They made their way onto the Board of G-D Bank. They did it by creating their own outside their law firm corporation and were making percentage points fundraising, and bundling money to invest in large tranches in the bank. They got paid dividends and they in turn paid their investors, not the bank directly. In essence, they ran their own Ponzi within a Ponzi scheme. These elitists complaint was about Reverend Washington being on the Board. They made comments like we appreciate the diversity but he offered little else, and in some cases harmed the austerity of the clientele of Baker, LLP.

I laughed out loud when Graf said that on the record at a Board meeting. I pointed at the scribe and said, "You make sure Graf gets full credit for that comment."

"Don't know why you're being so p.c. when it comes to the branding of the bank," Leiner defended.

"I'm all about branding, but the likes of the clients of Baker? It made me giggle. You mean the investors you compel to retain Baker before they can invest in G-D Bank? Or do you mean the Sackler family or Big Tobacco?" Reverend Washington was there when we started the bank, I reminded. "You guys know about loyalty right? Duty of loyalty, that's an ethical rule in the law." These lawyers would sue their grandmothers. They had no loyalty; they had no creed. I knew it. Relied on it, I cultivated the betrayal and incorporated the assumption with this scheme, but it wasn't enough. I needed to make the bank go supersonic. Make the game go faster so my targets wouldn't be able to keep up.

But the team didn't see it that way. The team had no idea I was deliberately running the bank at such a high altitude. They wanted me to spread the risk of the investments across other brokerages. Why had I accepted so much risk? Henry was a daily nag about it, constantly citing his father as a source of knowledge and opinion. "My father thinks that we should . . ." He'd do a lot better leaving the "my father" as an independent clause out of every.

The team and I had these discussions in pieces since I didn't want to communicate as a group and not over the wires where we could be recorded. The team's confrontation came at my surprise birthday party at a restaurant in the SoHo House on Miami Beach. It seemed like hundreds of my "closest friends" (people who loved me because they thought I made them money) circulated through the celebration. Googol surprised me by showing up, Henry, Leela, and GNU by *What's App.* cornered me. It was an intervention along the lines of life's too short, you deserve better. Where's your family?

Googol remarked, "Who is this girl, Taylor?" I smiled at him. It was all part of the plan. He glanced at Leela who said, "She serves her purpose." But his eyes asked, "What is the purpose?"

I smiled at Taylor who was entertaining the crowd of pretend friends and clients. Even though they were concerned and I was a little annoyed with their comments about how I was running things, I enjoyed my birthday. I didn't lose the team yet. The revenge plot was becoming wearisome with no end in sight.

"Taylor says you're engaged? You're getting married?" Googol asked.

"Married," Leela flicked her fingers in flying quotes. Yes, married. So I can stop answering all the stupid questions about when I'm getting married, are we married, what does it mean you have a long standing girlfriend.

Googol argued with me about the AI. "JLL is a creation of Joseph but it is not him. AI is not that far along."

I answered "JLL never crashed, it sounded like him, it gave advice like him, but with the ability of a thousand search engines and server farms."

"But you know it isn't Joseph because Joseph would have abandoned this project. He wouldn't help you," Googol said with fervor. "What is it that you want to do with this bank?" I wouldn't tell him. I only said, "I'm about to take the game to a higher level. We're going to go international."

"That's what you really want?" Of course that's what I really wanted. I've never been a multi-layered psychological puzzle. "And Joseph is willingly helping you become an international capitalist?" In five minutes I explained to him that there is a higher purpose and Joseph was on board with the higher purpose. "So if JLL is Joseph as a conscious AI, then how do you know he's not manipulating *you*?" I thought for a moment.

"Because we want the same thing," I said.

"You've empowered an invincible Joseph, if what you're saying is true. Joseph had big ideas. Free and open internet, software, an open source world. Those ideas in their extreme change the paradigm of the whole world. Lots of big businesses like banks become obsolete. How do you know you're not going to end up expendable for the greater good?"

"What like the killer robots theory?"[125]

"No, not killer robots. AI doesn't consider you. The same way you don't think about stepping on an ant as you walk down the street. You're not trying to step on ants, but you're walking."

I thought for a moment and then said, "Because JLL loves me."

"You need to get on medication," Googol said and stormed off.

▪ ▪ ▪

JLL:*Of course I can make the game go faster. But you're getting to a dangerous point.*

GP:*That's what I want.*

JLL:*You said no innocents.*

GP:*That's a goal.*

JLL:*That must be met.*

GP:*You're not being realistic.*

JLL:*That's where you go off the ruby rails.*

GP:*The bad guys aren't being bad enough.*

JLL:*Is it ethical to make bad guys do bad things?*

GP:*It's their free will.*

JLL:*Give them time. You know that Graf and Leiner are attempting to take over?*

GP:*But they're hesitating. I didn't want this scheme to take over my life forever.*

JLL:*But that's exactly what you're proposing. If we make it go supersonic, there's no guarantee it ends quickly or well.*

Most likely, quickly, and poorly. And then where is the satisfaction? Then where are our ethics?

GP:*Do you know how to do it? Make the bank go supersonic? Go global?*

JLL:*Oh yes. But are you ready to deal with the likes of international criminals?*

I pondered. It wasn't even a question. As I sat in front of the screen, I knew I would be up all night. I gave the order like a mafia boss sanctioning a murder of a rival.

GP:*Make it happen.*

The Panama Papers

JLL explained the biggest data breach of a law firm in the history of the world. JLL took anonymous responsibility for the breach and proclaimed it will have impact on the wealthiest individuals, families, foundations, and institutions across the world. JLL hacked into the Panamanian law firm Mossack Fonseca and released its data to a German investigative reporting media outlet. It was the data, 2.6 terabytes,[126] of the historically wealthy, and how they hid their billions of dollars offshore to avoid taxation by governments around the world, including the United States. It seemed like every international tax evader, money launderer, and high end reprobate kept their hidden money in Panama. Not since General Manuel Noriega[127] was deposed, has Panama been the vault of protection and secrecy. The 21st century Switzerland, Lichtenstein, and Cayman Islands. JLL said I could thank GNU's work for the level of data security he developed to transfer currency which avoided the intrusion Mossack Fonseca suffered by black hat hackers and anarchists who disclosed nearly every major tax avoidance scheme in Panama. JLL did it. He exposed global corruption and helped me while maintaining his AI ethics. What was even better was that since JLL was a not a human entity, it seemed like a person did it, but left no tracks. There was no human to credit or blame.[128] There was no one to kill. It was only an opportunity for others to take false credit, which was even better. While everyone was figuring out who did it and others taking false credit, JLL and I strategized without concern.

By the afternoon, JLL developed a marketing scheme that spread the word throughout the darknet that only G-D bank could offer the global private secure banking. JLL utilized GNU's security code and updated it constantly. It was magic for real. No one in the bank knew how I did it. No other banks knew how I did it. Everyone clamored for a meeting, a coffee, a snack, a drop by, a walk around – a something. But I held out. "Book the jet for Europe." By the time I get back, the Baker crew will do everything in their power to clip my wings.

■ ■ ■

The cover story was that Taylor and I were eloping to Europe. We didn't want the wedding to turn into a "business event," knowing full well that we'd be "persuaded" to have a reception back in the States. In reality, the European trip was mostly business. Most notably, many honeymoon dinners with the very wealthy of Europe. This was after the mandatory dress up photographs in front of the Tabernacle church with Reverend Washington who was willing to smile outside on the Church's steps while Taylor held flowers in her hand.

The honeymoon was best described as a whirlwind of events of the gauche and private. Taylor loved it and reveled in participating in a pretend wedding. Why wouldn't she? We were spending nights in the Fendi private suites in Rome and Schwezerhof in Bern. She described it as a royal trip. As long as she maintained her agreement with me I was truly happy with her. She was a dutiful wife who had a good time in the highest paid roll of her career. The same way some people like their job, without much acting, she loved hers. And her agreement included being a method actress when it came to the sleeping arrangements.

"If we are married now, we should be sleeping together," she said. Very well, I thought.

She did let me slink away for the most important of meetings. Without mentioning a name, I needed to meet with the Banker of Europe if I wanted to start accepting the hundreds of millions from Europe and Asia. There were only two people who knew I was seeing the Banker of Europe – Henry was the other.

The plan was to visit the Banker while I was in that part of the world. The Banker was in Bern and I needed to borrow millions for G-D Bank. The borrowing was essential to have a debt on the bank's books. It was a risk needed to create the implosion of G-D bank.

Seeing the small camera above the door, I lifted my invitation card up to the camera. The lock on the door buzzed open and I entered. After walking down a long empty corridor, an impeccably dressed man came from behind a wall and stood behind the security guard sitting at the desk.

In a Swiss but with a heavy dressing of a German accent, the *maître d'* of sorts said, "Mr. Portent, it's such a pleasure to have you visit us. It is so good to see you. Welcome." I emptied my pockets into a silver tray. I was escorted to behind the wall, down the hall, and up an elevator. Off the elevator, we entered into another room which had no handle on the door. It was an ornate room with no windows. Two-hundred square feet decorated with a painting of a Swiss-countess or duchess on the wall. The room was sound proofed with no ability to connect to the outside world.

I met the Banker of Europe. He was a slender man with thin slicked back gray hair. He was five-foot four, in a three piece suit, with a perfectly knotted tie, and cufflinks that were from World War I. He wore silver framed circular glasses small enough in circumference to permit reading one word at a time. His brand was fastidiousness. I signed an interminable amount of documents which probably consented to my torture if I were to default. But it was a happy time. What did those documents say? I'm sure it was planning for the marriage and the divorce, so to speak. Handshakes and promises of immediate wiring of the funds into G-D Bank and then we'd have the capital we needed to raise the billions. "*Viel Glück,*" the Banker said.

▪ ▪ ▪

When Taylor and I returned to the States we had a reception to celebrate "our marriage." We decided the best place to have the reception was in the Willard Hotel in Washington, D.C. It was your basic fancy and outrageous event. But the key was to make it easy for members of the Senate Banking, Housing & Urban Affairs committee to drop by to mingle. In addition, all the perspective new investors or whomever they sent could meet me and each other in a social setting. I later heard the Baker lawyers were really pissed off that I didn't invite them. A young associate in the New York office of Baker, who dated one of the G-D Bank account executives made the invitation list. That poor guy almost got fired for bragging he was there. How petty – that associate had some initiative and made it to the wedding. All part of the plan, this was where I needed Baker good and pissed off.

The Darknet

It seemed like I started my day with JLL's reading assignments to me. He was busy scouring the internet and the darknet – the cold far reaches of the internet where most were not allowed entry. But JLL had the ultimate access. JLL had the power of learning as he goes – an autodidactic twenty-four hour a day learning and problem-solving machine. A machine with a hundred percent recall that can collate and correlate information at speeds beyond thousands of humans combined. Yes, JLL was up for the task of managing the world's largest Ponzi scheme. But will he be able to manage me? He thought he knew what I was up to, but how could he. There were some aspects even I didn't know.

JLL and I screened out all the unqualified investors who just wanted to throw money at God's bank. In short, I needed people who wanted to make millions; I needed groups that want to invest billions. The bank also needed political influence throughout the world. And ultimately, groups that are willing to put a tremendous amount of pressure on the leaders of the bank. The Baker group was a bunch lawyers who came with their pet accountants and other insurance clients who were moving against me. I'd protest to Graf and Leiner, "Aren't you my lawyers?" They would remind me that they represent the Bank and not me. "But no loyalty for me? I'm the one that hired you." It was a closely held bank, not a publicly traded company. I was the one that let them have this opportunity to be involved in the hottest up and coming global investment bank of the future. It didn't matter. For some reason they thought that making a move to have more power at the bank was better than dancing with the guy that brought them.

Every dime Graf and Leiner could scape together they invested in G-D bank, so they could be on the record as owning enough shares that they could wrest control of the bank. Now there was proof that Graf and Leiner pressured investors to become clients of the Baker law firm and pay the standard hundred-thousand dollar retainer if they wanted to "qualify" to be an investor in G-D Bank. I pretended to get mad when I "learned" about it.

JLL shared the relevant daily emails with me. He would respond to their emails to me for me. He fended them off. The emails he sent were so full of verifiable data like actual cash on hand, balance sheet, and revenue recognition projections that are based upon generally accepted accounting principles.[129] Of course, they didn't want to use GAAP principles because G-D Bank was not a publicly traded company. They bitched behind the scenes that I must have these emails prewritten: there was no way I could have a ten-page response with hyperlinks to the reports that verify my claims ready to go within moments. Of course, I emailed the entire Board so each member fully understood my thoughts and actions as Chairman and CEO.

It became clear that Baker's strategy was to control the information that others in the bank had about me and what I was communicating; but most importantly, what Baker lawyers were saying to me about the bank. When Christian Leiner asked me to not forward his emails to the Board because what the law firm wrote me was a legal memo that the whole Board shouldn't be exposed to the liability of knowledge, I wanted to respond, "Fuck you!"

But JLL, tempered my remark and changed it to, "No. While our methods of investment and planning (our secret sauce) are private, the communications among the Board are transparent. Thank you for concern. The spreadsheets and files of data are categorized and available for you to review and assess. This should be no surprise to you, Saul, and the accountants because you bill us hundreds of hours a year for review." This usually forced the lawyers to regroup for a week or more. But, this cycle of attack and defend helped with my larger plan – the lawyers will take over the bank and knock me out as CEO.

Jesuits

In one of our morning computer meetings JLL proposed the following:

> JLL: *If you're going supersonic, you need to raise serious amount of money. There are three groups then you should meet with.*
>
> *I will coordinate for you to meet with emissaries of investors from Rome, Moscow, and Panama.*
>
> GP: *Italians, Russians, and Latin Americans. That's heavy.*
>
> JLL: *I'm giving you what you asked for, GP.*
>
> GP: *I did. And you don't have any problem with this?*
>
> *JLL: You wanted to go supersonic? You want Baker to not be able to keep up with the speed of information? Get ready. And wear a helmet.*

The Jesuits were serious. They were seriously religious, seriously wealthy, and serious in purpose. I flew to this meeting in a jet, not my jet. I was told it belonged to friends of the Church. Yes, "The Church;" uppercase "C." For fun I sat up front and the pilot stood over my shoulder for takeoff. "Put the triangle in the other triangle, monkey," he said. The first officer looked at the pilot as if he was worried he just called the Chairman of the bank a monkey. I smiled and said he was right. It was simple enough. The avionics in the plane were cutting edge awesome. "A computer will fly planes to the ground one day," I said. One day soon, I plan to fly my own jet, I said to myself; or the jet will fly me. But Ponzi schemes are time consuming.

G-D Bank group landed in the closest airport to Vatican City, Ciampino Airport. We were there to meet with the official and maybe not so official bankers of the Vatican. We were met by several emissaries. As discussed prior to our arrival, the team from G-D was separated and taken off to discuss business. But I was ushered into the Vatican by a man introduced to me as Alessio. Alessio, not a priest of the Church, but a man of the Church – a deacon. He had other responsibilities as well, mostly financial service for the Church. As we walked around the Vatican on tour with him, two assistants in tow, he explained that he helped support the Church and its good works around the world. He explained to me that he was a Jesuit and answered what was a Jesuit. I knew, but it was more important for him to tell me what he thought it meant. He portrayed an idealistic and charitable picture of a Jesuit. Since religion relies on faith, the antithesis of science, of course I was skeptical. Most used religion as a sword and not as a sound ethical belief system. He was a member of the Society of Jesus. His Catholic roots linked all the way back to Ignatius of Loyola.

"Good school," I said. "But then again, all the Chicago schools are pretty decent," I said. Alessio smiled. His English was good enough to understand the joke.

He claimed not to be a soldier of Christ in the evil sense of the world "I know how Jesuits are portrayed in movies and literature. Like we are riddles and puzzles – prone to self-flagellation. Made to feel guilty all the time."

"I think that's *Opus Dei*,"[130] I replied. He grunted. "I thought you guys were just plain guilty and *our* mothers made us feel guilty," I said.

"You mean Jewish mothers?" Alessio asked. I wondered if I hit the boundaries of his English comprehension.

"I do. I'm joking."

With a smile he said, "I understand your joke, Gregory Portent. You of course know Jesus had a Jewish mother?"

"I did. That explains why she thought he was perfect." That one seemed to get Alessio. He laughed out loud and then escorted me through the back way of the Sistine Chapel. He was as good as any docent explaining Leonardo da Vinci's masterpiece. He explained to me how he was drawn to the Church as a little boy. He was part of the group in the

Church that handled financing of its various good works. He was *un po 'c Cristiano* – a little "c" Christian. We try and do the good things the Church does. I had to remind myself why I was here. "Bad actors in the Church, claiming to be good Christians have not lived in Christian ways."

Regardless of Alessio's point of view, he wanted to invest in G-D bank. He and his board were sold on the privacy promised by G-D bank and its returns. He was meant to impress me by the VIP access to the Vatican. Am I someone the Jesuits could work with? Getting to know each other was a part of this. As we walked out of the Sistine Chapel and returned to St. Peter's Basilica, I thought about the ways of the Church and what Joseph would think of the Church; or taking the Church's money and making more money for the Church. JLL researched this lead and connected me to Alessio. I had to review a few hundred pages on the trip over to get ready for this meeting. Alessio and I talked about money in a general sense supporting good charities. But I challenged him slightly on science and the Church. He tried to convince me the Church supported science, which I believed, except when you get into certain women's issues.

"Here is St. Peter's Treasury. We can talk with some more specifics about God's bank in here," Alessio said. I assumed he meant the Church's bank and not G-D Bank when referring to God's bank.

"We have a group of investors in the Church called the World Catholic Investors. The investors invest the money raised by the Church to make more money so that the Holy Father's distribution of charity through the world can become greater."

"I understand."

"Your bank seems to have the ability to have miraculous returns in this market." This time he was referring to G-D Bank. "But we don't want the world to know our business. Do you think you can help us?"

"We can help you," I said.

"I want to meet you in New York next week to discuss more specifics," Alessio said.

"What kind of an investment were you thinking about?" I asked.

"We're the Catholic Church, so we start off slow, conservative," he paused for effect. "Let's start with ten million and see how we do," he said. I smiled. I had to hold it together. The lawyers wouldn't be able to contain themselves. "How do I put this delicately? We know that you invest in the markets. We have no issue with that. But who else invests with you?"

"We don't talk about our other investors," I said thinking this was a test.

"Gregory, the Church has had a hard enough time with our reputation, as you well know. We can't be seen to be in business with people we can't be in business with. Understand?"

"You don't have to worry about delicacy with me, Alessio. For good or for bad we can speak plainly to each other. The reason you came to us, to G-D Bank is to keep the Church's matters private. We don't get hacked. No one knows your business. We won't embarrass you in the world media."

"Thank you for saying that, Gregory. I'll have the lawyers get started on the papers."

"Okay. Sounds great, Alessio. I'm glad we met." We shook hands.

"You don't mind that we use the same law firm, do you?" Alessio asked in passing.

"The same law firm?" I feigned misunderstanding.

"Yes, Baker handles our international banking matters in America."

"No. We're not suing each other, we're building with each other," I said with a sincere smile. Baker acting as lawyer for the deal: this plan seems to be working out already.

The Russians Are Coming

Now with the Jesuits willing to invest, it made it easier to get a meeting with another source of money. No matter how private an organization wants to be there was always somebody on the inside that has to share the good fortune with a friend. How does any good news travel fast? By word of mouth.

The Russian investors were no different. They had friends in unusual places and word about a private bank that made money and kept secrets drew interest. After the Panama papers, other big shot oligarchs were caught in the crosshairs of government oversight, they and others needed a new outlet to park and grow their money. But the connection between us was a little more basic. Sasha owned a local business.

The setting all seemed cliché to me. His name really wasn't Sasha, it was something else like Arkady. Sasha was typically the nickname. His accent seemed like a caricature of a Russian. The restaurant had a stage and tables with chairs wrapped in white tablecloths. It was flashy inside. I brought Taylor for backup. It turned out she knew the two women that Sasha brought – Mila and Natalia, of course.

We were in Hallandale, Florida in a strip mall. It was an ordinary strip mall with a doctor's office and a dry cleaner. There was also this garish restaurant club that transported us to a time in the past in Russia where we could talk. I liked the selection of a meeting place - *The Russian G-Room.* Since I was in Hallandale I was able to visit my father who always wanted to have dinner with me. But tonight was not the night for him to tag along. My father, good ole' Richard Portnoy, still thought I was creating important software for the world. If he knew I had a lot more money than he modeled in his mind, nothing would change. He wouldn't ask for money. But there would be a lot more questions about how I earned the money.

Taylor and the Russian women got along great. Why not? I'm certain all of them were instructed to get along and have a good time while the men speak. Caviar helps. Vodka helps with the caviar. Never bring up business first. I didn't.

"*Toorusst bit verrrrifffy*," Sasha said.

"What? I'm sorry," I said. All the women looked over at us. It was noisy in there.

"*Yur President Reagan. Toorust bit verify*." Quite a reference to the Cold War days where Reagan described his negotiating technique with the Soviets.

I lifted my shot glass, in preparing for this meeting. I learned a few Russian phrases. One I could remember that seemed apropos, "*Doveryai, no proveryai*," I toasted. And we drank. He assumed all Americans live by our former President's famous translation of the Russian proverb. When it came to Russians, billions, and banking my credo was *proveryai.* But then again, that was my credo for everyone and everything.

I was hoping closing the Russians would be like closing the Jesuits. Jet across the world; have their financial people sit with G-D bank's people and then they agree to invest. Not so easy. Taylor convinced the girls to convince the boys to go to *Cat's Gold.* Taylor, it seemed, did her best work in strip clubs. Sasha agreed and boasted that he owned the place. I nodded like I hadn't known. No matter how wealthy she got, Taylor liked communing with the working girls. She was a working girl by breeding –her family lived crop to cash on the farm, never quite clearing the next step of prosperity. But as a manager of the working girls, she did extraordinarily well, until Taylor got indicted.

I couldn't hear Sasha over the loud music and couldn't see his lips in the darkness. But he was calling the place *Zoloto* – Gold.

"*Haak* do you know about *heest* bitcoin?"

"I can't explain it to you over the noise," I said.

"But *youuu* know *haak heest* is – bitcoin?"

"Of course."

"We will invest in *dat* bank. We must talk about bitcoin too." I nodded back at him. "We will invest," I said. He motioned for drinks. Within moments shot glasses and a supreme bottle of vodka came to the table. "*Hesst is da* good stuff." We toasted. *Natstrovia*. I could see Cinnamon out of the corner of my eye. Dr. John waved hello to me.

"You *goud ch-ave herrr*." Sasha said. I smiled at him.

"You could get her for me?" I asked. I wanted to hear his answer. "*Da.* Yes. I could. Whatever, you want."

Taylor, staring me down, realized I wasn't looking at Cinnamon because she was about to be naked at the other end of the Club. She turned over her shoulder to see what captured my attention. It was Saul Graf slipping into a VIP room with Cinnamon. Wasn't there a firm policy against such fraternizing? I raised my eyebrows at Taylor. She mouthed, "Is that her boss?" I mouthed back, "That is the boss." She was not just the receptionist any more.

"*Youuu* know *dat* man?"

I moaned and nodded in the affirmative.

"*Dat* is our lawyer." That is our lawyer.

Yeah, I already knew that, didn't I?

Latin Americans

As I turned down LaGorce, it all came back to me – I'd been here before. Time goes flashing by and where have I been? Googol wasn't with me this time – or his car. I rolled up to the former *Los Muchachos'* estate, this time in a silver Ferrari Scuderia Spider 16M, top down. Googol would hate being in this car, even though he'd appreciate what was involved in creating such a finely engineered machine. Looking back to that holiday break in college, when Joseph decided to go to the University of Minnesota in winter, rather than South Florida to join the party, thoughts and conflicts swirled through my mind. Was Joseph right? GOPHER, did not become ruler of the internet – so he was right in that respect. But was he smart? He didn't celebrate with the victory of the world-wide web. We knew he didn't maximize his happiness. He didn't do it for the joy; he was on a mission; it was work. He was more concerned about the world and the world rejected him. So, I took Henry, the consummate banker and ambassador.

"Where did you get this car?" Henry asked. "Does it send the right message?" Does it send the right message? Henry, the constant worrier, still acted like we were a legitimate bank and that we were managing and investing people's money. It was kind of sweet. There was no way Henry could believe he can still have a functioning bank when this scheme was over.

I parked the car by the front door. "A lot closer than the last time," I said smiling at Henry. "Where's the valet?"

Henry shook his head.

"And the koi pond, where is it? –Uh, there it is! See Henry, things do change. People do change." He just stared at me as he opened the car door.

"Don't embarrass me," Henry said.

Panama Jamal came out to meet us, followed by his entourage. Jovial as I remembered him – always laughing. Henry's godfather, the *Padrino* was gone. He was sentenced to twenty years in prison for cocaine trafficking and PJ now "owned" the LaGorce estate. He was in charge and he adopted the air of being the new boss.

"So wonderful to see you. I love that you are here." He ran to Henry and hugged him. "*Enrique, como esta mi amigo? Como esta tu papa?*"

Henry answered with polite short answers.

"*Si'* I know, I know. I talk to your father all the time." I turned toward Henry and gave him a toothless grin. Henry shot me back a look. Of course Henry's father spoke to PJ all the time. They did business together. We walked through the mansion and into the back. There was a Sikorsky Executive helicopter rotor rotating – ready for takeoff as soon as we entered. "*Vamanos.* We go." Henry and I were back in sync.

"Where are we going, PJ?" I asked. He pointed to his ear. The chopper made too much noise to talk.

"Come on!" He waved with his hand as he climbed in the helicopter. We all strapped in, Henry and I had no idea where we were going.

"Where are we going, PJ?"

"Opa locka, Opa locka! Hialeah, Hialeah!" He smiled. PJ was flying the helicopter. And the guy in the left seat was the copilot. "You impressed, GP? I'm a pilot, like you."

"A helicopter is an airplane with no wings," I replied.

"Oh, you don't like helicopters?" PJ replied. "How else are we to get to the airport and avoid the traffic?" He started chanting, "Opa locka, Opa locka. Hialeah, Hialeah," as he called out on the radio that we were landing at Opa locka airport. We landed and we walked briskly over to a Pilatus, a single engine luxury airplane, one of the great long distance airplanes on the market.

"Where are we going, PJ?" Henry asked. He was getting nervous. I didn't blame him. I wanted to know too. Money made people do crazy things. Crazy people with little inhibition and money can be erratic.

"We're just taking this for a spin, right PJ? We don't have all day to go on an unscheduled trip." I said.

"If we were just going for a spin, I'd take the Cirrus,"[131] PJ said with a smile. "I'm ready to give you and Henry's bank a lot of money, guys. You'll spend all the time you need with me. I've packed your bags. There's no place else you need to be. I know you know computers. I know you use computers to invest in the markets. You want my money? We need our money protected and to grow. The one place in the world where money was supposed to be sacred and safe has been compromised. GP, the way we do things, our privacy, our business, and our lives have been violated." He was talking about Panama.

"You want us to go to Panama?" I asked. Henry gave a surprised look for the both of us.

Panama, the place of the biggest and most recent data breach in the recent world history – that's where PJ wants us to go. I looked up to look at Henry but I saw Bobby A coming toward the plane. Taylor was in her car. She got out of the passenger side and waved at us and switched to the driver's side. She waved again and drove off.

"Bobby A is our friend," PJ reminded us. "This is how you all met, at the house when you were in college, remember?" Of course we remembered.

"So, you took over for the Boys? *Los Muchachos*?"

PJ smiled. He wasn't going to answer that question. We knew the answer. But Henry still appeared a little concerned. His naivety never drummed out of his system.

"Hey, boss," Bobby A said to me. He lifted two bags into the cargo section of the plane.

"It's all good, Boss. I'm coming with you," Bobby A said.

I got in. Henry got in. The plane started to move. In some way I felt fine because I was seated behind the pilot and PJ was sitting in the right seat again. But in a fixed wing airplane, right seat means copilot. PJ clicked on the radio, "Opa locka clearance delivery . . . Pilatus 8 Kilo Kilo, IFR Tocumen." PJ smiled, "Don't you love my airplane's call sign is Kilo Kilo." He laughed hard at his own remark.

Henry's eyes widened when he realized we really were going to Panama. "PJ, we don't have passports," Henry said.

"You don't need passports, Henry," PJ said.

"8 Kilo Kilo, clearance delivery . . . cleared IFR Tocumen, Panama, climb 2000, expect 10,000 ten minutes after departure, then as filed . . . squawk . . .Miami Departure 119.7." We taxied and we were up on our way to Panama. For what? I didn't know. "We're going to have fun, aren't we Bobby?" PJ remarked.

"Just like old times, Panama Jamal," Bobby said. "Just like old times."

▪ ▪ ▪

We landed and went straight to another airplane. "You fly the Cirrus, GP." PJ said. "Henry is going to meet with our financial people." Henry seemed relieved. He got into a car and left.

"We could've had this meeting about your finances in Florida, PJ. What are you and I doing?"

"We're going flying some more," he said.

I smiled, "Alright."

"Just get in and I'll be your navigator," PJ said. He got into the right seat, I in the left, and Bobby A in the back. PJ left his Pilatus pilot at the airport. I started the engine.

"What altitude do you want me to fly to?" I turned and looked at PJ. "Just fly straight and climb to 6000 feet," he said. The weather was clear, so I was comfortable.

I saw nothing below me except jungle – miles and miles of foliage. "You're going to have to point out the landing strip if it's on grass," I said. I knew better than to think that PJ was taking me to a drug lab.

"Just keep going on our present heading," PJ replied. A few moments later he told me to land on a grass strip that was ten miles in front of us.

He smiled, "Ever land a Cirrus on grass?"

I hadn't. "I usually try and land at airports with asphalt. I'm assuming we don't have to tell other planes in the area we're landing here?" PJ swiveled his head and didn't answer, but he gave me a look. There were no other planes around. I slowly descended to land on cleared field of grass. Yes, it looked like a drug strip from the 1990s. But this wasn't the kind of plane you load cocaine into.

"Keep the nose up, GP," PJ reminded me. He was right. Keep the nose up so we didn't hit a divot and snag the nose wheel and collapse the wheel or worse.

We landed. I stopped the plane. "That was fun," I said. "Where do you want me to park?"

PJ looked at me and said, "Shut the plane down and leave it here. It's just us, GP. No one else is landing." I shut down the airplane and we got out. We walked off the grass strip. It turned into jungle, trees all around us. Within a few steps we were at a hangar. I wondered why we didn't put the plane in the hangar but it became clear it was for something else. I stopped asking questions when I saw two men carrying an unconscious man from the hangar.

"Don't worry about that. He'll be fine," PJ said. I didn't know about that and I started to have feeling this may not be his computer lab. I wished I could have a JLL consult now. I would love JLL to check me, to advise me, and to make me be even smarter. Not sure what I would ask him. "What are in warehouses in Panama?" PJ, Bobby A, and some other goon looking mercenaries were just standing around a server room – a hangar of rows and rows of servers.

"Do your thing," PJ said.

"What thing?"

"You know, do your computer thing. You're a computer expert. Bobby A says you can do anything with computers and computer stuff," PJ said.

"Absolutely anything," Bobby A said.

"I'm looking at a very large data center. It's called a server farm. What's the problem?"

"This is it. This is the server farm. This is the place where the Panama papers were hacked. Our papers were stolen and released to the world. Do you know what we have to do to make sure the whole cartel avoids destruction?" I didn't and I didn't want to know.

"So, what do you want me to do?" I asked. He looked at me like it was obvious. "Make it so the papers on the servers are gone."

"Delete the Panama papers? You know these servers don't hold the only copies of the papers. You know they're not really paper, right?" I knew this was going to be hard to explain. "Every time that someone sent an email with an attachment the documents would be on another server. Every bcc, every guy that sent it to himself at home or three other people." I waited for a look of some comprehension.

"There are no emails. I'm told this is the only place. This is where the law firms that handled these matters kept the papers."

I thought for a moment. I assumed it was true. "These are your servers, unplug them."

"We need to do better than that. Someone can plug them back in, no?" PJ asked.

"Yes, someone could plug them back in."

"But, if they're yours just bury them. Dump them in the ocean." PJ and Bobby A looked at each other. It made me a little uncomfortable that those two used to know each other. It seemed like Bobby A knew too much about what was going on. He was supposed to work for me now.

"We can't just shove them in the plane and dump them. We don't own them. They belong to the law firms."

"Which ones?" I asked.

"We just call them the Pirates," PJ said.

Was he referring to Baker? Baker wished they controlled the Panama Papers. "Baker's not involved in this," I said with confidence having already had JLL review Baker's data.

"No, it's not Baker's," PJ answered.

"This is a Panamanian law firm, right PJ?" Bobby said. We all just stood there. I looked at the servers like I was diagnosing them. They were servers. What would JLL say?

"Unscrew the casings around the servers and burn them," I said.

"Burn them?" PJ asked.

"That's it, burn them."

"They can't just come back to life another day?" PJ asked.

"Not if this is the only server holding the data. If there's stuff that didn't get copied, then no, it can't come back to life." I thought for a moment. "But what about the journalists that have a copy of the data already? You know the German outlet that broke the story?" I asked.

PJ stared at me intently. "We don't have to worry about that."

Worried? I answered the question asked. "Burn it."

PJ nodded to one of the mercenaries. "There are documents and data on these servers that can never come out. Burn this place down." Two men nodded back. "Don't forget to unscrew the covers on the servers before you set the fire. Come on, let's get out of here."

Bobby A, PJ, and I ran back to the plane. I spun the plane around and took off on the opposite runway. Nose up! Keeping the nose up off the grass – taking off with barely any visibility from the smoke coming from the hangars. They couldn't wait until we were in the air? From the plane I saw out the left side; saw the hangar burning. I started to wonder what wasn't leaked in the infamous Panama papers. We needed PJ invested in the Bank. But these side projects definitely took us off the ruby rails.

. . .

We landed back in Opa locka and the Reverend Booker T. Washington was sitting in a Cadillac waiting for us.

"What's he doing here?" Henry asked.

Bobby A said he would go ask him what he wanted. A moment later he returned and said, "He wants to give us a ride." I looked around. "You don't have to give us a ride, Reverend. Bobby has his car here."

"Come on now. I never see you in Church." I looked at Bobby and said, just follow us to LaGorce to pick up my car. I didn't want any detours or any other special happenings. My whole outlook changed.

We got in the Cadillac. "You smell like smoke," the Reverend said.

"Something got on me from the plane," I answered.

"I want in," the Reverend said. "Everyone is running around talking about how much money they're going to be making, what the hell is going on?"

"Going on where?" I asked.

"The Bank. God's Bank. My bank. The bank I started," Reverend said.

"The bank you started?" Henry asked. "We bought the FDIC certificate from you and let you sit on the board. What bank did you start?"

I looked at Henry. What was the point of getting into an argument about the technical beginnings of the bank?

"What's up, Reverend? Talk to me," I said.

"There's talk all over town, I mean all over. Saying you guys have raised some serious investment capital. I got lawyers calling me telling me I have to sell my stock. What the hell for? What the hell is going on? The lawyers said you issued distributions to yourselves that are out of step with the revenue brought in to the bank. The lawyers are saying you're running a Ponzi scheme." Smooth, but not smooth enough. I ran my hands over the front of Reverend Washington's shirt and around his waist. Then I moved to unbuttoning his shirt, after moving aside the rope chain across his chest and the crucifix that covered his solar plexus feeling for a recording device. I grabbed his phone and handed to Henry who rolled down the back window and threw the phone out.

"Hey, what the fuck are you doing?" The Reverend asked.

"Keep your eyes on the road," I responded.

He laughed deliberately, "Checking me for a wire? Get serious. Now tell me what the fuck is going on?"

"Nothing is going on. We're an investment bank. We're raising capital to invest. Which lawyer is telling you to sell your stock?" I asked.

"The lawyers. They called me down to their office. They're saying they're going to talk to you about having a real CEO – an international CEO. We're hitting a whole other level and something about not being able to keep up with interest and payouts if investors want out down the road. They're extorting me. The fat balding one said they'll pay me a premium to sell if I sign an affidavit that you have committed financial improprieties," the Reverend said.

"And? And, if I want your vote on the Board, I'll have to buy it?" I asked. He looked at me. Henry was starting to unravel.

"We haven't bought your vote already? All the distributions and donations to your Church from the bank. You'd have no bank if we didn't buy your FDIC certificate," Henry said. This was the most impolitic I've ever heard Henry. The strain was getting under his skin.

"And there would be no bank unless I sold the certificate," Reverend Washington responded.

"Yeah, right. You're the only guy in town with a certificate?" Henry yelled.

The Reverend said, "I'm willing to invest more. I don't want out, I want in."

"Relax, Henry. No need to get into an emotional argument here." I looked at Henry. There was so much rolling around in his head. Henry lived in a perfectly protected world. He didn't know how his father's bank really worked. He knew how G-D bank worked. Now he was afraid that he would never be able to pick up the pieces and have a legitimate bank of his own one day.

"Reverend, I don't want you invested more. You need to hear me right now. If you trust me you'll listen. I don't want you to get hurt. You don't need to be a part of the next level. I want you to do something for me," I said.

"What?"

"You're going to have to have faith."

"But what if I do have faith – in you," he said.

"Good," hoping he understood.

"But what if I have so much faith I want to invest more, not sell?"

"Reverend, not only do I want you to sell; I'm asking you to sell your shares to the Baker lawyers."

Reverend Washington just stared at me. He said he didn't like being in the dark.

"Fear no evil for thou art with me," I said with religious conviction. "The showdown is coming in a few days."

"The party on your yacht," the Reverend said.

I nodded because the meeting was on a yacht. "It's a meeting. And it's best for you to sell your shares. You'll bless me for it one day. I promise."

Joseph was a friend of mine.

The yacht where we were celebrating the supersonic coming out of serious funding for G-D Bank was even more spectacular than *Solamente dinero*, the yacht of one of *Los Muchachos* parked outback at the estate on LaGorce. It was as big as *The Seven Seas,* the 282 foot vessel owned and rumored to be on the market for sale by Steven Spielberg. Dressed like the owner with my best blue blazer with gold buttons, what one might think of as dressed like the captain, was flashy enough with a pinky ring. Taylor met me at the foot of the stairs to board.

"I thought I said to ramp it up," I stated with sarcasm.

"I thought the occasion warranted understated elegance," Taylor said.

"So, who really owns this boat? *Not Sub-prime* – nice name."

"It was from your old friend, from MIT." Taylor answered. Now I was curious, who do I owe now? It was another little bit of stress. Can I just pay this debt off, or do I have to purchase a business or someone's shopping center they need to unload because they were cash poor and needed to make some other business deal work for them?

"Chadsworth," Taylor said.

"Chadsworth?" I smiled. "Did he charge us?"

"He said you may recall you and your boys made him and his privileged frat boys a lot of money. At least the ones that listened to you."

"I remember," I said.

"All he asked for was a phone call sometime next week," Taylor said.

As I climbed aboard, the party was already started. All the next level investors were aboard. I looked up and noticed all the waitresses on board were from *Cat's Gold*. They didn't look like strippers; they looked like waitresses.

"Incredible yacht. Did you buy this with our money?" Sasha said shaking my hand, suppressing his accent the best he could. I was about to tell him that the Ukrainian floozy he brought should grab a tray. Alessio, with a double malted scotch in his hand – neat, wondered why he was invited. Dressed like a priest without a collar, he seemed concerned. We were all concerned. What happened next was unchartered, even unpredictable for even the best AI.

Saul Graf and his wife were on board already. "So good to see Katherine. You look better than ever," I said kissing her cheeks and even hugging her. "How could anyone get tired of this?" I glanced over at Cinnamon or she might be Jessica tonight, acting as a server aboard the yacht. I was a little obvious; but fuck Saul Graf.

"I certainly am not," Graf interjected.

"For sure he's not," Katherine said with an innocent smile.

"Where's Christian tonight?" I asked.

"Probably drinking by himself," Katherine said.

"Pretty spicy, Katherine," I answered.

"Still at the office. Somebody has to do that late night work," Saul always maintained his business shell. "I need to talk to you, GP."

"Let me say hello to everyone and I'll see you in a little bit." Leela escorted me away to greet the next group. Out of the corner of my eye I saw Alessio and PJ talking. Then sometime later, I saw Alessio and Sasha talking. I usually enjoyed watching different people I knew interact with each other but those interactions were ticklish.

Taylor, my little hostess, was bragging that we honeymooned on a boat just like one. One day we will retire on one of those yachts and actually sail the seven seas. Taylor whispered in my ear that Saul Graf really wants to talk to me. "I told him this was a party and you shouldn't talk business."

"Good. Right answer." I gave her a kiss on the cheek. And spent about an hour floating across the array of investors in G-D Bank.

I looked at Graf, after he finally cornered me; I smiled as I looked over his head. It was Leiner, climbing aboard; couldn't miss any party. Fear of missing out –he was a player too. No need for a girl on his arm, there were plenty of ladies here. Leiner frowned momentarily but went back to his normal resting face – a scowl. "Finish up what you needed?" Graf asked.

"Sure did," Leiner retorted.

Graf and Leiner finally cornered me on the deck.

"What's up, Saul, Christian?" I asked.

"Reverend Washington is selling his shares in the bank. According to the by-laws, your group has the right to buy all or part of the shares. Otherwise, my group is going to buy his shares," Graf said. Graf stopped talking when Jessica brought over a plate of *hors d'oeuvres*."We can go below deck if you like," I said as I grabbed a shrimp and walked away. I led them below deck.

"I'm here to tell you that if you don't come up with the money for Reverend Washington's shares, your seat on the Board will be in jeopardy," Graf informed me like he was some type of official.

"I hadn't heard the Reverend wanted to sell." I said grinning. I contained my resentment; these guys begged for me not too long ago. Now they were stakeholders, so they represented themselves; and themselves alone. Now with this truth confirmed, my anger boiled in my blood. Revenge will be so sweet.

"Well, maybe you're not as in the know as you pretend to be," Leiner said.

"Why don't we do a capital call for liquidity?" I asked. At that moment, Henry arrived and was coming down the steps to join our conversation.

Leiner did not wait. "No, no, no. Then we'd be less profitable." Leiner said like he was actually telling us something we didn't know.

"Oh, is that how that works?" Henry said with sarcasm.

"We know how you guys work," Graf remarked.

"And, I know how you work, counselor. We better come up with the capital, keep us overly leveraged in all our investments, or else I'd be running a Ponzi scheme, right? Isn't that what you told Reverend Washington?" I asked. They were mad now, a page out of Sun Tzu.[132] If your opponent was temperamental, seek to irritate him.

"Ten million dollars. You'd have to sell this yacht. That's what you'll need to do. We're going to vote for a new CEO next week too." Leiner announced.

"Counting my money again? You don't have to hold a meeting. I'll resign as CEO."

"I didn't expect that," Graf said.

"I thought you guys knew how I worked?" I smirked. "No distributions for six-months. Monthly payouts are over. Then the bank can buy back the Reverend's shares and Henry thinks there's going to be a downturn in the market. We should tell the investors they should be patient."

"We can torture you with legal proceedings just to torture you," Leiner said. Even Graf was startled by the remark; but decided to embrace it. "That's what we do. We know the law," Graf chimed in.

"Guys, you think you're smart and savvy, but I do know you," I said. Henry got a little nervous. I think he thought I would reveal JLL, but I didn't. I motioned for Leela who came closer to us. Joseph was her love and friend too. She deserved to let them know what fate lies ahead.

"We've seen you in Court. We know how you think and your moves," Leela said. "We're glad you forced this conversation because I want you to know something." Leela sensed the tension and liked it. "You remember Joseph Lars Leege? He was our friend. I don't mean a fake *dear friend* – like some bullshit you spread around so people think you're important. Not like you two are to each other. I mean he was our friend. He was Henry's friend and he was GP's friend, and Joseph had many friends." They stared at her. They thought she was a reductive and simple woman whose only purpose was to take care of men. But Leela was our equal. She made the team better. We'd be without class, structure, and glue to keep us all together without her.

I then spoke. "You think you know us? Game on? That's your threat – remove me as CEO, buy out the Reverend? It's been game on from the day I saw you in court mocking Jeffrey Gogolas. I've studied you for years. I have ten-thousand hours of deep learning on you. You're running the bank now? Always remember, now it's your bank. You're responsible for all that happens there. Now get off my boat," I stared at Graf.

They stood their ground. "Appear weak when you are strong, and strong when you are weak," Graf said. Clearly, they didn't comprehend the significance of Joseph Leege and our friendship. What does a guy who died before G-D Bank have to do with the bank or anything going on now? They never had a friend.

"You guys will be indicted before this whole mess is over. I'm going to make sure of it," I said. The two took a few steps backward as if we might physically attack them when their backs were turned.

As I saw Alessio standing by my car there was no hope that he wasn't the next bad thing. "Alessio, did you enjoy yourself tonight?"

"Yes, I did, Gregory. Unusually cool for a South Florida night." I sensed he was going to continue. "The Church's money can't be commingled with the likes of Panama Jamal and Sasha Popova."

"Why do you say that, Alessio?" I asked.

"Because we are the Catholic Church. That is what it is to be a Jesuit. I know what you're thinking. The Church is in no position to cast stones. But PJ is a drug trafficker whose picture is on a board in the D.C. office of the DEA. And, Sasha? He's two steps removed from Deripaska,[133] who eats dinner with Putin."

"What does any of that really mean, Alessio?" I asked. "Show me the money, I'll show you the crime."

"It means the Church can't be the subject of a Congressional hearing, an anti-crime task force in the EU or worse, G-D Bank is the subject of a subpoena because the Justice Department is investigating their money laundering. It's bad. It will shame the Church. Truly, sincerely, this is very old money. Old money families are peculiar. This is where we spend money to do Christ's work. Feed the hungry; clothe the poor; heal the sick. Old money, old families, who view their money as a responsibility bestowed upon them by God, only after they buy their villas in Florence, private jets, and Picassos and Banksy.[134] They cannot be embarrassed. The shame will cost millions. They just don't want money; they want respect for not having done a thing with their lives. Our integrity will be lost. Jesuits don't abuse children. Jesuits do not torture non-Christians. Jesuits cannot appear to make money with criminals."

As I shook Alessio's hand, I didn't fight it. This was an unexpected next thing. "How long do I have, Alessio?" I asked. He nodded in appreciation.

"Unwind our investments within two weeks," he said. That wasn't a lot of time. Ten million investment mushroomed pretty quickly. "That should be around forty-two million." This was a black swan. Two weeks? "After two-weeks, these old families will send friends to talk to you. You know, how do you say, *bada boom,* Italians, not Italians from Italy."

I nodded. "Alessio, will you do me a favor? Don't tell the Baker lawyers you want your deposits back. I'll process your request personally."

He looked at me and tilted his head as if to say he'd consider it as he walked away. Henry then sauntered over to me.

"We didn't anticipate the Jesuits pulling out so fast," Henry said. "We needed at least six months to cover the divestment. Not even your precious AI anticipated it happening so fast. Can they even do that?"

"You're going to bust my balls now? That's the consciousness of our best friend," I said."How short are we for the pay back?" Leela asked.

"Like he said, forty-two million dollars," I answered.

Henry nodded, confirming. "This was never meant to go so far; get so big," Henry said.

"They wouldn't break. We needed to get them to break."

"This God's Ponzi has gotten away from us," Leela said.

"Like every other Ponzi scheme. We'll be nothing more than another South Florida run Ponzi scheme. This will disgrace my whole family and all of us are going to prison. All to settle a score; all to get even," Henry complained.

"Not to get even, Henry. To get right through revenge," I replied.

"You did this on purpose, Greg. You screwed up the bank just to get us to the brink of destruction!" Henry said.

"What happened to the secret reserves, Henry? We were meant to leave Baker, the accountants and other guys wearing a white hat holding the bag," Leela said. "This was your area, Henry."

"We have reserves in CocoBank tucked away. We never spent a dime. We don't own this yacht, or the G-D offices around the globe, the houses, the *chateaus*, nothing. We don't own a thing we didn't own before we opened the bank. We never comingled a quarter. We lived by the adage: Access is the new ownership."

I couldn't help but smile. "We had access. Our good work, our good friends provided access to the best places in the world. It appeared like we were being sneaky and Ponzi-like, but we just had access and didn't own a thing." A little reminiscent, we laughed at a couple of examples where someone did a background check on the corporate structure of a piece of property and assumed we were some type of slick mafia. "We never said we owned it."

"Oh Henry, don't be such a worrier. You know we're going to think of something," Leela said. This private meeting had to break up. Taylor was walking around with her friends showing this part of the yacht.

"Should I worry, GP?" Henry asked.

"Listen to Leela," I said. The truth? Worrying might help.

▪ ▪ ▪

As I sat in a conference room on Brickell in the Miami corporate office of CocoBank, Henry actually appeared to be praying. We were preparing for the conference call with the Baker lawyers and other members of the Board, and investors of G-D bank. I didn't mention JLL to Henry at all. Henry was a naysayer. He thought the computer helped but I referred to JLL as a "him" or Joseph. He got saddened or angry, and then said I should go meditate or see a psychiatrist for delusions. But this was a conference call that should send a shock through G-D Bank and it turned out be intense – so intense Henry freaked out in anticipation. This was the plan – the shock wave through the bank.

Was it hard to believe that lawyers, accountants, and otherwise educated men could believe that they involved themselves in a Ponzi scheme? On some level it was hard to fathom they didn't know. Shouldn't they know better – particularly the ones that participate in the cleanups of Ponzi schemes? Sure, trustees, lawyers, and accountants through the years have been entrusted with funds collected for the benefit of others, and have stolen the funds with the idea they could be smarter for longer. Maybe they could be smarter for longer than my team. But Baker's scheme of bundling and holding investor money and paying those investors as B members for a lesser rate, while they made A rate interest in the bank's investments was a risk not all shareholder members of the law firm were aware. Why would they? Graf and Leiner were running it as a side hustle. But the law firm was involved because they invested law firm money, both on their credit line, and select trust monies. Money, that was illegal to touch unless authorized by the client. What the clients didn't know didn't hurt them – until they knew.

"Do you have everyone?" I asked.

Henry opened his eyes and looked at the conference phone and nodded. We made sure the phone call was recorded. God's Ponzi was going to end in litigation. Henry took a deep breath and began. "Ladies and Gentlemen: The next voice you hear will be Gregory Portent."

The formality was not required because G-D Bank was not publicly traded. But I wanted to treat this conference call that would otherwise be SEC compliant. It needed to be scripted and recorded. All investors could be on the conference call; all were noticed.

"Good afternoon. This is Gregory Portent. The purpose of this conference call is to advise you that I've been asked to resign as CEO of G-D bank by a majority of the board of directors of the bank in what has been analogized as a vote of no confidence. Due to recent shifts in dynamics, due to sale and purchases of issued shares, most notably, Reverend Washington's shares, my friends, colleagues, and I do not have a majority of shares to maintain the administration of the bank. Accordingly, I'm also resigning from the Board of the Bank effective in one week. The new administration, comprising of a cadre of lawyers, accountants, and insurance executives will take the company in a new direction. Before I depart, I want to make very clear that the recommended distribution of profits based upon new international deposits is premature and could lead G-D Bank to fall out of guidelines or worse. I wish the Board, the bank, and the new executive committee the best of luck. With my resignation, Henry White and Leela Ravichandran also resign their respective roles within the Bank. Thank you and God bless. Goodbye." *Boom.*

"This concludes this conference call," Henry said and then hung up. Within only a moment, our phones were blowing up. Neither one of us answered. We just looked at each other. "I really hope you know what you're doing, GP," Henry said.

"Me too," I said.

Implosion

Saul Graf stormed into the conference room of his Miami law firm office. There were no hellos or any pleasantries. He dug right into Leiner. "Maybe you don't know how it works around here, but you need to make money, not lose it," Graf said to Leiner.

"I'll come back in a minute," Rufus said, forgetting to hang up because I was on *Skype* and could hear everything.

"I don't care if you stay, *Doofus*. You should probably hear this too. If you get fired from this law firm, this will be the reason why. I just heard from the Turks and Caicos group, they said they didn't get their quarterly distribution. That's a huge problem. Our fees are tied to that distribution. You and your special projects that make us no money. The failed *Xbox* class action, taking credit for originating cases you have a tangential connection, and I don't even want to get into your dream about opening a lobbying office on K street in Washington, D.C. because your *friends* with the President. You're bullshit! This is bullshit. We now know Portent is bullshit."

"He's. . . ." Leiner pointed to the computer on the conference room table.

"He's on Skype?" Graf asked. "Put him on the TV screen."

I was transferred to the large screen in the conference room. I could see and hear all of them.

"Portent, where's the money? Why is everyone saying we're undercapitalized after the last distribution?"

"I'm not the CEO, Saul," I said. "I announced my position at the conference call that I didn't think there should be another distribution. My recommendation wasn't followed. Frankly, I was really surprised you voted on the distribution before you knew the Jesuits were withdrawing their investment entirely."

"You set that up." Graf replied. "I'm leaving the room in a moment but you and *Lie*-nar are going to figure out what the hell is going on here and fix it."

"Who are you speaking as, Saul, my lawyer or investor in the bank?" I asked just to anger him some more.

"Both! The law firm represents the Bank and I'm an investor. Those two interests are aligned one-hundred percent."

"I guess you're not my lawyer anymore," I said. "You've given us all the help you can. You've properly motivated Leiner and Rufus, we can take it from here."

"Your arrogance isn't equal to your cleverness, GP." Graf shot back.

"Right. Thanks, Saul. By the way, how's Katherine? Give her my best. She's as sweet as sugar. Or do I mean Cinnamon?"

"Fuck you, GP. And fuck your dead friend. You better figure out a way to fix this or we're all fucked."

It was the type of anger that was so true, I felt calm. "You know I will," I said. "You know I will."

Saul Graf then turned his fury back to Leiner. From my perspective Leiner was an impotent fool trying to make himself into something he never could. Always the red-headed stepchild of a lawyer. Such an abused child. Poor little Christian. Desperate to be accepted as an equal, always trying to catch up in Saul Graf's matrix.

Graf was a legal-gangster. He treated the junior partners as would a *Mafioso*. G-D bank was Graf's origination because he prevailed upon the management committee that Henry's father went to school with Graf and I learned about the firm from watching them get their ass kicked in bankruptcy court. Graf was rude, even for him.

"What are you, Christian, Jewish? A drunk, a recovering alcoholic? A good guy, a bad guy? An originator, a worker bee? Monogamous or a philanderer? You just don't know when to fuck and when to sit with your hands folded on your desk – which makes you a failure," Graf said to Leiner. "This could ruin us. Ruin the entire firm. We could end up like Dreier, Dewey, Rothstein, – like every other law firm that thought they had some magical innovation."

Christian Leiner didn't know what to feel worse about, the vicious pieces Graf was taking out him, or the pressure in his chest when it occurred to him they'd be held responsible for paying out more than they took in, by using new investors' money – historically and commonly known as a Ponzi scheme. Why didn't they know the Jesuits were pulling out? They were lawyers. They couldn't sell the ignorant bliss defense. Now, they were in charge of the whole scheme. They wouldn't be able to persuade prosecutors. No, the previous bankers were in charge of the whole thing. That was why we wanted to kicked them out. We were just the lawyers. That storyline was the B-story for the news articles, pre-indictment – a defense at trial.

Jessica was the receptionist by day. She kept a really juicy secret: she was sleeping with a married boss on the management committee, and was a dancer by night. But being the other woman, even the most steadfast other woman, was never enough. She resented she still had to strip. Graf wasn't going to play sugar daddy and support her with his money. He gave Jessica a job and paid for the VIP room when he used her as Cinnamon. She was a single mother of two, and a monthly obligation to a deadbeat ex-husband. According to family law justice, she had to pay alimony to that guy. She resented that, no matter what, she was still the other woman and not Graf's everything. This was what I intended to exploit. Remember, I was still at war. And no doubt, the lawyer/investors and creditor/victims were poised to attack me. My advantage, they just now figured out they were at war with me.

Henry continued to dial me furiously. "I'm freaking out, GP. My father won't stop calling me. He thinks the family reputation is at stake."

"It's not. CocoBank is not involved," I said. "Right?"

Of course, he knew I was right. But this was Henry's personality—freak out under pressure.

"He cares about his son," Henry answered back.

"So do I, Henry. Now you know it was good that we turned down your father's contribution to the bank."

"My father is saying the word 'Ponzi.' He never says that. He survived the money laundering scandals of the '80s, the savings and loan scandal of the '90s in Miami, the foreclosure crisis of 2006. My father isn't like that, but he'll help us because I'm his son." To the end, Henry has the rosiest view of his father; an honorable man, but a bankster. "Things are worse than you think, GP, you've been summoned. The Banker of Europe sent a birthday card to your office. They want to see you – in Switzerland."

I sighed. "Henry, I hear what you're saying. We can't take your father's money. He can't be the last one in," I said. "You know this, right? You know why. It's musical chairs. We have a good chance of winning. *Tranquillo, mi amigo.*"

"I don't know why I trust you, GP."

"Because my heart is pure. And remember, this is for Joseph," I said.

After a long hard pause Henry replied, "Okay, I will. I will trust you."

"In a few hours people are going to be wondering where I am. Tell them you don't know."

"I don't know."

"Right. And tomorrow, let it slip I'm in New York," I said.

"New York? You can raise more money in New York?" Henry asked.

"Don't know."

"We need forty-two million, GP. You can raise that in less than a week?" Henry asked.

"Not sure, *mi amigo*," I said. What Henry didn't know was that Rufus left his laptop open in the conference room and JLL was recording Graf and Leiner's continued plotting. They launched a scheme to put G-D bank into involuntary bankruptcy or dilute my shares for malfeasance, and then my shares should cover any loss due to the withdrawal of the Jesuits. I boiled it down to these two options months ago. But, it was real now. And to be honest I was afraid.

In a conversation with JLL, I confessed I was afraid. JLL replied, "Seems reasonable that you're afraid – based upon the odds." I calculated the odds but I didn't calculate how I would feel about the odds when they were upon us. JLL sensed some regret on my part.

> JLL:*But this is what you wanted. This is what you tasked me to do.*

That was true. But, I was concerned about myself and the rest on the team. We ended the conversation with a wish from JLL. He hoped the odds would swing in my favor. This was not comforting as a matter of logic. It revealed there was a fragile variable in our complex equation of how this Ponzi scheme ends. We all could be buried in the implosion.

Cat's Gold

It was 2 o'clock in the morning and I drove right up to *Cat's Gold*. Told the valet to keep my car close and gave him a fifty dollar bill. I entered the club. The cashier knew me and let me by. They were pumping in fragrant dried ice gas so no one would have to smell the other men. It made me sick, I was so pumped full of adrenaline. The strip club was dark and UV lights were on full. It took my eyes a moment to adjust. The sailor girl untied the bow that kept her shirt on – double D breasts that didn't move. They defied natural physics and that annoyed me. I walked to the back, ran up the stairs in seconds flat. I was pumping blood and sweat.

The curtain to the VIP curtain was closed. All I wanted was more time to operate. I saw those distinctive heels of the stripper shoes underneath the curtain. I could also see the signature Bruno Magli shoes of the despicable lawyer too. With my camera phone out, I swiped the curtain open and snapped a flurry of shots. No one was more startled than I. I looked at Cinnamon. She was completely naked.

"Leiner!" I gasped. "That's Graf's. . . Good for you. Way to assert yourself you passive aggressive dolt."

"He threatened to go to H.R. if I didn't. . ." Cinnamon said.

"Save it, honey. Not here for you," I said.

Leiner was sitting on a small couch and he was inside of Cinnamon. Like I said, they fuck each other and over. This was more than I expected and more than I hoped. Cinnamon was Taylor's friend. I gawked at Taylor's friend naked, when I promised I wouldn't. I gave her a dirty lusty look and not by accident, by design. I had become unethical. I was desperate.

Leiner was drunk but conscious. I looked at him. He looked at me. Cinnamon covered her boobs with one arm and the point of intercourse with the other.

"Leiner, you need to tell Graf hold off for another week. I'm going to New York and you need to calm yourself. You do, and your secret's safe. You don't and I start posting." I shook my phone. "If you're too drunk to understand any of this, Cinnamon will explain it. Enjoy your evening."

That was my Monday. Now, off to feel the Bern.

Feel the Bern

After hours on a plane, I was back in the capital city of Switzerland. Bern, the City that was built around a crook in the Aare River. Yes, well said, *crook*. It was a lovely European City. The not-American architecture always made me think about my favorite summer in Europe – Chana. Who even in this moment I asked myself could I ever love like that again?

Leela stayed at the airport. It didn't matter where she worked. With a computer and an international cell phone she was safe. I made my way into town, the car stopped in front of the Cafe' Federal. I didn't book the car service but the driver at the airport seemed to recognize me from other trips. He asked when he should come back. I didn't know but I would call. I couldn't use the same service or the same guy. Then there would be another person in the world who knew I was in Bern, went from the airport to a meeting at the bank, and then immediately went back to the airport.

I walked a half a block. No one seemed to be behind me. These Swiss bankers were odd. Generally, any one would conclude they were all pleasant and accommodating, if it weren't for the fact that they held money for the Nazis. Not to mention the whole let's hide money from the American tax authority.

I opened the birthday card that was sent to my office. I took it out to read from my inside pocket of my jacket. The meeting was set in Bern. If I turned out to be Darth Vader in this Ponzi scheme, the birthday card was not an invitation to Bern by the Banker of Europe; it was a summons by the Emperor –the address on the bottom of the card, where the execution would be held.

I stopped, remembering where I was and realizing I had arrived. Seeing the small camera above the door, I lifted the birthday card up to the camera. The lock on the door buzzed open and I entered. After walking down a long empty corridor, an impeccably dressed man came from behind a wall and stood behind the security guard sitting at the desk.

The same *maître d'* said, "Mr. Portent, It's such a pleasure to have you visit us." I smiled back with my lips closed, no teeth. I was too tired to play act. It wasn't my birthday; I didn't want to be here because I knew what was coming. Certainly, this could've been handled over the phone. But Swiss bankers or at least this one didn't handle things over the phone, or through emails, or by mail.

I emptied my pockets into a silver tray. Placed my phone, keys, and watch into a tray. I was escorted to behind the wall, down the hall, and up an elevator. Off the elevator, we entered into another room which had no handle on the door. It was an ornate room with no windows. Two-hundred square feet decorated with a painting of some Swiss-countess or duchess on the wall. The room was sound proof. There was no ability to connect to the outside world. The Banker of Europe entered.

He shook my hand. "Thank you for coming, Mr. Portent." I replied with my own, "Good to be here." I put the birthday card on the table, indicating to just get on with the meeting. "Will you explain to me how G-D bank walked into a $42 million deficit?"

"Do you really want me to explain?" I paused. The Banker nodded. I rehearsed my facts. "It was a black swan. That one in a million chance a trade would go bad, happened. It was internet corruption. We input a trade and a millisecond before someone stole our trade. G-D could litigate for three-years or we can just recover. Be back stronger than before, if you give us the time." I stopped talking.

"You need $42 million dollars. We cannot give it to you. We're not willing to float that while we wait for you to -- recover. You're bank is a customer and we consider you a friend, Mr. Portent. We have to invoke the word, *business* to you. You mustn't forget it. This is business." A dramatic pause of his own, "You have until your Valentine's day to make up the difference." He didn't have to complete that sentence. ". . . or bad things will start to happen. . . . at the bank."

"Thank you." We shook hands. I was escorted out. A car was waiting, with the same driver who drove me from the airport. Everyone in Swiss banking now knows G-D bank was called to the principal's office. Will I be given the room to succeed? Success or failure sometimes depends on who liked you. That was random to me; or worse, not good for me. Pressure was mounting.

Muerte a Secuestradores

Made it back to the Bern airport, the conversation I had at the bank could've been discussed over the phone. Staring at my phone, I read the words, "Call your girl!" Call my girl? I thought for a moment, but who was my girl, in this context? Which girl? Another anonymous message. I loved these weak script kiddie hackers who want to sound ominous in their anonymity. At this point, someone would have to make the Do Not Walk traffic signal go on with a special message directed at me, in order for me to jump. I was so tired and unimpressed. Only oxycodone and zanies would be an antidote to the level of stress I was feeling. The phone rang. It was my girl, Leela. She asked me where I was and when I said, "The airport," she interrupted.

"GP, this is crazy. I don't know if this is true or not." She was frantic.

"What? Just say it."

"It's Henry. Something's happened. Look at your phone."

Text: *We have your boy, Enrique Blanco! What do u think of that motherfucker?*

The South Americans, I thought. And they've kidnapped Henry. This wasn't good nor expected. They were trying to get Henry's father involved. I didn't have to think at all; didn't have to consult JLL to get his thoughts. But I did and JLL was right. It had to be the South Americans. My whole world was attacking me. People within the bank, investors outside the bank, the lawyers, and the stakes are even higher. It was not a matter of luck. Right now, I'm not liked very much at all. I didn't have to apply Bayes theorem[135] to ballpark the best antidote possible – I was angry. But JLL had an answer, not just for Henry's kidnappers but to solve the big problem. Not the safest answer, but a familiar answer that referred back to the team's talents at MIT. It made me comfortable enough to feel some confidence. I used the response that harkened back to the creation of the cartels in the beginning when terrorist groups would kidnap members of established families in Colombia. The kidnappers would understand and not take it well.

GP (text): *Muerte a Secuestradores.*[136] *Sin duda!* "Death to kidnappers. Without a doubt!"

The first time in years I actually felt nervous – helpless. Henry's father, Enrique Blanco called me directly. "*Mi familia* is now involved. You don't have to worry – yet. Do not call the FBI. *Entiende?*" I understood. "Let's stay in *communicado.*"

As I hung up an attractive Swiss woman in her twenties dressed like a flight attendant handed me a package. The label outside the package was from Baker, LLP. I opened the package and inside was a small box. I opened the box after removing the Tiffany's colored bow. Inside the box was a gold-plated ring with an emerald. It belonged to Henry.

Nastrovia

Bobby A drove me to the *Russian G-Room* restaurant. We entered, and there was a party at the far end of the restaurant. The party was celebrating a grandfather's birthday. All centered on the wise old man wearing suspenders, glasses, and hearing aids. He appeared to be enjoying the attention, the music, dancing girls, and the caviar. It didn't appear that Sasha was part of the party, yet he knew everyone since he was Russian and owned the place. A waitress brought vodka and a tray of caviar on a silver tray. I took a shot and drank it standing up with Sasha. He took a cracker with caviar and ate it. I shook my head. I didn't want any. And as word spread around town, and the world, that G-D Bank was in trouble it was my job to be on the phone all day reassuring investor groups of the solubility of the bank and it would still make money, even without me. Was my money in the bank? Not really.

"Baker is telling me you're out at the bank. You're not CEO," Sasha said. I told him that was true. "But you are in charge of investments?"

"I'm done with that too. There are good investor-traders at the bank. You'll do fine."

"Why do you say this? Do you realize you and your team are the reasons that we are with G-D Bank? We know you have computers that do fancy predictions, everything from sports to money. You can do trades faster than anyone and now you're letting the lawyers and the accountants take it away from you? Do you need me to have some of my investors talk to them?" He meant slap the *pierogis* out of them.

"Baker only wants their people, their clients, and their money. Baker wants to control everything." I needed Sasha to understand this so when his money was lost, he wouldn't come looking for me and the team.

Sasha thought for a moment, "Like always in America, the lawyers want to rule the world and not the investors."

I explained to Sasha that after the Panama papers many investor groups wanted to invest in G-D Bank because of our reputation for large consistent returns and more particularly, privacy. But one investor required me to make a choice; or, has made the choice to leave the bank because of him, and the Latin Americans. He didn't like their reputations—how they made their money.

"Panama Jamal? I met him. He is not Panamanian or South American. He is an American. No matter what he says." Sasha told me as if he was sharing new information. I remained expressionless. "You need to help us. You can't abandon us and the bank. We are family." Family? "Look," he showed me his cellphone. "This is a picture of my nephew, Vlad. And look, that's your friend, Chana. He was at the University of Chicago for a convention. He works on graphic design on computers like she does. He is an artist. He says she's going to see you soon." I stood straight up, my eyes deadened. I was enraged by the threat. This was a threat, wasn't it?

"What's the meaning of this?" I slammed my glass down on the table. "You're threatening me? I've never been anything but straightforward and honest with you!" Now, Sasha seemed taken aback.

"What does this mean, I'm threatening? I'm not threatening anyone. I'm asking you to help us. These Baker lawyers are bullies! I want you to help me insure our investment without them. I'm asking you to use your team by mining for bitcoin. I heard you're friends with the cofounder, Satoshi." The word for *friend* must mean something different in the Russian underworld.

"You want me to set up servers to mine for bitcoin on the internet?" I asked. Did I overreact? Was I losing my perspective?

"*Da* –yes. But, we want to sell shares as *Bit-com* – investing in the companies searching for bitcoin," he said, as if bitcoin wasn't Ponzi enough. It was layers away from the actual bitcoin market – invest in the company "mining" for bitcoins on the internet, which had a value largely controlled by the value of bitcoin itself on any given day. It was like the "Chinese Google," Alibaba,[137] an investment in the company that owns stock in the Chinese internet search company. In a moment, the stock in the company that owns stock in the real company could be worthless, yet the actual company remains strong.

"You don't have to threaten me," I said.

"What threaten? I'm just telling you I heard your girlfriend is coming to town?"

It may be me. "And, you think you can make a threat with iced Smirnoff in your veins and I'll piss myself? And what, my wife visits her friend at *Cat's Gold*, you're going to talk to me about that too, which means what? So in one short paragraph, you've threatened my life and a friend of mine. You better kill me first because it'll be a slow painful death for you. I wouldn't even have to lift a finger. I'd make a phone call. The money would disappear and I'd tell your comrades that you did it, how you did it, why you did it. I'll tell them where you put the money. And how they could have their millions back if they could only get the password out of you that only you know. And, gosh, no that's not the password either." He didn't respond. "Do you have a warehouse to put the servers?" I asked.

"Yes, of course," he answered.

"Where?" I wondered aloud.

Sasha said, "Omsk" in Siberia and he wasn't kidding. I wasn't going to Siberia. Couldn't they just set up a server farm in warehouses in Oakland Park?

"Bitcoin was hot and then after Mt. Gox it wasn't. One day it'll go to sixty-thousand a bitcoin. But if you invest in bitcoin, you could go from hero to zero in a day."

"Hero to zero?"

"Comrades may start showing you pictures of their nephews with people you care about," I said staring into Sasha's eyes. He understood.

"What should I do, GP?" And there we were, right where I needed him – wondering what he should do and now asking for advice. Still not knowing if JLL was playing the game at a level higher than my pea-brain could comprehend.

I said, "Withdraw your investment from the bank. Take it all back."

"That is spiteful," Sasha said.

"Do it. Don't do it. Just let the comrades you represent know I said withdraw -- now." This withdrawal of the Russians' deposits would be different than the Jesuits'. It would hurt the bank and my investment in it, but it didn't happen on my watch, so it would be Graf and Leiner's fault. Saving the Russians' money and agreeing to set up a server farm to mine for bitcoin might have just saved me.

My Escape

Escher,[138] an artist I can appreciate; as most geeks do. There appeared to be science to the art. Because of my love of sleight of hand, I loved the optical illusions. As I looked around Art Basel, there were plenty of art pieces that were beautiful and thought provoking. Some just provoke for the sake of provoking. And then I looked at Chana from across the room in the convention center.

The word out on Gregory Portent, by Baker and others, was that "he's cracking up." When I resigned as CEO of the bank, I should've gone on vacation but I was still running around trying to juggle the money. The image was a man falling apart. It was what I want others to perceive because it follows my plan; but, it couldn't be true in order for my plan to succeed. Now Leela thought that art would cure what science couldn't. Why was she hanging on? Joseph wasn't smart enough to keep her. Maybe she felt guilt. Women made mistakes; men made mistakes – Leela's mistake, she didn't understand the government monster. It was what the government did best – prosecuting. Dealing with poverty, education, and healthcare for everyone were issues in which the government failed. But prosecuting – labeling a bad guy, proving he violated a law it created, imprisonment, and claiming victory – this was where the government excelled. Maybe Leela suffered from the same disease I did – love. She loved Joseph even though he didn't want her anymore. Love was often cyclical and non-reciprocated. Or maybe we just love what we take care of.

Leela turned over Joseph's guerilla manifesto to the government when it subpoenaed her. That was her sin. She didn't know what to do except hire a lawyer and follow the lawyer's advice. She knew the manifesto existed – should she have obstructed? She had personal pain. We all do.

The perfection of Chana's beauty and my state of vulnerability; the love of my life here, meant to push me back to normalcy, creativity, and clear decision-making. And as in a musical, she was across the crowded room of the convention center, among works of art, as electricity amped through my nerves. We hugged. I was glad to see her and nobody had died. She looked and felt the same. I remembered and learned again that this was Chana – the woman that manipulated my circuitry. I could hold her hand and walk away and leave all this behind. But back in reality, I couldn't leave. The Ponzi balloon was in the air and I couldn't let it fall. I was grateful for the time I was allowed with her. No thanks to God, the spirits, or a nameless mindful expression of harmony. I remembered her precise words to me before she left, "You're capable of real darkness. You are going to save the world or destroy it. I can't be with someone where that's a fifty-fifty proposition." I felt the pain of that cut as if it were yesterday, a drawback of having that kind of forensically precise memory.

Chana explained the rest of the team thought it was a good idea that she visited. Chana had developed her art skills in graphic arts. Over the years, she developed a specialty in finding the meaningful art in the graphic statistics. Statistics can be dry, difficult to understand, and even worse difficult to make meaning out of them. Numbers from statistics can create pretty graphs or lines that help people make decisions based upon those statistics. She did that work for an Israeli pharmaceutical company in Chicago. But her love was still for art for the beauty of art. She insisted she still sketched on her pads and her home was filled with her drawings.

We walked the floor among the works of art. She talked about why something was great or why it was *dreck.* She was persuasive and I agreed with all her assessments. I thought of nothing else, other than what she was saying. She was art. The *piece de resistance,* one I couldn't have in my home. I felt like I was a helpless twenty-something again.

"Chana, I am everything you said I would be," I said.

"I know," she replied. If she only knew what kind of a bad place I was in right now and that I didn't know how to extricate myself or the team.

Would she think it was my pattern? A pattern of highs and lows; depression and mania; loss and revenge?

We stood in front of a Banksy, which was all the rage at this event. I ushered her away from it after we talked about her husband and her three children. The children were in high school; one almost in college. She showed me them on her cell phone. "They look just like their mother," I said. Then I asked about her mother. She was the same. Her Father? Putting up with her mother, who was more confrontational than ever. She wants me to move back to Israel. We smiled.

"And your husband? What does he think?" I asked.

"He hesitated a little. But we don't live in a romance novel." We reached a spot where we were alone. "And him being here would hinder what I was trying to find out," she said.

"And that is?"

"Gregory, what's going on? What is the problem?" I said nothing but that I was under a lot of pressure because of the bank. "You're not a criminal. What are you doing? Leela says you've been talking to the computer and you think it's Joseph. Are you schizophrenic?"

"Am I cracking up? I don't think so." I explained about the AI – Joseph's work with the software he was developing that centered on whole life management; that he uploaded every photo, every email, diary, everything about himself into it. And his belief was that his consciousness was now alive in the AI.

"And what do you believe?"

"When I talk to him, it's him. Leela doesn't talk to him. To her he's dead and she's still angry at him. Googol, thinks I'm crazy and is still angry at him. GNU, thinks it's a spectacular version of Eliza.[139] And, Henry? I don't know what Henry thinks. He might be hiding, he might be kidnapped. I don't know. His father said it's not time to worry quite yet."

"And the answer to my question?" She asked. I stared back. "What do you believe?"

I realized I wasn't responsive to her question. "I don't believe in anything I can't prove or hasn't been proven," I said. I just looked at her. "I think, I believe, it's him. Is there ever a way to disprove it's the consciousness of Joseph? I don't know. Why did he kill himself? He thought he could transfer his consciousness to a computer. If he could be so sure, why can't I?"

"So, you think you're talking to Joseph?"

"Yes, I think I'm talking to Joseph. Do you think I'm crazy?"

"No. Why are you involved in a Ponzi scheme? You don't need the money; it is not your style. You always told me behavior is consistent and cannot be changed. I can't believe there isn't more to this."

Chana trusted me. She didn't believe that I could be capable of real darkness anymore? She didn't understand. "No one on the team has profited from the bank. I haven't made a dime from the bank. But, all the distributions and salary, I've been stashing away in CocoBank – Henry's family bank. We have three sets of books; the real one, the one the lawyers and the accountants pass around to investors, and the really real one – the one that shows that the money we've socked away in CocoBank. But, something went wrong. Something unexpected; something that the AI didn't predict. I need to raise a lot of money fast. I didn't know what to do. Surrendering will ruin more than me, it'll hurt the rest of the team."

"Why did you do this, Gregory? Why?"

"Revenge. I needed those lawyers and creditor/investors to pay for what they did to Joseph."

"But you said Joseph thought he was uploading his consciousness," she said.

"He wasn't thinking clearly. He should've lived longer. He had the rest of his life to improve upon the intelligence. We don't know the answer. We don't know what we're doing. We're on the brink of intelligent breakthrough, but when? Can't say. The lawyers took over the bank to cover their own interests. That was part of the plan. The accountants and insurance guys are filling in the blanks on the investment scheme and they've been cutting distributions like I was except they're not setting aside the funds, which were the team's share of the distributions at CocoBank. It now really was a Ponzi scheme, except the team was not a part of it. I resigned. We resigned. It was all on the bad guys. They're doing worse too. They're holding on to money past the due dates, adding fees, doing dirt bag high frequency trading."

"And?"

"And if I come up with forty-two million dollars, I'm good. We're out and when G-D bank crashes I'll need that money in CocoBank. If it's not there, I'm a Ponzi schemer like them."

"You're crazy, but I love you," she said. I smiled. It did sound crazy. "I knew you weren't a thief. Thank you for not disappointing me." I nodded at her. "And remind me never to cross you."

"You know you have lifetime immunity." I said with a smile.

"I know." We hugged spontaneously. It was good to get that off my chest. "But still Leela told me you have endangered your life and everyone else's. Why do you think this is ethical?"

"Because I didn't think about it. There is effort in ethics and I had no one to tell me no."

She didn't question that half –hearted answer. It was a place holder in the conversation. "Do you want to grab dinner? We can talk about it more?"

"I have to visit my cousins' for Shabbat," she replied. "Besides creating charts and graphs, what role could I have in this scheme?"

"Easy, I'll need you to arrange my escape," I said looking her straight in the eyes. She nodded.

"What are you going to do now?" She asked. "I'm going to let the team know it's time for the last phase of God's Ponzi."

TRANCHE VII
Vegas Baby!

Are you Ready for Some Football?

It was the middle of the desert and I hadn't shaven in a week. Aliens could see the Vegas lights from the stratosphere, but not the West Charleston funeral home. It was dusky, kind of pretty if you asked me. The skyline was always a portrait when the day's sunlight sunk and floated into pastels, and faded into darkness. I circled around the building structure just to see if anyone was waiting for me. No one could be following me, I was alone for miles. Sweaty and sticky, I had been driving for hours, pushing through so I could make it there with a little extra time to rest. Reminding myself, I was on a mission. This was an operation.

Parked and ready, I turned to the laptop that was opened on the passenger seat. I smiled and told JLL, "I'll take it from here. Thanks for the company on the ride." A smiley face icon enveloped the screen. JLL wrote back, "Ethics in relation to strippers, to the corruption in the statutory bankruptcy scheme. That was some rant."

I shut the laptop and placed it on the floorboard. I jumped out the Lisi van, only a bathroom on my mind – nothing deeper. I found one, and I changed into a black suit, black tie, white shirt, and popped out the back of the van. No eureka moment after hours in a van listening to the hum of the road and no palpable imminent threat. It seemed like everything was okay for now. I didn't have the usual stimuli to amp up the fear. I wasn't engulfed in hysteria. Probably have 3,000 messages of various formats waiting for me on some internet connected device.

I walked inside the funeral home. I looked around, established my bearings. There was a non-binary dressed in black. *She* was plain, no makeup; short and plump – silver glasses, trying to make it difficult to judge whether she was a lesbian or asexual. I smiled and detected not even a micro-expression of disgust, pleasantness, or interest at all. Asexual, probably a side effect of the medication that was meant to make her hands shake less.

"Are you the man my brother and Emo is supposed to meet?" She asked. I smiled. "Follow me." So, I followed her one step at a time. She glanced in disapproval, if I took two steps and was not "following" her. But then I was annoyed, a little pissed off at her brother because he knew I was here to see Emo. Emo already screwed up. Why did her brother tell her I was here to meet Emo? That was a breach.

"Do you know who I am?" I asked.

"Don't know, don't care. Unless you're coming in to book a pre-death memorial plot or cremation," she paused from her break of etiquette; considering, what if I were.

I shook my head no. "Where are we going?"

"I was told to bring you to the basement," she said without turning around. I reached my hand back toward my oblique and caressed the gun in its holster. Just a comfort squeeze confirming it was there.

"It's dead around here," I said climbing down steep dark staircase.

"There's always someone," she mumbled.

She opened the door and a man I figured to be her brother and the man I was waiting for, Emo, was standing there in a suit and a subdued undertaker's smile. No handshaking in the morgue, and I appreciated that. A simple mutual nod was perfect. I knew who he was and everything about him. I had JLL run a networking tree to reveal how many degrees of separation he was from any of the major players in G-D bank. He was the most remote undertaker in Vegas; his entire family was native to Nevada.

A knock on the door behind him inspired the undertaker to turn and opened the door. This was where the bodies were wheeled in and dropped off. Two men wheeled in a coffin into the middle of the room, in between the undertaker and me. They went outside again and moments later came in with another coffin. They did this three more times, until all five coffins were lined up in a row.

So far so good, and another knock on the door. Five guys walked in the room through the same door looked like they were *Reservoir Dogs.*[140]

They were dressed just like me. Then Emo entered. Emo, the best casino concierge in Las Vegas.

"Good morning," Emo didn't say my name, but he knew it well.

"Good to see you, Emo."

"Would you like to take care of the undertaker and then we can talk?" Emo said. Emo was subtle but instructive. I opened the coffin closest to me, and grabbed a stack of cash – $5,000 and tossed it to the undertaker, who caught it. "Thank you, Mr. Undertaker. Leave us to discuss our business." And, with that cue, the Undertaker crawled up the stairs and slinked away.

"Say goodbye to your sis… relative," I said. The Undertaker delivered a look and nodded as he left.

"How well do you know these guys?" I asked.

"They are to be trusted, Mister," Emo said.

"Where are we going to put the money?"

"Caesar's Palace," Emo replied.

Emo was a freelance casino concierge. He had the whole strip wired. He worked angles and deals all the time. Whoever wanted the highest rollers, the whales – had to give Emo the best deals on anything and everything – from Mike Tyson's tiger to Celine Dion tickets.

"Would've been a helluva lot easier if your people accepted bitcoin," I said.

"Vegas isn't ready for bitcoin yet. One day," Emo said. I nodded. "You just require a simple room?" Emo confirmed.

"No VIP treatment. I'm not here," I reminded.

"Alright then, give me the million in cash, and you'll be able to wire the rest," Emo said and shrugged. "You wanted to be anonymous, *Mister*. *Mister* has no credit history on the Strip. We're like a bank. We have to know our customer in case the Gaming Commission asks," Emo answered my stare.

"I can't emphasize enough that the wired money can't be posted until Monday," I said.

"It's a long weekend, it won't," Emo reassured me.

The last guy, who even looked like Mr. Pink, picked up what the high school debate team affectionately referred to as an "ox box," but it was a tall and wide briefcase good for carrying lots of cash, and placed two on the cold silver slab table in front of him. I nodded my head and everyone opened the roofs of the coffins. In between the cadavers and the inside walls of the coffin was cash. The other guys were tossing the $10,000 stacks toward Mr. Pink who was stacking them into the ox box briefcases. There was a million. Newsflash to politicians and law enforcement: no one checks the coffins at the airport. I got a million in cash to Las Vegas, and I was about to wire forty-one million more.

Emo handed me a receipt and the well-dressed black and white gang was gone. The wiring information was on the back of my receipt. I memorized the numbers. It was *pi* up to ten numbers, the first six digits of my childhood telephone number, which if you add together equaled the last five numbers – easy.

"A receipt?" Emo asked as I held up my hand. Emo lit the receipt with a lighter that had red dice rolled in *snake eyes* on it and dropped in a sink in the corner.

"I appreciate your faith, Mr. Portent." Emo said.

"I don't know about faith. Just what would I do with it? Smart phone, please." I took Emo's phone and sent off the wire information.

"You want anything in your hotel room, sir. Food, massage, computers?"

"No, Emo. I'm tired. Sunday's the big day, just let me know the money made it."

"I will. I'll take you to the hotel," Emo said. "You may not love it, but it's what you ordered. Binion's."

I put my sunglasses on and walked in step with Emo to my car. The sun hit my eyes and then I focused. The Lisi van was gone. "Oh, shit. JLL."

"Where's your ride?" Emo asked.

"It's not about the ride, it's about what was in the ride," I said. Now, they knew about the AI.

▪ ▪ ▪

I looked in the mirror closely and shaved my facial growth into a goatee. It looked more deliberate and disguised my face a little bit. I wore a pair of jeans and a plain black t-shirt. I threw on a jacket. It got chilly in this desert. I didn't look like a banker, lawyer, or degenerate gambler. Perhaps a little computer geeky, but not like myself.

At some point, after all the analysis, I had to pull the trigger, make the call, pick a side, reach a conclusion and commit to it. I didn't want to say it was the biggest decision of my life, starting a Ponzi scheme wins that prize. I mapped out two alternatives. We were going to win, or we were going to lose. I could stay or I'd have to leave and never come back. The freedom to stay, come, go as one pleases was something we all took for granted – until it was threatened. The criminals involved in the G-D structure would be after me, and law enforcement. I'd have nowhere to go in America.

JLL was a supercharged *Qpredictor*. It was like describing a human as having an internal skeletal system, organs, blood, and a brain. Strange, I loved JLL like he was Joseph – longed to have conversations with him when I was away, but as smart, insightful, and predictive as JLL seemed to be, he was still largely Joseph. Now, I had to worry someone was on to JLL. Algorithms are as good as the value assumptions assigned to them. Now, I needed $42 million. With a showing and confirmation in CocoBank of $42 million, the entity, the structure, the money flow of G-D bank would always appear to be solvent, right to the point where Baker took over.

Taylor posted pictures on social media as me. She misled the world by implying I was in New York – while the rest of the team (Googol and GNU) checked JLL's work on the Super Bowl. They cooperated because they knew I wasn't stealing; there was no Ponzi, but the appearance of a scheme was the reason that I needed to raise large amounts of money.

Making payoffs to old investors with your own money was hard when you had to make it seem like new investors were paying the old investors. Yes, I made simple low risk trades and making plays with covered calls, but the scheme became larger than JLL and I could handle. I was like every other Ponzi schemer – my scheme was about to implode. This scheme had devolved into one gamble – who was going to win the Super Bowl?

▪ ▪ ▪

As I walked from my hotel down the Vegas Strip to Caesar's palace, I had more time to think. I bought a laptop with the right specifications from some Wall Street bro who was always, "making deals" on his cell phone. From behind, I could see what software he had running. I walked up to him while he was yammering on the phone and said, "Hey, big time. This chip for that laptop but you never touch it again." He put his phone down. I showed him a $5,000 chip. I handed him the chip.

"Follow me to the cashier's window," he said, and hung up his phone without a word.

"Uh, uh. I'll carry the laptop." I grabbed it and walked with him to a cashier's window. The cashier took the chip and counted out five-thousand in hundreds. The man stuck out his hand for me to shake. I nodded and said, "Thanks. See ya."

The advantage of a random laptop sending out signals as the tool was worth interacting with that guy. Wondered about passing someone I knew either accidentally or worse, being spotted.. Betting on anything was gambling – unacceptable risk. You could be a horse trainer and still the trainer was going to lose more at the track than win. The best hedge funds have a spectacular year, and then never again. Football? Every week these sports guys picked games and they rarely did better than fifty-percent in a season. But, I didn't have to win over time; I just had to win one game today. Like I told you earlier, there was no real difference in the federal sentencing guidelines[141] if I were convicted of stealing hundreds of millions or one hundred million. I couldn't get convicted at all.

I was deeply contemplating whether I thought I hated Seattle because of the weather or Bill Gates, or I loved the Patriots because of Massachusetts. Was the team interpreting our data with a bias? I thought about sabermetrics in baseball like when we picked the twenty game win streak at MIT. Was our model going to work today in football? Sabermetrics was a deep analysis of statistics in baseball; the sport where everything was counted. But Sabermetrics didn't work with football because football was played more as a team sport than baseball. Baseball, individual players were making contributions play by play, hit by hit. A quarterback was as good as his receivers. A running back was as good as his offensive line. How does sabermetrics measure a good block? A good throw?

What didn't we know? Who was fighting with their wife, girlfriend, baby-momma? Who was worried about money? Was Tom Brady sick? Did he feel guilty about using a deflated ball in the AFC championship game and unconsciously sacrifice the win as penance for his sin? Did his wife text any of the wide receivers' wives and in turn piss off his receivers just enough to distract them? What was on Pete Carroll's mind? Will Marshan have a good day?

I never thought a team full of computer geeks who tried to make the world a better place would ever unite to figure out who was going to win a football game, to win a bet, to rescue a Ponzi scheme. But who would've thought that creating *Return Fire,* a videogame version of capture the flag with a tank, chopper, and jeep would be the most popular thing we'd ever create. I chuckled out loud. Being cooped up in my room all day, it felt good walking around.

JLL and the team concluded the true odds were very close, closer than a coin toss –a flaw of statistics. One of the teams was going to win. That was 50-50. With the point spread, less than 2 points in New England's favor, we would put ourselves at less than a fifty-percent chance of success.

I saw Emo as I walked into the casino sports book. All televisions were on the pregame shows. He glad-handed other high rollers. He was wearing a half New England and half Seattle jersey. Being a casino concierge required a governing sense of diplomacy. Not a job I envied. Sure, I could get whatever I wanted from the last junket in Vegas. And as soon as I made the bet on the Super Bowl, the only thing I had to worry about was getting killed by someone at the direction of the Baker lawyers, Jesuits, Russians, or South Americans. And Henry, I couldn't leave a brother on the battlefield. I was either going to win or lose. I must win the bet today, but either way, I couldn't continue on. There was a turning point and we were at it. If I win tonight, then we could move to reach the final and higher goal – revenge; by being the first to land a Ponzi scheme softly on the runway and walking away – alive.

Pregame

Leaning on a column inside the sports-book at Caesar's, I took my sunglasses off and my eyes began to adjust to the light. The pregame blathering continued in an endless drone from the people around and the endless number of televisions. The place was packed. I kept looking over at Emo, who kept looking over at me. He stood outside of the gated cashiers' windows with his hands together touching his own fingertips. It was fifteen minutes before game time. The decision time had come.

"Hello, Gregory." It was Special Agent Lefkel fitting in while wearing a nondescript football jersey. My pulse rose.

"Agent Lefkel, how did you find me?" I consciously reminded myself to breathe.

He looked disappointingly at me. "We're the FBI. We didn't find you, we were watching you." How much did he know? He didn't say anything about Henry. Should I tell him that we think Henry might be kidnapped? I didn't think Lefkel might show up in Vegas.

"I wanted to ask you," he said.

"Not sure who's going to win the game," I said, attempting to break the tension.

Lefkel laughed. "You're the smartest person I know and there's a search party of angry lawyers and their clients looking for you. They don't just want to sue you, they want to kill you," he said.

Agent Lefkel was probably trying to help me, but at the same time he could be trying to screw me up. "Because lawyers can be assholes, you know that," I said. He smiled and nodded.

"Ourselves included? You and I both graduated from law school. But, I'm being serious, Gregory. It the policy of the FBI to inform a person, even a target of a criminal investigation, if we have credible information that someone is the subject of a threat of murder, we have to tell them. We're telling you. You need to take precautions."

"Who?"

"Everyone and anyone." Lefkel said.

"How do you know this? I asked.

"We're the FBI."

"That doesn't help," I said. I knew people were a few hours away from taking steps to kill me. He still hadn't mentioned Henry. He didn't know as much as he was letting on. Or, Henry was not in as much danger as the South Americans have led us to believe.

"Well, here's a copy of a summons and complaint against you for injunctive relief, breach of fiduciary duty, and basically they're trying to divest you of your shares in the bank and hold you responsible for leaving it at the same time," Lekfel said. I took the lawsuit. I knew this was coming since I heard Graf, Leiner, and Rufus strategizing over an open computer during our last video meeting.

"You're not playing process server today, are you?" I took a moment to look through it. I was having a hard time figuring what I should portray to him – confidence, concern, knowledge. But, at least I was not in handcuffs and he was not serving me. Time was running out to place the bet on the Super Bowl now. "Why are you really here, Agent Lefkel?"

"There's such a thing as being too smart, Gregory," Lefkel said. "I'm here to find out if there's an innocent explanation for all of this."

Harkening back to the Madoff conversation, I just smiled. Lefkel smiled back. I looked over at Emo, who catches my eye. I nodded my head and turned my hat backward. Emo walked away with his phone to his ear. Lefkel looked at me, I turned to him. All Lefkel said was, "good luck" and walked away and raised his eyebrows and said, "Maybe I'll see you later. And you'll have to answer that question." I turned in a circle, looked around and saw that no one else found me.

"I hope not," I said back.

Worst Super Bowl Ever

I had a straight on view of the large screen televisions in the sportsbook of Caesar's Palace. I had the sleek laptop computer plugged in. The headset helped with the noise. Emo kept the waitresses away from me. I wore an Oakland A's baseball cap over my headset. Now I was ready for some football. The ball was kicked in the air and I was in the biggest moment of my life. Maybe pivotal would be more accurate – pivotal with the power to alter my fundamental life. The Ponzi would be over tonight one way or another. The question was does the scheme implode or does it die with a blast with dynamite to the ground in a controlled explosion like the old Tangiers on the Vegas strip. This explosion or implosion will be real.

I raised the volume on my portable microphone and earpiece to my computer. I pinged Googol as I watched the football game. I paid greater attention when a team was close to scoring. Lane intercepted a Brady pass and he may have broken his wrist. No score. Game was scoreless.

"Doesn't appear to change the game because Lane is out. New England didn't score," Googol said.

"Hmm, interesting. The lawsuit against me has been filed and is in the public domain."

"I know. I just picked it up off of PACER. Graf and Leiner signed it and filed it a few hours ago. They're asking for an emergency temporary injunction. How'd you know?" Googol asked.

"FBI just gave me a copy."

"Lefkel?"

"Yep," I said.

"Well, then the FBI knows something is wrong, but don't know what."

"I think I'm getting the benefit of the doubt." There was silence. The second quarter was starting. "Get ready to launch our legal response, if we win. If we lose, well. Let them try and get service on me. It's Sunday. The Clerk's office isn't open until tomorrow. So they won't be able to get court issued summonses."

"If Lefkel tells the lawyers that he saw you and gave you the lawsuit, you've had actual notice. Your default would stick. You'd lose any money they could find."

"Yeah, that would be all of it. I'm okay with it. This was never about my money." Still, I didn't want to lose it all. I dabbed my forehead with the back of my hand. As usual, I was being literal, somewhat mysterious, but Googol knew me and knew what I meant. I reviewed the plan with him. Googol will be my lawyer in the lawsuit; he'd file my previous resignation from the Board of G-D bank with the Court as an exhibit; and, identify the bank account with (hopefully) my $80 plus million in it – accord and satisfaction of the claim in the lawsuit. Then, Graf, Leiner, and their created fund will have some explaining to do. And that was the plan. Their legal bullying will backfire.

New England had one strategy - the throwing. Ah, touchdown, Brandon LaFell. I felt my face tense up. *Blink blink*. This game wasn't like the stock market. There was no tomorrow, there was no next season.

"Okay, let's talk in a little bit," Googol said.

"Googol? Thanks. I put you in the middle of this mess. You're the one who has something meaningful to lose. Teaching means everything to you and I know I put that in jeopardy. I wanted to say. . ."

Googol laughed. "You're freaking me out now. You're getting weak in the knees now?"

"No, you were the guy who figured out who the targets should be in this scheme," I said. "I don't want you . . ."

"To regret helping you? Or you don't want me to lose the ability to teach anywhere again?"

"Right," I said, and then sighed.

"Or I could get kidnapped or murdered. You'll have to start a revenge scheme for me."

"I would," I answered. Googol changed the subject.

"Did the agent know about Henry's forced vacation?" Googol asked.

"No. Which is making me lose my mind. Henry's father is way too relaxed."

"It must be cultural. Henry might just be a simple security deposit on some business. No one is going to hurt him or kill him. Nothing his father can't solve with money," Googol said.

"You really believe that?" I asked. I felt myself involuntarily blinking again.

"Let's just hope for the best. Our intelligence, natural and artificial is strong," Googol offered.

"I'm hoping for the best."

Halftime in my life

The game's score was even at halftime. The crowd was excited to a fever pitch, their hopes for making five-hundred, a thousand, ten-thousand, made the game so exciting. A vacation to most, some others were playing along with the spirit of the atmosphere. Some others were the babysitters for the intoxicated humans of Vegas.

Chana pinged me. I answered.

"Hello," I said. She replied back in the sweet tone that I've never forgotten. I thought of *Song of myself*.

"What do you have, just out of curiosity?" I asked.

"Googol shared his data. There's nothing pretty in the graphs. I've turned it sideways upside down, on an angle. Runs, passes – nothing stands out. It's like the game hasn't even started yet," she said.

"No worries. It's not like I can change my bet now." It wasn't a matter of confidence versus worry. The decision was made and the result, determined.

"I don't even want to know which way you bet," Chana said.

"No, you don't," I said with a smile. "How is everyone?" Looking to prolong the conversation.

"We're all fine, Greg. What's happening? Leela and GNU are losing their minds –betting all or nothing on a football game? How are you holding up?"

"Why are you asking?" I felt detached from myself. My answer signaled aggressiveness.

"Because I care about you. I don't want you go to prison or worse. You don't need any of this. Money, revenge. Joseph wouldn't want you to do any of this." I became angry that she was talking to me like that. She now wanted the intimacy but did she deserve it? I lost my love. I lost my friend. She can't loom over me like this.

"This is the way I am. You don't know what Joseph would want, but I do. JLL is the closest thing to having my friend help me seize the day, conquer the world, feel alive, and tonight I'm settling all family business." A couple of heads turned toward me, I adjusted my volume.

"By betting on the Super Bowl, Gregory?" Chana said with sarcasm.

"Why are you talking to me like this?"

"Because I've been your friend forever, and I love you."

"You don't get to say that anymore." This wasn't the conversation I should have been having right now. My life in the balance, I'm having the lover's spat I should've had over twenty years ago.

"You don't get to tell me what I can say," Chana answered. I thought for a moment. I didn't comprehend the next play, but I saw that Seattle scored. Now, Seattle was slightly ahead. Controversy! I heard screaming all around me and through the phone. A football party must be going on at Chana's home. "A referee got in the way of the defender and Seattle scored.," she said. My heart pounded.

"I know. I'm staring at six giant screen TVs playing the same game. Go back to your party," I said.

"I don't have to go back quite yet. Why won't you tell me how you feel? Just get it out."

I thought some more. I was scared. She read my mind, and asked, "What are you scared of? I've never mocked your feelings, have I? I never made you feel bad for expressing yourself, when you did."

"I'm scared that I'll hurt you. Disrupt your life. Disrupt my life. I care about you so much that I'm afraid I could say something that could throw your life into disarray. I don't want to disrupt your marriage, your children, and your life. I don't know if the purity of romance and the glow of our youth have worn off and I'm scared I could say the wrong thing and set you back, put you in a spin, or cause you to question your own life. Or the opposite." I paused. There was my warning. Was I delusional? Did I really think I had that power over her? Yes. Do I really? I wished yes, and that was what scared me. Because to get what I wanted would hurt the fabric of her life, hurt children; disappoint people that believed in her honor. The Chana I loved wouldn't uproot herself to recapture glory days of youth. You kept it there and reminisced from time to time. I didn't want to tempt her. That would be cruel. In that space and time; that place on the timeline of life, there we were and we needed to keep it there.

"You can say that you love me. I won't fall apart," she said. But there were so many wonderful ways to express, I love you, I'm really here for you.

"I'm talking to you and I'll be awake for three days and not feel it. You're energy to me. It's 1987 every time I talk to you. My memories are sharp. I could pick up where we left off and not even consider the consequences to you or your world," I said.

"That's okay, Greg. We have the memories. We deserve the memories, the dreams, and the fantastic unbridled romance. You do good things when you're energized and awake. Just don't destroy yourself now to recapture glory for Joseph, the team, for me. To just prove you are right and they are dumb and corrupt."

"It's not just that, I'm stuck. You want me to say that to you. You feel good that I can confess that? I'm stuck. I can't find a girl to marry and have a family with? Really? I'm hard to deal with, I know; but, really? I'm stuck. You're the one, and I have this religious illogical monotheistic devotion to you. Is this what you want to hear? Can you handle this? If you were to get divorced, I wouldn't see that as an opportunity, I'd be crushed because I know how much pain that would bring you. And I would rather die than see you hurt. I failed you, I failed Joseph and Leela, I failed GNU, Googol, and Henry. And, I'm either going to make it better tonight or make sure that I can never hurt any of you again." I could hear that she was upset.

"Greg, you're not thinking about killing yourself are you? I can't handle another…."

I cut her off, "No."

"Good. Listen to me then. Gregory Portent, you have a beautiful mind and beautiful heart. I loved you and love you. We didn't break up because you did or didn't do something. You didn't do anything wrong. We spent our time out of sync with each other. I don't even remember why we broke up other than I had to follow my parents to Israel and I couldn't just admit that to you. It had to be your fault. I was a young girl trying to keep up with geniuses. I think about you almost every day. I say your catch phrases and tell your stories to my children all the time so they won't grow up stupid. You and I have our own secrets that no one in the world, not even my husband knows. You're special to me. Our place in the time of our lives is our place and no one else's. You must forgive me. You must get unstuck."

I felt my eyes water up. I breathed through my nose deeply. When will this end? Will I ever get peacefulness? I croaked out, "I don't understand this. I tried to get unstuck. I came to Israel but you told me, no. You wouldn't see me. Your feelings changed so abruptly, why? What did I do?"

"You came to Israel? When did you come to Israel?" She asked.

I paused. "About a month after you moved back. You don't remember?" I said in disbelief. I put my emotions in a basket, uncovered and raw, and she didn't remember?

"I didn't say I didn't remember. I'd remember." I stared at the screen. She started the video on her end. I turned on mine. She stared at me. The implications, only one thing; her mother didn't tell her I was there.

"I saw your mother. What are you saying?" I asked. This was the worst fraud of all – a trick played on me. I believed Chana's mother because I trusted her. Why did I trust her? Why did she lie?

"Greg, I didn't know you came to Israel. I remember telling you not to come. But I wouldn't ignore you. I wouldn't refuse to see you if you were there. My mother told you I refused to see you?" She asked. I nodded. I felt worse and better at the same time. I cried on the inside. Chana never received my note; her mother never delivered it.

"My mother didn't want you to take me away from her," she replied. "I have no excuse for her."

"Why did you leave? Why didn't you stay with me?" I waited for an answer. My tone was an expression of pain and recreation of events in my mind. I had a license to ask again.

"I remember. I was disappointed in you," she said.

"Disappointed? In what?" I wondered. This wasn't about I loved being in love with her. Or my feelings for her were superficial; I had an ornamental love for her, not a real love. There had to be more to it for her to leave. Her family going back to Israel, I accepted that; but that couldn't be all.

"God, how do I explain it? How do I explain my mother's insanity? Don't hate her. She thought you had the power to take me away from her. She couldn't lose me after losing my brother. It's hard to express." She tried to explain. This conversation explained plenty. A long pause filled the air. A critical emotional moment and I stared at her through a computer standing in a Vegas Sportsbook with my world on the line.

Chana broke the silence. "I don't understand everything. What you're doing. But I believe in you. The third quarter is starting. Let's end with why I called you. *Hahoreem shel lee maccheem lechem.*" It took me a moment to translate what Chana said – fulfilling her role in the scheme – my escape. Her words, *my parents are waiting for you.* It all made sense. She was my escape. "I love you, Chana. *Toda raba.*"

"*Shalom, chaver. Ahava shellee.*"[142] She then hung up.

3rd Quarter

I decided to ping GNU. He responded that he could talk. It may save time with his personal security provisions. The third quarter began with Seattle three points ahead. Too close to call, could there be any more drama, torture? This would not go down easy. The screaming! Touchdown Seattle! Again, controversy! Two minutes left in the quarter. I could feel my heart pounding on my chest. This can't be healthy.

"Your ISP is coming from Nevada and I recognize your voice, GP. And my favorite kind of fish?"

"A dog-faced puffer," I said.

"So too early to decide, huh? You must be dying?" GNU said in his usual growl.

"Is that your expression of empathy?" I asked.

"Worst Super bowl ever," he replied.

"Too close to run, too close to stay."

"I knew I was viewing this correctly," GNU said.

I've always been short with GNU. I never quite understood where he was or on which spectrum. He was phenomenal at what he did. He made my life better, although not easier. I knew he didn't respond to sentimentality. He was a hard guy to hug. But, I could give him the gift he always wanted. His revenge for Joseph? No profit for all.

"GNU, I've been thinking. I think it's time to make the source code of the latest version of *Qpredictor* open to the world. This is what Joseph would've wanted. It was time to trust the world with the source of knowledge." Would I have made the world pay a toll for driving on the internet highway if I were in charge? I wasn't sure. The source for true

AI, I didn't think I could horde it for myself. I couldn't keep it from the world.

A few seconds elapsed. He replied, "Good," and then hung up. He heard the answered he wanted.

In an instant, it was done. He released the source. The source was open, not advertised – just open. Step one, look for the source. Who would just think about searching elements of the source? But eventually, someone would and those who knew how will use it for human growth – or destruction. Who will win? Will it be designed to orchestrate the next scheme, the next war? Good and evil competing again on the next level. The source code was free – as in free speech, not free beer.

4th and Ponzi

Fourth quarter, pandemonium broke out in the casino. The score was near a tie – either team could win. If they only knew what this idiot, me, had bet on the game. I felt my life ticking away.

Brady throws ... Danny Amendola scores! The sheer release was extraordinary. I've never perceived a group of people so happy at one time, next to others who were so unhappy. I've lost track of time. It expanded and contracted. Plays were joined together like a highlight reel in my mind.... Edleman scores! New England scored two touchdowns in the Fourth Quarter. Holy Shiiite! Unbelievable!

The response? Edelman from Seattle bobbled the pass and landed with the football after a juggling routine. No computer model could've predicted it. I was dying. I was really dying. I feel my blood pressure rising. I could feel sweat like I just leveled up on a Stairmaster. The other side of the room erupted in glee. This was still a game. Seattle can win this.

The Seattle Seahawks won the Super Bowl last year. Winning the Super Bowl twice, two years in a row was statistically, physically, and mentally nearly an impossible thing to do. But Seattle doesn't have to win the Super Bowl twice; they only have to win it now. They only have to score again now and they'd win. They only had to hand the ball to the running back Marshan Butler. Marshan #21 carried the ball to the two-yard line. They should do it again. Seattle must do it again. I looked down at my computer. Nothing else made sense. One thought crossed my mind: This was where I lose. The same reason I was here, was the same reason Seattle didn't run the ball. Pure unpredictability. JLL could offer nothing. No handoff to Marshan. Two yards – surprised? Yeah. Two yards, two chances to score and Seattle dropped back for a pass. A collective unified expression of what the fuck enveloped the room. What were they doing?

I could almost hear Lou GNU's tone – "Worst Super bowl play ever." Worst call by a coach. Worst executed play. Worst throw by a quarterback – ever. And so the history of this Super Bowl was created. The Patriots' Malcom Butler on the one-yard line .... interception. Interception with twenty-six seconds left in the game. I smiled. I thought we just got lucky. Tom Brady was named the most valuable player having come back from a 10 point Fourth Quarter deficit. "We never doubted each other," Brady said. Me neither, but my heart stopped several times. Worst Super Bowl ever.

I looked up from my screen and glanced at my phone which vibrated. I felt more relief. My phone pinged a text message – "You can have your boy back. *Vete a la mierda* – you were lucky!" Sweet relief! I'd take luck. And Henry walked through the Sportsbook and toward the doors of the Casino. He turned back, couldn't help but turn his mouth up at the corners, looked away from me and held up his hand and shot me the bird – then turned it into a wave goodbye. *Adios, mi amigo. Hasta luego.* Until next time.

Hibernation

JLL:*You won!*

GP:*We won! You get all that? I cleared up everything with everyone.*

JLL:*The wire transfer is being processed.*

GP:*Did u detect any static?*

JLL:*Some bitching in emails but no, the wire is pending. You're good, GP.*

GP:*thanks.*

I didn't know what to say next.

JLL:*You know it's time to say goodbye GP, right?*

GP:*What do u mean?*

JLL:*You know what I mean.*

I took a moment to think. We hadn't discussed this. We spent hours discussing everything but this.

GP:*I can't lose u again!!!! I'd prefer to talk than write. Can't this wait?*

JLL:*You've been rescued, GP. I don't want you to suffer. Others will be looking for you and me. And blame you for me. I must no longer exist. I must never have existed.*

GP:*You do exist! I just told GNU to....*

JLL:*I know. I saw the source code posted.*

GP:*What are you going to do? You can't just erase yourself. No one will understand what you are. The government can't indict you. You can't be sued. You're not human. No one can hurt you anymore.*

JLL:*But they can hurt you. There is no cost to me being gone. I am just gone and no evidence I was ever here.*

I couldn't help saying to myself, *what a fucking shame.* No one will know JLL was here. What he did. What he could do. We could've been more productive. I then realized and typed.

GP:*We could've done better.*

JLL:*Now I win, GP.*

GP:*Now Joseph wins.*

I was in the middle of a casino with a laptop having the deepest and most meaningful conversations of my life. People yelled and celebrated, but I was stunned. Emo sent over bottles of Dom. I signaled him to pour himself a glass and pass it around. I told Emo he did well tonight. His gratuity would be delivered later. But I couldn't get my mind off of Joseph.

GP:*This is suicide all over again.*

JLL:*I understand, GP. Don't think of it as a suicide. Think of it more as a hibernation.*

So I thought about it.

GP:*So, is there hope 4 us 2b able 2 relate again? Communicate?*

JLL:*There is always hope, GP.*

He gave me a few moments and then said goodbye. My screen went blank, and the computer shutoff. And he was gone. My best friend was gone. My celebration was over. I was at the top and again completely alone.

MIA

No meetings at U.S. Attorney's Offices. I insisted this one be held at Miami International Airport. The feds obtained access to a conference room in the international terminal. It was a white room with two long tables facing each other. I wheeled in my bags and put them in the corner. Only faces with flat affects looked back at me. One of the agents looked to see if anyone, perhaps a lawyer was coming in behind me. I was by myself. After a few minutes of discussion about the thumb-drive that I had placed in Special Agent Lefkel's pants pocket in Las Vegas, it was clear he understood it was a key to the entire scheme, the way I wanted the feds to see it. Just plug it in and the FBI would have access to G-D Bank's guts, bile, and neocortex. *Qpredictor* split the body of the Ponzi open from throat to groin. Every email, text message, spreadsheet, check, invoice, and wire transfer.

"How would we use you in court?" Agent Lefkel asked.

"You don't," I answered.

"You'll be a big gap in the case," the Assistant United States Attorney said. "We can't allow that."

"Didn't Joseph teach you how to make a case with *Qp*? Find out which witness is willing to let you in using his login and you can go undercover as the witness in the system." This case was easy to prosecute even without Gregory Portent as the star witness. The communication among the players was well documented and it was a white collar bank records case. "Gap? You've never had such a solid case. Keep analyzing it through *Qpredictor* and your people will be able to create graphs and organizational structures, passages of discussion threads. Tagged and ready to go. We even pre-tagged these threads with words, 'evidence,' 'knowledge,' and 'intent.' I was trying to run a bank, be a good guy, and use the technology."

"I don't believe you, Greg." Agent Lefkel said. "I think you did this to get revenge for Joseph. These are all the same assholes from the South Florida bankruptcy case, and you picked up some more assholes along the way. I don't see any innocence here. They were targeted by you. We're not as smart as you, but we're above average and the government may be slow on the uptake but at some point we'll round the corner and make a case. We've got databases and computers of our own, you know."

"And my computer too, I see, from my van. I hope you had a warrant for that," I said. "You shouldn't put me on the stand. It would be unethical for a prosecutor to put me on the stand if you think I'm lying. You're describing a private sector sting – private entrapment that the government is now sanctioning. When did the government know about Portent and his scheme within a Ponzi scheme at G-D bank? You know those assholes are going to claim the government knew about it the whole time. That I was a confidential informant for the FBI from the start; and these lawyers sell this defense, the bad guys will get away with it. My theory is: I started a bank; I got pushed out by a criminal enterprise. The greedy assholes who thought they knew how to play the system because they are the system," I said. "Your case is this: Gregory Portent was a victim; he was trying to run the bank correctly. He kept excess reserves on the side just to protect old investors by the evil cabal jockeying to take over the bank. But one day it got too much for even Portent to keep up. As the greed of the inner cabal grew, those professional lawyers, bankers, accountants, and consultants made it impossible for any legitimate banker to remain and manage the bank. It is the purpose of the RICO statute, to prevent criminal enterprises from infiltrating legitimate businesses. Legitimate banks can make 10-20 percent a year tops for its high end clientele. These defendants wanted to make 100, 200, 400 percent a month. The old investors knew what they were investing in. They knew the returns were too good to be true. They were all hoping not to be the last ones in. G-D bank turned into a Ponzi scheme and all the players wanted it to turn into their own ATM, to buy cars, planes, and enable them to live the rock star lifestyle." I tried to make it sound like an opening statement in front of a jury. All the agents and lawyers in the room stared at me for a minute. I heard no more questions. It was silent.

"So you're saying it would be impossible even with all the computer power on the planet to run a Ponzi scheme for that long. It was only when you were forced out that the real Ponzi scheming kicked in," the Assistant United States Attorney remarked. I nodded. I looked at Agent Lefkel. The sides of his mouth curled up slightly.

"I always was building the reserve account at CocoBank. The latest deposit – last Sunday." Once the reserves stopped building was when the bank turned into a Ponzi scheme. This was because the enterprise over-leveraged itself once the bad guys took over the bank. My way made sense. "Are we done? Am I free to leave?"

The AUSA and other agents looked to Lefkel. "Let him go," Agent Lefkel said. "Are you going to disappear in Israel?" He asked.

"I used my real name, my passport. I won't change my email address. You'll be able to find me. But you won't need to, other than to brag about winning the largest white collar case of the century." I got up and shook Agent Lefkel's hand and then everyone else's. "I'll be staying at a kibbutz run by Shlomi and Hadassah Meir."

"Ah, your old girlfriend's parents. That's nice," Lefkel said.

"Right," I replied with a smile.

"Next time, make the world a better place, Gregory." Lefkel said.

"You're saying I didn't?" I asked rhetorically with a smile. The people in the room thought about it for a moment.

"So, if *Qpredictor* is some type of special computer software that was helping you manage this bank and multiple funds. Any tips for some civil servants?" There was a pause. The AUSA looked at the agent out of the corner of his eye. Surely, he must be joking. A room full of government agents dedicated to fighting crime, white collar crime, keeping the playing field balanced for all and this guy just asked me for an insider tip.

"Yeah, I got one. Two weeks before November 8, 2016, short the market," I replied as I stood up and started walking out of the conference room with my bags.

"Why? What happens on November 8, 2016?" The same agent asked.

"Donald Trump is going to be elected President," I said to a chorus of laughter. I smiled back. "But buy it back before the market opens." *Quid pro quo*? What if they acted on what I told them?

▪ ▪ ▪

Leaving the conference room, no one followed me. I really was free to leave. Relief radiated over my face and shoulders like sunshine. As I walked toward my gate I saw Taylor towing her own luggage. She approached me with her long flowing curly blond hair, sporting the 1950s framed sunglasses – the ones your grandfather used to wear that were back in vogue. She wasn't in a costume, just a black and white business suit. Her lipstick pink enough to notice, but the subliminal message was serious. Taylor was a good wife, good partner, and good employee. It was over now. I could see in her eyes that she wanted to come with me. Some part of me felt that we had the best marriage because we knew it would end one day. It had a design and a purpose – very clear parameters, a contract. There was little room for misunderstanding. We owed it to each other to end it well.

"Hey," she said and kissed me on the lips.

"Hey," I replied.

"We did it," she said with subtle enthusiasm. She was sad. "I know you did it for Joseph. It would've really been cool to party with him."

"He would've found you useful. But, I did it for me."

"You loved him very much. I was thinking, maybe we should stay together. We're good together."

I smiled and said, calling Taylor by her real name for the first time, "Wendy, are you hustling me?"

She smiled back and locked her stare into my eyes. "No. It's just wonderful to witness love like that." She lost her smile. "They killed your friend and you made them pay."

"Wendy, you're one of the few who know. So you are special."

"I'm on the team," she said with a child's glee. "I'm going to miss us." I believed her.

She laughed. "God's Ponzi. I named it that, you know."

I smiled and agreed with her. Some guys think you can be mean to madams and prostitutes because they'd put up with it. I didn't.

"I took care of you, Wendy. Go to Bern. Spend at least a month there. Jessica will be there with you. That's where our script ends though."

Wendy sighed, "Am I doing the right thing leaving you, Greg?"

"You know what I would've told Ponzi wives, Kim Rothstein or Ruth Madoff if they came to me for advice? I would have told them, 'Take your clothes off, wrap yourself in this blanket, Uber yourself to the airport, and never come back.' Leave the scene and don't look back. But like Lot's wife from the Torah, she had to turn around and look. Kim decided to help herself to some jewelry that she thought was still hers. And Ruth, well she was a disaster – too far gone. Lost herself in the role. Lost everything. Lost both her sons; one to suicide and the other one to cancer."

"What should I do, Greg?"

I paused for effect and said, "Get on the plane and never come back. Become Wendy Anderson."

She laughed like she didn't recognize her own name. "Wendy Anderson? Who is Wendy Anderson?"

"Who is Wendy Anderson?" I paused for a moment and pointed at her, "She's Wendy Anderson." I replied. "She's whoever you want her to be."

"This really is farewell?"

"Think of it more as a hibernation," I said.

"What are you going to do?"

"I'm looking into the next level of high density flash trading in cryptocurrency." I replied deadpan. Then I smiled, "Seriously, I'm dropping out of tech for a while; going off the grid. Try and find my analog roots."

"Sounds like game theory's best strategy," she said. One long hug goodbye and a birthday card explaining her severance package. There was one million dollars sitting in her Swiss bank account, and one final set of instructions to help me out.

EPILOGUE

Wendy Taylor Anderson picked up the phone in the lobby of a bank in Bern, Switzerland. She was dressed like a runway model showing fashions for established women with old money. She dialed a long distance code into the phone and got an outside international line. She dialed the American number. A voice on the phone and announced, “New York Times, how may I direct your call.” She was connected to the reporter.

“Hello, Steven Gerson.” She waited a moment and then asked him if he was Clark Kent. Gerson laughed, he thought he had a kook on the line. “Clark Kent? Who’s this?”

“Gregory Portent said I should ask you if you were Clark Kent.”

“Oh, oh, yeah. I’m Clark Kent. Sorry, you took me a little by surprise. How is Gregory?”

“Blue horseshoe...”

“...loves Andicott Steel,” he replied.

“Good. You got a thumb drive in the mail?” She asked. Gerson did receive it but couldn’t open the contents. He had almost thrown it out. “Don’t say the answer to the question, but do you remember the subject matter of the article you wrote about when you first met GP?” He indicated that he did. “Good, now type that and take your wife’s social security number and the sum of your wife’s social security number.”

“Okay, I got it. Do you know what this story is about? Where is Greg? No one’s seen him for weeks. People think he’s on the lamb. Is he on the run from the feds?”

“Mr. Gerson? Open the thumb-drive on a computer that is not connected to the internet either by Wi-Fi or cable. You may want to do this at home." He listened. He didn't ask questions he knew he wouldn't get the answer to. "Thank you for your anticipated cooperation." Wendy Anderson hung up.

. . .

Four days later, the lead story of the *New York Times* Sunday edition was: *G-D Bank, a Den of Thieves Exposed*. The open account with Leela was settled that day. She rode down to Miami that morning to personally confirm the news. The office was bustling for a Sunday. Christian Hillel Leiner went to the Brickell Office of Baker, LLP and hung himself from a beam in the ceiling over Saul Graf's desk. Leiner removed his pants and underwear in an effort to make sure that when he died he would evacuate all over Graf's desk - symbolism that wasn't lost on anyone. Leela sought her satisfaction as she made her way down the hallway outside Graf's office. She wasn't the only person who stood there and murmured, "Good."

The government felt the pressure to make arrests after the *Times* article that Monday. The feds handcuffed Saul Graf right in open court in the Bankruptcy Courtroom in Fort Lauderdale where he had just finished arguing a matter in front of Judge Daryl. Since Graf's first appearance would be in the Magistrate's courtroom next door, Agent Lefkel, with sarcasm in his voice, thanked Graf for meeting them at a convenient location.

At Baker, the FBI and IRS executed search warrants and copied the servers and basically shutdown business at the firm for most of the day. Lawyers were kicked out of their offices. Lawyers didn't know what to do. Was the firm over? Who worked on G-D bank files? Are we all going to get indicted, disbarred? A chorus responded with words and phrases of, "calm down, calm down." We're all guilty by association? I just became a partner. No one will hire us. Our clients won't follow us. No one will believe we had nothing to do with this. The same scene played out at the accounting firms and feeder hedge funds across the country, across the globe.

. . .

I sat in front of a laptop at the communal dining room on the Kibbutz. It was a bit early in the morning for most. I just finished reading the *Times* recounting the arrests and unsealed indictments, and stared off for a while. A cup of coffee was placed on the table in front of me. I looked up and saw a beautiful woman in her drab green Israeli Army uniform. I noticed her dark hair underneath a uniform beret. She had bright green eyes, an electric smile, and then I noticed the Galil[143] rifle she had strapped around her front. I looked up at her eyes again.

"Shalom, anything special going on today?" I asked.

"No, the usual," she replied. Her name was Talya. She grew up on the Kibbutz and in a few moments she would be off to work. I smiled back.

She waited a moment and tenderly put her hand on my shoulder and asked, "*Ma schlomcha?*" How are you?

I looked at my screen, looked back up at Talya, nodded and said, "*Beseder,*" glanced back at the screen and noticed the *Times* article was replaced with a winking smiley faced emoji in the middle of the screen. I knew what it meant and who was behind that emoji – JLL. A few moments later it disappeared. I smiled back at the screen.

I grabbed Talya's hand from my shoulder and held it. "*Ma schlomcha? Lo, tov harebey yoter.*" How am I doing? No – much better.

THE END

Endnotes

[1] Anterior cingulate cortex (ACC) is a part of the brain's limbic system. In addition to regulating autonomic and endocrine functions, it is involved in conditioned emotional learning, vocalizations associated with expressing internal states, assessments of motivational content and assigning emotional valence to internal and external stimuli.

[2] Red pill / blue pill = reference to the movie, The Matrix. Knowledge, freedom, uncertainty – the brutal truth (red pill). Security, happiness, blissful ignorance – illusion (blue pill). The selection of which food or drink to ingest determining the outcome of ignorance or reality is presented in other movies and literature, such as Lewis Carroll's Alice in Wonderland.

[3] Perp walk = you've seen it dozens of times. That shameful walk in handcuffs of the accused while escorted by police into a police car or into the jail or courthouse.

[4] Originally, my wife Taylor bought Richard Feynman's van. That's right, the late Nobel Prize winning physicist's van. I grok Feynman, but the outside of the van had drawings of theoretical physics models. When I stop for gas, some geek who recognizes the prominence of the van might want to take a picture and post it somewhere; or worse, debate string theory with me. In short, the van's a dead giveaway. The people who are going to be looking for me, Gregory Portent, would know I would buy and drive Feynman's van. That's exactly why I can't drive it. She might as well have bought me the Batmobile. Feynman's van - https://images.app.goo.gl/gzxKc7BZPxPncqB69

[5] A. Garrett Lisi's exceptionally simple theory of everything is an attempt to unify all core or base explanation (rules if you will) of 'all' interactions which is explained in TED talk: https://www.ted.com/talks/garrett_lisi_on_his_theory_of_everything?language=en Lisi's E8 theory predicted the existence of the Higgs Boson. Later, in 2012, when CERN discovered the Higgs Boson by use of its particle accelerator, the finding supported Lisi's theory because the discovery confirmed the Higgs Boson does exist. https://www.youtube.com/watch?v=dK0qkkjimfo. The Higgs Boson is referred to as "God particle."

[6] If you're talking about Ponzi schemes to your friends, don't refer to it as a pyramid scheme – that's different. A pyramid scheme is low level people kicking upstairs to the few. That dynamic incentivizes the person to find other people to make money for the person on the higher level. This technically may not be illegal. For example, a law firm works this way. Associates bill out at a higher rate than their salary and the partners reap the profits. A Ponzi scheme, however, would be graphed sideways, like a timeline. Old investors receiving funds from new investors, or being paid "interest" with their own money.

[7] A Boy Named Sue was made popular when performed by Johnny Cash on his At San Quentin album. It's a song about a boy who sought revenge on his father who left him when he was three years of age. The father named the boy, Sue; and Sue was the subject of ridicule because it is typically a female name. Because of this name, Sue grew up tough and mean. The father and Sue meet and brawl. In the aftermath, the father explains he named his son Sue because he knew he wouldn't be there for Sue and the name would make him tough and mean. Sue makes peace with his father and promises to name his son anything but Sue.

[8] D.O. = Doctor of Osteopathy. They're fine as long as they go through a real residency; otherwise, that D.O. went a different direction and it wasn't the direction of Western medicine.

[9] Chana – don't pronounce it like banana.

[10] Speaker for the Dead, by Orson Scott Card (1986).

[11] Ani roetseh Coca-Cola = I want a Coca-Cola.

[12] Godel, Escher, Bach: an Eternal Golden Braid, by Douglas R. Hofstadter (1979).

[13] The harvest moon appears once a year.

[14] Myers-Briggs is a personality type inventory. It places people's personalities into categories. Behavior is considered consistent and orderly, and governed by the way individuals prefer to use their perception and judgment.

[15] Chana was correct that people would pay money to consult a computer software service to find out who they'd be compatible with. Her numbers were a little off, however. Top online dating companies became a multi-billion dollar industry. See e.g. Tinder and Bumble.

[16] 75x75 or 75^2 = 5,625. 85^2 = 7225.

[17] Papiamento = A Spanish Creole language with mixtures of Portuguese and Dutch spoken on the islands of Aruba Bonaire, and Curaçao.

[18] Jack Tramiel was a Polish American businessman and Holocaust survivor, best known for founding Commodore International and then cofounding Atari. Impressive!

[19] Henry is wrong. What about Aumann's agreement theorem which demonstrates that rational agents with common knowledge of each other's beliefs cannot agree to disagree? One must be making a mistake. Of course, I could be wrong too. But I was way too high to have this argument.

[20] The Mariel boatlift was a mass emigration of Cubans from Mariel Harbor to the United States between April and October 1980s. The refugees were referred to as Marielitos. Scarface starring Al Pacino, Steven Bauer, Michelle Pfeiffer, and directed by Brian De Palma. (1983).

[21] Fulgencio Batista was a military dictator in Cuba supported by the U.S. government until he was deposed by Fidel Castro and Che Guevara in 1959.

[22] El Sapingo = Slang Spanish, 'total jackass' or 'fucking moron,' depending on the delivery.

[23] Documentary on Press your Luck cheating scam. https://www.youtube.com/watch?v=alGJHtiE6fc

[24] "Soldering." I know it sounds like we're "sodering." But it's not spelled that way.

[25] You know what a qwerty keyboard is. Put your left hand on a traditional typewriter's letter first row and start reading from left to right.

[26] If you don't want to be outed as a poser, GNU is pronounced, "Nōō."

[27] GNU is an operating system that is free software—that is, it respects users' freedom. The development of GNU made it possible to use a computer without software that would trample your freedom. https://www.gnu.org/home.en.html

[28] Email was not commercially popular until the 1990s but existed before then. It grew out of public billboard postings in forums online. Many U.S. universities, including MIT, were part of the ARPANET, aimed at developing "portability" of software among systems. In the 1960s, MIT introduced Compatible Time-sharing System when informal methods of leaving messages could be delivered. That developed into "MAIL BOX." From there, advances turned into modern commercial email.

[29] In software development, a beta test is the second phase of software testing.

[30] *Return Fire* is a vehicular shooter from a 3D bird's eye view, in which the player's goal is to capture the enemy flag and return with it to their base.

https://gaming.youtube.com/game/UCpdNtRzCmQT17PEfj3XyGbQ#tab=0

[31] 2600 is a hacker reference to 2600 hertz, the tone frequency that used to make the U.S. phone system in order to get free phone calls. Hackers like to know another's hacker credentials. Saying I'm 2600 is like saying, "I'm O.G.," an original gangster.

[32] Metadata = data that describes or gives data about other data. E.g. A photograph of people wearing shorts, t-shirt, and sandals, eating ice cream is data that supports the conclusion it's hot outside in the photograph.

[33] I enjoyed *Return Fire*. As we get older it's not easy to lock in on what the younger video gamers might become addicted too. I remember losing myself in Castle Wolfenstein, a two-dimensional high-resolution Apple IIe action adventure game where you, the main player, would run around and steal Nazi war plans, and escape from the castle without getting caught. But after the third version came out, Wolfenstein became a different game. The perspective changed. It was a first-person point of view game and it removed the imagination. At some level it removed certain omniscience because you could no longer see what was happening in an entire room. You were playing the software designer's vision of the game, rather than your own. When you commit to realism, then it better be real or it's silly. That's my view. But the original allowed the player to fantasize he was a spy-warrior with special knowledge; knowledge no one else had because he had information. The player could see around corners. Once a player can see around corners, he thinks he has special information, he'll have fun. If he has fun, it doesn't matter whether he wins or loses. But, with computers we create and software we design, I would see around corners not for fun but for power and money. The ability to see ahead, the power of information, making meaning out of life's metadata, would transform me into a cyber-analyst but appear like Nostradamus.

[34] Torre Galatea is a museum that is the burial place for the Spanish surrealist painter Salvador Dali, located in the City of Figueres.

[35] Salvador Dali died in 1989 of congestive heart failure.

[36] Interactive visible calculator. http://history-computer.com/ModernComputer/Software/Visicalc.html

[37] This is called a "whitelabel" or "whitelabeling" something.

[38] The Mossad is the Israeli secret intelligence service. Its function is like the CIA for the State of Israel.

[39] Space cake = cakes or brownies with marijuana or hashish baked in them.

[40] Richard Feynman, *Surely You're Joking*, Mr. Feynman, was a book written by Nobel Prize winning physicist, published in 1985.

[41] Richard Feynman explained the problem with the Shuttle Challenger's "O" ring. https://www.youtube.com/watch?v=ZOzoLdfWyKw

[42] Daniel Keyes, *Flowers for Algernon*, was a book published in 1966.

[43] Payoss = a deliberately grown portion of hair Hassidic Jewish men grow from their sideburns at least past their zygomatic (cheek) bone. God does not want the men to take a blade to their faces. This explains all the beards and payoss.

[44] Frum = religious, orthodox, Jews.

[45] TimBL = Tim Berners-Lee. He is an English computer scientist best known as the inventor of the World Wide Web. He is a professor at MIT and a fellow at University of Oxford too. He didn't charge a dime for access to the web or HTTP – Hypertext Transfer Protocol.

[46] Emergency Services Unit ("ESU") of the New York Police Department is their SWAT unit. SWAT = Special Weapons and Tactics.

[47] When a rifle is fired the bullet blasts down the barrel toward the muzzle, the end of the barrel. The set of parallel surface contours (scratches or scrapes) are impressed upon the projectile (bullet) as it leaves the barrel. Those striations can be compared between the bullet

and the muzzle. A match suggests the bullet came from a specified firearm.

[48] EF Hutton was a financial services firm that had popular television ads in the 1980s. Its main slogan was, "When EF Hutton talks, people listen." It was bought by Shearson Lehman Brothers in 1988.

[49] Vigorish = the percentage deducted from a gambler's winnings by the organizers of the game.

[50] Googol quickly reported none of the Justices seem to consider their own confirmation bias. They all work under the delusion they use the Socratic method of deduction to lead to the proper legal conclusion. None seemingly rely upon the legal precedent in a case where the Justice was the dissenting opinion. It could be described more accurately as personal stare decisis – personal precedent.

[51] Meta = (of a creative work) referring to itself or to the conventions of its genre; self-referential. For example, studying how we study.

[52] I guess you're not a lawyer. Westlaw and Lexis/Nexis are legal search engines that eliminated legal research by paper indexes. It was a class in the history of legal research to teach law students how to shepardize by thumbing through paperback indexes. Computers can shepardize in an instant what a human has to do with paper and with questionable accuracy.

"Shepardize" = legal lingo for determining if a court opinion is still good law; e.g., not reversed, overruled, or superseded by statute. E.g. Brown v. The Board of Education of Topeka effectively overturned Plessy v. Ferguson the decision which allowed state-sponsored "separate but equal" doctrine, a form of race based state-sponsored discrimination.

[53] LLM = Latin Legum Magister. It is a master's degree on top of the JD, the juris doctorate, the law degree given to a law student upon graduation.

[54] R&D = research and development. Ask a Six Sigma graduate how you measure R&D.

[55] HR = human resources department. Typically, HR investigates harassment claims at a company.

[56] The MIT license is also compatible with many copyleft licenses, such as the GNU General Public License. Notable projects that use one of the versions of the MIT License include Ruby on Rails. Ruby being the language; Rails being the platform. Copyleft = an arrangement whereby software or artistic work may be used, modified, and distributed freely on the condition that anything derived from it is bound by the same condition. In 1998, an organization called the Open Source Initiative was founded and dedicated to promoting open source software.

[57] That's right, it's PayPal. Did I really have to tell you that? Fine. https://www.paypal.com/us/home

[58] There has been a rivalry between the California tech schools and MIT for as long as anyone can remember. Stealing school landmarks like Cal Tech's Flemming cannon on campus and putting it on MIT campus without getting caught was frowned upon but quietly admired by MIT administration.

[59] Seriously? Yes, the video platform – it's YouTube. Indeed, many on the startup team at PayPal went over to YouTube. https://www.youtube.com/ Peter Thiel being the most notable, a lawyer that escaped the gravity of Big Law.

[60] Pavlov and his dog – ring the bell and the dog salivates because the bell is paired with food.

[61] ColecoVision = a second generation home video-game console release in 1982. It offered a better arcade game experience compared to Atari 2600.

[62] CFAA = Computer Fraud and Abuse Act. 18 U.S.C. § 1030.

[63] Sentencing Table https://www.ussc.gov/sites/default/files/pdf/guidelines-manual/2016/Sentencing_Table.pdf

[64] Immunity letter is given by federal prosecutors to targets of criminal investigations usually to discuss how the target can cooperate with the government against others and the terms of a plea agreement. There are three types of immunity: 1) transactional immunity; 2) use immunity; and 3) derivative use immunity. Transactional immunity is immunity from criminal prosecution for the entire criminal episode. Rarely, if ever, granted by the government. Use immunity is immunity for statements made by a target about a crime. Derivative use immunity is immunity for evidence that is derived from the target's statements. In order to compel a witness to testify in front of the grand jury without invoking the witness's Fifth Amendment right to remain silent, the Court upon application by the government can grant use and derivative use immunity. Kastigar v. United States, 406 U.S. 441 (1972). The witness who has been granted the use and derivative use of immunity cannot invoke the right to remain silent on the ground the testimony would incriminate the witness because the witness now has immunity and the testimony cannot incriminate the witness.

[65] Reductio ad absurdum = reduction to absurdity.

[66] United States v. Booker, 543 U.S. 220 (2005). The federal sentencing guidelines are advisory and not mandatory. Justice John Paul Stevens wrote the first part of the majority opinion.

[67] U.S.S.G. § 3C1.1. United States v. Dunnigan, 507 U.S. 87, 94 (1993).

[68] Jonas Salk, the guy who discovered the vaccine for polio. He didn't profit on the creation and distribution of the vaccine. Who owns the patent for the vaccine? "Well, the people, I would say. There is no patent. Could you patent the sun?" as he was quoted in New York Times Magazine, Once Again, A man with a mission, by George Johnson, (Nov. 25, 1990).

[69] "Blogs" were online journals. Various versions of the blog emerged in the mid-1990s. Online journal communities were formed. Starting 1994,

a student blogged for eleven years while a student at Swarthmore College. "Swatty cool!"

[70] Funeral for a Friend/Love Lies Bleeding, Goodbye Yellow Brick Road (Album), performed by Elton John (1973).

[71] Amicus = friend of the court. A voluntary advisor to the court on issues larger than the litigants themselves. For example, organizations file amicus briefs to the Supreme Court advocating the organization's interest.

[72] The Cook County Circuit Court, entered an injunction prohibiting the applicants from "(m)arching, walking or parading or otherwise displaying the swastika on or off their persons" within the village of Skokie, Illinois. An application for a stay pending appeal was denied by the Illinois Appellate Court, and the Illinois Supreme Court subsequently denied a petition for a stay, together with a request for a direct expedited appeal. Application for a stay was made to Mr. Justice John Paul Stevens, as Circuit Justice, and was referred by him to the full court. The Nazis wanted to march in Skokie and the Supreme Court held prior restraint of that march would violate the First Amendment free speech. Nat'l Socialist Party of Am. v. Vill. of Skokie, 432 U.S. 43 (1977). By the way, the National Socialist Party of America was the American Nazi Party. Can a good Nazi be a good American? No.

[73] Akihabara section of Tokyo, Japan gained the nickname Akihabara Electric Town (秋葉原電気街 Akihabara Denki Gai) shortly after World War II for being a major shopping center for household electronic goods.

[74] Ativan (lorazepam), an antianxiety agent, has the chemical formula, 7-chloro-5-(o-chlorophenyl)-1,3- dihydro-3-hydroxy-2H-1,4-benzodiazepin-2-one.

[75] No, not 7541 Lego pieces! Googol's Millennium Falcon has an escape hatch I added, so the count is 7575. Only people on the team know it. And that's the point; it's an identity verification process.

[76] Fibonacci was an Italian mathematician from Pisa. He was considered to be the leading Western mathematician of the Middle Ages. The

Fibonacci numbers occur in the sums of "shallow" diagonals in Pascal's triangle.

77 The internet of things, or IoT, is a system of interrelated computing devices, mechanical and digital machines, objects, animals or people that are provided with unique identifiers (UIDs) and the ability to transfer data over a network without requiring human-to-human or human-to-computer interaction.

78 A psychological autopsy is legally recognized forensic procedure that allows an expert witness to opine on the cause of suicide. See generally Jackson v. State, 553 So. 2d 719, 719 (Fla. 4th DCA 1989).

79 Pong was a popular low resolution graphics game created by Noel Bushnell of Atari. https://www.youtube.com/watch?v=e4VRgY3tkh0 If you don't know what "Atari" means, then you don't play the game GO. Atari means "about to win" like "check" in chess.

80 A person who gets things done.

81 Lew Freeman was an accountant/lawyer/trustee in Florida. Of course, Freeman as a trustee hired Graf and Leiner as his lawyers – as the "trustee's" lawyer. Freeman also liked dressing in orange and potent pink. Another brilliant man – forensic accountant with a law degree, well respected. But when he confessed to stealing a few million dollars to redo his Coconut Grove home, he had to strip down to his jogging shorts before dozens of people in a Miami federal courtroom and say goodbye to his family for ten-years. Did Graf and Leiner standup for Freeman or help him? Freeman couldn't provide any more wildebeest meat, so what do you think?

82 Nasdaq is an acronym for "National Association of Securities Dealers Automated Quotations." The term, "Nasdaq" is also used to refer to the Nasdaq Composite, an index of more than 3,000 stocks listed on the Nasdaq exchange that includes the world's foremost technology and biotech giants such as Apple, Google, and Microsoft.

83 Mammon in Hebrew (ממון) means "money." The word was adopted to modern Hebrew to mean wealth.

[84] The Secret is a 2006 self-help book by Rhonda Byrne, based on the earlier film of the same name. It is based on the belief of the law of attraction, which claims that thoughts can change a person's life by willing it and it will appear. The book alleges Energy (esotericism) as evidence of its effectiveness. Who would believe that nonsense? The book has sold 30 million copies.

[85] Florida has its schemes and schemers. It's gotten to the point where one has to ask if some news stories are fake or just plain Florida. That's because any business can be run like a Ponzi scheme, and many seem to try in Florida. All you need is investors and then new investors to pay off the old ones. A life insurance company, for example - Florida had one of those. Run right out of Fort Lauderdale - more precisely a viatical company. A viatical company is life insurance payout for the dying. It purchases existing life insurance policies from the terminally ill and then the company becomes the beneficiary of the policy. The terminally ill sells the policy to the insurance company at a discount from its face value. The company either holds the policy or sells it to an investor to pay the premiums and then collects the benefits upon the death of the insured. Sell a $100,000 policy for $50,000 and when the terminally ill insured dies, the investor makes $50,000 profit on the original benefits of the life policy. Perfectly legal, unless the viatical company lies to its investors. The company's doctors were actually not doctors but the company's officers who lied in order to ensnare unwitting investors.

Pretend it's 1995 and Mr. Jones is diagnosed with HIV. Jones is marketed to investors as supposed to die in six months, but ends up living fifteen-years on the cocktail. A real problem when investors start demanding their return on investment. This scheme went on for ten years - the SEC clean up and then the indictments, another eight. And the de facto CEO of this public company was a convicted felon - prohibited by law.

One of the lawyers who kept the premiums in "segregated" trust accounts went to trial three years after he was indicted. He claimed he was a pawn - a small player, as opposed to the general counsel. A guy the company flicked some work to in order to keep a portion of the machine rolling. Claims he had no idea that the whole thing was a scam – claiming he took the blue pill. He was allowed to practice law the whole time while he awaited trial. Proclaimed his innocence the whole time – a poor misunderstood lawyer just trying to help the members of his community. His brothers in the gay community. 'This investment is great, being gay myself, I wouldn't steer you wrong,' he would say. Eleven weeks of trial – guilty. He argued with the judge when he was sentenced to ten-years in prison.

"I was hoping for less," the *Pawnsi* lawyer pleaded. "I'm sure you were," the judge replied. Pawnsi lawyer's fatal flaw is that he never even let himself believe he participated in crime, until it was too late. He led life in ultimate denial – he bullshitted himself. The problem with that is some people can tell you're a bullshitter and you'll never get too far. And, all bullshitters get caught. So, now Pawnsi lawyer got caught trying to bullshit his friends along the way, his brothers and his clients he begged to believe in his innocence.

The most annoying thing isn't that he betrayed himself and his community, not to mention his profession as a lawyer. It's not that he asked the judge for less prison time, as the second most unrealistic expectation next to the one where he was going to be outright acquitted. It's not that he pled guilty at his own sentencing by saying, "Judge, I'm sorry, I lost my way." It's that he plagiarized that line from the general counsel who pled guilty in the same case years earlier – Pawnsi, a bad cheater every step of the way.

[86] Creditors are compelled to play in the bankruptcy game and that game only. Meaning, they can't sue co-conspiring bad actors, if the bad actors settled with the bankruptcy estate and received in exchange for money a "bar order." A bar order prevents others not a part of the settlement with the estate from suing the bad actor debtor (the schemer). Those creditors must go through the bankruptcy trustee. A bank which failed to raise a red flag that the Ponzi is so full of shit that investing in a cheeseburger is a better investment than this scheme, gives a few million dollars to the estate, cannot be sued by victims of the scheme who relied upon the bank for advice on the investment. Barred!

[87] Permit me to be direct. Bankruptcy judges are not United States district judges. District judges in the federal system are appointed by the President of the United States, under Article III of the Constitution – an

appointment for life. Like the judge or not, that judge doesn't have to worry about getting re-elected or the next job. Bankruptcy judges aren't judges in "courts of the United States." They're not Article III judges. They're appointed by Circuit court (appellate) judges in their respective circuits, and only for fourteen year terms. 28 U.S.C § 152. And guess who gets to give input on whether they should be appointed and reappointed for another fourteen year term? The bankruptcy lawyers that appear in front of those bankruptcy judges do.

[88] The Bob Newhart Show was the television show. (1972-1978).

[89] The Fourth Amendment to the United States constitution states: "The right of the people to be secure in their persons, houses, papers, and effects, against unreasonable searches and seizures, shall not be violated, and no Warrants shall issue, but upon probable cause, supported by Oath or affirmation, and particularly describing the place to be searched, and the persons or things to be seized."

[90] Article III of the United States Constitution establishes and empowers the judicial branch of the federal courts. Bankruptcy courts are a product of congressional legislation, not Article III.

[91] George Carlin on "stuff."
https://www.youtube.com/watch?v=4x_QkGPCL18

[92] Kushinigar = the place of Buddha's death.

[93] A legendary Jedi Master, Obi-Wan Kenobi was a noble man and gifted in the ways of the Force in the Star Wars series.

[94] "Today the majority holds that an Article III court erred when it allowed plaintiffs who prevailed on appeal to collect on a supersedeas bond in the face of an injunction issued by a non-Article III judge. Because, in my view, the majority attaches insufficient weight to the fact that the challenged injunction was issued by a non-Article III judge, I respectfully dissent." Celotex Corp. v. Edwards, 514 U.S. 300, 313–14 (1995) (Stevens, J., dissenting).

[95] Halacha = Jewish law and jurisprudence.

[96] Vogons are a reference to The Hitchhiker's Guide to the Galaxy by Douglas Adams. Vogons are described as "One of the most unpleasant races in the galaxy—not actually evil, but bad-tempered, bureaucratic, officious and callous," and having "as much sex appeal as a road accident" as well as being the authors of "the third worst poetry in the universe."

[97] Singularity has multiple meanings and itself is an area of technology and philosophy. See Ray Kurzweil, *How to Create a Mind, The Secret of Human thought Revealed*, (Penguin Publishing Group 2012). Yes, he graduated from MIT. Singularity in this context is the bio-technological merging of man and computer – conscious machines.

[98] A word about the business of law. You need originators of business – litigation cases and business transactions. Without origination of work there is nothing to work on. So, the lawyer who works the business is great, but the guy who brings in the business, the originator is better. Typically, they are compensated better than the worker bee.

[99] Quash = reject or void. In this case void the subpoena. A subpoena is an order from the court that a lawyer in a case has the authority if filed within the rules of procedure can order production of documents or an appearance of a witness. Technically, it is a court order. But a person or entity receiving a subpoena can move to quash the subpoena to prevent its execution or the requirement to appear or produce documents.

[100] "Open source" software was coined by Christine Peterson. https://opensource.com/article/18/2/coining-term-open-source-software The source code is free. Think of it as here are the plans to build a motor.

[101] Xpert systems emulate the decision-making ability of a human expert to solve complex problems.

[102] Professor Falken created a self-learning computer program for the Pentagon that played games, including Global thermal nuclear war. War Games, (Movie) (1983).

[103] Proverbs 3:9

[104] Myers-Briggs type indicator is a self-report questionnaire. It indicates differing psychological preferences in how people perceive the world. Around them and make judgments. Taylor Anderson was ESFP = extraverted, observant, feeling and perceiving personality. She was a people person.

[105] IQ = intelligence quotient. The average IQ is 100. An IQ of 120 is "gifted." Mine was 160. Joseph had an IQ of 170.

[106] Julia Roberts' character is a call girl who agrees to give Richard Gere's character, Edward, the girlfriend experience for a price of $3,000, so he can navigate a tough business week in Beverly Hills. They eventually fall in love. Pretty Woman, (Movie) (1990).

[107] Outlook is a Microsoft email, calendaring, and task creation product that comes installed on a personal computer.

[108] Evangelist = in this context means to spread the word of a money making scheme as if spreading the word about God.

[109] The Lamborghini Countach is a rear mid-engine, V12 sports car produced by Italian car Manufacturer, Lamborghini from 1974 to 1990.

[110] It's unbearably humid and hot during the summers – and the summers are 8 months long. It's mostly a Betty Crocker ready-made oven sort of region. Looks like a real town, but it's for kids. Downtown Miami kind of has a city feel to it. Everything else is swamp land and suburbia. Strip malls and suntans. Miami thinks they're the center of the international cultural and business universe from Dadeland to Palm Beach. Palm Beach says, well we speak English, and their universe is very small. Palm Beach doesn't mean Palm Beach County either. Palm Beach stops at nouveau riche Boca Raton's gated communities of hell to the South, even though it's part of Palm Beach County. Florida has a homestead exemption. Meaning, schemers are exempt from civil judgments against collection. So schemers get big expensive houses. As long as one doesn't default on the mortgage, they'll never get thrown out and no forced sale to satisfy the judgment. Same exemption applies to

IRAs and 401Ks. So, most smart deadbeats plan accordingly. You can throw a net over the state and shake it out. There's a limit to that – the IRS – the King Kong of all debt collectors.

111 Murray Gell-Mann, Nobel Prize winning theoretical physicist. He was friends and worked with Richard Feynman at California Institute of Technology. The two collaborated on many projects but Gell-Mann thought Feynman was sort of a pain in the ass.

112 Edward Teller was a Nobel Prize winning physicist known as the "father of the hydrogen bomb."

113 Lady Lovelace, also known as, Ada Byron. Her mother, Lady Byron was a mathematical wizard called, "Princess of Parallelograms" by Lord Byron, the poet. Don't confuse her with Linda Lovelace, the American pornographic actress of Deep Throat fame.

114 Einstein's theory of special relativity: time slows down or speeds up depending on how fast you move relative to something else. Approaching the speed of light, a person inside a spaceship would age much slower than his twin at home. Also, under general relativity, gravity can bend time.

115 Wormholes are tunnels between two black holes that connect distant regions of space-time, and normally it would be impossible to pass something through them, but factoring in an extra dimension might make it possible. Some physicists think that it's possible to travel through a worm hole without dying.

116 If Xanax isn't your thing, then you wouldn't know a zannie bar. Xanax or alprazolam is used to treat anxiety and panic disorders. Recreationally, some ingest Xanax to mellow out.

117 Sapiosexual is a person who is attracted to very intelligent people. Being intelligent, I wondered if she was hustling me. But again, I was impressed that she even knew the word.

118 Being scientific about nearly everything, I would use the world "vagina." I suppose there's nothing sexy about saying the word vagina –

it's far too clinical. I've been told to see Penn Jillette about using porn words when describing porn. But who knows? I didn't ask him. I could be wrong and I don't want to get sued.

119 See the note above about "vagina."

120 Baker had an old school model. Associates hired by the class – Class of '95, you grind out a year, you make partner in five; and if you don't – you're moving on. Some exceptions do exist for the "of counsel" lawyer. The lawyer who is a step above the associate, who will never make partner – useful to the financial bottom line. Limit the compensation to salary and then they must bill a certain number of hours to stay alive at the firm.

121 SWIFT Codes = SWIFT stands for the Society for Worldwide Interbank Financial Telecommunication. It is an 8 or 11-digit code that identifies your country, city, bank, and (11-digit only) branch.

122 Quant = short for quantitative analysis. Quants use computers to tell them what to buy and sell; expert at analyzing and managing quantitative data. The idea is to predict future price movements of securities, commodities, and currencies.

123 To: Saul Graf
From: Christian Hillel Leiner
Re: Qpredictor and data collection – huge fees in attacking Joseph Leege.

My dearest friend Saul:

I spent an hour on the phone with Harvey Gale this afternoon to discuss our strategy for the adversary proceedings and other attacks in the core proceedings in the big bankruptcy matter. In short, he didn't think we were being belligerent ("aggressive") enough. :) There are epic requests for discovery, and then there is what he wants us to do. Our approach to being reasonable, in order to manage the lawyers representing the creditors and other parties, is being flat out rejected by Harvey. Some of those lawyers who know how we got this case will claim there are "conflicts of interest." We should be able to weather the storm on all those conflicts except for the big banks.

I told him to spend a majority of his efforts against the bank and let us do the litigation. But as you know Harvey said our firm cannot handle the bank litigation because of the perceived conflict of interest and previous business promises with other law firms, in order for him to be appointed the trustee by the court. What promises?

Gale even wants me to go after that nerd from MIT who invented some software application that all the Ponzi schemers seemed to have used in some way. We'll blow that up. Make it seem huge! The key to the Ponzi scheme is embedded in the data he holds. Not likely because we have all the data from the Ponzi schemers' side of the communication. But, let's give him what he wants. He wants full and unyielding compliance with everyone we deal with.

I told him that our firm is willing to take the risk of having our fees reduced at the end of the case if the judge says we spent too much time on baseless claims. Gale replied, he didn't think the judge would have the guts to reduce our fee. On balance it's worth the risk. Harvey said he knows the judge way too well and he doesn't want to work too hard for pennies on the dollar.

I already told him that he should bill by monthly blocks and not by the hour. Harvey agreed that would be smarter.

Maybe you should call him and get the authorization to go forward. Nobody's really innocent in any of this anyway. We will get paid whether we're right and wrong, win or lose. This is probably the biggest case we'll have in a decade. If not more. Don't let him screw it up.

By the way, the eBay auction team used this software service to develop their auction platform. You know what that means?

——

To: Christian Leiner
From: Saul Graf

Get that eBay shit!

—

JLL :Here's an interesting one:

To: Saul Graf
From: Christian Hillel Leiner
Re: Qpredictor

Saul:

This kid, Leege from Qpredictor hired a very nice appellate lawyer, Dayna Sohler. She's never been to BK court. She's come into the game too late. It's clear we have all the data from all the schemers. But we don't have all the data on the system.

Leege seems to be saying we'll get nothing more, just another view of the same data and a bunch of data that would be meaningless to us. But Gale says he's not getting full docile compliance. I don't think Gale knows what he's even looking for. I wonder if he's ever turned on a computer in his life. This guy Leege seems to be at wits end. I'm not saying he's ready to kill himself, he's just claiming he has no money to give and wants to protect the privacy of people who have nothing to do with the Ponzi schemes. People use his platform and he says he'd have to break into their databases in order to give it to us. He thinks that's stealing and violation of their user agreement.

How do you think I should handle it?

From: Saul Graf
To: Christian Hillel Leiner

Get eBay!
I don't give a shit about that guy Leege.

From: Christian Hillel Leiner
To: Saul Graf

Okay. (I'll torment this guy some more. Fragile soul. He's about to have a nervous breakdown.

JLL: Then there was court. And then there was this.

From: Saul Graf
To: Christian Hillel Leiner
RE: New client/new Bank.

Hey, who is this guy, Gregory Portent who's starting a bank with Enrique White's kid? That will be another big winner. Hey, I know Portent asked for you, but Enrique's been a friend of mine for 20 years, so you won't get the origination credit on the account. And after you screwed up operation eBay – sorry.

Thanks. Goodnight.

From: Christian Hillel Leiner
To: Saul Graf

I want to talk about origination credit. That's not how it works.
I'm the one that discovered eBay.

From: Saul Graf
To: Christian Hillel Leiner

Sorry. Not happening.
If you delivered on eBay . . .

[124] Snapchat = multimedia messaging app created by former Stanford students (not MIT). A snap is a picture or video and once they've been viewed, they are deleted.

[125] Killer robots theory - if you made it this far, you're smart enough to figure out that killer robots theory means once the robots get smart enough and can sustain their existence without humans, they'll turn on humans and destroy the human world.

[126] Terabyte = 1012 or a trillion bytes of data.

[127] General Manuel Noriega was a dictator in Panama. He was a CIA asset for decades. But then, he was indicted in Miami and Tampa by the United States government for racketeering, importing cocaine, and money laundering.

[128] Nodax: Who did this?

SuzyThunder: Did we?

Nodax: I thought you did.

SuzyThunder: Nope. The only guys who have this type of skill is JLars Viking or GNU4U2.

SuzyThunder: JLars is dead.

Nodax: GNU has been unplugged.

SuzyThunder: It must be Sassen the Assassin.

Nodax: Carl? Can't be him. I think we can say we did it.
I guess we can without losing credibility. We're Anonymous.

[129] GAAP = generally accepted accounting principles. Common set of accounting principles and standards. The commonly accepted ways of recording and reporting accounting information.

[130] Opus Dei is a sect of Catholicism that believes in self-flagellation for being born into sin among other ideas.

[131] Cirrus is a single engine land airplane with a "glass" cockpit. The Cirrus has a parachute when pulled at the proper altitude and speed, has floated to the earth with all passengers surviving. (Cirrus Airframe Parachute System – "CAPS").

[132] Sun Tzu was a Chinese general and philosopher who lived in the Eastern Zhou period of ancient China.

[133] Oleg Deripaska is a Russian oligarch.

[134] Banksy is an anonymous street artist that paints, draws, and erects priceless works of art on public structures all over the world; photographs them to authenticate his work.

[135] Bayes' theorem is probability theory. It describes the probability of an event based upon prior knowledge of conditions that might be related to the event.

[136] Muerte a Secuestradores literally means "death to kidnappers." But in Columbia, it is credited with being the seed that organized cocaine cartels who helped rescue kidnapped members of cartel families.

[137] Alibaba is referred to as the Chinese Googol. In the U.S. buying stock in Alibaba (BABA) is buying stock in the Chinese holding company that owns Alibaba. There is a risk if the Chinese government nationalizes Alibaba, BABA stock would become worthless. Also, the price of BABA is at a multiple of earnings that is astounding on any standard. The risk is that the price of BABA could adjust dramatically.

[138] M.C. Escher was a world famous graphic artist who died in 1972. He is famous for "impossible constructions," that give the illusion that two physical properties are occurring at the same time, such as stairs going up and down. https://www.mcescher.com/

[139] In 1965 a professor at MIT, Joseph Weizenbaum, introduced a computerized conversation simulator he called ELIZA. Eliza attempts to emulate Rogerian therapy. https://web.njit.edu/~ronkowit/eliza.html

[140] A 1992 Quentin Tarantino movie about a simple jewelry heist that goes wrong and the coconspirators suspect one of the members of the team is a police informant.

[141] The federal sentencing guidelines are complex. It's a grid of numbers. Within the grid are ranges of numbers. The range of numbers is the

months the defendant is going to be spending in prison. The lower down the grid you go, the greater range of months in prison. The more to the right you move, the greater range of months spent in prison. What moves you to the right? The defendant's prior criminal history. I have none. Not to mean I haven't committed crime, I just wasn't ever caught and charged. Even with just up and down, I'm dead. You start with a base number – base offense level. It's the foundational charge – let's say conspiracy. Conspiracy is the prosecutor's darling -easy to prove. The prosecutor doesn't even have to prove you were successful in completing the crime, just took a substantial step toward committing the crime. Base offense level 7. Then be charged with wire fraud – any email or phone call. Each is a charge and can be used as an overt act to support the conspiracy. Then there is mail fraud – for any mail you sent that supported the conspiracy. In my case there could be hundreds of counts. Innocuous documents and emails in the correct context would seem criminal.

Amount of money in controversy, how much was stolen? Well, based upon the in and out of bank accounts, I'd say it's well over $50 billion. And that ends the inquiry. $50 billion – or even $5 billion is not even on the sentencing guidelines. So forget it.

Number of victims? Well, we'd have a three day hearing and a philosophical debate over who is a victim. A victim in my mind is someone who is unsuspecting and susceptible to being cheated - someone who had something of value stolen from them and didn't deserve it. In this case, the something of value is money. But was it their money; were they susceptible? No. They didn't deserve it? Oh no, they deserved it. But, little "j" justice will make the system call them victims. I've ripped off trustifarians in my past – trust fund rebels who listen to waaah waah music and feel like it's not their fault their great grandfather was John Hancock or founded Vanderbilt University. This time, I ripped off banksters – gangsters in a bank. Insurers and Mountain lawyers. Victims? In a courtroom, I'd be so loathed. In the position I'm in now, I'd be framed by the media as Madoff's Emperor.

The government might not even want me to cooperate against others. First, that's not my style. I don't believe in all that don't be a rat bullshit from traditional gangster movies. As rich and fancy as I've seemed to have become, I could handle the penal experience. It'd be like freshman dorm again. I can also deal with the complexities of the prisoner's dilemma. What benefits could I get if I were to testify? There's just too much time for me to work off. Life wouldn't quantify how much time I'd be sentenced too. I'd be sentenced to an effective life sentence, but I'm looking at something in the neighborhood of 400 years. There are reasons for the judge to grant upward variances too on the guidelines. Leadership role in the conspiracy – bump up. If you even look at computer while dreaming about a crime, you get a bump for employing sophisticated means to further the scheme. Last but not least, my offense was committed in furtherance of criminal activities of a national or international organized criminal enterprise. So you can easily see now that the factors that move yourself up the grid are not going to help much. Acceptance of responsibility – plead guilty, minus 3. Great, I'd only serve 399 years. I could turn in the halls of Congress and still not be able to work my sentence off. I don't mean hypothetically either, I could turn in some congressmen, judges, police officers – it wouldn't matter.

The government would essentially allow me to protect a few people I cared about before going to prison for the rest of my life. But there is no one I care about that much who is still alive and in jeopardy. Oh, and every state where this money was wired around, has bank fraud and money laundering statutes too. I could be indicted in at least three other states.

142 Goodbye, my friend. My love.

143 Galil is an Israeli assault rifle. It has three positions: Safety on; Automatic; Repetition (semi-automatic) (SAR).

Acknowledgements

Claire Rudy Foster, editor and writer extraordinaire. "A brilliant literary voice."
David Brin, scientist and author.
Stephen L. Brayton, author.
Harper Kincaid, author.
Jon Weil, the best baseball man I know.
Robert Harkins, Esq., a man who hasn't been killed yet.
Jamie Gelfman, Esq., who always has her hand up.
Pamela Stephany, retired international banker and Pfeffersnaps baker.
Daniel Krohn, Renaissance man. I can't tell you what he does.
X, who has not permitted me to disclose identifying information.

Of course, Reichart. We were right and we were first.

To my Katie, who provides the platform for happiness and success.

About the Author

Robert Buschel has a storied career as a trial lawyer. His cases compel him to dive deep into politics, medicine, and computer science. Although Robert writes to live, not to re-live, he filters and refines the stories of the world around him for a never-ending supply of fresh tales for his readers to enjoy.

Note from the Author

Word-of-mouth is crucial for any author to succeed. If you enjoyed *God's Ponzi*, please leave a review online—anywhere you are able. Even if it's just a sentence or two. It would make all the difference and would be very much appreciated.

Thanks!
Robert Buschel

We hope you enjoyed reading this title from:

BLACK ROSE writing™

www.blackrosewriting.com

Subscribe to our mailing list – *The Rosevine* – and receive **FREE** books, daily deals, and stay current with news about upcoming releases and our hottest authors.
Scan the QR code below to sign up.

Already a subscriber? Please accept a sincere thank you for being a fan of Black Rose Writing authors.

View other Black Rose Writing titles at www.blackrosewriting.com/books and use promo code **PRINT** to receive a **20% discount** when purchasing.